Baby
Come
Back

Also by Maeve Haran

Having It All
Scenes from the Sex War
It Takes Two
A Family Affair
All That She Wants
Soft Touch

Baby Come Back

MAEVE HARAN

LITTLE, BROWN AND COMPANY

A *Little, Brown* Book

First published in Great Britain in 2000
by Little, Brown and Company
Reprinted 2000

Copyright © Maeve Haran 2000

The moral right of the author has been asserted.

*All characters in this publication are fictitious and any resemblance to
real persons, living or dead, is purely coincidental.*

All rights reserved.
No part of this publication may be reproduced, stored in a retrieval
system, or transmitted, in any form or by any means, without the
prior permission in writing of the publisher, nor be otherwise
circulated in any form of binding or cover other than that in which it
is published and without a similar condition including this
condition being imposed on the subsequent purchaser.

A CIP catalogue record for this book
is available from the British Library.

HARDBACK ISBN 0 316 85179 5
C FORMAT ISBN 0 316 85180 9

Typeset in Berkeley by M Rules
Printed and bound in Great Britain by Clays Ltd, St Ives plc

Little, Brown and Company (UK)
Brettenham House
Lancaster Place
London WC2E 7EN

For my father, the late Dr Tom Haran

Acknowledgements

With many thanks to Norcap for their vitally useful information on tracing adopted relatives.

To Ariel Bruce, who intrepidly searches for both lost mothers and lost children. She has brought about some amazing happy endings.

To Diana Quick, who only needs to walk into a room for one to understand that great actresses are different from the rest of us.

To my agent and friend, Carole Blake, and my editor and friend, Imogen Taylor, and all at Little, Brown for their enthusiasm and commitment.

And, of course, to my family, who remind me every day of the importance of a sense of belonging.

Chapter 1

'Oh, shoot!'
The button vainly attempting to contain Molly Meredith's newly voluptuous breasts parabola'd across the room and landed in the half-eaten box of Thornton's Continental Chocolates in front of the television. Molly tossed her equally unconfined red hair, the colour of polished brass, her grandmother used to say, though Molly thought it more like rusty bed springs, and went to hunt for it, putting down her staple gun as she descended the ladder.

Till she'd had a baby six months ago her bosoms had been like two small tangerines, but post-birth, they had become positively melonious and had taken on a life of their own. Egged on by a raucous friend from her childbirth group, Molly had even engaged in a wildly unladylike contest of spurting, worse than any competition between small boys over how far they could wee. Molly had won boobs down.

There was no time to sew the wayward button back on if she wanted to finish the curtains in time to surprise Joe. So, ever resourceful, Molly picked up her staple gun and applied it to her shirt before bounding back up the ladder to finish the pelmet. She had just banged in the last staple and was standing back to admire her handiwork when Joe's key turned in the door.

1

She so wanted Joe to like the curtains, their small flat, and every aspect of their life together.

'What do you think?' Molly gestured grandly towards the dramatic curtains in exotic purple and jade made with cheap fabric from the market in a bold attempt to disguise the view of a car park and two tower blocks.

Her husband Joe gave the window his fullest consideration. The extravagant curtain display was so totally Molly. Colourful, wildly over the top, and utterly unsuitable for a box-like flat conversion with two small bedrooms and a tiny kitchen. Yet it worked brilliantly and somehow transformed the whole room.

'Gorgeous,' he concluded. 'Just like you. How did you guess my secret wish to live in a Louisiana brothel?'

'It's nothing like a Louisiana brothel,' corrected Molly sternly. 'A *Turkish* harem perhaps . . .'

'I don't suppose there are too many Turkish harems in Peckham. You ought to be a set designer one day. You're easily talented enough.'

'It is a bit outrageous, isn't it?' Molly agreed gleefully. 'I've draped the sofa with the rest of the fabric so I can lie here eating chocolates while I feed Eddie.' She lay back and stretched out luxuriously.

'Tell you what,' Joe approached her with a meaningful look. 'Play your cards right and you could be my favourite wife. Have me every night of the year.'

Molly laughed and pretended to run away but he caught her and pushed her back on to the newly draped sofa. 'Starting now.'

At that moment their baby, Eddie, started to wail from the other room.

'The joys of parenthood,' Joe conceded wryly. 'Just as well they don't tell you at childbirth classes that you'll never have sex again. You might change your mind about the whole thing.'

'A bit late by then,' Molly pointed out.

'Shall I fetch him?'

Molly nodded. She adored her baby but was always delighted to have five minutes' peace. 'And I'll get us a drink.'

She hummed as she bustled round their tiny kitchen, opening a bottle of cheap white wine. She still could hardly believe that she and Joe were actually married.

Joe had been the handsomest and most stylish student in their year, or any year for that matter. With his dark, brooding good looks and amazing bright blue eyes, he'd seemed like a member of a different species from the rest of them. That and his periodic flashes of Byronic moodiness and reserve, which had made some students find him stuck-up. Once at a drunken party in the student bar he'd confessed to her that he never felt he fitted in, not in college, nor in life. 'Maybe it's because I'm adopted,' he'd half laughed, nervous she'd dismiss him as self-pitying, but she'd glimpsed the pain in his eyes and it had touched her heart. After that all the other men she met had seemed boringly uncomplicated.

Molly was one of nature's optimists, down-to-earth and practical. Molly believed she could fix things, and Joe was one of them.

But the moods hadn't gone away; if anything, they'd deepened. There were times when Joe would simply disappear. He'd taken up running and it had seemed to help, to give him a focus and an outlet for his restless energy.

And then Molly had got pregnant. The thought had appalled her at first. Surely Joe would feel trapped into a marriage he didn't want? But her news had had the opposite effect. Joe had been thrilled and insisted they get married at once. While all their friends were still wondering what to do with their lives, Joe had got himself a job producing handbooks for car buffs.

She sighed as she twisted out the cork. He seemed happy enough with their life together, but his sudden glooms had been the one thing Molly hadn't been able to fix after all.

She picked up the wine glasses and padded across to the small bedroom adjoining theirs. Joe had lifted Eddie out of his cot and put him on their bed. He was staring down at him, his eyes alight with tenderness.

The resemblance between the two of them was so amazing that it always took her breath away. Father and son shared the same dark hair, a sheeny shade almost of plum, the same pale skin and astonishing eyes, the dazzling blue of a jay's wing. Even their hands were the same, down to the square-tipped fingernails and deep cuticles.

'He's so like you,' she breathed, full of love.

'I know.'

Unexpectedly Joe turned away, as if the emotions he felt were too deep for words. His face seemed to close over.

'I'm going for a run.'

Molly was about to protest that supper was ready, but she knew the signs of one of Joe's moods and decided to let him work it out in his own way. His gaze caught hers and he tried to smile in apology but the pain she'd come to recognise was there again. 'Sorry.'

'That's all right.'

After he'd gone she lay next to the baby on the bed and stared into his eyes as if they might hold the answer. 'Why's your dad so unhappy? He loves you but even that doesn't seem to be enough.' Molly lay back on the bed and fought against the tears. Why had she thought that she, Molly Meredith, had the power to heal Joe's wounds when nothing else had been able to?

She drank her wine, fed the baby, and, without even bothering to get undressed, fell asleep.

It was dark when she woke up. Eddie slept peacefully beside her in the crook of her arm. There was no sign of Joe.

Molly felt the sudden stomach churning of panic. Had something happened to him? Yet she knew at the same moment that nothing had. But perhaps something had happened to *them*. Maybe she wouldn't, after all, be able to reach into Joe's darkness. And maybe Joe saw that too.

She sat up, cold and stiff and miserable, just as the front door opened. Carefully, so as not to wake him, she put Eddie back into his cot.

She heard Joe clattering about in the kitchen, but felt too tired even to leave the bedroom and join him. He arrived moments later, bearing tea and biscuits and a smile of such genuine apology it felt like the sun coming out.

'I'm sorry I've been so long. I was thinking.'

Molly's heart hammered. What had he been thinking about? That their marriage wasn't working, despite Eddie; that he had to be alone?

'I've come to a decision.'

Again that thud, jarring and painful.

'These bloody depressions of mine. I'm sure they're something to do with being adopted, so I've decided to look for my real mother. Do you think you could help me?'

Chapter 2

Molly's relief was so intense it almost hurt.

He wasn't thinking of leaving them; he wanted her help. And it made so much sense. The need to know where you came from was so powerful she was surprised he hadn't considered it before.

Joe read her thoughts. 'I did think about looking for her when I was eighteen, but you know what Pat's like.'

Molly did indeed know what Joe's adoptive mother was like. Pat had built her whole life round Joe and would be devastated at the thought of him tracing his birth mother. The word *betrayal* was an understatement where Pat was concerned.

'On my eighteenth birthday I went and got a book out of the library on tracing your relatives and hid it under the bed like a dirty magazine.'

'Pat would have preferred a dirty magazine.'

'Yes. Then she had her breast cancer scare and I just couldn't put her through it. So I took the book back to the library and forgot about it.'

'Except that you didn't forget about it.'

'No.' He cuddled up to her on the bed. 'I thought maybe when we had a baby that would sort it out, but in a way it's made it worse. He and I are so incredibly alike that it makes me wonder if those genes came from my mother. And I can't help wondering where she is.'

'And now you want to try and find her.'

'Yes.' He turned his intense blue gaze on her, full of touching hope. 'Do you think I'm stark staring mad?'

Molly turned to him, losing herself in the blue depths of his eyes. 'No, it makes absolutely perfect sense.'

'The thing is, you're so good at stuff like this. I remember when you helped the kid next door with his history project.'

'Digging up facts on the Norman Conquest is a bit of a far cry from finding your mother,' Molly replied.

'But you're so practical and thorough and determined.'

'You make me sound like a public librarian.'

'And charming and convincing and irresistible. You're the only person I've ever known who's talked themselves out of a parking ticket when it had already been printed.'

'I lied. I said I was going into labour.'

'Exactly. You're unscrupulous too. A perfect combination. As well as extremely sexy.' He pulled her gently and firmly towards him. 'I love you, Molly. Please help me.'

Molly knew there was no real choice. 'Of course I will. C'm here, my lovely, gorgeous, scrumptious husband . . .'

The next morning Joe was the first to wake. He leapt from the bed, naked, and lolloped towards the kitchen, whistling. Molly was amazed at the change in him.

'Watch out!' she warned. 'Old Mrs Jenkins next door is always looking out for the milkman.'

Joe stood by the kitchen window and leaned out giving their neighbour his most dazzling smile. 'Hello, Mrs Jenkins. How's your Bert's lumbago?'

'Better, thank you, Joseph,' came the octogenarian's cheery reply. 'You'd better put some clothes on,' she added gleefully, 'or you'll catch your death.'

Molly hid her head under the pillow. 'You'll give her a heart attack, poor old dear.'

'Nonsense,' Joe laughed, pausing to pick Eddie up from his cot in the other bedroom. 'She's seen it all before, hasn't she, Eds?'

Molly watched her two men lovingly and thought her heart might burst with happiness. It was going to be all right. Molly had always operated by instinct, and she had a really strong feeling about this.

She waved Joe off to work, still in her dressing gown, and thought about what to wear. Life was getting better by the minute. Not only had she and Joe come to a momentous decision, but she was meeting Claire for lunch today and she could share the excitement with her.

Claire was Molly's closest friend, her ally, her confidante on the subject of men, misery and mothers-in-law, and her comrade-in-arms at the local wine bar, when words were no longer enough.

They must have chosen each other, it often struck Molly, on the principle that opposites attract. While Molly was tall and willowy – apart from the newly acquired developments on her chest – with tumbling russet hair so unruly she had to confine it with three separate scrunchies, Claire was gamine and short-haired and barely five foot tall. What she lacked in height, though, she made up for in ambition. While Molly was perfectly happy with husband, home and baby, Claire wanted to conquer the world.

When Claire, sensing all was not utterly well with her friend, had suggested the lunch, Molly had thought about taking Eddie with her, but Claire said the restaurant didn't allow babies, even babies with Gold Cards, and then Joe's adoptive mother Pat had offered to come up from Essex for the day and look after him.

It would be Molly's first entirely child-free lunch, and she had to admit she couldn't wait.

'Molly, dear,' Pat requested, as soon as she'd taken off her coat, 'where do you keep your Dettox?'

Pat removed a pinny from her handbag and donned it like a soldier about to go over the top.

She found it alarming that Molly was a rather haphazard shopper who tended to buy Cookie Dough Ice Cream and Mr Kipling's

Almond Fancies instead of sensible things like Ajax and washing powder. Molly hated supermarkets and preferred to shop daily, or sometimes twice daily, at the corner shop. She had developed a mutually rewarding relationship with the shopkeeper, Mr Sawalha, as well as his extensive family, who remained unfailingly cheerful in the face of English weather, racist harassment and the arrival of out-of-town superstores. Mr Sawalha would always ask after Eddie at great length, then hand Molly some sweet or other for him. In the background his wife would smile and raise her eyes heaven-wards at the ineptitude of men who had no idea that babies didn't eat penny chews, fried eggs made of sugar, or something like an elongated fruit pastille which rejoiced in the name of an Astro-Belt.

'I'm sorry, Pat, I don't have any Dettox,' Molly pointed out. 'I just use washing-up liquid and an old J-cloth.'

'My goodness,' commented Pat with relish, 'your surfaces must be a germ paradise.'

Molly contemplated this fetching description. It sounded rather like a tropical holiday for bacteria.

Pat disappeared off to the shop and emerged armed to the teeth with sprays and scourers and something that promised to go round the bend, which was what Molly would do unless she left the flat pretty damn quick. Any moment now the bugs would be coming out with their hands up. The thought of Claire and the smart restaurant was getting more inviting by the moment.

Molly knew that when she got back the whole flat would have been spring-cleaned from skirting board to cornice (even behind the wardrobe, which it took three strong men to shift) and that she ought to be deeply grateful. It was just that she would have pre-ferred to be asked first. As it was she had to accept the none too tacit suggestion that their flat had looked like shit in the first place.

'Eddie'll probably wake in half an hour,' Molly explained. 'There's some expressed milk in the fridge.'

Pat pursed her lips in disapproval. Whether this was because Joe, being adopted, had been bottle-fed, or that Pat found the whole process distasteful anyway, Molly didn't know. She suspected that if she ever attempted to feed her baby in front of her adoptive mother-in-law, Pat would spray Molly's chest with Dettox first.

'I have brought up a baby, you know,' Pat pointed out tartly. 'I expect Eddie will survive a day with his Gran. Are you going out wearing that?' Pat's tone implied that Lady Godiva was better dressed.

In point of fact, Molly had given a lot of thought to her ensemble of white cargo pants and plain T-shirt. She didn't want to pretend she was competing with the sharp-suit brigade and this had seemed perfect.

'See you later then, Pat. And thanks for looking after Eddie.'

The bacteria in her flat might not agree, but Molly did appreciate it that Pat had driven so far to allow Molly to have her girlie lunch. Molly couldn't imagine Pat ever having had a girlie lunch in her life, but maybe she and her friends got together and confessed to not scouring the bins and occasionally ignoring the dust under the coffee table.

'Enjoy yourself,' Pat waved her off. 'And don't worry about Eddie. He'll be fine.'

On the spur of the moment Molly gave her a hug. Joe's sudden decision to try and find his real mother was going to be toughest of all on Pat. They would have to be incredibly careful how they went about it.

When she arrived at the smart restaurant there was no sign of Claire. Molly decided against perching at the bar amongst all the smart career girls dishing the dirt on other smart career girls, and headed for the loo. She was perfectly happy being at home and would have hated to hand Eddie over to a nanny, but in this ambition-orientated atmosphere she felt one step up from a leper. In fact she might have done quite nicely standing outside with a collection box marked 'Full-time mother, give generously so we can eliminate this curable disease'.

By the time she'd brushed her hair and touched up her make-up, Claire had arrived and had ordered a bottle of wine.

Molly had to confess, it was bliss to be in a grown-up environment, totally child-free. Lately the only menus she'd been reading

were in McDonalds, meeting other mums with babies and tod-
dlers. She studied her friend for a moment. Claire had always been
small and petite, with a touch of the tomboy, but since she'd got
this job, the polish of working on a big newspaper had rubbed off
on her and she had taken on the rather daunting patina of success.

'So, what news on the home front? Not bored out of your skull
yet?' Claire poured the wine.

'You're only jealous because your life's an empty desert, marked
out by the meaningless milestones of ambition and disappointment,' Molly quipped.

They both cracked with laughter. This was a game they always
played. The truth was, there were things each envied about the
other's life, yet both were relieved to be leading their own. A highly
satisfactory basis for a friendship.

'We always seem to talk about me, but how about you?' Molly
quizzed. 'What's happening in the backstabbing world of
Amalgamated Newspapers?'

Claire looked momentarily dashed. 'Well, actually, things aren't
that brilliant. There's talk of redundancies.'

'But not you, surely. You've been doing so well.' Molly nudged
her friend slyly. 'Anyway, aren't you, er . . . with your boss?'

'Emotionally involved?' Claire supplied helpfully. 'That's a joke.
I've never understood why "emotionally involved" means you're
bonking someone. "Physically involved" would be much more
accurate.'

'Whatever you call it, doesn't it help?'

Claire looked deflated. 'I'm not sure even if I had the sexual
skills of a Bangkok hooker it would make any difference this time.
I was last in, and that means first out, unless I can come up with a
real humdinger of a scoop. But enough of me and my selfish, shallow concerns. How's motherhood treating you? You seem different,
more cheerful. Like you look when you're on one of your crusades
to tidy Peckham's pavements or Adopt a Granny or something.'

'Well I am, sort of. Joe's asked for my help with something that
really matters to him, and it's such an amazing relief. He's been so

moody lately I thought he might be on the point of leaving or at least having a secret affair.'

'Joe'd never leave you. I remember the day you got married. He went round looking as if he'd won the lottery. It made me really love the boy.'

Jealousy had etched every detail in Claire's memory. Molly in an ivory *belle époque* dress she'd made herself (complete with staples, she later confessed), the folds of the silk disguising the gentle swell of her already pregnant belly; Joe in an embroidered waistcoat, his dark good looks making him every inch a modern Mr Darcy. And Claire convinced she'd remain on the shelf forever.

'So what's this big thing he's asked you to do? Not join a glee-some threesome with a St Bernard or something?'

The waiter chose that moment to hover discreetly at their elbow.

The man didn't bat an eyelid.

'Sorry, we haven't decided yet,' Claire announced.

'As a matter of fact, he's asked me to help him try and find his real mother.'

'Bloody hell. When did he come to that decision?'

'Yesterday. After a two hour disappearing act. I was on the point of phoning the police station when he came back and announced it. Actually, I'm really pleased. I've always felt that if he could find her it might help him a lot, especially since we've had Eddie. It's human nature to want to know where your nasty little mannerisms come from. Everything's down to genes these days.'

Despite herself, Claire was impressed at the daring of the venture.

Molly was amazing. She thought she could mend anything, from a broken toy to a broken dream. It was what made her so engaging – or infuriating, depending on whether it was your life or someone else's she was fixing.

'Joe's always had this moody side – he disappears off into a world of his own and it's like the barriers are three feet thick. You just can't get through to him. And yet it's not like he's a depressive or anything. I *hate* it. I used to tell myself it was just his need for space.'

'Very sixties.'

'But it sometimes feels like being slapped in the face. He's so loving the rest of the time, it only makes it worse. I know there's a reason. That's why it was so amazing when he asked for my help.' Molly was warming to her theme like an early saint drunk on wildfire, oblivious to the curious stares from the next-door lunchers. 'I've been reading up on the subject, Claire. Lots of adopted people feel like Joe. If I can find his mother and she persuades Joe that he meant something to her, and that she loved him, it could make all the difference. I mean, she could have been some poor teenager, pressured by her parents. There are some terrible stories . . .'

'Molly, hang on,' counselled Claire, alarmed at how quickly all this was going. 'What if it wasn't like that? What if she really didn't want him, or it was rape or an affair? Not everyone would want their long-lost son, or their long-lost son's wife for that matter, blundering back into their life. What if she doesn't want to know him? There could be a million reasons why she gave him away. She might reject him again, and what would that do to him? Look, we write about this stuff. It isn't all happy endings and tearful reunions.'

But trying to stop Molly when she was on a roll was like trying to trap a whirlwind in a bottle. 'If she doesn't want to meet him,' Molly insisted, as if it were the most obvious thing in the world, 'then I'll have to persuade her. After all, it'd probably help her too. Unless she's a completely heartless cow.'

Claire felt momentary sympathy for the heartless cow when Molly did find her. Molly tended to see the world in terms of black and white.

'Of course, if I find her and she really doesn't want to meet him, I suppose I could always pretend I hadn't found her.'

Claire reached a hand across the table. 'I love you dearly, Moll, but you don't think you're playing God just a bit here?'

'Claire, I think this is really going to help our marriage.'

'In that case, I'll drink to that.'

Molly clinked glasses and looked round the room. 'Look, I'll probably get nowhere. You're always accusing me of being brain dead, stuck at home with a baby while you're out in the world thrusting. This'll give me something really worthwhile to do.' She changed the subject with an audible clunk that brooked no further discussion. 'Now, what are we having to eat? And more important, Claire, are you paying, seeing as you suggested this place? I couldn't even afford the olives on the bar.'

'Of course I'll pay,' Claire reassured. 'I can't exactly put Pizza Express on my expenses, but they'll accept this place. Now, who shall I say my guest is today?' She winked at her friend. 'In this light I'd say you look a lot like Kate Winslet, or maybe Minnie Driver.' Molly tossed her head and laughed. 'No, definitely our Kate.' Claire raised her glass. 'Good luck in your quest. To Molly the Mother-Finder!'

Then she put down the glass and swivelled rudely round to watch the progress of a stunning dark-haired woman.

The crowds in the small bar adjoining the restaurant seemed to melt before the new arrival like the opening of the Red Sea.

'Hey, isn't that Stella Milton?' Claire whispered loudly, her journalistic instincts perking up at once. 'God, she's even sexier in real life. My boss Tony nearly has an orgasm every time she does that ad for the car with all the leg-room.'

Molly craned her neck, trying to pretend she was hiding behind the giant menu as Stella swept past them, the embodiment of womanly chic, her dark hair cut so that it angled into her chin, accentuating the chiselled hollows of her cheekbones. Her upper lip protruded over the lower in a slope of subtle sexual invitation.

Other actresses were more beautiful, but there was only one Stella Milton, Shakespearean sexpot. Her whole presence suggested tangled white bed-sheets and hot erotic afternoons.

'How does she get those cheekbones?' demanded Molly, pursing up her face in an attempt to find her own. 'Do you suppose she holds her breath all the time?'

'Stop it, Moll. You look like a constipated prune, not a sex bomb.'

'I was watching her on daytime TV the other day,' Molly confessed. 'That programme where they have lunch and chat. Do you know, she can wrap pasta round a fork while telling funny anecdotes at the same time.'

'Not the only skill she's supposed to possess.' Claire delved in her handbag, leaving Molly to imagine the murkier waters of sexual stimulation her friend was hinting at. Sometimes she was glad she was stuck at home.

'Or it could be,' Molly murmured to herself, 'she's a bloody good actress and other people are jealous.'

'Do you think I dare go up and ask her for an interview?' Claire was half out of her seat. 'Look, she must have had cosmetic surgery. No one looks that good at her age, unless they're Tina Turner or they've sold their soul to the devil.'

'Why don't you go and ask her?'

But it was too late. Stella Milton had disappeared, and a wall of other lunchers, all too sophisticated to stare, came between Claire and her prey.

Chapter 3

On the other side of the restaurant, Stella's agent, Bob Kramer, with whom she was lunching, raised an eyebrow and waited for his client to arrive. Over the years Stella had developed the capacity to be acutely aware of her impact, without ever showing it. She could saunter into places with her eyes fixed on the *maître d*'s back as if he were the most important, enthralling man in the universe, thereby avoiding the glances of anyone sitting at other tables without ever looking snobby or superior. It was part of her skill to create a myth of approachable sexuality without ever having to talk to anyone. But even Stella's powerful allure couldn't go on forever. The truth was, she was reaching the end of her siren's shelf-life and Bob wished she could bring herself to admit it.

He wondered exactly what today's invitation was all about. This lunch had been a royal summons at very short notice. She'd insisted he cancel whatever plans he'd had. Bob wasn't quite sure whether his client was still sought-after enough to justify such imperiousness. Catherine the Great had had the Russian Empire to justify her attitude, Stella only had her beauty, sensuousness and considerable acting ability. Up till now, that had been enough. Could any woman over forty demand such treatment?

The spotlight above his head reflected on his polished skull as

Bob pondered on these things. 'So, Stella, my love, to what do I owe the surprise and pleasure of your company at such short notice?'

Stella blessed him with an ironic curl of her full lips. Bob was one man she had never tried to charm. An agent was of far more lasting value than a lover, but it was a useful card to have in reserve. Stella's whole life had consisted of always having cards up her sleeve; sometimes she even felt disappointed at not having to use them.

'There's a role I want.'

'Mmm. Of course there is. And who has it at the moment, poor unsuspecting lamb?'

'I don't think it's been cast yet. It's playing in New York with Suzi May.'

'Ah. *Dark Night and Desire*. But Stella, the lead in that show is a blonde.'

'I can be a blonde.'

'Darling, she's under thirty.'

'I can be under thirty. I've seen them do it in Italy. Waiter, could you get me a rubber band?'

The waiter who was just passing with a tray of drinks looked as if he would go to the ends of the earth to find one for her. Fortunately the cash desk was a little nearer.

Customers at the adjacent tables tried not to gawp as Stella captured a strand of hair each side of her temples and pulled, thereby administering an instant face lift. 'The actresses there all do it, and none of them remind you of reheated corpses like they do in the States after cosmetic surgery.'

'The trouble is, Stella love, I heard a rumour that they've already cast it.'

'Then get them to stop. Tell them I'll read for the part. Tell them I don't care about the money.'

'Hang on, Stella.' Bob had never seen her so determined. 'Some things are sacred. The competition's hot for this part. Old-fashioned glamour's back in style and a lot of these young actresses have the knack of it.'

'They're only pretending,' Stella insisted, reaching for the coat draped over the back of her chair. 'I'm the real thing. Get me the part.'

'Aren't you eating?' Bob had just been working up his appetite at the sight of some of the entrées. 'This was supposed to be lunch.'

'Got to stay thin for this part.' Stella dazzled him with her thousand-watt smile, but fortunately, as the agent of some of the most beautiful actresses in London, Bob was inured to it. He preferred food to women. It might make you dyspeptic, but at least it didn't wake you up in the middle of the night and ask for sex.

'I'll see what I can do.' He got up to accompany her to the door.

'I'm sure you will. Goodbye for now.' Stella, as usual, appeared not to notice the eyes that followed her progress through the restaurant, but she could have drawn a plan of who was and who wasn't watching.

Outside, Bob summoned her a taxi – easy to find since most smart lunchers had only just sat down – and closed the door gallantly. 'You don't think, Stella my love,' he leaned in at the window and dropped his voice, 'you ought to give up chasing parts for twenty-eight-year-olds?'

Stella pretended not to have heard and waved goodbye. She had been intending to go back to her flat and see Richard, her patient and generous lover, but some impulse directed her towards Victoria Station. It was a reaction against Bob's negative attitude. What she needed was a dose of her astringent mother, Beatrice. Bea was already eighty and still saw herself as young.

She might not have been the most available of mothers, Stella reflected – Bea was an actress too and had spent much of Stella's childhood travelling the globe on musical comedy tours – but there was a no-nonsense immediacy about her that Stella found comforting. Her mother still saw the world as a simple place of good and evil, right and wrong, and didn't hold with introspection. Analysing yourself, Bea always said – and even worse, anything that involved couches – was the curse of Stella's generation.

'Excuse me,' the cab driver interrupted Stella's reverie, 'but aren't you the lady who does the advert for that car?'

Stella felt a bristle of annoyance that after twenty-one films, countless Shakespeares and an early 'art' movie when she took all her clothes off, she should be remembered solely for that advert. 'Yes,' she answered pithily, 'I am.'

'Hope you've got enough in my cab,' he chortled.

Stella looked blank.

'Leg-room, I mean.'

Stella smiled faintly and reminded herself how much she'd been paid for the ad. Enough to accept a pittance for *Dark Night and Desire*. If she got the part at all.

Stella enjoyed journeys. There was a safe, cosy feeling about being between two places. Nothing was expected of you. When a car was sent to take her on location or to do some TV show, she very often wished she could stay in it instead of arriving and turning on the glamour. It was hard work being a legend.

The first part of the journey was the train to Cliffdean. They were so used to celebrities on this line that the barman almost gave you *his* autograph. All the same, Stella kept her sunglasses on and hid behind a judicious copy of the *Guardian*. She changed at Brighton for the few stops to Ovington, where she took a taxi for the final miles to Lower Ditchwell, where her mother lived.

Lower Ditchwell was a downland village of around a hundred houses, so postcard-perfect that it had graced table-mats, playing cards and the occasional chocolate box. There had never been, as far as Stella knew, an Upper Ditchwell to explain its prefix.

It was June already, and she'd been so busy working she hadn't even noticed. In Lower Ditchwell it was impossible *not* to notice the time of year. Once the place had depended entirely on the whim of the seasons for its very survival. Its cottages might look notelet-pretty, with their roses round the door and pebbled flint walls, but a hundred years ago each one had been tied to a job with manor, church or farm. Mostly they would have run with damp, giving the labourers a permanent cough, boasted almost no furniture except perhaps an upright chair and rough table, and been filled with so many children that only the cottage pig, cared for better than any of the labourers' offspring, came between them and starvation.

The cottages' original occupants would have fainted at the sight of their former homes today. Now each tried to outdo the others in its profusion of hanging baskets, ornamental wheelbarrows stuffed with busy Lizzies, add-on conservatories and white patio furniture.

These days not a single cottage-owner had any relationship with the land, except perhaps the gay garden designer in the converted school-house who made his living from garden schemes according to the principles of *feng shui*.

One cottage alone resisted all this suburbification, though 'cottage' might be too simple a word to describe the elegantly proportioned golden stone house with its white front door, shaded by a decorative carved lintel. This was Bea's house, the fruits of a lifetime spent touring the ex-colonies with Noël Coward revivals and evergreen musical comedies like *The Boyfriend*. If her mother felt guilty about being abroad for Stella's entire childhood, abandoning her daughter to the tender mercies of the nuns at boarding school, she never showed it. The nuns had looked after Stella well, and became incandescent with excitement when, after three days of silent retreat, Stella thought she had heard the call of God and might have a vocation to join the order. When the sick feeling in her stomach which, at thirteen, Stella had interpreted as the voice of God turned out to be the onset of her period, the nuns had lost interest in her.

Stella smiled to herself. The nearest she'd got to being a nun since was playing the demented, sex-addicted Reverend Mother in a Ken Russell film. She hoped the nuns had never seen it.

'Stella, darling, what a lovely surprise! Why didn't you ring from the station? I'd have come and fetched you.'

Bea took off the floppy sun hat she always wore for gardening and embraced her daughter. She had teamed it with faded jodhpurs, ancient riding boots and a frilly white blouse. She still kept on the amazing false eyelashes of her stage days, and looked like a disconcerting mix between Vita Sackville-West and Barbara Cartland.

Stella hoped that, unlike Vita, she wasn't having a wild affair with someone else's wife. Probably not, on balance. Everyone in the village would know, and besides, despite her advancing years, Bea loved the company of men.

'Hello, Beatrice, you old bat.' Stella and her mother had never gone in for maternal epithets. 'It's good to see you.'

'It's certainly that. You're just in time to help me make twenty-four glasses of orange juice.'

Puzzled, Stella followed her mother out of the bright sunlight into the cool, flower-filled sitting room with its low beams and palest yellow walls. Her mother, who had never been a genteel country lady, had, in the last few years of her life, developed an extraordinary knack for appearing to be one. Perhaps it was the latest in a series of many roles, and just like the others, Bea played it brilliantly.

'Why do you need twenty-four juices, for God's sake?' Stella asked. 'You're not expecting a male voice choir?'

'Just an outing from the parochial school. I let them come and use my old clothes and put on a little play for me. They'll be thrilled to have you as a co-judge. Though I doubt any of them are old enough to have seen your work.' She paused meaningfully. 'Fortunately.'

'Don't you believe it. The poster from that silly film about the girl biker is on every bedroom wall in the best boys' schools, or so I'm reliably assured.'

'Only because you've got nothing on under your leathers,' Bea commented a shade too tartly. 'Don't kid yourself it was your acting ability.'

'Actually I wasn't.'

Any further conversation was drowned out by the arrival of a boisterous horde of children, whooping and skipping as they emptied out of their minibuses and into Bea's peaceful cottage. Down the street, several Liberty-print curtains twitched with disapproval. Bea didn't appear to notice. It was typical of her mother, Stella mused, that she hadn't even enquired why her daughter had arrived out of the blue on a Thursday afternoon without even a phone call's warning.

But then, Stella asked herself, why *had* she come? If it was for reassurance that she wasn't too old for the part she wanted in *Dark Night*, then Bea was hardly the person to turn to.

The schoolchildren, by now dressed as Victorian ladies and assorted flappers, with one small redhead in Elizabethan ruff and doublet, trooped back into the room to stage an eclectic performance which featured the unlikely tale of Elizabeth I giving orders to Mrs Bridges from *Upstairs Downstairs*.

'Brilliant, darlings,' congratulated Bea. 'You're all wonderful.'

'Those clothes must be worth a fortune,' Stella pointed out as a ten-year-old Juliet stepped on a flapper's pink silk tap shoe, leaving a large mark. 'You should auction them, instead of letting all these kids loose on them.'

'I'd rather they had some use,' Bea replied.

'Now get changed out of my fine clothes before you have your juice, please.' Bea addressed the children with all the authority of a born teacher. 'And remember to hang them up so they're ready for next time!' She turned back to her daughter. 'You've never really seen the point of children, have you, darling?'

'Meaning?' Stella bristled.

'Meaning you decided you weren't cut out for motherhood. You were probably very sensible.' Bea's tone implied that she didn't mean a word of this.

Stella felt a fiery wall of anger leap up all round her. Her mother could never resist a crack. 'You've never forgiven me, have you, for having him adopted?'

'I thought you acted selfishly, certainly. There were other alternatives less drastic than adoption. We could have helped if only you'd asked.'

'*I* acted selfishly!' Stella could hear her voice rising, abandoning all the modulated vowel sounds she had worked so hard on in her training. '*I* was selfish? That's rich coming from you!'

All her memories of loneliness and abandonment in that damn convent, stuck there even during the holidays, welled up through the years, fuelling her fury at her mother's hypocrisy. 'You never bothered about me once! You just buggered off with Father to Woolloomooloo or Sarawak and assumed I was fine.'

Bea looked momentarily stricken; the folds of her thin neck seemed suddenly to pile one on the other like hula hoops. 'I had to. Your father couldn't get work here. The only plays I could get for us together were abroad.'

Stella indulged in a moment's bitterness for the father she'd never really got to know. And now it was too late. He'd died when she was in her twenties.

'He could have gone and you could have stayed.'

'That would have been the end of our marriage. Your father always had a roving eye. People felt you had to put your marriage before your children in those days.'

'You certainly had no problems there.' Stella hadn't meant to sound so bitter, but it was hard to stop now that she'd started.

Bea was just as irascible. 'Was it all worth it, Stella? For your brilliant career as an actress who takes her clothes off? How many times has it been now? Ten, twelve? And let's not forget that nude Juliet that started it all off.' She took her daughter's hand and held it fast. Do you ever wonder what happened to the baby. What kind of life he's had?'

The expression on Stella's face tore at Bea's heart. She looked like some expensive, cosseted animal that had been kicked by the one person it could depend on. 'Look, Stella darling . . . I shouldn't have said those things. You're right. I was selfish when you were growing up; the fact that attitudes have changed is no defence. I have no right to accuse you of being heartless.'

'Don't worry about it.' Stella's tone was so icy it could have rubbed the skin from your fingers. 'I expect you recognize the emotion.'

It wasn't Bea's beloved daughter who reached down for her jacket with exaggerated casualness and walked from the house, but the glamorous actress known to so many.

Bea watched Stella leave in silent pain, wishing she could take back some of her accusations and heal the jagged wound between them. But no words came. Everything she'd said had been true, and both of them knew it. Sometimes the worst thing about being a mother was that you were the only person who could dare to tell the truth.

Chapter 4

Later on in her small but much-loved flat, to which only the favoured few were allowed entry, Stella considered the life she had created for herself. The flat was tiny but brilliantly positioned in the heart of Covent Garden, so she could walk to any theatre she might be appearing in. It had a roof garden with a small conservatory she had filled with jasmine. Here she could sit, drinking in the heady perfume and watching the stars while still listening to the sounds of the city she loved below. It was not the kind of flat you would bring children up in, just as Stella's pair of vermilion art deco couches were not the colour that you would choose if there were to be sticky fingers in the vicinity.

Why, Stella asked herself angrily, should success only be defined through having children? Didn't talent, hard work, instinctive understanding of what a dramatist was getting at, count for anything? Could life's value only be measured by adding one more soul to the already overcrowded population?

How dare her mother suggest her life had been a failure. Her mother with her outrageous fake eyelashes, her voice that sounded like sandpaper scraped through honey, who had spent her whole acting career in far-flung flea-pits, a ridiculous figure, always trying to compensate for obscurity by dressing outrageously, the parody of an actress. Stella remembered how she'd tried to roll herself up into a ball of embarrassment, like a hedgehog scenting danger, each time Bea arrived to pick her up from school in some new and dreadful ensemble that looked like something left over from a production of *The Mikado*. Her mother had simply not noticed or cared.

Well, neither did Stella. Why should she mind what anyone else thought, especially her mother?

She dialled her agent. Bob often stayed at the office later than anyone she knew, which was reassuring in an agent. And if he wasn't in the office he was always out at some show featuring a client, or schmoozing someone who might be useful to another. Bob seemed to have no private life at all, and not even to miss it. While some people had mid-life crises and decided to jack in their jobs to embrace Buddhism or country living, Bob just bought a new and more efficient gadget to update his contacts book.

Tonight he was at the office. 'Bob. It's Stella. Did you find out the score about *Dark Night*?' Stella never wasted time with niceties like asking how people were.

'Yup. Sorry, love, but it's cast in stone. Roxanne Wood's got it.' Roxanne Wood was not only one of the new hot actresses, but the young and beautiful daughter of a stage dynasty.

'But she's a child! She hasn't even lived yet. They'll have to age her ten years.'

He might have said 'Easier than subtracting ten.' But he didn't. The thought lay there somewhere, though, between them. 'What they were wondering,' he paused, waiting for the fireworks to erupt, not sure he should even go on, 'is whether you'd consider playing her mother.'

'I hope you told them to go and fuck themselves.' Stella slammed the phone down furiously.

'Yes,' Bob confided to the dead telephone, 'I did. Only I put it slightly less politely.'

Stella was still shaking with anger when the doorbell rang. Richard stood outside with a huge bunch of scented white lilies.

'Exotic and perfumed,' he smiled, 'like you.'

The irony was that although Richard seemed quiet and low-key, he had depths invisible to the normal human eye. Not many men, however macho they might seem to the rest of the world, were strong enough to take Stella on. Men assumed, not entirely correctly, that she would be as experienced at sex as she seemed on film or stage. No matter how sophisticated they might be, they still believed that Stella Milton really made her nipples harden by rubbing them with ice-cubes, which she then ate, as she had done in *Whatever Gets You Through the Night*, or that she actually had had an affair with her own father, as in *Daddy*, or, more daunting still, that she indulged in the somewhat exotic habit of personally embalming the lover who had betrayed her, as in a black comedy entitled *Guess Who Stayed For Dinner*.

It might simply have been that Richard lacked imagination, but he was the one man who had been able to understand that she liked eating pizza in bed, rather than screwing hanging upside down from the lightbulb, and watching an occasional video on a Saturday night just like the rest of the population. Especially if it didn't star Stella Milton.

Stella opened a bottle of wine and they sat on the terrace together. 'I love London,' Stella breathed. 'How anyone could live buried in the countryside with nothing to do with their brains except gossip and garden beats me.'

'Been to see your mother, have you?' Richard guessed. 'How was Dame Beatrice?' This was Richard's pet name for Bea, of whom he was extremely fond.

'Imperious. Batty. She had a houseful of screaming children borrowing her valuable stage clothes when she could auction them for a packet.' The image brought back vividly the pain of her mother's accusations.

'Is that all that's annoyed you?' Richard knew her well enough to sense there was more.

'No. Let's go to bed.' The announcement took Richard by surprise. Normally it was he who suggested lovemaking.

Without waiting for an answer, Stella disappeared into the small bathroom, which had the brightest lighting Richard had ever encountered this side of the London Palladium.

He began rapidly undressing before Stella changed her mind. The bathroom door was open, and moments later Stella, stark naked, leaned on the jamb, illuminated by about five hundred watts. 'Richard, tell me the truth. When I take my clothes off, do I look all right, or do people think, "Oh God, not those tired old tits again"?'

'Not if they're anything like me, they don't.' Richard lifted the covers and showed her the evidence.

It wasn't quite the answer Stella was looking for. But it would have to do.

'Richard,' she asked suddenly, in a voice so uncharacteristic it made him turn to her, 'do you think we're too old to have a baby?'

He opened his arms and she came into them. 'Maybe not too old, but certainly too selfish.'

Stella buried her face in the duvet. Why did everyone always use that word in relation to her?

Earlier that afternoon, Molly and Claire had finished up their buffalo mozzarella and roasted pepper salads, and Molly had given in to the temptation of a tiramisu ice-cream. Claire resisted on figure grounds, but was delighted when Molly succumbed. At least the waiter wouldn't curl his lip in that 'We *are* cheapskates, aren't we, madam?' way so familiar in posh restaurants when you just opted for coffee.

To Molly's astonishment, when they came out, Joe was sitting outside on the kerb, with Eddie in his buggy next to him.

'What on earth are you two doing here?' she asked in delight.

'I had a meeting in town so I went home and relieved Mum. Thought we'd give you a surprise. Did you have fun?'

'We saw Stella Milton, and she's stunningly beautiful,' Molly enthused.

'What grand circles you move in.'

A gypsy passed with a pathetic-looking strand of dried flowers wrapped in foil. 'White heather for luck, darlin'?' She pushed the flowers towards Molly.

Claire's mouth was open to say no, but Molly handed over a pound and took the flowers, raising them to her nose to sniff. It wasn't heather at all, but sea-holly dyed white, with no scent whatsoever.

Seeing Molly's look of disappointment, the gypsy took the bedraggled bundle back and sprayed it with some foul-smelling cheap perfume. 'It'll be all right,' the toothless woman whispered in Molly's ear as she handed it back, her breath so disgusting that Molly almost turned her face away. 'You're doing the right thing.'

Molly watched open-mouthed as the woman disappeared without a second glance off towards Oxford Street to accost some more shoppers. What the gypsy had said was so general it could mean anything, but Molly, being Molly, decided to take it as a miraculous omen, and she felt absolutely wonderful.

Claire watched as her friend undid the kicking baby's safety strap and enveloped Eddie in a tender hug. Although she didn't want children herself, or certainly not yet, Claire couldn't fail to be moved by Molly's pleasure in her son, and was even a little envious.

A whiff of nappy brought her back to her senses.

'Phew!' Claire fanned the air between them. 'Rather you than me!'

While Molly looked around for somewhere to change Eddie, Joe turned to Claire. 'How's our thrusting journo these days?' He and Claire were fond of each other, reflected in the scathingness of their banter. 'Knocked the editor out of his job yet?'

Claire didn't confess that her worries were more about staying there at all. 'Not quite. I'd better dash. See you soon, both of you, and you, you lump of scrumptiousness.' She tickled Eddie's toes and he chortled delightedly.

Molly waved goodbye before turning back to Joe. 'What a lovely surprise, you turning up.'

'I just wanted to say I'm sorry to both of you about the way I've been.'

'It's all going to be fine,' Molly breezed. 'The gypsy just told me.'

'Did she?' Joe laughed, and ruffled her hair. 'Oh, that's all right then. Did she also happen to tell you the name of my real mum?'

'That probably costs more than a quid.'

The next day, in the drowsy half-moments between sleep and waking, Molly had that precious feeling, like knowing you have a present but haven't unwrapped it yet, that there was something wonderful waiting for her. Then she remembered. Today she was going to start the search for Joe's real mother. Today she was taking the first step towards making everything all right.

She studied her sleeping husband's face next to her on the pillow. The bed was too small for both of them but it was the only size that would fit in the room if they wanted to have anywhere to hang their clothes. In fact, Molly liked it. It meant she could feel Joe's warmth and the imprint of his body next to hers. She knew even without stretching out that he was next to her and it made her feel safe.

Molly kissed him, then went to bring more tangible proof of her feelings in the form of a cup of tea.

'You're a goddess,' Joe murmured appreciatively. 'Aphrodite in a pink towelling dressing gown.'

'They're standard goddess issue. Now get up or you'll be late for work.'

After he'd gone, Molly tidied the small flat, gave Eddie his breakfast and strapped him into his buggy. The library opened at 9.30, and she intended to be outside it by 9.29. She stopped at the newsagent's and bought a notebook, telling herself she mustn't get too excited, that her search might never bear fruit and that if it didn't, she and Joe would have to deal with the fall-out of that disappointment.

The reference library was on the first floor, and there was no lift, so she had to carry Eddie and the buggy all the way up. No one offered to help. From the look of them, most people had come here either because they had nowhere else to go, or to scan the job columns for a post they'd never get. Lethargy and despair hung heavily in the air. Molly refused to let herself be ground down. She had a purpose.

With the rather grudging help of the librarian, she amassed a pile to work through for as long as Eddie would let her. She started with a book called *After Adoption: the Burning Search for Self*.

Molly's heart hammered. It was all there. The restlessness Joe felt, the moodiness that swept over him, his unease at having to create himself from scratch.

Sitting in the sad silence of the reference library, Molly felt the tears sliding down her face as she understood for the first time the depths of Joe's loneliness. He had always hated people who felt sorry for themselves and blamed their backgrounds, yet he was clearly to some degree a victim of his. How awful it must be for no one to ever say – infuriating though it was when they did – 'You're just like your father' or that you had your uncle's nose or your aunt's jolly temperament. People secure in their web of cousins, brothers and sisters might find comments like those irritating beyond belief, but they located you at the centre of a structure that shored up your sense of self. She wished Joe were here so that she could hold him and tell him it would all be fine, because Molly would make it so.

At that moment, Eddie, who had been dozing, woke and smiled.

'We're going to find your real granny,' she promised him. 'And when we do, everything's going to be all right.'

She felt a new lightness to her step as she returned the books and ordered more for another session. She had been riveted by what she'd read and couldn't wait to find out more.

She was so happy that she stopped at the coffee shop and indulged herself in a caramel shortcake and an outrageously fattening vanilla milkshake.

'Here's to our research, Eddie,' she toasted him, and he kicked his little feet as if he already knew the answer to their enquiries, and it was good.

Later on she was meeting Claire, who had been digging around at the paper for the names of some experts Molly could consult.

The *Daily Post* was on the corner of Ludgate Circus, just teetering on the edge of the City of London. Its location was the envy of all the other newspapers, once clustered together in Fleet Street, now banished to lonely complexes miles from the centre. The *Post* had fabulous views down the river in both directions.

Even the atrium was splendid beyond Molly's imagining. She had to psych herself up just to approach the huge reception desk, behind which a daunting-looking lady of about fifty held terrifying court. She felt self-conscious in her dungarees, pushing her buggy, in that temple of thrusting competitiveness.

The receptionist seemed determined to deal with everyone else before Molly, and to make things worse, Eddie, unusually for him, began to wail so pitifully that she had no alternative but to pick him up.

At the sight of the miserable Eddie, the receptionist seemed to melt like an iceberg in July. 'Aaaah, isn't he gorgeous. Just like my little grandson. How old is he?'

A line of important-looking people built up as the receptionist, ignoring all of them, emerged from her marble console and asked if she could hold him.

Molly was quite relieved when Claire finally appeared, carrying a box file, and the woman was forced to hand Eddie over and get back to her duties. 'You know, Claire,' the older woman remarked, 'you should get one of these. It would suit you.'

Remembering the pong of Eddie's nappy, Claire backed off like a virgin confronting a vampire. 'No thanks. I'll stick to being single and miserable.'

She whisked Molly off to the staff canteen and bought them the cheapest coffee and muffins Molly had ever encountered. 'They're subsidized, that's why, and the view's thrown in free,' Claire pointed out, leading Molly out on to the terrace. 'Pity we have to pay with our souls. Is it OK out here? A bit chilly, but more private.'

After they'd sat down, Claire opened the box file. 'There you go.' She produced a great wodge of photocopies and handed them over. 'Everything you've ever wanted to know about adoption. Plus quite a lot you didn't. Now, how much have you got to go on?'

'His date of birth, obviously, and after that, not much.'

'You don't have any idea of his birth name?'

Molly shook her head.

'Or the place of birth?'

'No. Though I assume it's probably near where Patricia and Andrew live. They're very pro everything local. I'm sure they'd have gone somewhere nearby.'

Claire put her hand briefly over her friend's. 'Molly, gorgeous, I'm all for life's adventures, but have you thought about how Pat and Andrew will react when they find you're looking for his real mother?'

'Of course I have. I know how hard it'll be for them both, that's why I'm going to tread incredibly carefully. Andrew will understand, but Pat's a different matter. She's invested so much in Joe and she won't hear a word of criticism of him. As far as she's concerned, there's only one problem in our marriage. And that's me.'

'Then you'd better start with Andrew. Ask him for whatever details he can remember; nothing's too small, it'll all help. And find Joe's birth certificate; he must have needed it for your wedding.'

'I think they've still got it.' Molly's hand crept up to her neck. Thinking about it from Patricia and Andrew's point of view made her see how sensitive all this was going to be.

'Will that have his mother's name on it?'

'Not if it's the one he was issued after adoption.'

'You'll have to start with the official channels.' Claire handed Molly a blue booklet called *Searching for Family Connections.*

'This'll show you some short cuts, but it's going to be tough. Though it's much easier than it was, and easier still if Joe's mother actually wants to find *him*. There's something called the contact register. It's a list of parents who've said they want to be contacted if their child ever decides to look for them.'

'Is that common?'

'It happens quite often. Giving away a baby is something that haunts a woman. Some people never get over it and can't wait to find their child again, but a lot of women feel it's morally wrong, that it's unfair to the child or their new family to actually look for them. If they put their name on this register, it shows they want to be found. Joe will have to register as well though.'

As she walked back to the tube station, her bag bulging with press cuttings, Molly tried to picture Joe's mother, Eddie's grandmother. Would she have been some poor teenager from a council estate who couldn't cope? Someone who went on to get married and have more children, but who perhaps never forgot Joe? Someone who, even now, still ached for her lost child and yearned passionately for the joy of a reunion?

Inspired by this happy thought, Molly decided to get Joe to register and to try and find out if Joe's mother had been in touch. The thought of taking action at last kept her spirits up. And it also, she had to admit, took her mind off how Patricia and Andrew were going to react.

Despite its wonderful location, paranoia lurked behind the VDUs of Amalgamated Newspapers. It surfaced most often in the corridors, where little groups clustered away from the open-plan atmosphere, or in the ladies' loo, or on the front steps where the diehard smokers gathered for a fag. A certain level of anxiety was accepted, par for the course in a profession where the supply of bright young graduates far outweighed the number of jobs on offer, but ever since word had got around that job losses were on the cards, the level of gossip, innuendo and sheer funk had thickened like smoke on a battlefield.

'It says here,' Claire read out from her screen, where she had been whizzing through the Press Association's bulletin of news stories, 'that Media Studies is now the most popular course at university and that in one year more new graduates are produced than there are jobs in the whole of the media.'

'Shut up, Claire,' requested her neighbour at the next desk, 'and read us something cheerful. Aren't there any nice reassuring axe murders on PA?'

'Tony wants you, Claire!' someone bellowed from the other end of the features section.

Claire pinched her nose between her finger and thumb as if she were about to jump into a swimming pool. It was a childish gesture of anxiety that all the big-girl toughness she'd managed to assume hadn't quite suppressed. What the hell did Tony want with her? She'd already been allocated her story and would have to rush to file before the deadline since she'd taken all that time out with Molly.

Tony was the executive in charge of features, and also Claire's married lover.

She hadn't intended to fall for a married man, had indeed sworn to avoid them for her own as well as the wife's sake. Then, six months earlier – and Claire couldn't believe the corniness of this – she'd got drunk at the Christmas party and ended up necking with him in his car. The fact that he'd been dressed as Santa Claus at the time, after giving out the department's Christmas presents, was her only excuse to explain her disgraceful behaviour. She'd always loved visiting Santa as a child. Fortunately in those days Santa hadn't put his hand down her blouse like Tony did.

Claire smiled at the memory, especially the bit when he'd sat her on his knee in the back of his Range Rover and asked: 'And what would *you* like for Christmas, little girl?'

It could have been grounds for sexual harassment if she hadn't been so entirely willing. The affair ever since had lacked the initial drama of that moment, but she'd gone and got fond of him, stupid fool that she was.

Today Tony was playing the Big Desk game, which meant he stayed behind it, trying to derive some authority from the six feet of solid yew that separated them.

'Look, love,' Tony glanced round his office as if he might catch sight of some concealed microphone in the yucca plant, 'I shouldn't be telling you this, but I saw a list of proposed redundancies.' He smiled in sympathy, then reached out his hand and squeezed hers, looking hideously embarrassed. 'You were number two.'

'But I'm just as good as the rest of that bunch of hacks out there,' she protested angrily.

'Far better, probably, but you were last in, so you have to prove beyond argument you're worth keeping or you'll be out. This is nothing to do with talent, just the size of the redundancy cheque. Your talent might be bigger but your cheque would be smaller than theirs.'

'What can I do?'

'Come up with a story that's so bloody amazing, so scorchingly readable, so totally exclusive to the paper that they have to fire someone else instead.'

'Right.' Claire felt her hand creep towards her nose again and had to stop herself. 'I'd better get moving then.'

'Can I come round tonight?'

'I'll be too busy looking for that scoop.'

'Come on, Clairey, you can sit on Santa's knee again.' He tried to look appealing and signally failed.

'Hasn't anyone ever told you,' Claire said tartly, 'that Santa doesn't exist? He's just a figment of the marketing men's imagination.'

'You could have fooled me,' Tony responded with such a woolfishly endearing expression on his face that she weakened.

'Nine o'clock then. And no saying you'll miss your train to Godalming.'

Claire went back to her desk, trying to keep up her spirits and think how the bloody hell she was going to find a story so good it could possibly save her job.

*

Early summer in London was always a pleasure, it seemed to Molly. All bright blue sky and red geraniums, with people smiling and sitting outside wine bars. The parks were still fresh and green, not yet worn and threadbare as they would be in a couple of months. Every day Eddie kicked his fat bare toes in the paddling pool in their local park, which had just been filled with clean water and had not yet acquired its oily garnish of discarded ice-cream wrappers and foil crisp packets. Each morning before she took him there, Molly ran down to see if there was a letter on the mat telling them the joyous news that Joe's mum wanted to contact him. But none came. Finally, as sultry July shrugged off the fresh delights of June, a letter did arrive.

At that moment Joe bounded down the stairs, late and reminding Molly of a scruffy schoolboy. He had been busy at work and preoccupied. So preoccupied that he almost stood on Eddie, who was crawling around on the mat, and didn't see the buff envelope at first. It was from the Adoption Department of the Registrar General's office in Southport.

'Go on, open it,' Molly urged, holding her breath. It was the first bit of real feedback they'd had and they both needed the encouragement.

Joe's shoulders slumped. 'No dice. She hasn't put herself down on the register.'

Molly hugged him extra tight and tried to bury her disappointment. It would have been so much easier for everyone if she actually wanted to be found.

There was another question. Did the fact that his mother had failed to register mean that she actively *didn't* want to be found?

Molly sighed. Now that she knew Joe's mother hadn't tried to contact him, she was going to have to go a step further. On Sunday, as they did every week, they would be having lunch with Joe's adopted parents, Patricia and Andrew.

Did they dare ask for their help?

Molly knew Pat found her daughter-in-law disconcerting. Molly's wild curly mane of hair, her paint-splattered dungarees and her tendency to spray her dining table lime green or build an entire kitchen were so different from anything in Pat's quiet and dependable life. Nor could Pat see how a young married woman was allowed out to noisy wine bars with her girlfriend to get up to God knows what. Molly had even once beat Joe in a downing a pint of beer contest, making Patricia announce, shuddering slightly, that Molly was like no housewife Patricia had ever met.

It also irked her that her own husband, Andrew, had such a soft spot for his spirited daughter-in-law. Molly'd won him over on their very first visit by her genuine interest in Andrew's beloved tool collection.

The first time Joe brought her home she'd spent a full hour with Andrew in his shed asking questions about the efficiency of his Workmate and the relative merits of Black & Decker versus Bosch drill bits. Patricia, who considered drill bits about as interesting as the football results in Norwegian, had polished her surfaces in tight-lipped silence.

'Come on, love,' her husband had teased, 'you'd love it if she was asking about your new washer-drier.'

By Sunday lunch Molly and Joe still hadn't decided whether to broach the subject.

Pat was waiting for them, as she always did, standing in front of the picture window of their bungalow in the small town of Mere-on-Sea.

Mere-on-Sea was the classier end of Westbeach-on-Sea, if Westbeach could be said to have a classier end. An hour's drive from London, it had become the point of exodus for the most colourful and, in Pat's view, commonest *émigrés* from the East End of London. Mere-on-Sea, at least, did have an aura of dignity that its noisy neighbour lacked.

'Hello, Molly love, good journey?' Andrew, Patricia noted waspishly, had also been looking out for Molly and Joe, from the superior vantage of the tool-shed.

'Great, thanks.' Joe hugged Andrew with obvious affection. 'Eddie slept all the way. Must have been the double brandy we slipped him.'

Andrew cracked with laughter. It was always the same, Pat thought. Andrew had a way with him that people, even their own son, responded to.

Feeling excluded, she took a step backwards into the shadow, almost tripping over the coffee table in her desire not to be seen.

'Hello, Joe dear,' she said stiffly when she emerged again a few moments later. She surveyed Molly's muddy Nikes. 'Do you want to leave those in the hall?'

Everyone in the Meredith household had to take off their shoes to preserve the 'new' beige carpet. The fact that it had been there over five years now escaped Patricia's attention. This didn't surprise Molly in someone who still kept the plastic covering on the seats of her dining-room chairs. It always amazed Molly that Joe had grown up in this house. It was so hard to imagine a grubby-kneed, wellie-booted boy running about the place.

'Do you need to feed Eddie before lunch? I've left a towel out in the spare room.' Patricia didn't hold with boobs being whipped out anywhere but in the privacy of a chilly bedroom.

'It's all right, he's asleep at the moment.'

'Right. Shall we start lunch then?'

Sunday lunch at Patricia's was always exactly the same, and that was how her menfolk liked it. It was still roast beef, despite all the scares about BSE, which Patricia had no time for. The only concession was buying it off the bone rather than on, and only then because the Government had banned it. There were roast potatoes, a single vast Yorkshire pudding, sprouts, carrots and shop-bought horseradish sauce. The two men, whose palates were as finely tuned as Escoffier's, even detected the difference if Patricia changed the shop.

Molly glanced at Joe. She could see he was building up his nerve. 'Actually, Mum, there's something I wanted to ask you and Dad.'

'But the meat'll be overdone,' Pat stated, as if Joe had asked to alter the time of the Lord Mayor's banquet.

'We can always turn the oven down,' Andrew suggested, realizing something important was coming. Let's all sit down.' He led them into the shiny sitting room. Joe began as soon as they were seated.

'The thing is, Mum . . .'

'You're not splitting up, are you? Not after so short a time?'

'Nothing like that,' Joe said quietly. 'It's something I've been thinking about for a long time, but I didn't want to hurt either of your feelings. You've been such wonderful parents.'

Pat looked suddenly like an old football flattened by a lorry in the road. 'You want to look for her, don't you? That's what all this is about, isn't it?'

Chapter 5

'It's not a criticism of you, Mum,' Joe said quickly. 'You and Dad always gave me all the love I could ever have wanted. It's just that I need to make sense of myself. Find out why it happened.'

The silence was so white and deep and glacial, Molly felt they might all plunge into it and never be seen again.

Finally Pat spoke in a small, tired voice. 'I thought you were a happy child.'

Joe bounded across the room and held her. 'You've been a wonderful mum . . .' he began, but Pat cut through his words.

'So wonderful you need to find her.'

She turned on Molly with so much vitriol it shocked them all. 'You've pushed him into this, haven't you?' Resentment fizzed through her words like molten metal in water. 'He's never even mentioned any of this to me, not once, till you came along.'

Andrew, always more in touch with unpleasant realities than his wife, looked as if he were about to interrupt, but Patricia swept on. 'You think you know it all, don't you, you college graduates with your *Guardian* and your pop psychology. The natural mother's got some kind of divine right, hasn't she, and the adopted mother doesn't count!' Pat, alarmingly, had jumped up clutching a bowl of mixed nuts to her breast like a shield.

'You can't even imagine what it's like not to be able to have children,' she hissed at Molly. 'Every month you pray, you tell God you'll do anything, pay any price, and nothing happens. You start the tests. They scrape you and poke you and stick things up you. And then they patronize you. And you have to put up with it. Every sodding humiliation.' Molly flinched at Patricia's swear word. On her prim lips it seemed like the worst obscenity imaginable. 'And then some tart falls pregnant up against a wall and dumps her baby on the scrapheap.' Even Andrew was shaken by the strength of his wife's venom. 'And do you know what? Even when you're allowed to take it home, this baby she doesn't want, that she's thrown away and you love with your whole soul, you have to wait months, can you imagine that, *months* before he's yours. She, the sainted mother, can change her mind and grab him back any time she fancies. You don't even dare love him. Can you imagine what that feels like? Can you? And now the bloody law allows him to go and find her.'

A wail of pain, animal rather than human, ricocheted round Pat's neat sitting room. She threw down the nuts and ran upstairs, with Andrew following.

Molly felt the blood drain from her face. She'd encouraged all this, helped lift the lid on this Pandora's box of emotions. She wished she could go and hug her mother-in-law, tell her she was sorry, that it would all be for the best. But would it? Not from Pat's point of view. Her world had changed already.

Eddie, who'd been sleeping peacefully until now, sensed the commotion and began to wail too.

A few minutes later Andrew reappeared.

'Dad, I'm so sorry.' Joe was fighting back tears himself. 'I didn't know how else to say it. Do you think I'm doing the wrong thing?'

'She's just had a shock. It's almost worse that she's always known it might happen.'

He walked over to the small polished wood bureau, the only piece of furniture of any value in the room, and opened a drawer. 'Here's your birth certificate. You probably haven't seen it since your wedding.'

Upstairs the crying had subsided.

'Can I go up?' Joe asked.

'Will she be all right?' Molly added when Joe had gone upstairs. 'This must be so hard for her.'

'Pat always wanted Joe to be different, to seem more like hers. She hated it when he ever talked about being adopted.' Andrew picked up a photograph from the mantelpiece and thought of the lovable, sometimes forlorn little boy, always reading his book, so different from his classmates. 'Pat doesn't like admitting it, but Joe always took being adopted hard. He wanted to tell the other boys at school because he believed in being honest, bless him, and they bullied him for it. I'll never forget the time he said, "When I go to big school, Dad, I won't say I'm adopted. I'll pretend to be like everyone else." He never said that to his mum, though. He knew he had to protect her. She didn't like even talking about it.'

'Do you think finding her might really help Joe then? Maybe there are other reasons why Joe's troubled, nothing to do with this.'

'He's always been a restless soul. I don't think he ever felt completely at ease with us. Pat knows that too, but she'd never admit it. Maybe secrets are best out of the closet.'

On an impulse, Molly hugged him. 'Whether you're his birth father or not, Joe was lucky to have you.'

Andrew picked up the birth certificate Joe had dropped in his rush to comfort Pat. 'I'm not sure how much use this'll be. It's the post-adoption one. We weren't allowed the one with his mother's name on it. Joe'll have to apply for that officially. If it's any use to you, we adopted him through the Sacred Heart Society, so maybe they could help. They have a branch here and another in Sussex. I think, from something one of the nuns said, he came from round there. Something else I remembered. His real name may be Lewis.' Andrew smiled gently. 'I ought not to know that, but reading upside-down writing's one of my useless skills.'

'Not so useless. Thanks, Andrew. I know this must be hard for you too. I love Joe and Eddie so much.'

'I know you do. And he loves you too. I know he can be moody. I don't want him to waste his best chance of happiness and I firmly believe you and Eddie are it.'

'So you think we should go ahead?' Molly realized how much they'd all come to rely on Andrew's quiet ways.

'You've already decided. Even if it's a dead end or the mother doesn't want to know, maybe it's a ghost Joe needs to lay.'

A little while later Joe came back down. 'Best you went home now,' Andrew told them. 'Leave her to have a cry and a sleep.'

'Maybe we should never have told her.' Joe bit his lip. 'I mean, it might easily be for nothing.'

'Better to prepare her. Don't worry, Pat's a coper. She'll come round. Just keep loving her.'

After they'd left, packing the baby and all his gear back into the car and starting off on their subdued journey back to Peckham, Andrew went upstairs.

Pat was lying on top of the pink candlewick bedspread, staring out of the window after them. Andrew lay down beside her.

Still weeping, Pat clung to her husband. 'I'm going to lose him, Andrew, I know I am.'

Andrew began to pat her back rhythmically, just as he did to Eddie and had once done to Joe. 'We never owned him, love. We always knew this could happen. We've given him all we can and we have to hope it makes a difference.'

All the same, once Pat had finally fallen asleep, Andrew wiped away a tear of his own. He wasn't a praying man, but there were times when he wished he were.

The question was, would it be better for all of them if the woman, whoever she was, acknowledged Joe or not?

'Are you still happy to go ahead?' Molly asked when they'd unpacked the car. 'I mean, we could easily stop if you felt it was too difficult.'

For answer Joe folded her into his arms. The extraordinary thing was that it had already brought them closer together. The sense that life wasn't always easy or happy had made them suddenly appreciate each other more.

'Would you like me to do that belly dance now?' Molly asked, shaking out her long hair. She wanted to cheer him up and make him feel loved.

'My God,' Joe teased, 'don't tell me my wife is trying to seduce me on the sitting room floor? I must look for my roots more often.'

'Good place as any. Our bed's usually got three in it.' Molly began to undo the belt of his trousers. 'There's one root I wouldn't mind finding straight away.'

Together they tumbled down on to the squashy old sofa under the dramatic curtain display and did exactly what one was supposed to do in a Turkish harem.

After Joe had disappeared for work the next day, Molly sat on the sofa again, this time fully clothed, smiling at the memory. Maybe, when she wanted to make some money, she should design erotic bed hangings. Still in her dressing gown, she tidied up the flat, arranging Eddie on a sheepskin rug, where he kicked happily. She felt wonderfully louche, and deeply relieved that she and Joe seemed to be so close to each other. She thought about ringing Pat, and decided to leave it for a little while. Maybe it was easier for Pat to make Molly the villainness of the piece. She put on some music by U2, her favourites, and began to dance to the music, her dressing gown slipping off her shoulder.

When the door bell rang she was sure it was going to be one of the neighbours complaining about the noise. But it wasn't the neighbours. It was Claire.

Claire took in the decadent dressing gown and the look of smug satisfaction on her friend's face. 'Ah ha, do I sense a happy family reunion with celebratory fuck thrown in?'

Molly giggled. 'What on earth are you doing here at this time? Don't you have a job to go to?'

'As a matter of fact, I'm researching hookers in Streatham. Since the hookers were all busy having their pussies waxed, or whatever it is hookers do with their mornings, none were in. So I thought I'd drop by.'

'But Streatham's miles away!' protested Molly.

'It's all south London,' Claire dismissed airily. 'You don't mind pretending to be a hooker, do you, so you can give me a quote or two?' She surveyed her friend. 'Come to mention it, you even look like one in that get-up.'

'Since when have hookers worn dressing gowns and white socks?' Molly protested.

'You'd be surprised. Punters pay extra for white socks. And that come-on look would have them reaching for their credit cards.'

'That come-on look is relief. Look,' she steered Claire towards the kitchen, 'make us both a cup of coffee while I get dressed.' Claire was the opposite of domesticated. 'That's if you can manage instant coffee?'

'So how was it? Did she blame you?'

'Of course she blamed me. Actually, it was awful. Poor Pat. But Andrew was incredibly helpful. He gave us this.' Molly pulled out the birth certificate. 'But even better were the titbits of information. Joe was adopted through a society called the Sacred Heart, possibly their Sussex branch, and his mother's name may have been Lewis.'

'Moll, that's brilliant. You've got more to go on than you'll ever get from the authorities, more than a lot of people ever have, actually.' Molly believed her. She knew from the books she'd already flipped through what a bureaucratic process it was.

Claire tickled Eddie's tummy. 'You know,' she confessed, examining her sheer tights for snags as she stood up, 'sometimes I envy you the brat and everything.'

Molly laughed. 'You certainly have a way of putting things. Anyway, you're not yet the brat type. Still the prat type. Speaking of which, how *is* your boyfriend, the executive features editor?'

'Warning me, as he whips out his willy, that I'm for the chop if I don't find myself a really good story.'

Molly was appalled. 'Thank God I'm at home. Newspapers sound horrible.'

'I think he meant it kindly.'

In the end Molly made the coffee herself, as Claire had shown no inclination to do so. 'Claire, I need to borrow your journalistic skills. If it were you looking for your mother, where would you go from here?'

Claire thought for a moment. 'Write the Sacred Heart Society a really nice letter explaining that you're Joe's natural sister and you're desperate to find him. Say you're coming in three days' time. Don't leave an address, otherwise they'll write and put you off. That'll throw them into a tizz. They'll look up his file. Then, when you get there, they might see you. And if they see you, they might let fall some clues. Then pray to the Sacred Heart.'

'My God, Claire,' marvelled Molly, 'you're good at this.'

'So I bloody well should be. I spend all day trying to find out things that people don't want to tell me, and throwing all the stuff they *do* want to tell me in the bin. The question is, am I good enough to keep my job? I'd better get back before my desk's been allocated to someone cheaper.'

As soon as Claire had left, Molly did exactly as her friend had suggested. She wrote to the Sacred Heart Society, signing the letter Molly Lewis and telling them she would be coming to see them in three days' time. This was her first actual lie, but Molly was ashamed to admit that while she had some misgivings, there was also an undeniable frisson of excitement. What if Lewis wasn't, in fact, the right name? Molly plunged ahead anyway, Andrew rarely got things wrong.

Chapter 6

For the next three days, while Molly found herself boiling with excitement, it was almost as if Joe had lost interest in the subject.

'Shall I go then?' she asked him on the day she'd undertaken to drive to the foster home run by the Sacred Heart Society.

'Up to you,' he hedged, leaving the car keys very visibly right in the middle of the kitchen table.

'I'll take that as a yes, shall I?'

The journey to Sussex was not promising. The roads in south London sweated heat, Eddie whinged, the traffic was worse than a bank holiday, and when Molly missed her exit off the motorway and had to drive an extra fifteen miles she wondered if it was an omen.

Turn back, Molly Meredith, and stop interfering would probably appear miraculously in one of those flashing speed-warning signs any minute.

Finally she found the place. The Sacred Heart Society's foster home was in a small village inappropriately called Plumpington. The name made Molly smile even while she recognized that few mothers about to give away their babies would see the funny side.

In fact, the epithet 'village' was an exaggeration. The place, though countrified, was more like a straggle of unprepossessing modern cottages, a farm with a corrugated-iron roof instead of the usual mellow russet tiles, and a dilapidated concrete bus-shelter. The foster home itself was hard to miss. It was an ugly, purpose-built 1960s building. Outside was a noticeboard sporting an ominous bright red heart pierced by a knife and dripping drops of dayglo-red blood.

A nun in modern dress, but still as recognizable as if she were wearing a white wimple with butterfly wings, answered the heavy wooden door. She was Irish and friendly, not at all the disapproving, tight-lipped type Molly had been expecting. She had rounded, weatherbeaten cheeks and unusually pale blue eyes, which could easily have been cold and forbidding had not the warmth of her smile belied the effect. Molly wondered if she would be turned away on the spot. Instead the nun beckoned her in.

'You must be Miss Lewis,' she greeted Molly, chucking Eddie under the chin. 'We always used to scare the babies in our old get-up. I'm Sister Mary, by the way. I used to be Sister Assumpta before we went modern, so that's another improvement. I've cleared the parlour for our chat.'

Molly followed Sister Mary along a long red-tiled corridor, which was spotless and smelt strongly of carbolic soap. 'I use Flash when it's my turn,' confided Sister Mary, 'but it's Sister Bernadette's day today and she prefers doing it the hard way.' To Molly's amazement, the nun winked.

At one end of the passage Molly noticed a curious arrangement of rooms. On either side were two identical doors. Each gave on to a smallish room beyond, both with an outside entrance.

Sister Mary paused. 'The mothers and babies lived upstairs until the baby was old enough for adoption. This was where the exchanges were made. The mother brought the baby in that side and gave it to the nun in charge, who took it to the opposite room, where the prospective parents waited. We used to call that side the Sad Room and the other the Happy Room.'

Molly stared into the Sad Room and shivered, almost able to feel the cloud of grief and loss that still hung miasmically in the air even though it was painted white and fresh. She imagined the young girls getting their babies ready to give away, wrapping their love inside the shawl or the matinée jacket along with the baby, holding it or kissing it one last time, before going slowly downstairs with a granite-faced parent and the awful, terrible pain of parting. Perhaps they sometimes felt a sense of relief that they would have their young lives back, but how many would have left with red eyes and backs bowed at the realization that they would never, ever forget that moment no matter what might lie ahead for them?

Molly found herself wiping away a tear, and clutching Eddie extra tightly.

Sister Mary patted her. 'Your brother would have come through here.'

For a second Molly, carried away with the emotion of the moment, almost said 'What brother? I don't have a brother,' but saved herself in time.

'Of course, we don't handle adoptions here any more,' said Sister Mary. 'Not enough babies. Girls are wiser now, they know about contraception and abortion.' The nun paused, contemplating a world where girls were familiar with strawberry-flavoured condoms and morning-after pills. 'And a very good thing too,' she added briskly. 'I saw enough tears here to flood the Red Sea.'

'Were they unwilling, then? To give away their babies?'

'Some of them were dragged in here kicking and screaming.' Sister Mary touched the cross round her neck. 'It was an awful process, inhumane. The new parents would hear the mother wailing and screaming when her baby was taken from her, and they felt guilty at stealing her child. The Spanish Inquisition couldn't have designed a better system. They wanted these girls to suffer the wages of sin.'

'Even in 1975, when my brother was born?'

'Morality changes more slowly than you think. I hear all this sounding-off about how immoral the world's got, and I think, "Good thing too!" It might mean fewer babies for adoption but a lot less heartbreak for those poor girls.' The nun seemed to remember herself. 'I'm not sure the Mother Superior would go along with that, now, or the Pope. But morality's not always a kind thing, whatever the Church has to say.'

They'd reached a small scrubbed parlour, its walls as white as a Grecian monastery, which smelt faintly of incense from the adjoining chapel, and beeswax from the polished furniture. On one wall was a small crucifix.

'Enough gabbing from me,' apologized Sister Mary. 'My family had to send me away to the nuns, not because I'd get into any trouble – would you look at me, is it likely now? – but because I couldn't keep my mouth shut even then. And I can't now, thirty years later. What was it you wanted to know about your brother?'

'He was adopted through the Society, almost certainly through this branch, in February 1975,' Molly gabbled on, hoping the nun wouldn't push her on amy inconsistencies.

'So if this baby was your natural brother, does that mean the lady who had him adopted was your mother?' Sister Mary watched her closely.

Molly thought quickly. 'Yes. Yes, that's right. She was my mother.'

'Not much of a family resemblance.' The nun turned away, as if she'd said too much.

'You remember her then?' Molly's heart hammered in her chest, but she tried to keep the excitement from her voice, in case it discouraged the already indiscreet Sister Mary from telling her more.

The nun glanced up at the crucifix, as if for guidance.

'How could I forget her? She was so beautiful. And completely different from all the others.'

'Mum's always stood out,' Molly bluffed. 'I'm sure she'd be touched you remember her so well. I'd love to hear about her then,' Molly pushed gently. This was Joe's real mother the nun was talking about!

'She was older than normal for a start. Self-assured. Middle-class. And she had no one with her. That was unusual in those days.'

Molly felt a small shiver of apprehension. This wasn't the image she'd held of Joe's mother at all. No pathetic young girl forced by a furious father into giving her baby away. The nun was painting a picture of someone in charge of her own destiny.

'But then her family were different from everyone else round here. Sophisticated people. Londoners.'

'You knew them?' Again Molly felt a shock wave. 'It must have been terrible for her when they took my brother away?'

Sister Mary sighed. 'Everyone shows pain in different ways. She didn't want to look at him. Just got up and left.' The nun sounded as if she were back there in that sad, bare room. Then, as if remembering that the young woman was Molly's mother, she added: 'I'm sure she had her reasons. Have you tried to ask her?'

Molly jumped again. 'She doesn't like talking about it,' she lied.

'It takes a lot of people like that. You mustn't be too hard on her. It's the only way some women can deal with the loss. To pretend it didn't happen. It's not an easy subject; you shouldn't condemn. Pain and loss show in many different ways.'

At that moment Eddie, who had been sitting quietly in his baby chair, woke up and yelled, reminding Molly that it was time for his feed. Molly wished she'd had the foresight to drop him at Pat's instead of bringing him. Except that she wasn't Pat's favourite person at the moment.

'And of course,' Sister Mary added, 'we didn't get too many Amandas.' Molly's heart leaped like a salmon in cold water. Joe's mother was called Amanda! 'And none as lovely as her. I always wondered what happened to her.' She looked Molly up and down. 'I'm glad she settled down and had more children. Funny, you don't look like her, but resemblances are strange things.'

'No. I favour my father's side.'

'Your son does, though. He's very like her. The same dark hair and those extraordinary eyes.'

Molly hung on to Eddie, trying to contain her excitement. Joe and Eddie's startling looks obviously had to have come from somewhere, and she'd always suspected it had to be his mother. 'I can't give you any details of the couple who adopted your brother though. That would be wrong. You'll have to write to the Register. Maybe he's trying to find you.'

'Thank you, Sister Mary I'll do that. You've really helped me today. I feel a lot better about everything.'

'I'm glad you came. I've never forgotten your mother. There was something special about her. I hope she's happy.' As she was showing Molly out, the kind nun paused and took her hand. 'I've told you too much, but that's my choice. Of course, you should have applied officially and I'll probably get into all sorts of trouble, but I'm too old for all that palaver. I've never believed in institutions anyway, nasty male things, or I'd be Reverend Mother by now. God can punish me if he wants. And reunions can be such happy events. I hope you find your brother, be careful, though, dear. I know your motives are for the best but it's dangerous territory you're in now. An emotional minefield, you might say. You have to be sure this is what your mother wants. Not just you.'

Back outside the sad silence of the home, Molly felt elated. Andrew had been right about Joe's mother being called Lewis, but Molly now knew her full name, and that she was extraordinarily beautiful. Since she must have lived near here, there would be people who would almost certainly remember her. The excitement at getting closer was heady and overpowering. She decided to explore the area a little.

The next village down the road was only a couple of miles away, but centuries apart in mood. Molly was surprised that the foster home, with its sprawling urban architecture, had ever been given planning permission so near to the timeless Garden of Eden that was Lower Ditchwell. Perhaps it was something to do with rival local councils.

She could just imagine the kind of rivalries that existed between the larger spillover commuter towns and their peaceful upmarket neighbours, terrified of the corrosive effect of starter homes or executive estates blotting their landscape of English rural peace. The Sacred Heart home must have been one in the eye for the snobby Ditchwell dwellers, with God's seal of approval thrown in.

Molly parked in the pub car park, hoping the publican wouldn't notice. Like all pretty English villages, Lower Ditchwell had nowhere to park, having grown up in an era where no one travelled unless they absolutely had to, and even then probably only the six miles to the nearest town by horse or carrier cart. Four-wheel drives with rhino bars were still a distant unimagined nightmare.

The village consisted of a hundred or so houses, some thatched, some with grey stone roofs, the tiles made by splitting heavy slabs of stone. Most of the cottages were flint-faced, with white front doors. On this sunny morning the scent of honeysuckle and old-fashioned roses was overpowering.

In amongst the cottages, Molly noticed a tea shop, and headed straight for it. Tea was the natural accompaniment for gossip, and Molly could bet that all the gossips for miles around congregated here to dish the dirt over the china cups and the home-made Victoria sponge.

The tea shop was crowded, and Molly felt self-conscious carrying a grizzling baby. Everyone here seemed more the age to be grandparents, and grandparents of extremely well-behaved children at that, and disappointingly, the place was far too crowded to start asking questions.

The lady running the tea shop took pity on her and carved out a small place in the corner for them to sit down. Molly searched in Eddie's baby bag for the emergency bottle of expressed milk she carried, sensing that at any moment the whingeing might turn into a wall of sound.

'Want me to pop it in the micro?' asked the owner kindly. 'I know you're not supposed to, but we always do for my grandson. It's fine as long as you shake it properly.'

'Thanks.' Molly handed over the bottle gratefully.

When the woman returned, Molly asked if she could borrow a phone book. She had the ambitious idea of writing down all the

Lewises in the neighbourhood, but to her dismay there were over a hundred listed.

'Is there anywhere I could photocopy this?' she asked, jiggling Eddie on her knee and trying to stop him chewing the phone book.

'Quite a handful, isn't he?' Molly tried to look for the positive connotations in this description. 'The Stores might. They're a post office. Doreen,' the woman bellowed, so that everyone in the place jumped, 'does the Stores do photocopying?'

'Yep.' A friendly, doggy-like face with a thick fringe appeared out of the steamy depths of the kitchen. 'I photocopied the vet's report for my Pet Plan.' The newcomer asked the question in everyone else's mind. 'Are you looking for someone, dear? Maybe we could help.'

'Actually,' Molly confessed, not at all sure this was a very discreet method of conducting her investigations; what if Joe's mother were one of these women sitting here enjoying a bun and a bit of back-biting? All the same she couldn't resist it, 'yes, I am.'

'Maybe we could help?' Ten or eleven fascinated faces stared at Molly. 'What's the name of the people you're looking for?'

'Lewis.' It sounded so odd to say it. She took her courage in both hands and went on, 'I'm looking for someone called Amanda Lewis.'

She held her breath.

'Lewis?' repeated the café owner. 'Wasn't there a Lewis over Polehampton way? Ran a riding stables?'

'He's dead,' chipped in the one old man amongst them, with relish. 'Died of a heart attack a week after retiring. Probably couldn't stand his wife.'

'What was her name?' Molly asked eagerly. 'The wife?'

'Mabel.'

'Did they have a daughter who might have been called Amanda?'

'Only dogs and horses,' the old man announced with satisfaction. 'They said they never had no time for nothing else. But if you ask me, he was more interested in sheep than women. Mind you,' he leered at the assembled gathering, 'the Southdown is a pretty-looking sheep. Better looking than his wife anyway.'

Doreen rapidly changed the subject. 'Weren't that couple near Weighaven called Lewis?' she demanded.

'They were brother and sister,' pronounced the old man.

'Brother and sister?' sneaked Doreen. 'They used to come in here holding hands. If I'd known I'd have chucked 'em out!'

The old man sniggered. 'Maybe they just huddled together for warmth.'

'Charlie Farlow, you're disgusting!'

'At least I keep me hands off me own kith and kin,' Charlie countered, still grinning.

'And looking at them, who could blame you?' Doreen turned to Molly, who was reeling from all this rural revelation. 'Sorry, love, it looks like there's no Lewises in this village.'

Eddie had finished his bottle and Molly, rather gratefully, got up to leave. She bundled all his things into his buggy and headed for the door, longing for sunshine and air. She wondered for a moment if they were having her on.

Doreen had followed her out. 'Don't pay no attention to Charlie, my duck. He's gone soft in the brain. Good luck with your search.'

Molly wheeled Eddie off along the narrow pavement while Doreen turned back into the tea shop.

'Here, Doreen,' piped one of the quieter old ladies, 'you never mentioned him up at Lewis's Antiques.'

Doreen clapped her hand to her mouth. 'He don't live round here, though. He lives in Cliffdean like all the rest of them poncey antique dealers.'

'He's called Lewis all the same, ain't he?'

'He is that.' She turned to see where Molly had got to, but Molly, once out of sight of the tea shop, had raced along the pavement at double speed back towards her car. She wanted to get back to dirty, drug-ridden old London, away from all these sheep-shagging, sibling-screwing country folk.

She had almost made it to the car when Eddie, not satisfied by the one bottle, began to bellow again. This time she would have to feed him herself. She looked around for a suitably discreet spot and noticed a wooden bus-shelter. Though a bit dark and smelly inside, at least it was draped in honeysuckle and wild roses. She had started undoing the buttons of her shirt when she noticed someone watching her from behind the trim hedge of the house opposite. It was a tall, slender woman in a floppy hat, wearing jodhpurs and a white lace shirt, almost like the male lead in a pantomime. She looked as if she were about to speak. Perhaps she would tell Molly that feeding a baby in a bus-shelter was just not on in the country. Molly planned her pithy urban retort.

Instead the woman said nothing and disappeared.

Moments later a shadow falling across the bright sunlight made Molly look up. The woman was now standing only a foot away. Molly was startled to see that she was old.

'Excuse me, my dear.' The voice was strong and husky, and reminded Molly of TV commercials for world cruises or opulent retirements on Portuguese golf courses. 'But would you prefer somewhere more comfortable to feed your baby? It's all cat's pee and condoms in here, I'm afraid.'

Molly, who had had enough of straight-talking country people who called spades shovels, was about to politely refuse when some instinct made her gather up her belongings and get clumsily to her feet. It really *wasn't* very salubrious here.

'There's a little summerhouse you could sit in.' The older woman led the way through a wooden gate which was locked in the dark, glossy embrace of an ivy bush. She settled Molly down in a garden chair with a comfortable chintz-covered cushion behind her. 'I'll just get you a cup of tea. I remember how thirsty all that makes you.' She gestured to the baby at Molly's breast. 'I always used to drink a gin and tonic. Absolutely *verboten* now, I know. Poor baby was probably permanently pissed. Would you like a biscuit? Of course you would.'

She returned with a plate of delicious Belgian chocolate biscuits. Eddie, perhaps scenting the new and alluring aroma of chocolate, turned his head away from Molly's breast towards his hostess.

The older woman started and almost dropped the plate of biscuits. 'How gorgeous he is,' she said quickly. 'About six months?'

Molly nodded, smiling like a madwoman in her maternal pride.

'And what extraordinary eyes. Ocean blue.'

'They are amazing, aren't they? Just like his father's.'

'And are you, or, er, his father from round here?'

'No, we live in Peckham.' There was something about the older woman's mix of warmth and outrageousness that encouraged confidences. She would, Molly sensed, be as unshockable as the Sphinx. 'But I think my husband's mother came from round here. I believe her name was Lewis. Amanda Lewis. I don't suppose you know her?'

Eddie chose this moment to grab a biscuit and try to stuff it in his mouth and Molly had to lean down and rescue him, so she missed the look of shock on the older woman's face. It was anything but Sphinx-like; rather it seemed as if a ghost had tap-danced on her grave.

A beat passed before the old woman spoke. 'Would you mind very much if I held him for a moment? He's such a lovely little thing.'

Molly hesitated. Eddie was just reaching that moment of separation anxiety when he liked only to be held by his mother, or failing that, his gran. Occasionally he even cried when Joe held him, which upset Joe hugely. 'All right,' she said finally.

Her hostess opened her arms and held the baby to her, tightly and confidently. To Molly's amazement, Eddie settled down immediately. The older woman stared deep into his eyes, as if beaming her being into his. Then she smiled.

'Gosh,' said Molly, stunned. 'He hardly ever does that, especially when he doesn't know you.'

'Maybe we met before in a previous life, didn't we, er . . .'

'Eddie.'

It seemed to Molly that her hostess held on to the baby just a fraction more than was usual, and a tiny shiver of fear passed through her. There was something strange going on here. What if the woman were a psychopath, or a babysnatcher with some tragic secret in her past?

Molly gently eased Eddie back into her own arms. 'I really had better be going . . . If I don't, I'll hit the rush hour and it'll take hours.'

'Of course.' Suddenly the woman seemed perfectly normal. 'Oh, by the way, I haven't introduced myself. My name's Beatrice Manners.'

'It sounds familiar somehow.'

'It might if you were thirty years older. I used to be quite a wow in musical comedy once. Noël Coward mostly. I don't suppose you know any Noël Coward.'

'Of course I do.' Molly put on a tight-clipped voice. 'Amanda, my darling, how lovely you look in blue . . .'

It took her a moment to register the name she'd chosen. How ridiculous. 'Goodbye. And thanks so much for the tea.'

'I'm sorry I couldn't help you.' And then, as if on a whim, 'I know, why don't you leave me your name and number, just in case anything comes to me?'

Molly wrote it down.

Bea watched the young woman with her flowing red mane and her spiky optimism walk down the lane towards the pub. She hadn't put the baby's sun hat back on and its dark, almost black hair stood up like a tiny beacon against the white of Molly's shirt, reminding her of another baby, years ago.

But was it a beacon of hope or a warning against impending tragedy?

Bea sighed. It had happened at last. In some ways it was almost a relief. She walked inside, out of the dazzling sunshine into the cool darkness of her hall. The telephone stood on a small round table next to an embroidered chair. Bea picked it up and dialled the familiar number.

When her daughter answered, Bea dropped her voice as if some-one might be eavesdropping. 'Listen, darling, I don't know how to tell you this, but a young woman just turned up on my doorstep asking for Amanda Lewis.'

She waited for a reaction but there was none. 'I think it must be his wife. It was quite a shock, I can tell you. Now listen, darling, what do you want me to do?'

Chapter 7

Molly tried to quell the silly sense of disappointment she'd felt when Beatrice Manners said she'd never heard of Amanda Lewis. Prising so much information from the very helpful Sister Mary had been enough of an achievement for one day. As the handbook she'd read on searching for lost relatives had warned her, she mustn't expect too much too soon. It was a long road, pitted with disappointments, and she'd had more breakthroughs than she could have hoped for. It had been extraordinary good fortune that Sister Mary had been the kind of person she was. Had Molly's letter fallen into the hands of the other nun, Sister Bernadette, the one who liked to scrub the corridors on her hands and knees from choice, Molly would probably have been sent away with a curt refusal and five Hail Marys to say as penance.

Eddie, satisfied by his feed and lulled by the warm sun, had fallen into a deep slumber. Molly was just about to lift him into the car when she spotted a small antique shop down an alley, almost hidden from sight. What a strange place to put a shop. Half the potential customers you might get would walk past without noticing. The economics of antique shops were always a mystery to Molly. Many of them seemed to be for 'Export Only' and were never open, or else their proprietors were out buying, or they were

61

closed because the owner had nipped out and would be 'Back in Five Minutes'. Except that they never were back in five minutes.

Molly adored antique shops, the junkier the better. Some of her best finds for the flat had come from junk shops, plus the occasional car-boot triumph, and once or twice from a builder's skip. She was the kind of person who infuriated her friends by finding art deco lamps at school bazaars, and brass bedheads at garage sales which she restored to their glorious finery.

Here was that notice again, or at least its second cousin: 'Gone to the Bank'. This probably meant 'Gone to the Pub', as it was lunch-time and the village pub was an inviting, wisteria-covered inn which Molly had considered herself.

She peered in the window. It was standard antique shop fare. A pine rocking horse, probably wildly overpriced, some china cider jars, a Welsh dresser adorned with pretty spongeware, and in the corner, a wash-stand with white water-lily tiles on the splashback. Molly could just picture it in the bathroom she'd stripped and painted herself to save money, with tongue-and-groove lining the walls. It would look fabulous. Then she saw the price tag and had to bite back her disappointment. There was no way they could afford it.

On a corner stand was arranged a selection of miniature china bells. Collecting china bells was Pat's one passion. She always bought one wherever she went, from Totnes to Thailand. Maybe it would help make amends if Molly got her one. She banged loudly on the door, but nothing happened.

Halfway through Molly's fruitiest insult, the door unexpectedly opened.

'I bet you say that to all the boys,' came a voice. The man in front of her was a curious character. Tall and emaciated, with shoulder-length light brown hair and a long black leather raincoat, like a seventies heavy metal star auditioning for the Gestapo. Despite this, there was an air of seedy charm about him, something to do with a gap-toothed smile one dental visit short of a yokel's.

He looked like the kind of man who would cheat you, then give you something free to make up for it.

'The door's open, you know,' he stated with an air of mild condescension, 'if you'd only had the nous to try.'

Molly's lips parted to remind him that removing the sign might have been a help to prospective customers, but he'd disappeared back inside.

Eddie was still sleeping, so she left him where she could see him, under a wisteria-laden tree.

Once in the shop she breathed in the evocative smells of linseed oil and beeswax. The stock, she noticed, was of a better quality than she'd expected. Other people's ancestors lined the walls, some of them looking quite old and valuable. She inspected a pretty pine chest of drawers, then drew in her breath at the price.

The shop's owner shrugged. 'They're Georgian. Quite early. A single piece of pine. With original handles.'

Molly tried not to smile. How would the antique trade survive without the description 'Georgian'?

She hunted through the selection of bells until she found the perfect specimen for Patricia. It was blue and white Delft. 'I was wondering how much this one was?'

'The price is on it,' the man pointed out. He'd gone back to sanding a bookcase at the back of the shop.

'Yes, but that's not the trade price. What's the best you can do on it?' Antique dealers, she knew, sold their stock to other traders cheaper than to the poor old public. Molly had never understood why. Personally, if she were an antique dealer she'd hate some other antique dealer to come and beat her down then go and make money on her bargain in their own shop.

'Are you trade, then?' His tone implied that traders didn't usually wear blue denim dungarees and push buggies around with them.

'Yes,' Molly said staunchly. Well, she sometimes had a bric-à-brac stall at the Scouts' fête.

He knocked off two pounds and Molly handed over the money. It was still quite expensive, but Patricia would love it and it might help mollify her. Plus, getting it two quid cheaper was almost worth it in itself.

She was halfway through the door, thinking that the shop's owner could do with a stint at the Lovejoy Academy for Fake Charm, when a sudden thought occurred to her. 'I don't suppose,' she held the door slightly ajar, enjoying the cool breeze from the alleyway, 'that you ever knew anyone called Amanda Lewis?'

The regular kiss of sandpaper on wood stopped momentarily, and he looked up at her. 'Now how would I know anyone with a posh name like that? Perhaps you'd better ask at the big house, where the county set live, or even at the cottage on the corner.' He leaned his head back towards the way she'd come.

'I've tried there already. The lady there doesn't know her.'

The man smiled to himself fleetingly and then resumed his sanding. 'Then I'm afraid I can't help you either.'

Molly felt the same sharp kick of disappointment she'd felt at the old lady's house. She scribbled down her phone number on an old price ticket on top of a Victorian wash-stand. 'Here's my number, just in case anything occurs to you.' He didn't even look at it.

It was early evening by the time she got back to Peckham and she was astonished to find Claire sitting on the steps leading up to their flat, as incongruous in her smart suit as a copy of *Vogue* in a pile of *Exchange & Marts*.

'Not more hookers in Streatham who happen to be out?' Molly enquired.

'No, actually. You invited me.'

Molly was about to deny all knowledge when she remembered Claire was right. The trouble with not going out to work any more was that you forgot to put things in your diary.

'Does this mean there's no Dom Perignon on ice waiting for me?' Claire helped her haul Eddie's gear up the front steps. 'Because if so, I might just have to find I'm double-booked.'

'Dozy cow,' Molly teased, thrilled to see her friend so that she could report her breakthrough. 'You can slum it with Safeway plonk. It'll get you used to how the rest of us live in case you really do get the chop.'

Claire's elfin face clouded over. 'Don't, Moll. It isn't a joke.'

'Sorry. I just can't imagine you with all your ambition and expensive tailoring staying long in a dole queue. Someone'd snap you up.'

'I'd rather not think about it.'

'You've always been the same, Claire. You never want to think about what you'd do if things went wrong.'

'We were always the opposites who attracted. You were the Boadicea of the sixth form and I was the bookworm anxious to get the grades and get out. Do you remember when you thought they were feeding us dog food and you staged a school-wide fast?'

Molly giggled. 'Yeah. And they hired an Italian cook and her lasagne really *was* made with dog food.' She banged the lift button again, hoping someone hadn't left the doors open on the top floor.

'So, where've you been then?'

'Actually,' Molly dropped her voice conspiratorially, 'I've just been to Sussex on the hunt for Joe's mother and come up with some pretty damn good leads.'

'To the Sacred Heart Society? Was my advice any use?' Claire followed Molly into the flat and flopped on to her sofa, where she took her shoes off and curled up like a small and pretty Persian cat.

'Do you remember you told me to write to them without giving an address and then just turn up?'

'Did it work?'

'Like a dream. There was this lovely nun who told me all sorts of things she shouldn't. She's a bit of a rebel, and I suppose since the place isn't handling adoptions any more she felt freer to speak. Andrew was right that Joe's mother was local; Sister Mary obviously knew the family. They were louche Londoners, apparently! And God, Claire, the most amazing thing. She was called Amanda.'

'Wow! Not quite the put-upon little teenager you expected, then.'

'She was stunningly beautiful, so this Sister Mary said. And Claire, the most gobsmacking thing of all, she said Eddie looks just like her! It was the most weird sensation. I felt so close to finding her, it was as if she were in the next room, waiting for us. I could almost see her.'

Molly closed her eyes for a second, trying to conjure up the image of a flesh-and-blood Amanda who looked just like her own son and husband.

'Did this nun know anything about the circumstances? Why she gave Joe away or anything?'

'No. Only that she didn't cry when she handed him over. And I got the strongest impression that the family came from somewhere near, but when I went into the nearest village, no one claimed to know any Amanda Lewis.'

'Maybe they don't like gossiping to strangers. Or she could be married, then she'd have changed her name.'

'Of course, stupid me. She might be called something completely different.'

'Or maybe they're covering up.' Claire raised her eyebrows dramatically. 'Maybe they were all implicated in the birth and don't want any outsiders knowing, like in *Rosemary's Baby*.'

'Claire Simpson,' laughed Molly, 'are you trying to imply that Eddie's granddad was the Devil?'

'You know what,' Claire suddenly leapt off the sofa, startling Eddie into kicking his legs and whimpering, 'you should write about this for the paper. It's more exciting than a detective story. Loads of people would be interested. You could take us through it step by step . . .'

'I'm no journalist.'

'It wouldn't matter, it's *your* story.'

Molly pulled her up short. Claire was always sniffing out stories, even when she was off duty, running with an idea without thinking through what it might mean for other people. 'Claire, I couldn't. This is Joe's life, not mine, he'd be . . .'

In their excitement, neither of them had heard Joe coming back.

He was hiding behind a bunch of roses he'd just bought for Molly. He held them out to her. 'A bit undernourished, I'm afraid. Picked before their prime.'

Molly kissed him. 'Yellow, my favourite! They're lovely, thank you. I forgot I'd invited Claire over and the cupboard's barer than Old Mother Hubbard's.'

'Don't worry, I'll nip down to the corner shop. Mr Sawalha will be thrilled at the blow against the retail giants. How are you, Claire, still door-stepping grieving widows?'

Claire ignored this. 'God, you *are* a gorgeous hunk. I always forget quite how. You're a lucky beast, Molly.'

'I know.'

'Look,' Joe protested, 'do you mind not discussing me as if I were a Chippendale?' He pouted. 'Even Chippendales have feelings, you know.'

'No they don't, they're made of wood.' Claire guffawed at her own joke.

'So how did it go today? Did you manage to discover anything about my true origins? Don't tell me, I'm really the lord of the manor, only I was born on the wrong side of the blanket.'

Molly knew Joe's jokey tone disguised his uncertainty at the whole scheme, but Claire, who knew him less well, didn't pick up the signals.

'Give your wife a hug. She's absolutely bloody brilliant. She's only found out your mum's called Amanda, is stunningly beautiful and probably lived in Sussex somewhere!' Claire, whose meagre sensitivity had been worn down by the rough and tumble of working in newspapers, hurtled onwards like a truck with the handbrake off. 'And what's more, she's going to write about it for our lucky readers!'

Joe's face changed. 'Molly, for God's sake. How could you?' All the laughter faded from his eyes. 'Surely there are some things you could keep private?' He thumped out of the room before Molly had time to explain.

'God, Molly, I'm sorry! That was incredibly dumb of me,' Claire apologized.

'Yes, it was,' Molly agreed, furious with herself at her own stupidity in telling Claire before she'd told her husband, and with Claire for blabbing on about the silly newspaper idea without even consulting Molly. 'And even dumber of me. Discretion's never exactly been my middle name.'

'Melissa,' murmured Claire.

'Sorry?'

'Melissa's your middle name.'

She took in Molly's wounded expression. 'I'll go then,' she offered.

'Look,' Molly relented, 'it's my fault. I shouldn't have told you before Joe. He's obviously still incredibly emotional about finding her at all. I should have explained how sensitive it all was. The funny thing is, he seems to be going colder on it the nearer we get.'

'And I should have kept my foot out of my big mouth. Look, I really ought to work tonight. I've got loads of interviews to write up.'

She hugged Molly as she said goodbye. 'One small question. Why *are* you so bent on finding his mother if he seems so unsure about it himself?'

'Because,' Molly was answering her own inner doubts at the same time, 'deep down he really wants to. Joe's always been restless and uncertain about who he is. He hates acknowledging it because he thinks it's making excuses, but I just *know* finding his mother is going to make a difference.'

'You make it sound like a fairy tale where the hero has to somehow break the spell.'

'Maybe it is a bit like that. The risk is that, like in fairy tales, it might all go wrong and someone will end up poisoned or turned into a flying swan.'

'I hope you're right about Joe. I'm *sure* you're right. You nearly always find the best solution. You're one of life's doers. You couldn't sit back and just let things happen if they paid you a million pounds, and that's what makes you Molly.'

Molly waved Claire off, listening to her expensive shoes click-clacking down the stone stairs of their rather tatty block. Was Claire trying to tell her that she should stay out of it? And if so, was she right?

A slight choking noise from inside the flat made her swing round in apprehension. She'd left Eddie on his lambskin. Thank God he was still there, but he'd managed to pull over her backpack and the paper bag that held the bell she'd bought for Patricia had rolled out. Eddie was eagerly chewing it. She removed it from his gummy grip and took out the bell. Unconsciously, in a habit inherited from her own mother, she smoothed out the brown paper.

She was about to throw it into the bin when she caught sight of the name of the shop. At the time she hadn't noticed any sign above the door. It was called Lewis's Antiques. For better or worse, Molly knew she couldn't stop now.

Chapter 8

Bob Kramer studied his client with interest. He'd rarely seen Stella this subdued. She hadn't, as he'd expected, blasted her way into his office all guns firing, demanding to know what more he'd done to get her the part she wanted in *Dark Night and Desire*. In fact she'd hardly mentioned it, just draped herself on his sofa in a manner that had a hint of defeat about it. He stole a glimpse at her while she was absorbed in the review section of *The Stage*.

She was wearing the black sheath dress she had worn in that car advert that had got her so much attention. It was entirely simple, with a square neck that hinted at rather than revealed her famous breasts, and so wonderfully cut that it took more years off her than a nip and tuck. As she leaned down to retrieve something from her handbag she snagged one of her stockings (he had no evidence that she wore these, except that Stella was the incarnation of seductive femininity and he couldn't imagine her in tights). Much against his better judgement, Bob allowed himself to imagine the top of Stella's thighs. They would be milk-white and firm, but with the smallest suggestion of flesh beginning to gather, cushiony to the touch, especially at the tender junction where her thighs met. He thought of all the young men who would envy him sitting here, the thousands of pubescent boys who had imagined Stella leading them up to their bedrooms and slipping her hand into their trousers.

'Tell me *exactly* what they said about Roxanne Wood.' Stella was beginning to sound more like herself, collected, assertive, used to getting what she wanted. Bob was surprised at the relief he felt. He liked Stella; even her damn-it-all attitude secretly impressed him, though he would never admit it to her, since she needed no encouraging in that department.

'Stupid sods,' Stella rallied, 'how could they possibly prefer her to me? Her face is as round as a bowl of porridge and just about as interesting. And those tiny tits! They look more like chicken pox than breasts.'

'Come on now, Stella. You know the game better than anyone. It's just that she's hot at the moment and everyone wants her. She's the media's darling. There's one every year. They never last. They get overexposed. Between you and me, I think it was probably that double-page spread about her anorexia that clinched it.'

Bob was hunting under his desk for the copy of the newspaper where the revelation had featured, so he missed the swift look of anguish that briefly blemished Stella's lovely features.

'So I should spend my life with my head in the bog if I want to get a decent part, should I?' Stella demanded.

'Don't sound bitter, Stella. Not good for business. Anyway, that's bulimia. You know how the press works. Nothing they like better than a nice skeleton in the cupboard.'

He considered the almost Slavic triangle of Stella's haunting face, the pale skin and nearly black hair, jutting across her wonderful cheekbones, the full mouth with its pouting lower lip, and her spectacular blue eyes. He was grateful he wasn't a woman, and even more so an actress. The gift of beauty was hardest to bear when it started to fade, and acting was a cruel profession. He hadn't the heart to tell her that she'd been considered for a part in a film that was about to shoot in London and been dismissed as too old.

'It's the neck,' the trendy young director had confided to Bob. 'You just can't disguise it. After forty the face goes or the body goes. You can't have both. Of course, I'm one of her greatest fans. I used to cream my jeans over her in that motorcycle movie, but we're talking about fifteen years ago.'

No, Bob wouldn't tell her any of that. 'You don't have anything up your sleeve, do you, sweetie, that would get you all over the Sundays?'

Stella hesitated for only the briefest of moments.

'Not me, darling. I'm as boring as British Home Stores.'

Bob cracked with laughter. 'That's a pity. Your career could do with a nice little scandal.'

'Too bad.' She smiled, every inch the old, acerbic Stella. 'I'll just have to rely on my acting skills then, won't I?'

Molly had just given Eddie his puréed vegetables when Joe emerged from the bedroom. The next thing she felt was his lips on her neck. 'I'm sorry, love. I shouldn't have flown off the handle like that with you and Claire.'

She might be relieved but Molly wasn't letting him see it too easily. 'No, you shouldn't. You might have trusted me. You needn't have assumed that I'd expose your private secrets to the entire world.'

Joe had the grace to look ashamed. 'I don't know what the hell I think about anything at the moment. Where's Claire?'

'You've driven her away. She's gone to watch *Jerry Springer* on the TV so she knows what happy families are like.'

'Ouch.'

'I'm going to put the supper on. Why don't you stay and sing to Eddie for a bit? He loves your version of "I'm a Pink Toothbrush" more than Max Bygraves'.'

Joe laughed. 'Does he? Maybe I'll treat him to "Katzenellen Bogen by the Seeeee-ee-ee" as well then.'

In their small galley kitchen Molly chopped tomatoes and basil. Hearing the strains of 'There's a Tiny House', she started to relax. Joe was Joe again.

'He's fallen asleep,' Joe whispered five minutes later, helping himself to a beer and sitting down at the table in the open-plan kitchen/diner. 'Smells nice.'

Molly couldn't contain her excitement any longer. 'When I was in Ditchwell I bought a present for Pat in an antique shop.'

'She'll appreciate that.'

'Yes, but the thing is, I think the man who runs it knows Amanda and he just wouldn't admit it. I'd like to go down there tomorrow and see if I can worm it out of him.'

She'd thought Joe would be pleased; instead he stopped halfway through laying the table. 'Look, Moll, I know it's heady stuff, almost like being a private detective – but don't you think perhaps we should be a bit more tactful? I thought it'd take years and suddenly it's running away with itself. Maybe we ought to slow down and go through the proper channels.'

'Did you want it to take years. Maybe not even happen at all?'

They ate their meal in silence. Molly didn't say anything. She couldn't think of anything else *to* say. Finding his mother had taken up all her thoughts lately. Maybe Joe was right, it was a risky course of action, and maybe she was getting obsessed. But even as she thought it she knew she couldn't stop now.

'I'm sorry,' he said as they got undressed to get into bed. 'It's such an emotional seesaw. I'm just as scared as I am excited.'

When Joe had left for work next day, Molly opened the kitchen drawer and took out the brown paper bag that had contained the miniature bell. How ironic that it had been Patricia who had led her to that shop.

Her hands were shaking as she pushed the buttons on the telephone for train enquiries. Her instincts shouted that the man in the antique shop did know Amanda, even though he denied it. But surely Beatrice Manners would have told her if Amanda had come from Ditchwell?

This time she didn't take Eddie. She rang Pat and asked if she could possibly come to town and baby-sit. Pat agreed, perhaps glad of the chance to build bridges. Molly would give her the little bell and hope she took it as a sign of their affection.

Her mother-in-law softened somewhat at the gift. 'Oh, what a pretty one! It's got a little Dutch girl on it.' She tinkled it enthusiastically. 'So where are you dashing off to in such a tearing hurry then?'

'It's just an informal interview about some part-time work,' Molly bluffed.

'Doing what?'

Molly ransacked her brain. 'Helping an interior designer.'

Patricia sniffed, looking around her at the outlandish décor. 'I suppose you do have a knack. Provided you don't mind living in a circus tent.' She held out her arms to Eddie. 'Who's Granny's good little boy, then?'

Eddie kicked. 'He's got a little dimple on his knee. Just like me,' challenged Patricia, daring Molly to react in some way.

Molly didn't. 'Thanks a million, Pat. I shouldn't be late.'

'Good luck with the interview.' Patricia had been on the point of adding that *she* would never have taken a job when Joe was this age, but decided to try and be tolerant. Besides, it would mean she would get to look after Eddie more often.

She picked her grandson up and tattooed him with kisses. 'At least your mummy and daddy seem to have given up on that crazy scheme of hers of finding that nasty woman,' she confided to the smiling baby. 'And we're all relieved about that, aren't we?'

Eddie, unaware of anything except the blissful delight of having raspberries blown on his tummy, crowed in agreement.

Molly was thrilled to get to the station five minutes before the Cliffdean train was due to leave, just in time to pick up a coffee from the booth by the entrance to the platform and dash on board.

Fifty-five minutes later she changed trains at Brighton and chugged, stopping at every halt, towards Lower Ditchwell. To Molly, who was by now bursting with impatience, it seemed to take nearly as long as travelling back to London. At Ovington, three miles from Ditchwell, she got a bus. A taxi was too expensive and there was no other means of transport.

It was late morning by the time she arrived. While London had been sweating in sultry, scummy weather, by some extraordinary meteorological sleight of hand, Ditchwell dazzled in glorious, glad-to-be-alive sunshine and clear blue skies. It was as though the place had its own microclimate, smiled on by a selfish God who had chosen this little pocket as his own particular heaven. The sky seemed a deeper, almost delphinium blue here, the clouds fluffier and whiter, the hills greener and more lush. Roses trailed round the front doors of all the cottages, bees hummed in the Canterbury bells, hollyhocks nodded their jewel-bright heads over the flint-faced walls, like entrances to dozens of mysterious fairy worlds. Did people, Molly wondered, have to come from some special, blessed, enviable group to be accorded the privilege of living here?

Molly's mood of elation evaporated when she turned into the shady alleyway that was home to Lewis's Antiques. She couldn't believe it. The shop was shut again, with the same familiar sign. She flopped, momentarily depressed, on to the warm stone of the wall opposite. The man must be mad. He was never open for business, and today hundreds of cars full of potential customers would drive through the village, falling in love with it, and be eager to take some small slice of paradise home with them.

Molly jumped to her feet. The Boadicea of the school refectory wasn't giving up that easily. She remembered the pub. It would be open by now, and publicans always seemed to know everything, even about the locals who never darkened their door. Somehow, Molly suspected, the antique shop owner would not be one of those.

The Sun in Splendour had opened only moments before and there were few customers. At first the contrast between the bright blue day outside and the dark, dusty interior made her stumble awkwardly.

A bird in a cage near the bar squawked unnervingly at her intrusion. 'Who's a pretty girl then?' it enquired.

'Not me,' said Molly grimly, nursing a slightly twisted ankle. 'And don't you know the meaning of the word *sexist*?'

'Of course he doesn't,' tutted the landlord, emerging from behind a barrel, looking as if he'd like to cover the bird's ears in case it got corrupted, 'and I'd rather he didn't find out. That's London talk.'

He rearranged the pork scratchings hanging up on a card behind the bar to reveal even more of the model's left breast. 'Now, can I help you? A small sherry, perhaps, or a glass of dry white wine?' He pronounced it, in almost insulting tones, 'dray whaite waine'.

'It's a bit early, thanks. Actually, I'm looking for someone. The owner of the antique shop.'

'Anthony? He's in the lavvy. He doesn't have one at the shop, except one of them Victorian blue-and-white jobs and that has geraniums growing out of it. A bit of human fertiliser wouldn't do them any harm, as I'm always telling him.' Molly tried not to think about the implications of this. 'That's his drink over there if you want to wait for him.'

Molly glanced over at a small round wooden table with heavy decorative iron legs. It held a half-drunk pint of bitter with a second standing by. The man clearly didn't believe in wasting valuable drinking time.

Molly had just about worked up the nerve to ask the barman about Amanda when Anthony Lewis returned.

He looked Molly over suggestively. 'Hello, gorgeous. So, is it me or my chest of drawers you're after?'

'You've been giving that bird lessons. I'll have to report you to the RSPCA for corrupting mynahs.'

Anthony laughed appreciatively at her pun. 'Not bad. Not bad at all for a humourless Londoner.'

'Anyway,' Molly persisted, 'I love the chest of drawers but I couldn't possibly afford it.'

'Not even at the trade price?'

'You know I'm not really trade.'

'If it's not the chest of drawers, what can I do for you?'

'You told me you didn't know Amanda Lewis, but it strikes me that since you've got the same name, you're deliberately not telling me.'

'Not all Smiths know each other.'

'They would if they lived in a village this size.'

'Nonsense. Hyphenated Smiths wouldn't even give unhyphenated Smiths the time of day round here. Why do you want to know about this Amanda Lewis anyway?'

'I have good reason to believe,' Molly began, not quite sure whether she ought to be divulging this in a pub, which was, after all, the modern equivalent of the parish pump, but what the hell, 'that Amanda Lewis is the grandmother of my baby son, Eddie.'

Anthony Lewis spluttered so loudly on his glass of Tanglefoot that he choked, showering bitter all over the mynah bird. 'His *grandmother*, did you say?' He started to laugh, rocking backwards and forwards on his stool. It was a harsh, unpleasant sound. Molly couldn't help thinking of a large crow, alone on a post, cawing threateningly into the dusk.

'So you do know her then?' Molly quickly pressed her advantage home.

'I might have done. Once. A long time ago.'

Suddenly the reality of Amanda as a person seemed closer, actually within her grasp, and Molly held her breath. She had been about to ask how she could contact Amanda, but there was so much she wanted to know about this young girl, now a middle-aged woman who had so much power to change all their lives. A hundred questions rushed into her mind. 'What was she like?'

'Amanda?' Anthony Lewis shrugged. It was an expressive gesture, denoting the impossibility of capturing her personality in words. 'She was . . . unique.'

'As in uniquely wonderful?' prompted Molly.

He nodded. 'And uniquely awful.'

'Depending on what?' The landlord, she noticed, was polishing the same glass for the third time.

'Depending on whether she was getting what she wanted. And whether you were it. Being involved with Amanda was like the Andy Warhol saying: you got your fifteen minutes of fame, or in her case love, and that was supposed to last you a lifetime.'

The extraordinary thing was, Molly suspected, that in Anthony's case it had worked. His fifteen minutes of Amanda had indeed lasted him a lifetime. Unfortunately it seemed to be a lifetime of bitterness.

'Do you think we could go to your shop and talk undisturbed?'

'Undisturbed by customers, certainly.' The bitter smile again. He picked up his newspaper. 'See you, Trev.'

The landlord looked crestfallen.

'TTFN,' chirped the mynah bird.

'What's that mean?' Molly asked, intrigued.

'Ta-ta for now,' apologized the landlord. 'I'm afraid the stupid bird's stuck in the Jimmy Young era.'

'Rather like its owner,' grinned Anthony.

As they walked the few yards back to his shop Molly could sense the curtains twitching in their wake, though rather like Grandmother's Footsteps, she knew if she glanced round she would see nothing.

'Please,' Molly asked as he held open the door for her, 'tell me about her, everything you can remember. I need to understand her.'

'Don't we all. Not so easy, though.'

'When did you meet her? Did you grow up together?'

Anthony laughed. 'No, I'm a city boy. Amanda grew up here. But she didn't fit in, not with the horsy county types. She's never really fitted in. Part of her allure.'

Molly thought of Joe, who didn't feel he fitted in either. Maybe it was genetic. 'How was she different?'

'Her parents were oddballs. Thought they were a different breed, more fascinating than all the country bores round here. And people sensed it, so they left them alone. Amanda liked it like that. She was always a fantasist. Or, as she would put it, she had a rich interior life. She collected doll's houses. She had about twenty of them, all with their own elaborate little worlds. Amanda in charge and no messy real emotions to screw things up.' The professional in him woke up. 'They must be worth a fortune, those doll's houses. I wonder if she still has them.'

'Do her parents still live here?'

Anthony Lewis gave her a long, hard look. 'You really don't know, then?'

'Don't know what?'

'You've already met her mother. You told me so.'

'You must have misunderstood me . . .'

But Anthony Lewis was smiling at her with the look of a pimp introducing a boa constrictor to a nice young goat.

'You don't mean Beatrice Manners?' Even as she said it, Molly knew it was true; that there had been something strange about the woman's behaviour. Molly had liked her enormously, but had also felt a certain sense of withholding from the older woman.

'Was Amanda very beautiful?'

'There are probably women much more beautiful than her.' He picked up a delicate figurine which Molly hadn't noticed before. Something about it told her it was easily the most valuable thing in the shop. 'I've hung on to this. It reminded me of her somehow.' The figure was about eight inches high, with glowing white skin and lustrous dark hair beneath a Fragonard bonnet. 'Except that our Amanda was no Meissen shepherdess. You know those endless articles they have in newspapers trying to pin down sex appeal, and how it differs from straight beauty? They're all describing Amanda.'

There was something unexpectedly touching about this slightly down-at-heel man, time-warped in black leather and faintly flared jeans, hidden away in his shop with no customers, clutching the figurine.

Molly looked at her watch. She really ought to get back to relieve Pat.

There was a sudden appalling crash and the figurine lay at her feet in pieces on the concrete floor. Molly was sure the act had been deliberate.

'Oh dear, I seem to have dropped it. Time to stop living in the past, perhaps, and start again in the present.'

Molly decided to get out of the shop. She wasn't exactly frightened of Anthony, but wasn't it a gesture of being slightly unhinged to drop an immensely valuable figurine just to make a point?

'I don't suppose you know where Amanda can be contacted these days?'

A light of pure devilment beamed in Anthony Lewis's eyes.

'To break her the good news that she's a grandmother?'

'Among other things, yes.'

He started laughing again, making Molly wonder even more strongly if the man was entirely sane.

'Why the hell not?' He appeared to be asking himself, not Molly, this question. 'Why the bloody hell not? It's about time life caught up with her a little.' He got out a battered diary and tore a page out. There were no appointments on it. 'Here's her phone number.'

Molly's heart beat more wildly than a trapped bird's.

'The only thing is, she's changed her name.'

'To what?'

The man cracked up and started choking again.

'You'll soon find out,' he wheezed, sweeping up the shards of exquisite china from the floor and throwing them into the bin.

Molly's excitement lasted as far as Victoria station, when she remembered with horror that she hadn't, as promised, left two spare bottles of expressed milk in the fridge for Eddie. Pat would kill her. Instead of grabbing the bus to the Oval and getting the underground she hailed the first taxi she could. Even so, she expected to hear Eddie's cries halfway down the street.

To her astonishment a glorious peace reigned over their front steps. She dashed up the stairs and into the flat.

Patricia sat on the sofa, a waste-paper bin under her feet as an improvised footstool, watching *EastEnders*. Eddie wasn't howling. He was lying on his tummy, wearing only a vest and nappy, balanced in what looked a highly precarious angle over Pat's knee, blissfully asleep.

'God, Pat, I'm so sorry. I only remembered about the expressed milk when I was . . .' she realized she'd almost admitted her real destination today and hastily drew back, '. . . . coming back from town. How on earth did you survive?'

'I went out and bought some formula.'

'But he isn't weaned yet.'

'He is now,' Pat announced with hardly hidden smugness. 'I've probably done you a favour.'

Molly felt the painful ripping of an invisible bond, the first pang of Eddie's independence from her. It was mad to blame Pat when she had done the only sensible thing. The smugness was another matter, but Molly, feeling guilty about the real nature of her visit today and the impact it would have on her mother-in-law when she found out, made herself be generous.

'Thank you so much for stepping into the breach. It was really kind of you. Let me take Eddie. Gosh, he looks comfortable.' She peeled the small body from Pat's knee. He didn't stir.

'I put a teaspoon of whisky in the formula, just as I used to do with Joe.'

Molly shut her eyes, telling herself it wouldn't do him any harm. Except that after this, offering him the breast would probably be like trying to tempt a wino with a healthy glass of orange juice.

Pat put on her coat and picked up her John Lewis bag stuffed with knitting. She had an extraordinary capacity to knit elaborate patterns while watching TV and not a drop a single stitch, while Molly and all her friends were almost totally ignorant of knitting, sewing, darning or any of those thrifty skills their grandmothers prided themselves on. Knowing how ludicrous it was, Molly envied Pat slightly in the very same moment as she was grateful to be part of her own throwaway generation.

She felt a wave of sudden tenderness for her prickly mother-in-law and her spotless suburban home, and gave her a hug. Pat might have disapproved of Joe for leaving the town he grew up in and coming to live in London, even for marrying Molly herself, a tempestuous, unknown quantity given to bordello-style décor and mad, impetuous schemes like the one she was currently undertaking, but she had created a secure and loving life for Joe, which was more than the beautiful but obviously selfish Amanda had done.

Pat, unused to such unexpected displays of affection from Molly, wobbled slightly and had to steady herself. 'You're not annoyed with me then?' she asked. The smugness had been replaced by a touching sliver of anxiety.

'Of course not. I expect he'll sleep like a baby.'

They both laughed at the silliness of the words.

'I'm sorry I snapped at you the other day.' Molly had hardly ever heard Pat apologize before, and certainly not to her. 'I'm sure you felt you were acting in Joe's best interests.'

'Maybe I was just blundering about as usual.' An unfamiliar sense of truce descended on the two women, only slightly dented by Molly's knowledge that there was a piece of paper in her back-pack on which she'd written down the telephone number of Amanda Lewis.

Of course, having it in her possession didn't mean she had to use it. Did it?

The whisky certainly worked.

Eddie dreamed peacefully in his cot, not even offering any of his usual restless little grunts. So peacefully that Molly must have checked on him half a dozen times while she was making supper, even holding a mirror to his tiny mouth to see if it steamed up. It did. Eddie was blissfully asleep, not dead of alcoholic poisoning.

The evening wore on, but there was still no sign of Joe. Unusual, since he mostly rang if he was going to be late. On an impulse she laid the table as if for a celebration, which in a way it was.

She flipped on the TV but nothing caught her fancy. She was in one of those fizzy, can't-settle frames of mind when her attention was suited only to flipping through a fashion magazine, but with all the travelling this week she hadn't been able to afford one.

She caught sight of Amanda's phone number again. Not sur-prising, this, since she'd taken it out of her backpack and put it on the kitchen counter where she could hardly miss it. Even Molly couldn't persuade herself that noticing it had to be an omen.

But how did she know it was genuine, that it actually belonged to Amanda? She knew it had to be Joe who made contact, but what would be the harm in Molly ringing the number until it was answered, then putting down the phone, just to check its authenticity? Of course, Amanda would be able to dial 1471 and find out the number of the person who'd just rung her. On the other hand, she didn't sound like the kind of person who'd spend her time checking numbers.

Where on earth had Joe got to? The pasta sauce would be spoiled soon, a congealed red mass.

She grabbed the telephone before she could change her mind. It rang four times. With each ring she was tempted to slam it down, but she made herself hang on. After the fourth ring it switched over to an answering machine.

The message on the machine was in a throaty female voice, the kind advertisers pay thousands for, but it was the words themselves that made Molly freeze with shock and disbelief and a sense that, for good or ill, their lives were about to be changed completely.

Chapter 9

'Hello, this is Stella Milton speaking. I'm out, obviously, so please leave me a message or, better still, talk to my agent Bob Kramer. Bob knows more about me than I do myself. Bye for now.'

Molly stood still, the receiver in her hand, while the silence yawned at the other end. She felt entirely unable either to leave a message or to put the phone down.

The thought that it might be a mistake flashed briefly into her mind, like the relief on waking from a frightening dream and finding it wasn't true after all, but a sixth sense told her that she was fooling herself, that it was entirely true.

The devilish gleam in Anthony Lewis's eyes made sense now. Amanda had hurt him at some time in her life and now he had the chance of making her pay. Besides which, the Manners household, sophisticated and actorish, was just the right seed-bed for a Stella Milton.

Molly wondered when exactly Amanda had become Stella. Perhaps not long after she had abandoned Joe at the foster home? Single mum was hardly the image Stella Milton would have wanted to carry around.

The memory of that cool, self-possessed, glamorous woman

she'd seen at the Ivy came into her mind. Someone like that could have given Joe an amazing life! Anger scorched through her at the thought of Joe as an embarrassing secret, a squally baby who would be sick and spoil her figure and wreck her sophisticated image. Damn her!

Sister Mary had said how unusual she was, how different from the other young mothers. Beautiful and self-assured. Self-assured enough not to even cry when they took her baby. Those other mothers might have been less lovely and sophisticated, but at least they cared.

She was so preoccupied with her anger that she hardly heard Joe's arrival.

The expression in her eyes made him rush to her and hold her in his arms. 'God, Molly, what's the matter?' He took the phone gently from her hand and replaced it. 'What's happened? It's not Eddie?'

'No, no, nothing like that.' She didn't even know how to begin to explain.

He took her silence as a reproach. 'I'm sorry I'm so late. Graham caught me just as I was going out of the door. That man has a grudge against anyone who wants a home life. Just because he never wants to go home himself. Come and sit down and I'll get you a drink.'

Molly collapsed on to the sofa, trying to stoke up her courage. Could she possibly have made a mistake with the number?

He came back with two glasses of wine and sat down next to her. 'Now, tell me what's happened.'

'I don't really know how to. Or even if I should.'

'Talk sense, for heaven's sake, Moll. You're not trying to tell me you're leaving?' The sudden panic in his voice was wonderfully reassuring. 'I mean, I know I'm pretty bad at picking up signals and I slam doors a bit, but I thought we were basically all right.'

She touched his face. 'No, I'm not leaving you. It's nothing like that.'

'What then?' Before she could answer, he worked it out. 'You've been down there again, haven't you? For God's sake, Moll, I thought we were going to leave it for a while? Look, I know this means a lot to you, and I'm touched, but I've been thinking about it too. About what actually finding her would mean. To Pat. To all of us. And I've decided I'd like to drop the whole thing. If she'd wanted to find me it would be different, but I can't go blundering into some middle-aged woman's life. She's probably got a family of her own. I've already hurt Pat and Andrew, I don't want to do any more damage. This is my problem and I've decided I ought to stop whingeing and get on with life. I'm a lucky sod with a lovely baby and a fantastic wife. If that's not enough, someone ought to shoot me!'

Molly twisted the tassel of a cushion round her fingers. Would it be possible to just leave things, knowing what she now knew? To keep quiet about who Joe's mother was and put all her energies into getting on with their marriage?

Molly knew she couldn't do it. Not now.

'Maybe I should never have gone back, but I did and something happened.'

'What?' Joe had a wary look in his eyes.

'The man down there admitted he knew Amanda Lewis and after a bit of persuasion he gave me her phone number. I can't believe I didn't put two and two together before, I mean they even share the same surname.'

The import of this gradually sank into Joe's mind. 'And this is the woman we think is my mother?'

'Yes, it is. When I asked him for the number he laughed hysterically and said it was time life caught up with her. Then he told me she'd changed her name. Now I can see why he was behaving so weirdly.'

'Moll, you've lost me. What are you on about?'

'Joey, I rang the number . . .'

'What the hell were you planning to say?' Joe exploded. 'I mean, she might have slammed down the phone and that might have been it. She'd never agree to meet me.'

'I wasn't going to actually speak to her. I was just checking the number was genuine. I didn't want to give it to you and get your hopes up and then find it was the wrong number. The thing is, I recognized the voice of the woman on the answering machine.'

'You mean it's someone we know?'

'In a way, but not the way you think.'

'Come on, Moll, you're not making sense. Who was it, for God's sake?'

'I think you'd better listen to her message yourself.' She dialled the number and handed the receiver to her husband.

Chapter 10

Joe's features flashed through incomprehension to disbelief. Slowly he replaced the receiver and turned to Molly.

'But that's Stella Milton's answering machine. Are you trying to tell me that Stella Milton's my real mother?'

'I know it must be an incredible shock, but yes, I really think she is. Only her name wasn't Stella Milton then. It was Amanda Lewis. Stella Milton is her stage name.'

Joe sat down next to her and they both conjured up their private images: Stella walking naked towards the camera in *The French Mistress*; Stella seducing her own uncle in *Family Ties*; Stella in that motorcycle outfit in *Deceptive Bends*.

'Holy shit, I had a poster of her on my wall when I was in the sixth form. She was in motorcycle gear, with her zip half undone.'

He threw himself back against the sofa, staring at the ceiling, his mind a jumble of confusing images.

'Jesus, Molly! Are you sure about this?'

'Almost. Stella Milton's the only person who can really say if it's true.'

'So what do you suggest I do? Ring her up and say, "Hi, Mum, I'm the baby you gave away twenty-five years ago. I'm a big boy now. Want to meet me"?'

'Maybe you should be a bit more guarded,' Molly offered, hating the bitter irony in his tone. 'Tell her enough to let her know you're who you are and leave the rest of her.' She turned to him, reaching out her hand to his face. 'You don't have to do anything, you know. You could just think about it and decide what's best.'

'Have you ever tried to sleep with an unexploded bomb under your pillow?' Joe demanded, jumping up. 'That's what this feels like.' He turned his face away from her. 'I can't decide this now. I'm too tired. I'm going to have to try and sleep on it.'

Molly looked at the ludicrously laid table, with its candle and best napkins, and blew out the flame. She dumped her lovingly prepared tomato sauce into the bin and poured herself another glass of wine. What had she expected? That Joe would fall into her arms, cover her with kisses and thank her for this bombshell?

Slowly, as though each step were across deep shingle, she walked round the kitchen tidying up and removing every sign of their celebration meal, then sat down heavily at the kitchen table, alone.

In the bedroom Joe stripped off his clothes down to his boxer shorts and flung them on to his chair. Normally he might have made some attempt to tidy them, but not tonight. He turned off the light and punched the pillow until it was comfortable, but it was almost like having a painful allergy. He couldn't settle. He became aware of odd itches and minor discomforts that he normally never noticed. And then there was his heartbeat. It seemed faster and louder than he'd ever heard it. Somewhere, hidden under the layers of apprehension and anger at Molly for taking his dream and actually *doing* something about it, there was a small flame of excitement. Molly believed she'd found his real mother, and she was someone who was beautiful, exciting and glamorous, someone from a world he knew nothing about.

Joe sat up. Without giving himself time to think any further, he reached for the bedroom phone and dialled the number again. He held his breath. What if she answered in person? What the hell would he say? After four rings, which seemed to Joe to go on endlessly, the message cut in. A message in that breathy, extraordinarily sexy voice he'd heard selling everything from cars to cosmetics.

His mother's voice.

The message ended and was followed by a beep for him to record his own. He almost slammed down the phone. Instead the words came to him, slightly cryptic and hesitant. 'Hello. My name is Joseph Meredith and I was born on the twenty-fourth of January 1975, in the Sacred Heart Nursing Home in Sussex. I have reason to believe we might be related and would be very grateful if you could contact me.' He left his number and the message clicked off just as he was finishing, leaving Joe feeling even more foolish. Had he even managed to leave his whole phone number before he'd been cut off? He wondered if he should ring back, but didn't have the nerve. He couldn't go through with it twice.

He tried to sleep but could only think about when she would get the message and what her reaction would be.

He jumped out of bed and softly padded to the small adjoining room where Eddie slept. He leaned into the cot and picked up the sleeping infant, holding him tight to his chest and breathing in the clean, faintly antiseptic baby smell. A tear slid down his face and he wiped it away. It was the first time he'd ever cried for his mother. 'I was even smaller than you, Ed, when she gave me away. What on earth was wrong with me that she didn't want to keep me for herself?'

'How about a nice relaxing neck massage?' Richard offered. He began to knead Stella's shoulders, which emerged enticingly from a simple black crêpe dress, gently, as if she were made of very precious dough.

They had just got back from the preview of a new play. It had been a fascinating evening. An entertaining mix of people from different fields, not just actors droning on about who had or hadn't got the last part, and then the play, a new one by Harold Pinter. Now, what Richard really meant, Stella knew, was did she feel like going to bed, but he was suggesting it in the accepted code they'd

developed together. This had the dual effect of protecting his feelings and drawing a veil over who actually drove the relationship.

'I don't think so, darling,' Stella replied gently. 'Not tonight. I'm
just going to collapse into bed with a hottie and a good book.'

'Why do you want a hot-water bottle? It's blazing summer.'

'Because I won't have you, darling,' she smiled gracefully, 'to
keep me warm.'

'You'd better say goodbye for now.'

She looked puzzled.

'I've told you, Stella.' For once Richard's voice crackled with
impatience that she didn't listen to him. 'I'm off on tour with *An
Inspector Calls*. Leeds, Bath, Bristol, ending up in Richmond. I'll be
away for six weeks.' If only she cared.

'Have fun then, darling, watch out for all those juve leads.'

Richard shook his head. Stella wasn't in the slightest bit jealous
of any young women he might be playing opposite. As he kissed
her good night he asked himself, for about the thousandth time, if
he ought to be tougher with Stella and force himself into the centre
of her life. She had kept him hovering at the fringes, like a mongrel
who doesn't quite make it to Crufts sniffing around in a rather disgusting way, for almost a year now. The trouble was, he couldn't
imagine life without her. Possessing half of Stella, or even a quar-
ter, was what millions of men only dreamed of.

After he'd left, Stella opened the door to her jasmine-filled balcony and breathed in the exotic, slightly sickly scent. She too felt
guilty about Richard and understood perfectly that he wanted more
from her. She just wasn't sure she could give it. He was a good man,
and they were few enough. If she gave him up he could have a nice
wife and kids who appreciated him. She suddenly remembered the
question she'd asked him the other night, whether they were too
old to have a baby of their own. No wonder he'd been shocked.
Where on earth had that thought come from?

A cold shiver of fear ran through her. She already had a child.
He was twenty-five and, according to her mother, he was already
looking for her.

Stella quickly stripped off and showered, luxuriating in the fierce charge of her American-made shower. First hot, then icy cold, to keep the skin supple. Her nipples stood to attention as she stepped out of the shower, reminding her of the time she'd played Ophelia in a swathe of transparent silk, leaving every man in the theatre in no doubt that Hamlet really *was* mad to send her to a nunnery.

She dried herself with the thick white bath towel that never failed to give her pleasure, and anointed herself in expensive anti-ageing unguents, contemplating the lengths humanity went to to stay young. Picasso had drunk the urine of pregnant mares, she'd once read, for its youth-giving qualities. He'd certainly stayed young, seducing women and fathering children until other men were grandfathers. But maybe that was his pure male selfishness, not the hormones he so expensively imbibed. She'd always believed that selfishness was necessary to art. Great artists nearly always had spectacular doses of it, a ruthless dedication to achieving a goal that stood no dilution by guilt, the demands of family or even love. All their energy was saved for the white-hot purity of their achievement.

'Stop making excuses, Stella,' she reminded herself with unusual candour. 'You may be good, but you're not that good.'

As she slipped into bed, she reflected how bloody unfair acting was for women. For it was women, no matter how talented, who were judged by their looks, and Stella was beginning to find herself marooned in mid-life: too old for a sexpot, too young for a crone. Had it all, in the end, been worth it?

Her thoughts were interrupted by the ringing of the telephone beside her bed. Thankfully the answering machine would pick it up. She kept it permanently switched on so that she could hear who was calling and decide if she wanted to answer or get Bob to reply for her. She rarely interrupted the machine and admitted to being in.

But this time there was something about the voice that made her sit up and listen. The tone held a kind of proud defensiveness, an ignore-me-if-you-dare quality that put her instantly on her guard.

Stella didn't take in much of the message. Just the voice, and that date.

He had rung.

Of course she'd known he would, ever since the girl had turned up at her mother's house. Perhaps, more than that, she'd known all her life that this moment might occur, that her past, hidden away in some secret part of herself, might break through the steel-mesh barriers she'd so carefully erected and fight its way into her present.

Stella found she could hardly breathe. She had a son. A son who was now a grown man. A son who would probably hate her, and who might never forgive her for the wrong she'd done him in giving him away.

Like a dog biting its own wound, her mind gnawed away at that long-buried memory, the memory she'd tried so hard to forget.

The irony was, the harder she tried to forget, the clearer the imprint seemed to be. She could see that day as clearly as a snapshot. The weather had been beautiful, the kind that gladdens the heart and makes you grateful to be alive. Except that she wasn't. She'd wanted to die. And the weather had just seemed like a sick joke.

When he'd been born she'd felt she was drowning. Things just didn't happen to her that she couldn't control. Other people of her age, much younger even, coped with being mothers, but she couldn't. Maybe it was because she'd never felt she had a mother herself. Bea had always been somewhere else, giving audiences a good time, making *them* laugh, but not her own child. The result, in Stella's case, was to stop her being able to depend on anyone at all, in case the person she depended on abandoned her.

Was that why she'd given her baby away? Because she might invest all her love in him and he might, too, abandon her? Or was it, sadder still, because she didn't have the capacity to love at all? She had used the excuse of her brilliant career, that she needed every ounce of her energy for that, but where had her career got her? A nice flat, a set of white bath towels and the dubious accolade of being lusted after by half the male population.

She allowed herself a rare flash of self-indulgence. What if she had kept him? She'd seen it in friends' eyes, the joy that came from having a baby who adored you, who saw you as the source of all goodness and blessing, who accepted you totally as you were. She'd watched as those friends blossomed like buds in spring and had been amazed and more than a little jealous.

But they'd never been the same afterwards. They'd lost that laser beam of ambition that was so fundamental to acting success.

Now, with the distance of the years, Stella could admit it. That day had been the worst of her life. When he'd been born she'd shocked the nuns by saying that she didn't want to see him. They hadn't believed her, they'd been convinced she'd soften, but they didn't know Stella, or the strength of Stella's belief that none of this was really happening to her. Not seeing him was part of that belief.

But the nuns won in the end. They insisted that if she wanted him adopted she had to bring him down to the rooms where the hand-overs were made herself. She never knew whether it was the truth; she suspected it might have been a malicious diktat designed to make her suffer and confront her sins. Or it could have been a well-meaning but crass attempt to make her change her mind. It was the kind of thing that nuns believed, the fairy tale that if you only once saw the baby you wouldn't be able to part with it.

Stella ducked her head suddenly between her knees, trying to crush out the sudden pain that filled her mind. He had looked so helpless, swaddled so tightly that his arms were pinned to his sides and all that was visible was a little triangle of face. He'd made her think of a tiny, inscrutable mummy.

When she'd protested that he couldn't move, the nuns assured her that babies were happier like that, it made them feel secure. But he didn't seem secure. The look of anxiety in his dark, long-lashed eyes pierced her heart and kicked at her carefully constructed defences.

She'd asked to cuddle him, just one time. And for those few brief moments time had stood still.

Then she'd laid him down gently and unwrapped him. His legs, suddenly freed, had kicked with pleasure, or with anxiety, she never knew which. Unable to help herself, she'd stared at his tiny hands, with their miniature doll's nails, and his tiny feet. He was perfect, apart from one small darkening of the skin on the inner wrist, an almost imperceptible birth-mark. She'd kissed him, once, on the faint marking and tried not to cry.

And then she'd tucked her sorrow away inside his shabby hospital shawl and reverted to the other Stella, the one who was to make her mark on the world and knew it. She sat pretending to be composed and ready to give away her baby forever.

'Time to go now,' the nun had said, a different one this time, Irish, kinder, one who seemed to see that life wasn't the simple game of black and white that people might wish. 'Best to get it over with. They're good people he's going to.'

Under the table Stella had caught sight of a tiny sock. She had reached down and picked it up. 'Sister . . .'

'Keep it,' the nun replied, all the sadness of the world in her voice. 'He'll have plenty more in his new home.'

Now Stella slid off the bed and walked across the deep cream pile of her carpet to the chest of drawers. Her jewellery case was in the third drawer down, hidden beneath her underwear. She had never possessed any jewellery of real value, preferring stylish and dramatic pieces to valuable ones. The case, a present from Richard, was of cheap, brightly painted wood, with little drawers for rings and bracelets and larger ones for necklaces. She had kept the fourth drawer empty apart from one or two letters and an envelope. She wasn't sure who she was hiding these things from, a thief or herself.

She opened the envelope carefully and shook it. A tiny white sock fell out on to the greater whiteness of the carpet.

Stella slipped to her knees and silently wept.

What in hell was she going to do about that call?

The next morning, like every morning, Beatrice Manners was up early. She didn't fit the bill of languid ex-actress rising at noon and lying on a day-bed. Her alarm always went off at six a.m., summer or winter, and she drew comfort from following precisely the same ritual each morning. First, a cup of tea. She didn't hold with Teasmades and went down to make a proper one in the kitchen. While waiting for the kettle to boil she threw open the back door and surveyed the weather. The house was back-on to the morning sun and she had become as adept as any weatherman at predicting what the day held. One of the reasons she rose so early was that nearly every day was fine before seven; it was only about nine or ten that the day's glory dissipated into dull greyness.

She looked up at the reassuring honk of a Canada goose. A swallow dipped down over the small stream bordered by her lovingly tended rockery. Bea hadn't been patient enough to be a good mother to Stella, one of her deep regrets, but she found in old age she was finally patient enough to be a good gardener. The swallow was a bad sign. When they swooped low like that it was usually to catch the midges that supplied their food, and the midges stayed down close to the water when rain was approaching. Midges might be nasty biting creatures and pretty pointless in most ways, but their one useful function was as a barometer.

After her cup of tea, her next habit was to walk down to Black's Farm and pick up her quart of milk in its miniature milk churn. There had been a lot of scares about unpasteurized milk lately, but Bea ignored them. She hated all the petty regulations that hemmed farmers in and made everything so regimented. The farmer's wife, Eileen, used to make a delicious goat's cheese until she'd been told she had to buy industrial-grade equipment and gave up altogether.

On the swallows' advice, Bea took a light jacket with her for her fifteen-minute round trip to the farm. On beautiful mornings, or when the mushrooms were in the fields, or she wanted to get to the blackberries before they were all picked, she would make it a longer walk, but today she decided against it.

Sure enough, on her way back the sun disappeared behind a black cloud and it felt as if some giant bucket were being emptied over the village. The villages round here all seemed to have their own distinct weather patterns and it amazed Bea how it could be fine in one village and wet in the next.

She jammed her felt hat down further and turned up the collar of her coat. Like this she could stride quite comfortably for hours without feeling too much like King Lear on the blasted heath.

She had passed the pub when she almost tripped over the exhaust of Anthony Lewis's ancient Volvo, parked so far up on the pavement that it was impossible for a pedestrian to pass. Anthony carefully laid the grandfather clock he was removing from his boot back in the car and watched Bea's approach, a knowing smile making him look even more like a German bit-part in a war film than usual. Why on earth was he grinning manically at her like that, as if they were both sharing some fabulously funny joke that no other lesser mortals were privy to?

'Hello, Beatrice,' Anthony greeted her. 'You're out early.'

'I'm out every morning at this time,' Bea replied briskly. 'Best part of the day. *You're* the one who's up early. For you, that is. We never normally see your shop open till lunchtime.' *If at all*, she added under her breath.

'How's Amanda these days?' he enquired, pretending to fiddle with the clock.

'She's fine.' Bea ignored the sudden use of Stella's real name, but still felt unnerved. Anthony hadn't used it for years. 'Very busy, as ever.'

'I know,' replied Anthony. 'I read about her in the gossip columns. "The *Times* Readers' Pin-Up". What do they think they mean by that? Charlotte Rampling meets Barbara Windsor?'

'Really, Anthony, I don't think you can compare Stella with a peroxide barmaid type with huge breasts and a silly giggle.'

'I wouldn't dream of describing Charlotte Rampling that way,' countered Anthony.

Really, what had got into the man? Bea had to confess that she'd never liked Anthony. He was charming enough, in a wolfish way, but there wasn't the substance. He reminded her of a lot of second-rate actors with no determination she'd come across, the kind of men who took the easy option.

Bea squelched up the narrow lane beside her house, past the delphiniums in various shades of blues and pinks and whites, so weighed down with the rain that they drooped their heads, and admired her sunflowers. She'd tried them in red this year, but she wasn't sure it was a success. There was something about an original form that was always lost in the modification. God knew better than the gene manipulators when it came to nature. Bea shook the rain off her coat. It was so heavy it had even begun to penetrate the waxed coating. At least the garden would appreciate the change after a spell of almost Spanish weather, though she hoped it wouldn't knock the petals off all the roses. English weather had a habit of doing that the moment the roses achieved their supreme perfection.

At the far end of the garden path, not even taking shelter under the meagre cover of the stone lintel, her clothes soaked against her skin, her hair in rats' tails, looking more like a waif than a sex goddess, stood her daughter.

'Stella, darling,' Bea demanded, 'don't you possess a raincoat? You'll catch your death.'

It was a silly question, Bea knew. Stella was the kind of woman who never walked in the rain, in fact never walked anywhere. And yet here she was on Bea's doorstep, looking as if she'd stepped out from under the shower, her eyes clouded with misery.

'You've heard from him, haven't you?'

Stella didn't need to answer the question.

Bea unlocked the door and shepherded her in. 'Here, take off those soaking clothes, I'll get you my dressing gown. Good job it's only a summer downpour.' She took off her mac and ran upstairs, grateful for a moment to think.

So that explained Anthony's sly smile this morning. She knew from the look on his face that Anthony felt he was finally getting a chance to even old scores. The girl with the baby must have somehow found him and discovered about Stella. How thrilled Anthony must have been, and how helpful.

As she hunted for the dressing gown, Bea knew Stella had come to her for advice. What should she tell her? Bea had always been a believer in fate. Maybe it was all those years travelling round the East, but she had imbibed a sense of things happening because they were meant to, and believed that nothing the individual could do made much difference. This attitude very much annoyed their local vicar, who branded it positively unChristian, but Bea only laughed and went on arranging the church flowers better than anyone else.

She had to admit, Stella had been selfish. She knew this because she recognized the identical quality in herself. Bea wasn't much given to introspection, but it had struck her uncomfortably that she might have had a hand in creating her beautiful daughter's self-absorption.

Acting suited Stella, just as it had suited Bea, because it required passion and commitment, but also because it offered her the chance to hide her real personality behind the parts she played. It gave her the chance to somehow evade her own personal demons because she could always pretend to be someone else. And it rewarded her with a generalized adulation which required no emotional commitment from her. Stella, it seemed to Bea, had an overwhelming need to be loved, matched only by an inability to return that love to any one individual.

It hadn't been the recipe for a happy life.

Had you asked Bea ten, or even five, years ago if any of this mattered, she would have said that talent, and the capacity to be different, were what really counted in life. Now she wasn't so sure. The last few years, living here, in a predictable and comfortable rhythm, had been the happiest she'd ever known. If she could turn the clock back, she would have tried to give Stella a sense of undemanding security and reliable love, things that had been notably absent from her daughter's childhood.

She grabbed the dressing gown and went downstairs.

Stella had stripped off her clothes and sat in a dark blue velvet chair wearing only a lace bra and pants, her dark hair dripping down her back. Shot by one of the moody foreign directors Stella liked to work with, the scene could have been erotic, but her empty expression and the painful droop of her shoulders made it simply sad.

'You poor girl. Is it awful?' Bea wrapped her dressing gown round her daughter.

'I can't believe I mind so much.' Stella looked away. 'After all, it was so long ago.'

'I always worried that it seemed too easy for you.'

'But then we both know how to close off our emotions, don't we, Ma? You never seemed to mind much leaving me.'

Bea inched forward in her seat. If the stiffness which often arrived in wet weather hadn't prevented her, she would have liked to kneel at her daughter's feet and hold her. 'Oh, but I did! I hated it. I thought about you every day. I longed for us to find work here so I could be with you.'

'I wish you'd told me that.'

'My generation didn't talk about emotions like yours do. Besides, you were so prickly, so self-contained.'

'And it never struck you there might be a connection between that and you leaving me all the time?'

Stella huddled inside the fluffy pink dressing gown, suddenly looking absurdly young and vulnerable.

'I'm sorry, darling,' Bea said, leaning towards her daughter, 'that I let you down so badly. But in the end we all just have to get on with our lives and stop blaming other people.'

'I know.' Stella smiled a small, sad smile. She reached out a damp hand to her mother and Beatrice gripped it.

'You should have heard his voice, Ma.' Stella's own voice was low and anguished. 'It was all spiky and I-don't-need-you-ish.'

'He was probably trying to protect himself. It must have been a hard call to make. You might have told him to get lost. The poor boy must be terrified.'

'What if he hates me, though? I don't think I could bear it.'

'I doubt he does. More likely he needs to find you to make sense of himself.' She almost added that it might do Stella good to feel real emotion, but that would sound cruel and uncaring. If this boy really did get to meet her, Stella would soon find out what it was to feel something she couldn't control.

Bea smiled gently. 'It must be a bit of a shock to him to discover his mother's a sexpot.'

'And what about *me*? I'm trying desperately to get this part from Roxanne Wood. She's only about twenty-five herself. How's it going to look if it turns out I've got a son who's the same age?'

Bea could sense the barriers coming back up and the old Stella reasserting herself.

'So what are you going to do? Tell him that you'd rather not meet him?'

'You think I should see him, don't you?'

There were times when Bea knew her daughter better than Stella knew herself. If she said yes, Stella might rebel and refuse to meet him, even if that wasn't what she really wanted.

'I think you'd be perfectly justified in refusing. You've got too much at stake. As you say, if this got out it might be very bad for you.' She hoped to God Stella didn't take her at her word.

Stella thought about this. 'You don't think that might be a bit unfair? That I owe him the chance to meet? After all, I am his mother.' She hesitated on the unfamiliarity of the word in connection with herself.

Bea concealed her smile. 'I hadn't looked at it like that. Perhaps it wouldn't do any harm to meet him just the once.'

'As long as the press don't find out.'

'Why should they, if you're careful about where you meet? Does he sound the kind of young man to sell his story?'

'Ma,' Bea could be infuriating sometimes, 'I've only heard his voice on an answering machine. He might bring along a photographer from *Hello!* magazine for all I know.' But she didn't think so. There was something about Joe's voice that made her feel he could be trusted. That all this mattered too much to him to be a commercial exercise.

And if Stella were honest, deep inside her heart there was a small flicker of love just beginning to burn.

Chapter 11

When Molly opened her eyes, she found Joe propped up on one elbow contemplating her.

'You look beautiful when you're sleeping. A pre-Raphaelite beauty waiting to be painted.' He twirled one of her long russet curls round his finger.

'Unlike the shrewish, interfering, nagging old bag that I am when I'm awake then?' There was something different about Joe this morning that confused her. Last night he'd been furious. This morning it was as if the storm had been a passing one, leaving sunshine and bright blue sky in its wake.

'I called her after I went to bed last night,' Joe confessed.

'Stella Milton? My God, Joe why didn't you tell me?'

'I don't know. I did it on the spur of the moment, before I could change my mind.'

'What on earth did you say? That you were her son?'

'No. For once I took your advice.' His wry smile lit up her heart. Here was the Joe she loved. 'I just said I was born on January the twenty-fourth at the Sacred Heart and had reason to believe we were related. I tried to sound as matter-of-fact as I could so I didn't scare her off. Then I left our number.'

'Joseph Meredith, you're so brave.'

Joe pretended to dismiss her admiration, but smiled all the same. 'I didn't have much choice once you'd given me the number.'

Molly hid her head under the pillow. 'Oh God, it's all my fault. You wouldn't have done any of this if I hadn't been digging up the past like a demented gopher.'

'I might have wanted to, though. That's the difference between you and me. You're the doer. Maybe that's why I married you.'

He removed the pillow and began kissing her. Molly didn't know if she was imagining it, but there seemed more passionate intensity in this kiss than he'd shown for many months.

They melted together, both glad of this chance to give something to the other, and started to make love. Their climax came quickly and gratefully. In his room next door Eddie, sensing something was going on from which he was being excluded, joined in with a lusty roar.

'Just in time,' breathed Molly, and they both laughed.

'I'll get him,' offered Joe and bounded out of bed. He came back with Eddie in his arms and placed him gently in the bed between them.

As Molly watched her husband and son she felt an overwhelming feeling of tenderness, and not even the slightest shiver of apprehension at the thought of the Pandora's box she might have unwittingly opened.

Molly's friend Claire was having a bad day.

Tony, her boss, had stormed out of the editorial meeting in a most unloverlike manner, informing her and her fellow feature writers that the editor thought their ideas were crap and that they had better bloody well come up with some better ones unless they wanted to find themselves working on *Fly Fishing Weekly*.

Claire did what she usually did when she was desperate for a story. She rang all her contacts, even from her training days, scoured the other newspapers and a couple of the more switched-on locals, then spun through the PA stuff on her screen and

Celebrity News to see if anyone faintly interviewable was in town. Unfortunately, the dead season of summer was upon them. Rock stars had retreated to their French châteaux, no big films were being released and even the TV companies had started saving their interesting shows up for the autumn. Zilch. Claire felt herself coming out in a cold sweat and had to go the loo for the ninth time. Her best hope was a minor soap star who had agreed to spill the beans, unfortunately already splashed across a double-page spread of a monthly magazine, about her recent marriage break-up. The fact that the marriage had only lasted six months might make it less interesting, but could be dressed up with a comment piece written by the paper's agony aunt and billed 'The Disposable Marriage: a Sign of Our Times?'.

She took the idea to Tony, hoping to God he wouldn't chuck it out. She certainly didn't have anything else up her sleeve.

Tony was unimpressed. 'I suppose this will have to do for today. But you'll have to come up with something better next time, Claire. This is local paper stuff.'

Claire returned Tony's glance with venom. He was hardly the hottest features editor in newspapers, executive or not. In her view she'd come up with some bloody good ideas, but Tony was too unimaginative to appreciate them. His inevitable response was 'We've done it before', but the truth was that journalism consisted entirely of things that had been done before. It was all a matter of the spin you put on a story, but Tony never gave you the chance to prove that.

Looking across his desk at her balding, soft-featured lover, Claire realized she'd had enough. Today was Friday and this would be yet another weekend when her life would be on hold, wondering if he would call or manage to get away. It wasn't worth it. *He* wasn't worth it. Molly was always telling her she could find someone who would be better for her than Tony, that she was wasting herself on a man who was too indecisive to ever leave his wife. Suddenly she longed to see Molly. Molly, who always knew what was right, who was brave and forthright. She somehow imagined Molly as the inspiration for a Renaissance painting she'd seen of some saint or other, dressed in armour, on horseback, riding into battle with virtue aglow and head held high. Nothing like the pathetic lump of failure Claire felt at this precise moment.

She was quite annoyed when Molly didn't answer the phone and the machine picked up her call. She realized she'd come to expect Molly to be always around, part domestic goddess, part battling idealist, but always available to be leaned on. The thought crossed her mind that maybe everyone did this to Molly, used her as their centre, a kind of human tent peg who would hold down their craziest fantasies or gee them up when the ground seemed shaky. It was partly because Molly seemed so strong and instinctive, not riddled with self-doubt like Claire, so that she felt she was disappearing up her own ambition. Molly seemed to be so firmly outside the insanity of office life, with her feisty attitudes and her fizzy optimism. Claire hoped Joe realized how lucky he was to have Molly to draw on.

'I'll pop round later, if that's OK,' she confided to the answering machine when it cut in, 'about six thirty. Byeeee.'

Even though there were about three hundred people in the open-plan office around her, there was almost complete silence. Only the feverish tap-tap of keyboards demonstrated the tension level in the air. The paper's deadline was fast approaching . . .

Claire swivelled round to face her screen and began jazzing up the interview she'd already written with the soap star. The agony aunt piece was actually quite perceptive. All the same, there had to be something more exciting to write about than this.

If only she could find it.

She had more or less finished when Molly called back to say they'd love to see her. Just as Claire was hoping, given the state of her fridge and her life, Molly suggested she stay to supper. At least the weekend would start pleasantly. Claire didn't like to think about what a rut she'd got into. Either she stayed in and was miserable or she made herself go out and was miserable. Something was going to have to change. Maybe if she was made redundant it would be all for the best. She might get a payoff, and she'd get away from Tony.

From nowhere a sense of panic swirled up in her, making her chest hurt and her breathing painful. She felt sick thinking of the yuppie-level rent on her flat and the impressive size of her credit card bill. Her family had been serious if-you-can't-pay-for-it, you-can't-have-it people. When she was ten she'd had to save up for thirty-six weeks for her bike. How she'd laughed at her dad when he'd refused to buy a packet of Old Holborn on the slate at their local newsagent because he'd forgotten his wallet. The shop owner had been almost insulted when Dad had refused. But he had stuck to his guns, saying he didn't believe in tick.

Now she wished she was a bit more like him.

After work, on her way to Molly's, Claire decided to economize and let a stream of alluring black cabs pass her in favour of taking the underground.

The journey was nightmarish. Travelling south was even worse than going north. The trains were so full that even after she waited until the third one she still had to plaster herself dangerously against the doors to get on. Everyone had that dead, glazed look, like fish that had been hanging around too long on the fishmonger's slab. Next to her was a large, sweaty man who seemed to have spent his working day sitting in the pub. Each wave of beery breath convinced Claire she might faint. Not that anyone would notice. Not until they'd trampled her to death in their enthusiasm to make the 6.32 from London Bridge.

Finally she got to the stop nearest Molly and Joe's flat. It was still a bus ride, but people on buses were friendlier. On buses, at least the muggers talked to you before they stole your purse.

The sultry weather had passed, leaving clear, hot blue skies that made her long to be anywhere but in a city. Still, Claire had to admit as she sat on the top deck of the bus, there was a cheerful air to the crowded, dirty streets. Every pub had convinced itself it was in Paris rather than Peckham and had tables and chairs and striped umbrellas outside on the pavement. Even the kebab houses had discovered their Turkish roots and splurged their furniture out into the street. Ragga music, with shades of jungle and techno – at least that was what Claire, unfamiliar with the vital subdivisions of youth culture, supposed it to be – blared from every open window.

By the time she rang Molly's bell she was prepared to believe London wasn't such a hell-hole after all. As long as you could afford to live here. Which she wouldn't, if she wasn't very careful, be able to do for much longer.

'Hello, gel,' she greeted Molly in a dreadful attempt at cheery Cockney, 'you're looking great!'

And it was true. Molly's clothes were no different from usual – cargo pants and a crop top revealing an endearingly sloping post-baby belly – but she was suntanned and looked really rather sexy, her hair wild and loose plus, for some inexplicable reason, a biro behind one ear with a plastic sunflower attached to it.

In her arms was Eddie, plump and brown and smiling.

But what was most noticeable was that the anxiety Claire had noticed in her friend's eyes seemed to have disappeared and been replaced by a dazzling glow.

'Don't tell me. You don't need to. Marital harmony has been restored – not to mention, by the look of you, great sex. Actually,' the journalist in her prompted, 'that's not a bad idea for a piece . . . "After the Great Quarrel, the Great Screw".'

'Ssh!' Molly pretended to cover Eddie's ears. 'Come in. Joe's just popped out to the shops. Do you ever worry about turning life, especially other people's, into newspaper columns?'

'The answer's no, that's why I'm good at it.' Claire sat down and put her feet up. 'You know, you really ought to take up interior design. This place always looks like it's straight out of one of those sickening features called "Decorating on a Budget". I won't ask how much it all cost. Less than my totally impractical designer dining table that sports little white rings where the wine glasses go, I'll bet.'

'I'm only good at superficial things. I'm not sure I could knock down walls and boss builders about.'

'What? I remember you sorting out that landlord who was over-charging us at college. He'll never rent to redheads again after you.'

'He deserved it.' Molly grinned at the memory of the man giving them their money back, plus ten pounds for her to go away. She'd enjoyed tearing the tenner up, even though they were all so broke it was perhaps a tad unfair to the others.

'Anyway, why *are* you quite so full of the joys of spring? You haven't won the lottery or anything?'

Molly put Eddie down on the floor – although now he was get-ting old enough to turn over and start crawling, soon nothing in the flat would be safe – and took a deep breath. She shouldn't really tell Claire what had happened, given what she did for a living. On the other hand, she was going to burst with excitement if she didn't tell someone. Claire *had* helped her find Stella, and despite being a journalist she wouldn't tell if Molly swore her to secrecy. She was Molly's oldest friend after all.

'Actually, the most wildly amazing thing has happened.'

Claire pulled herself into an upright position, galvanized by the tone of Molly's voice. This was clearly no run-of-the-mill bit of gossip about someone they knew killing their husband or having a lesbian affair with the au pair. 'God, Moll, what is it?'

'You know I've been trying to track down Joe's real mother.' Molly paused, struck with sudden indecision about the wisdom of her revelation.

'Of course I do. I told you to keep a diary, remember, because you ought to write something. Have you been keeping one?'

'Sort of. Do you remember I found out her name was Amanda Lewis? Well, I went back down to the village where she's supposed to come from to do a bit more sleuthing, and managed to get the owner of the antique shop to admit that he did know her. He told me she lived in London now. The thing is, when I asked how I could contact her, he just laughed hysterically and said, "Why not? It's time life caught up with her."'

'Bloody hell. He sounds a bit unhinged.'

'More bitter than unhinged, I suspect.'

'So he reckons this Amanda's not going to be exactly thrilled when Joe turns up on her doorstep. Maybe she's got kids. Or a husband who doesn't know she had a baby adopted.'

'No, none of that. She's never married, as a matter of fact; at least I don't think so.'

'You've found her, then.' Claire could hardly contain her amazement.

'Almost. Joe rang her last night and left a message. She hasn't rung back yet.' The first small dent appeared in Molly's enthusiasm. 'But I've got this really strong feeling that she will.'

'God, Molly, this is really gripping. What an amazing story.'

Molly couldn't help grinning. 'You haven't heard the best bit yet. Who Amanda Lewis turned out to be.'

'Who? Go on, Moll, this is killing me.'

'Stella Milton.'

Claire felt her breath speed up and her neck prickle with excitement. 'You don't mean *the* Stella Milton?'

'Absolutely. Isn't it completely gobsmacking?'

Claire felt her palms begin to sweat. Not only was it gobsmacking, it was an incredible, amazing, stunning, career-making, once-in-a-lifetime scoop!

Then the full horror of it hit her. Not only was it the best story she'd heard in her entire career, it was one she couldn't tell. To tell it would be to betray her oldest friend. As moral dilemmas went, she'd never been faced with one as horrible as this.

She heard the sound of Joe opening the front door and dropped her voice. 'You're sure she's really Joe's mother? Stella Milton, I mean.' With every word Claire felt the sharp hooks of temptation closing in on her.

'Not till she contacts us, I suppose. I just *know* she is. I feel it in my bones.'

'Not the most reliable of sources.'

'Besides, Joe's incredibly like her.'

'I suppose he is, if I try imagining her with her clothes on.'

If she'd had any sense Claire would have left it there, but being Claire, she was too excited. 'God, Molly, I just can't believe it.'

Joe plonked a bottle of wine down on the counter and looked at them both, taking in their sudden silence and their furtive air.

'You've told her, haven't you?' he accused, his face a sudden mask of white-hot anger. 'You've actually told Claire.'

'She's my closest friend. She's like a sister to me. We've always told each other everything.'

'And the fact that she happens to work for a newspaper didn't ring the smallest alarm bell in your head?'

Claire jumped to her feet, hoping he couldn't read her mind. 'Don't be ludicrous, Joe.'

'I think you should apologize. What you're implying is incredibly insulting to Claire.'

'And I think you're being incredibly naive. Telling Claire about Stella's like leaving a gram of heroin with a junkie. It's not even fair to her.'

'For heaven's sake, Joe, Claire's our friend. She knows how delicate all this is. You haven't even made contact properly yet.'

'Absolutely. The whole story might be rubbish. I'll probably get a call from this woman's agent saying it's all bollocks and if I don't retract it she'll sue.'

Claire, feeling acutely uncomfortable, searched by the sofa for her bag. 'Look, chaps, I really do need to get away. I just remembered I forgot to feed the cat.'

'You don't have a cat.'

'You know what I mean. I'm intruding. This is between you two and I think it's better I take myself off.'

Molly picked Eddie up and held him to her, almost like a talisman, something that could guide her through rocky waters. She'd lost the sense of ecstatic happiness that being close to Joe had brought, and it was her own stupid, tactless fault.

Claire was halfway across the room, her shoulders hunched with embarrassment, when the phone started ringing. They all stood there for a second, rooted. Finally it was Molly who picked it up. She held the receiver at arm's-length, trying to stop Eddie grabbing the cord and chewing it.

Her eyes flashed at her husband. 'It's for you, Joe. I think it's her.'

Chapter 12

'Hello, is that Joseph Meredith?'

Joe closed his eyes, frozen in panic. It was Stella! Her voice tied him up in its strangeness and familiarity. It was really her.

'Yes,' he replied, trying to stop his voice shaking crazily. He had no idea what to say next. Even the obvious stuff deserted him. Faced with the mother he'd hardly even dared to picture, he felt like a pathetic schoolboy.

Although she would have given anything to stay, Claire knew this wasn't a moment to be shared with an outsider, no matter how good a friend. But just as she was opening the door Joe nervously dropped the phone and an extraordinary sound reverberated round the room, a distinct sob of animal pain.

Claire stood frozen, while Joe picked up the reciever, not knowing how to respond. To his vast relief, a warm and friendly and much older voice had come on the line. 'Hello, Joseph, this is Beatrice Manners. I'm Stella's mother. Stella's a bit upset.'

The knowledge that his own mother cared enough to cry, whether for herself or for him, or simply out of shock, turned the key to Joe's own emotions. He felt not the anger he'd anticipated but an unexpected protectiveness. 'Look, tell her I'm so sorry. Maybe we shouldn't have done this out of the blue, it isn't fair.'

'Life's hardly ever fair, though, is it, Joseph? This is a shock for Stella but not altogether a surprise.' Joe liked the sound of the voice on the other end of the phone. It struck him with the wonder of revelation that this was his grandmother. 'Would you like to speak to Stella again, she's feeling a bit better now?'

'Yes please.'

'Joseph,' the voice held a forced calm, the calm of will power over emotion, 'I'm so sorry.'

'Don't worry, it must have been quite a shock. It was to me, I can tell you, finding out who you were.'

Stella laughed. It was a delicious, husky sound. 'I can imagine. So, when shall we meet?'

Joe felt his throat dry up and close over so that answering was impossible. During the last days and weeks he'd geared himself up for disappointment and rejection, but never for breezy acceptance.

Finally he forced himself to answer. 'Of course I'd love to meet.' He had no idea what he ought to suggest. 'Next week perhaps?'

'Next week?' Stella's voice rang with disappointment. 'I was thinking of tomorrow.'

'All right then. Tomorrow.' Again the faint panic in Joe's tone. 'Where do you think we should go?'

'Could you come to my flat? It's in Covent Garden. Unless you'd rather somewhere else.'

Listening to her daughter from the safe distance of the kitchen, to where she'd retreated, it seemed to Bea that Stella's usual imperiousness had deserted her. She rather preferred this new Stella.

'No, your flat would be fine.'

'One o'clock?'

'All right.' Joe was still in shock. 'See you then.'

'Hold on,' Stella laughed, her usual seductive charm re-emerging, 'you haven't asked for the address. It's 64 Old Flower Market. The top flat.'

'See you tomorrow, then.' Joe was about to put down the phone when Eddie, who had been sleeping peacefully on the scarlet sofa where Molly had deposited him behind a mound of protective cushions to stop him falling off, woke up. As if suddenly aware that something vital had been happening without him, he began to yell vociferously.

'What's that?' Stella demanded. 'It sounds like a wild animal.'

'In a manner of speaking. That's Eddie. Our baby. He's nearly six months old.'

'My God.' If a voice could blanch, then Stella's voice did precisely that. 'Goodbye, Joseph. I'll see you tomorrow.'

'I think,' Molly picked up Eddie to calm him, 'that Stella's just realized she's a granny.'

Bea had been sitting in her favourite wing chair trying not to interfere but desperate not to miss a single word of this extraordinary conversation. 'What's the matter?' she demanded of her stunned daughter. 'You look as if you've seen a whole firmament of ghosts.'

'There's a baby. You didn't tell me about the baby.'

'No.' Bea got up and ushered Stella into her own seat. 'Well, one shock at a time I always say. The girl brought him when she first came asking for you. He's the most gorgeous thing. I had a little cuddle. I suspect she thought I was a maniac child-stealer, but I couldn't help myself. He looks just like you.'

'But that means I'm a grandmother!' Stella sounded as if she'd been given the diagnosis for a terminal disease. 'Here I am chasing after a part that's been given to a girl of twenty-five and I'm a bloody grandmother!'

'Still,' Bea consoled mischievously, 'think of all those glamorous granny contests you'll be able to go in for now.'

'Shut up, you old bat,' squeaked Stella, throwing a cushion at her, 'and get me a double vodka.'

Walking along Peckham High Street, Claire let a stream of taxis pass her as she contemplated the worst dilemma she'd had to face. Here she was, deep in debt, on the point of losing her job, faced with the most incredible story she'd ever come across, and she couldn't write about it.

She felt like Charlie from *Charlie and the Chocolate Factory*, a sweet-toothed child let loose in a wonderland of goodies, but knowing deep in his soul that to eat anything would mean disaster.

The worst thing was that whatever course of action she took would have an effect on their friendship. Either she would have to avoid seeing Joe and Molly altogether or her journalist instincts would get the better of her, or continue her friendship with them under such strained circumstances that none of them would feel natural about it. What she didn't have the moral courage to do, she realized as she finally hailed a cab to take her back to overpriced civilization, was to pretend that none of this mattered to her. This was a story she'd *kill* for and she was the only journalist in London who even knew about it.

She huddled into the back of the cab, feeling gloomier than ever. Even the vibrant summer street life, the buzzy cafés, music throbbing from each one, the sights and scents of a colourful south London evening, couldn't cheer her. She would have to spend the evening alone and try not to think of the amazing revelation she'd just witnessed.

Gradually the journalist in Claire calmed down and she was able to feel the more appropriate reactions of Claire the friend. There had always been a streak of unlikely glamour about Joe. Even at college his dark good looks and his habit of wearing black had singled him out. And somehow the black clothes, which would have been an act of deep pretentiousness in someone else, seemed acceptable in Joe. Of course, it had helped that they were from Oxfam rather than Armani.

Once you knew about it, you could see the strong family resemblance between Joe and Stella. They both had eyes that were a startling bright blue, with slightly jutting brows that gave them both a faintly hooded look, sensuous as much as beautiful. And they shared a kind of natural grace. It was funny how, now that she knew he was Stella's son, she saw for the first time how much subtle sensuality Joe possessed.

The taxi lurched to a stop as a child on a bike tore across the zebra crossing in front of them.

Claire's heart lurched. All this was going to change Joe. He wouldn't intend it to, he might even struggle to keep his feet on the ground, but he wouldn't be able to help it. Until now Joe had worked, with reasonable diligence, churning out handbooks on cars, and living in suburban peace in an unprepossessing flat (no matter that Molly had used her considerable skills to beautify it) in boring old Peckham. Stella Milton came from a world of glamour and tension and creativity, of flash restaurants and first nights and heady reviews. And some of that was bound to brush off on Joe. Of course, it might be a wonderful opportunity. Or it might mean Joe was about to be seduced, not literally, but metaphorically, by his own mother.

As Claire jumped out of the taxi and paid the driver, she reflected how much love and effort Molly had put into this quest. And she hoped, fervently and passionately, that it wasn't one she would come to regret.

The next day Molly watched Joe get ready to finally meet his mother and thought her heart might, quite literally, burst. He looked so handsome and his obvious nervousness just added to his attraction. She tried to think how Stella would be feeling; whether the shock of suddenly acquiring a good-looking son who was clearly a grown man was something she would welcome or be appalled by.

'Goodbye, good luck. It doesn't matter how long you are, just get to know each other, and don't forget we're going to want a blow-by-blow account later, aren't we, Eddie?' She went on to her tiptoes and kissed him. 'She can't fail to love you, just look at you.'

'It didn't work last time.'

'And I'm sure she really regretted it. This is a new start. For both of you.'

Joe leaned down and held them both. 'Anyway, you're my family now. My own little unassailable unit. Thank you, darling Molly, for doing all this for me. This would never have happened without you and your pig-headed determination.'

'Get on with you or you'll make me start blubbing.' Smiling, she watched him walk off. Were they really his unassailable little unit? The superstitious part of Molly didn't believe that anything was unassailable. Especially love.

This was one role Stella Milton had had very little preparation for. The contents of her wardrobe were strewn over her bed in her hunt to find the appropriate clothes in which to meet her son for the first time in more than twenty-five years. The obsession with her appearance, Stella realized, was probably a means of disguising deeper insecurities. She actually admired her mother far more for daring to look eccentric and please herself than her own attempts to look sexy and chic. And yet, damn it, she wanted to look her best. She wanted to charm and dazzle, perhaps because it was a lot less painful than being judged.

In the end, given that it was another glorious summer's day, she chose white linen trousers and a loose, flowing white silk top with a deep V, plus wildly expensive white trainers that had as much relationship to real running shoes as a Jaguar car has to the furry thing you find in the jungle.

She was, she had to admit, incredibly nervous, and broke her own iron rule of no alcohol before midday with a Dutch courage-sized flute of champagne. When the doorbell finally rang she knocked back the rest of her glass and ran a hand through her glossy dark hair, smart yet rumpled. This was it.

The sight of the tall, dark-haired young man standing on her doorstep made Stella more apprehensive than ever. It was like looking into a mirror. Joseph had her eyes and lashes, an identical-shaped face to hers, the same way of holding his head slightly to one side out of shyness that she'd had to work so hard to eradicate in her acting classes. The shade of his hair, lustrous and almost

117

black, with a faint hint of plummy purple, was just the same as hers.

Stella struggled to keep a calm smile pinned to her face when inside her heart was beating like the wings of a caged bird.

Joe handed her a bunch of white lilies. She breathed in their heady scent, trying to calm herself down. 'How did you know I love white lilies best?' There was a small wobble of emotion in the question which she hoped he didn't notice.

Joe laughed. 'Actually, Molly bought them. She's good at things like that. Or maybe she read somewhere that you liked them. It's really weird meeting someone you feel you know already, when of course you don't. Especially,' he smiled shyly as she shepherded him in, 'when she turns out to be your mother.'

Stella had to repress a small twinge of annoyance that his wife had chosen the flowers. 'Now what will you drink? I've started on the champagne, I'm afraid. Will that do?'

Joe hardly ever drank champagne. Actually he was more of a Budweiser man, but he doubted Stella had any of that. The flat wasn't at all what he'd expected. It was beautiful and pale and lux-urious, certainly, but he'd somehow pictured it as stagey and exotic. In fact, his own home looked more theatrical.

There were no tributes to Stella to be seen anywhere. In his stereotyped idea of an actress's home, he'd imagined the walls clut-tered with playbills or film posters, a tasteful – or perhaps not so tasteful – temple to Stella's ego. In fact there seemed to be few clues as to who lived here at all, except that the owner had subtly refined taste, quite a lot of money, and no children. The other sur-prise was that there were no photographs, of Stella or anyone else. The panel on *Through the Keyhole* would have had their work cut out deciding whose home this was.

Stella had decided to take him to the terrace, and they were halfway across the sitting room when he saw it and was hard put not to spill his drink. The one memento she'd chosen to display was a huge framed poster, the one he'd had up on his bedroom wall: Stella with her hand on the zip of her black leather motorcycle outfit, the zip that every male in England over the age of eight had wanted to undo.

Looking at it again after all these years, Joe felt an uncomfortable sense of confusion. He didn't even want to *think* what he'd done in front of that poster.

Stella led him through the French doors on to her roof terrace high above Covent Garden. The scent of jasmine was overwhelming, even stronger than the lilies. Three sides of the terrace were closed in by trellising curtained in climbing plants, giving the impression of a scented bower. It was impossible to believe you were in the middle of the West End of London. The view over the rooftops was magnificent. Down below, the shoppers scurrying along Floral Street to Paul Smith or Monsoon had no hint of the paradise hidden above them.

'So,' Stella refilled the champagne flute he had drained far too quickly, 'tell me all about yourself. I don't want you to leave out a single comma.'

'That won't take long. I'm not a very fascinating person. I'm twenty-five . . . well, you know that.' He blushed a little, looking even more attractive – he really was the handsomest boy. 'I went to the local primary school, then on to grammar school.'

'You were clever, then.'

'Petrified, more likely. My mother . . .' he stumbled to a stop, looking hideously embarrassed, '. . . that is, my adopted mother, Pat, would have killed me if I hadn't got in.'

'And what about your adopted father? What did he think?'

'Andrew?' Joe laughed shyly. 'Oh, Pat wore the trousers in our home.'

'And where was that?'

'Essex . . . Mere-on-Sea.'

This obviously tickled Stella. 'My son the Essex boy. How sweet. And were you happy?'

'I was a bit of an introvert. Stayed in my bedroom a lot. Hopeless at sport. I even loathed football, so that cut out ninety-nine per cent of all human communication. I don't think I was the kind of son Mum – Pat, that is – had in mind.'

119

Stella's heart lurched sickeningly. The thought of this awful woman not appreciating her beautiful, sensitive son made her crease up with guilt.

'Don't worry, they were always incredibly kind to me,' he reassured, reading her mind. 'It was just that I wasn't really their type.'

'Well, you're certainly mine.'

Joe found himself grinning ridiculously.

'And when did you meet the lovely Molly?'

'At college. I was still quite shy and Molly decided to take me on, rather like one of her projects.'

'She certainly is a whirlwind of energy.'

'That's Molly.'

Stella was ashamed to find she felt quite jealous of the tenderness in Joe's voice. She'd only just discovered the emotions of being a mother, and already here were the even more complex ones of being a mother-*in-law*. Stella wasn't sure she was ready for that. 'What did you study? Did it fire you up with intellectual passion?'

Joe cracked with laughter. 'Electronic engineering doesn't tend to. It's full of nerds who dream of being Bill Gates and end up servicing computers.'

'But you didn't?'

Joe looked faintly embarrassed. 'No. I work for a publisher who prints car handbooks. Everything you've ever wanted to know about your Ford Mondeo.'

'How riveting.'

Joe searched her eyes for sarcasm, but her beautiful face was entirely earnest. 'They're mainly for DIY fans,' he added limply.

Stella looked blank. 'Do people actually mend their own cars?' There couldn't be a better illustration of the difference between their two worlds. 'Heavens. To think I can't even drive.'

This time it was Joe's turn to be shocked. He couldn't imagine a world where you could survive without driving. 'How do you get around?'

'I get cabs,' Stella said simply, as if it were obvious.

'And whereabouts do you and Molly live?' Stella found she wanted every detail to store away for later.

'In Peckham.'

'How wonderful. Like in *The Ballad of Peckham Rye*.' Stella only had the haziest idea of where Peckham was. She just knew none of her friends lived there. 'Is it lovely?'

Joe glanced around him at the subtle splendour of Stella's surroundings. 'Well, not *lovely* exactly. But the views are quite nice if you ignore the tower blocks and with Molly at home and us both managing on my salary, we're a bit broke, so we're lucky to have a nice flat.' He could have kicked himself when he shut up. He probably sounded as if he were asking for money, for God's sake.

Stella produced a second bottle of champagne and popped the cork so ineptly that Joe had to rescue her.

'You're not so broke that you don't know how to open champagne bottles,' Stella said archly.

'Maybe it's in the genes.'

Silence fell as if someone had dropped a fork at a state occasion, shattering their pretence at normality.

'Why did you do it?' Joe asked abruptly. He hadn't meant to. He had told himself they should get to know each other before he asked any of the heavy stuff. But it wasn't like that. There were emotions that wouldn't stay neatly in their box. 'Why did you give me away? I mean, you weren't broke, you had your mother to turn to.'

The fine lines deepened around Stella's mouth. For a moment she looked old. 'I felt I didn't have any choice. I was so young and naive.' Joe couldn't imagine the sophisticated woman before him ever being naive. 'I was just starting out. I wasn't ready to be tied down by a child.' Her eyes held his, begging him to understand, not to simply condemn. 'I suppose it just sounds selfish and heartless to you.'

'A bit. We have a baby. I couldn't contemplate giving him away, no matter what happened.'

121

'It's entirely different. You're settled and happy. I was alone. I couldn't have coped with a baby.'

'What about my father?' Joe demanded. 'Wouldn't he have helped?'

Stella smiled sadly. 'I'm afraid he wasn't in a position to. He didn't want to acknowledge you. Things were so different then, even that short time ago. It's another world now.'

The pain etched on Joe's face cut jaggedly into her like broken glass. Did he need a father so much? He'd just found his mother after all these years, surely that would be enough. But she saw that she'd wounded him again and tried to make up for it.

'The fact that I gave you away,' she faltered, her sophistication disappearing, 'doesn't mean I didn't love you.' Joe shrugged and looked away. She could hardly blame him. This wasn't something you could put right with a quick apology. 'Or that I haven't thought about you endlessly over the years.'

'But you never made the effort to contact me.' The bald words were intended to hurt, and they did.

'Come here a moment.' She led Joe back inside and into the bedroom, to her chest of drawers. It took her only a moment to find the tiny sock. 'The nun at the foster home gave me that. It fell off your foot just as they were taking you away.' She crushed it into her hand. 'Then there are these.' She sat down on the white-duveted bed and delved into her bedside cabinet, taking out a pile of identical letters, tied together with a purple satin ribbon. 'I wrote you one every year on your birthday. There are twenty-five. Maybe you'd like to have them.'

'My God.' Joe took the bundle of letters in his hands, choking back his tears. 'You didn't forget me after all.' They were all different shapes and sizes on varying coloured paper – sometimes a card, sometimes a letter, written in a spectrum of coloured inks.

It felt like being given the most precious Christmas present imaginable when you'd thought you weren't going to get anything.

Stella held out her arms and Joe put down the letters and launched himself into them, holding onto her as if she might disappear again from his life at any moment and this time he was going to stop her. They stayed there, limbs at a ludicrously uncomfortable angle for almost a minute. Finally Joe looked up. 'Hello, Mum,' he said gently, wiping away the tears from both their faces.

'Hello, Joseph.'

Joe's spirits spun like an old aircraft looping the loop. She loved him. She hadn't forgotten him or thrown him out like a bag of rubbish. She'd missed him and written to him each birthday, and gone on loving him. It was like a stone being lifted from his chest, one he'd carried round all his life.

In that moment it seemed so simple. She had loved him and had made a mistake. Now that mistake could be put right. But neither of them, locked in their own emotions, suspected quite how much heartache might yet lie ahead.

Joe hadn't even got inside the front door before Hurricane Molly whirled in his direction.

'So go on, tell me, tell me absolutely every word that passed between you!'

'There's not that much to tell.' Joe grinned, knowing Molly would kill him for his apparently laid-back attitude. 'She gave me away because she felt too young to cope. My father didn't want to know and she was just on the brink of getting somewhere in acting.'

'Was it extraordinary? Did you cry? I was thinking about you all afternoon.'

Joe gathered her gratefully into his arms. 'Moll, I wish you'd been there. The best thing is that she never forgot me. She's kept this tiny little sock that some nun let her have. And she wrote me a letter on my birthday every single year. He reached into his jacket pocket for the bundle of letters, his eyes glinting with unshed tears. 'She's given them to me to read.'

'Why don't I make you a cup of tea and leave you in peace to have a look?'

'Molly, I don't deserve you. This is all your doing. It's as though there's been a big hole in me all my life and finally, thanks to you, it's being filled up.'

At that moment Molly thought she might melt with love and happiness right there on the spot. While she was putting the kettle on, she saw Joe out of the corner of her eye quietly slipping into Eddie's room and picking the baby up out of his cot.

'Tell you what, little Edward, you've got a surprise coming. Not one granny, but two, and very soon you're going to meet her.'

The tenderness in Joe's voice made Molly feel that every cloud in their marriage was being chased away. If Stella could have this effect then she was a miracle-worker. The only remaining cloud – and it was a pretty thick darkness-at-noon one – was the fact that fairly soon Joe was going to have to tell Pat that they'd not only found his real mother, but who she'd turned out to be.

But not yet. For now Molly was just going to enjoy the wonderful feeling that things were going exactly as she'd hoped.

It felt like waking on Christmas morning, Stella told herself, or how Christmas ought to be, knowing that wonderful excitements and surprises lay ahead. The feeling was too much for her. She had to share it. She rang Richard in Leeds to tell him what had happened. He sounded as delighted as she was if somewhat startled to learn that she had a son at all. Secretly she was relieved he was away, because it meant she'd be entirely free to get to know her son alone. Then she departed for Sussex to spend the day with Bea.

Normally Stella claimed that country Sundays were unbearably dull, and would only compromise by catching the train and meeting Bea in Cliffdean, which was rather like London-by-the-Sea. But today, as eager to sing Joe's praises as her mother would be to hear them, a visit was irresistible.

Bea stood at the door excitedly waiting for her daughter to alight from her taxi. Few people would have thought Nicole Farhi white linen with a thigh-high split more often seen on Liz Hurley suitable Sunday-in-the-country wear, especially teamed with high-heeled sandals held in place by the tiniest of thin straps across the toes, not to mention a large floppy hat and sunglasses, but Stella had her *femme fatale* image to consider.

What hard work it looks, thought Bea. Wouldn't it be nice for her if she could just relax and be like everyone else? But then perhaps Stella hadn't had the kind of upbringing that encouraged her to be like everyone else.

'Would you like to sit in the garden?' Bea asked. 'There's some lovely shade under the apple tree.' Stella was very particular about not getting sunburnt. The sun, she maintained, was almost as bad for your skin as sharing the billing with a peachy-faced twenty-year-old. Both made you look like an old crone.

Bea, who was near enough to being an old crone not to care, adored the sun and spent hours lying with her face upturned drinking in its rays like a lizard on a lilo.

'So,' she demanded, settling her daughter in a wicker chair with a Bloody Mary, 'do tell. And don't leave a single detail out. I want the full unabridged picture. What was he like?'

A smile that would have made Oedipus blush lit up Stella's face. 'He was absolutely, totally, utterly, wildly gorgeous.'

'Go on,' Bea teased, 'he must have had *some* good qualities.'

Stella looked blank, leaving Bea wondering how she'd managed to give birth to a daughter with absolutely no sense of humour. Maybe God had concentrated all his gifts on the exterior design.

'Where did he grow up, what were his adopted parents like?'

'In Essex, for God's sake. The parents sound ghastly. Dull as a Sunday in Rochdale.'

'Kind, though?'

'In a boring sort of way, but he never felt he fitted.'

'No.' Bea contemplated the tragedy of a beautiful young man who should have been brought up in her own family, surrounded by love and eccentricity. But then, were they capable of love in her family? Both she and Stella had wanted, more than anything, certainly more than marriage and domesticity, to act. Maybe Joseph had been better off with the boring parents in Essex after all.

125

It was a truly beautiful day. The kind only an English country summer can offer. The air fresh under a bright blue sky, the grass still green, not dried out and brown as it could so often be in August, the rare red apples ripening above their heads, a wood pigeon serenading them with his calm chant of 'coo-coooo-cooo-coo'.

Bea, usually cautious, felt a sudden leap of excitement that her family had gained three new members.

'And what did you tell him,' she studied her glamorous daughter, or at least what she could see of her under the hat and sunglasses, 'when he asked you why you did it?'

'How do you know he asked that?'

'Of course he asked that, or if he didn't he will. What else would any child, rejected and abandoned by the one person who usually loves it, want to ask?'

'Don't rub it in, Ma.'

'It's true, Amanda.' The unexpected sound of her real name startled Stella. Her mother hadn't used it in twenty-five years. 'You'll have to face the truth one day, you know.'

'I am facing the truth.'

'Are you? So what did you tell him?'

'That I couldn't cope, but that I always loved him. I showed him the sock I'd kept. I wanted him to realize that he always mattered to me.'

Bea reached forward and took her hand. 'And do you think he believed you?'

'Yes.' Stella nodded. 'I think he did. Especially when I gave him the letters.'

Bea looked confused. 'What letters were those?'

'The letters I wrote him on his birthday each year and kept in case he found me.'

'Oh, darling, that's wonderful.' Bea had to repress a sob, devastated by guilt that she'd underestimated her daughter's feelings so much. 'I didn't know you'd done that.'

Stella looked away in case her mother guessed the truth. She'd known that Joseph would need some concrete reassurance that he hadn't been forgotten, and the least she could do was give it to him. So the day before Joe came to meet her, she'd written the twenty-five letters. It had taken her all day. And it had worked. He'd almost broken down with emotion.

'God, Ma,' the Oedipal smile was back, 'I can't tell you how lovely he was. All tall and sweet and shy. I can't wait to take him out and show him off. My great big handsome son.'

Alarm bells, faint but insistent, started to sound in Beatrice's head. 'Be careful, darling. Not everyone is going to understand your motives in feeling you had to give Joseph away.'

And Joseph would certainly be one of them, Bea admitted to herself, if the whole truth ever came out. She'd just have to pray that it didn't.

Chapter 13

Molly woke up first, as she often did, and listened to the early morning peace. There was no sound quite as peaceful as a house which usually rang with the cry of a child when that child was sleeping. Silence seemed almost to echo back on itself.

She watched Joe breathing for a moment, his long dark eye-lashes two waves of black beneath black brows. He was handsome enough to be a male model or a film star. *Like his mother*, came the thought, a small jolt into the room's tranquillity. There was a tiny pool of filmy white, the residue of sleep, in the corner of one of his eyes, and she wanted to wipe it gently away. Instead she contented herself with studying him. He was far too good-looking for her, but by some miracle she was the one he'd chosen.

Molly stretched and smiled to herself. Their flat might be small and box-like, but it had a certain charm, and they might not have much money, but they got by. And now that they'd found his mother and she seemed to want to get to know him, things could surely only get better.

She slipped out of bed and made tea in a plain white teapot, put milk into the straight-sided jug and got two white mugs from the

128

cupboard. She might like exotic colours for her decoration, but she preferred some things to be simple.

Behind her, in the hall, the post dropped on to the mat. Usually it was left downstairs in the communal area. Some kind neighbour must be saving them the trouble. There were several pieces of junk mail, a bill, and one handwritten envelope in bold italic writing. Molly propped it against the milk jug and carried the tea into the bedroom.

Joe opened an eye and smiled lazily. 'Is it time to get up?'

'We've got a little while. I woke early.'

'And the sleeping lion's still in his den?' He nodded towards Eddie's room. 'Looks like the perfect opportunity . . .'

Molly put the tray down, laughing, and slipped off her T-shirt, standing in front of him in just her narrow briefs.

'C'm here,' he ordered, looking at her as if she were the last chocolate eclair in the cake shop.

Like most parents of small children, they didn't waste time. You never knew how long you'd get. If it was only going to be five minutes, then it ought to be five minutes well used.

And this was one of the most memorable five minutes Molly could ever remember.

Afterwards she poured the tea and handed him the handwritten envelope.

'For you.'

'From Stella,' he explained.

'I worked that one out. You've already got twenty-five others.'

'She wants to take me to lunch. At the Ritz.'

'Doesn't she know you work?' Molly tried to repress the twinge of irritation she felt at this regal summons, and also perhaps the fact that she was excluded from it.

'We do have lunch hours, you know, even in my humble line of work.'

'Except that you work in Croydon. She obviously thinks life really is a Noël Coward play.' Molly couldn't keep a drop of acid from her tone.

'That's not very kind.'

'No, it's not,' Molly admitted, telling herself not to be churlish. 'Will you go?'

'Of course I'll go! I'll tell Graham who my hostess is and he'll be so impressed he'll give me the day off. Do you remember how he sucked up even to that third-rate DJ who came to open the new extension?'

'And will you tell him what your relationship to your hostess really is?'

He shook his head. 'I'll say I won it in a contest.'

'Congratulations.'

'Come on, Moll. I've never been to the Ritz.'

Molly smiled. 'I'd better iron you a shirt then. One thing, though,' she was surprised neither of them seemed to have confronted this, 'someone's going to find out soon. And before they do, you're going to have to break the news to Pat and Andrew.'

Joe hugged her. 'I know. I'll tell them on Sunday when we go for lunch.'

Molly nodded. This was one occasion she really wasn't looking forward to. Pat wouldn't blame Joe for falling into Stella's arms or Stella for inviting him there. She'd blame Molly.

Molly took a deep breath and tried not to feel guilty. Poor Pat, this was going to be tough for her. All her life, as she saw it, she'd done her best for Joe. And now someone had come along who could sweep him away from her in a cloud of fame and Christian Dior perfume.

Molly was just beginning to know how she felt.

Joe's office was in a business park just south of Croydon that had until a few years ago been a green-field site. It took him only forty-five minutes to drive there on a good day, since it was against the tide of commuters going into London. Even though the surrounding Green Belt was getting increasingly built-up, it still felt quite countryish, thank God. Joe had never relished the thought of working in a concrete jungle.

Today he looked up from his computer screen to find a cow staring at him through the plate-glass window, munching slowly.

'Sorry to disappoint you, mate,' Joe addressed it, 'Friesians don't drive people carriers.' He indicated the handbook he was currently working on. 'Though they'd probably make better drivers than most owners.'

'Talking to yourself, eh?' It was Graham, Joe's boss. Graham had thought up the Service-It-Yourself handbook and it had made him what he described as 'comfortably off', which, in Joe's view, was rather like calling the Queen 'a bit royal'. Graham was fat, fifty-five and childless. He could have retired to Jersey or the Cayman Islands but he was the kind of man who preferred work to home and saw the golf course simply as God's waiting room.

Once established, the handbooks had been a wild success. At the moment they had a rush on the guide for a brand-new people carrier which would be available this month.

'How's the copy going? Will it be ready by the deadline?'

'I'll stay here twenty-four hours to make sure it is.'

'Good lad. You sound like me,' Graham congratulated him.

'Like you before you got so bloody rich, you mean!'

Graham laughed. Joe was his favourite employee, more like a nephew, and he let him get away with murder.

'There is one condition, though.' Joe pushed his advantage while the going was good.

'And what's that, pray?' Graham enjoyed indulging Joe occasionally.

'I've been invited out to lunch on Thursday.'

'By one of the dealers?'

'No, as a matter of fact . . .' Joe hesitated, savouring the moment. 'Look, Graham, you're not going to believe this. By Stella Milton.'

Graham cracked up. They'd had a poster of Stella Milton in the first garage he'd worked in. The lads had thrown darts at the bits they'd most like to encounter in the flesh. 'Come on, be serious now.'

'I am serious. I'm having lunch with her at the Ritz.'

'And I'm a one-legged lesbian!' If this crazy story had come from one of his other employees, Graham would have refused to believe it. But Joe had always been like a silver spoon in a canteen of stainless steel. 'How could *you* be having lunch with *her*?'

'I won it. In a competition.'

'Here, lads, Joe's only gone and won a fancy lunch with Stella Milton, you know the sexpot in the Peugeot ad. What was it, one of those radio phone-ins? You jammy bugger!'

'Bloody hell, Joe,' weighed in Brian, the technical manager, 'I wouldn't mind changing *her* gears for her!'

Joe found himself blushing redder than the scarlet people carrier on his computer screen. 'Excuse me, Brian, I've just got to nip to the Gents a moment.' He couldn't stand this any longer.

'Aye!' Brian shouted after him. 'And we all know why! Maybe you'd better take this with you!' He handed Joe a glossy car mag. On the front cover was a photograph of Stella from the Peugeot ad.

Joe glanced at it then flung it across the other side of the office.

'What's up with him?' asked Brian.

'He's always had an artistic temperament. Maybe he thinks you're not taking his good fortune seriously enough.'

'You think he's really going then? It isn't a load of bollocks?'

'Joe's not given to practical jokes.'

'Bloody hell,' breathed Brian, retrieving the magazine and studying the cover. A chauffeur stood with the rear door open while Stella, in a fur coat with nothing underneath but stockings, suspenders and skimpy black underwear, stepped out. *Bring a bit of excitement to your life*, it suggested. The joke of the ad was that the scene took place in a supermarket car park, full of ordinary shoppers.

'Anyway,' Brian shrugged, flinging the magazine sulkily on to Joe's desk, 'I don't really envy him. She's old enough to be his mother.'

Molly was just giving Joe's shirt an extra-special iron when he got back, and wondering what it would be like to have a life where, on a perfectly normal weekday, you had lunch at the Ritz.

132

Normally Joe ironed his own shirts, partly because Molly's ironing left clothes looking as if an elephant had just slept in them.

'That's nice of you,' he said. 'Why don't I take over now?'

'Because you think it'll look like shit when I've done it?'

'Because I think it'll look like shit when you've done it,' he confessed, smiling tenderly.

'So, how was Graham about letting you off tomorrow?'

Joe grinned. 'Just as I predicted. Disbelieving, then grovelling. I've got to get her to sign a napkin for him.'

'What a sleazeball Graham is!' Another thought occurred to her. 'I hope nobody recognizes you.'

'At the Ritz?' Joe was laughing so much he almost burned himself with the iron. 'I'm sure Brian from Technical and Jim the motorcycle messenger will be propping up the bar just waiting to spot me.'

'I don't mean them. I mean anyone from a newspaper.'

She watched him dress next morning in the shirt he'd ironed again himself, greatly improving its appearance. The extraordinary thing was that Joe looked, quite naturally, like the kind of person who'd be at home in stylish places.

'Now I know why I'm irresistibly drawn to the most expensive thing on the menu,' he joked. 'It's obviously in the genes.'

'Well, don't let your genes run away with you and start whipping out your credit card. Lunch there is probably a week's rent. Have a nice time. And let her pay.'

'OK, I'll tell her my incredibly penny-pinching wife insisted I keep my hand firmly in my pocket.'

On the dot of twelve, Joe rounded the corner from Piccadilly and ran up the front steps of the Ritz, trying to look as if he'd been there a hundred times before. The liveried doorman was fortunately too deeply engaged in finding a cab for a pair of Germans dressed improbably in full hunting gear to pay him any attention.

He found himself in a panelled reception area, with a carpet so thick it felt as if he might drown in it. He stood for a moment, somewhat at a loss. Despite his striking good looks, he always relied on Molly in social situations.

The receptionist, who was fifty and female, looked up to see a young man, dressed entirely in black, standing silently in front of her, looking nervous. He reminded her of a fledgeling blackbird that had left the nest but hadn't yet learned to fly properly.

'Can I help you?' she asked, wishing she could give him a few lessons herself.

'I'm meeting someone in the restaurant.' He hesitated. 'Stella Milton, as a matter of fact.'

The receptionist tried not to look disappointed at the level of the competition. 'Miss Milton's already gone through to the dining room. The maître d' will show you to your table.'

Joe followed the direction the woman had pointed, down a wide corridor with a bar on either side. Everyone seemed to be drinking champagne. He recognized a couple of politicians and a sprinkling of faces he'd seen on TV. The dining room, when he finally reached it, was breathtaking. Amongst the elaborate stucco plasterwork were delightful panels of pastoral paintings. It was almost like eating in an elegant French château.

When Stella spotted him she jumped to her feet and waved, causing every diner in the place to stop eating and watch Joe's halting progress towards her.

'How lovely to see you, darling,' she gushed. 'Will you have an aperitif?'

Across the other side of the restaurant, Bob Kramer was also being shown to his seat, at one of the corner tables near the window. He'd come here not only because it was beautiful and impressed people, but because it was surprisingly good value. The cooking had also resisted being too nouvelle and tiny-portioned, which he appreciated greatly. And because it was beautiful rather than fashionable, you didn't risk being seen by every producer and agent in town. The last person he'd expected to see here was Stella. Especially Stella looking radiant and with a fabulously attractive young man half her age.

He watched them both for a moment from behind the cover of his menu. He hadn't seen Stella sparkle like that for years. Dull but sweet Richard certainly didn't have that effect on her. But who was the young man? Not an actor, or Bob would have remembered him. Those smouldering looks brought to mind the Fiennes brothers. Dark brows and almost black hair, except that instead of the brown eyes which would have been more usual, this boy's were a pure Delft blue. Anyway, who the hell cared who he was if he was having this effect on Stella?

Bob didn't have time to consider the question further because the business associate he was trying to schmooze had arrived and he had to turn on the eye-contact full beam. He was quite grateful he couldn't be seen from where Stella and the young man were sitting. No one else was looking at him either. Everyone in the restaurant was too busy stealing discreet looks at Stella and her swain.

It was after four, and most of the tables had emptied long ago, when Bob finally snapped shut his Psion organizer and said good-bye to his guest. Once upon a time in London, lunches would sail happily on into the late afternoon, buoyed up by a couple of bottles of wine and chased by brandy and cigars, before you checked briefly into the office prior to a six o'clock drink, usually followed by a client dinner. Now most people didn't even order a starter, drank mineral water and refused pudding in favour of a decaffeinated cappuccino, a drink suitable, in Bob's view, only for babies and sick children and even then only for breakfast. The whole lunch ritual these days could be over from start to finish in less than an hour. And in the evenings quite a lot of his clients – even actors, for God's sake – behaved like computer programmers and insisted they wanted to go home instead of sharing a pleasant dinner with their agent. Bob was having to think of joining a club or he would end up, horror of horrors, dining alone some nights.

True to form, the restaurant was now almost empty, except for himself and, over the other side of the room, Stella and her companion. So he picked up his cigar and the remains of his drink and headed in their direction.

'Stella, my love, how absolutely lovely to see you!' Bob cooed, as if he hadn't known for the last two and a half hours that she was sitting mere yards away.

'Bob! Good heavens!' Stella smiled with a slight hint of good-humoured drunkenness. Most people wouldn't have noticed, but Bob Kramer knew Stella a lot better than most people. 'Joe, this is Bob Kramer, my agent . . .' She smiled again, wickedly this time, like a bride who's behaving badly at her own wedding. 'Bob, I'd like you to meet Joseph Meredith . . . my son.'

Chapter 14

Outside the Ritz, Joe hailed a cab. 'Victoria Station, please.'

'I thought you lived in Peckham,' Stella remarked.

'I'm going to work now,' Joe explained.

'But it's four thirty.'

The gap between their two worlds yawned. The difference between liking to work and having to work. He could explain that if he went now the office would empty soon and he'd get all the work he'd promised cleared tonight. She'd probably think he was mad.

'People have to earn their keep in the real world, Stella dear,' Bob commented.

'I often work in the evenings when I'm in a play,' Stella said in injured tones. 'It's no different.'

'Except the pay, darling, and the taxi waiting to take you home afterwards,' pointed out Bob.

Stella held tightly on to the arm of her tall, handsome son. She knew, in her heart of hearts, that she wanted him with her all the time. She wanted to show him off, introduce him to all her friends. To shout, 'Look everyone. I made this. Isn't he wonderful!'

'Joseph . . .' She'd decided to call him that because it made her feel as if he belonged to her, and that he was a different person from

137

the Joe who belonged to Molly. She also knew she couldn't bear to say goodbye without knowing when she was going to see him again. 'Look, I'm going to a fundraiser next week at the Britannia Theatre. Nothing flashy, just a dinner and the play. Will you come? It's on Thursday. I'd really, *really* love it if you could come.'

Joe hesitated. 'I don't know. I have to tell my adoptive parents about finding you first. It would be awful if they just read it in some newspaper. Molly and I are going up to Mere-on-Sea this weekend to explain what's happened.'

Putting herself in the position of those less fortunate than herself was not a habit of Stella's. All the same, it struck her how unpleasant it would feel to be told the son you'd brought up as your own had decided to find his birth mother. 'Good luck. If it helps at all, I'd like to meet her and thank her for doing such a good job.'

Joe smiled to himself. He wasn't sure this was a gesture Pat would appreciate, even though it was well meant. Pat would probably prefer to pretend Stella didn't exist and boycott all her films at Blockbuster Video.

'That's kind of you, and thank you for lunch.'

As he opened the door of the cab, she finally had to let him go. 'See you soon, darling.'

'So,' she felt rather than saw Bob's gliding presence arrive at her side, 'no skeletons in my cupboard, she says. Not even a tiny one. I'm as boring as British Home Stores, she says. No little hint about a long-lost son, and a fabulously handsome one at that.' Bob's tones were purring with possibilities. 'My God, Stella, have you thought about all the amazing publicity you could get out of this?'

Stella, who was still watching the departing cab, suddenly found her agent loathsome. 'Fuck off, Bob, and just forget I ever told you.'

When Joe finally got home, Molly made no mention of the lunch, though he knew she was waiting to hear every last detail.

She merely kissed him and announced that she hadn't cooked supper, assuming he'd be full after lunching like a fat cat.

Actually Joe was starving and had to go down to the shop to buy eggs and some tired-looking mushrooms, plus a bunch of corian-der that looked as if it had given up on living. He slung them together and made a delicious omelette which they shared in front of the television.

'So, how was the Ritz?' Molly gave in finally 'Were you too nerv-ous to eat?' She eyed his huge heap of omelette.

'I ate all three courses, as it happens. And the petit fours. And most of Stella's.'

Molly tried not to mind the casual use of *Stella*. It didn't sound much like 'Mum'. But then Stella didn't look much like 'Mum'.

'Did she want to know about us? Me and Eddie?'

The funny thing, Joe had to admit, was that Stella had quizzed him about almost every aspect of his life, but she hadn't asked much about either of them. He knew Molly would be hurt, so he didn't elaborate. 'We were just finding our way round each other really. I told her all about growing up in Mere, and Pat and Andrew, and my job, and how I was a bit bored with it really.'

Molly shot him a glance. 'You've never told me that.'

'You've never asked me. I didn't think you were that interested in my job, as a matter of fact. Maybe I didn't even realize I was getting bored myself.'

'Till you met Stella.' Molly pointed out.

'I suppose it has made me think about a lot of things. Don't worry, love, I'm not intending to resign tomorrow and have us all thrown on the streets, it's just that I'd like to start thinking ahead. I never really intended a lifetime in car maintenance.'

Molly could see the logic in this, but her annoyance that it had only surfaced since Stella's appearance in their life made her sound sharper than she intended. 'What about Graham? He relies on you.'

'Graham would find someone else. I'm hardly irreplaceable.'

An uncomfortable silence fell between them, for which, Molly felt, Stella's unseen presence was largely responsible. If Joe had told her before that he was unhappy at work, she would have been more sympathetic. As it was, she tried not to feel irritated. After all, she had found Stella for Joe's sake. It was obvious that discovering his mother was a famous film star would have some effect.

'Moll, the most extraordinary thing happened. Her agent was there and he came up and introduced himself, and do you know what Stella did? She said, "Bob, meet Joseph Meredith – my son." God, Moll, you should have seen his face!'

Stella was also finding slotting back into her usual life tougher than she'd expected. She had a film script to read from a foreign director who wanted her to come and meet him next week when he arrived in London, but all she really wanted to do was see Joe. She'd also been asked to 'read on tape' for some Americans, but felt that being made to do that was a bit of a cheek. The director ought to get her films out and see what he thought of her, or at least be bothered to look at the show-reel of her best work. Reading on tape was a cop-out.

She had promised to sit in on the auditions for her old drama school, something she did every few years as a favour. One reason for this act of graciousness, she had to admit, was the masochistic opportunity to look over the youngest and prettiest of the new crop of actresses, and perhaps even discourage a few.

But today she felt restless, as if all the usual fixed points in her life had gone out of focus. All she really wanted to do was talk about how wonderful Joseph was. She sensed Bea's scepticism on this subject, and Richard was still away, not that he could be expected to sing Joseph's praises. The only person she could think of with whom to share her advanced state of bliss was Bob, her agent, so it was he who received an unexpected visit.

Bob's offices were in Chelsea Harbour, an odd concrete desert of a place, part glamorous location, part desolate outpost. It was like the set of a film whose budget had been cancelled as soon as it was built, leaving it marooned and out of place, stunning but not real.

Stella strolled through the vast atrium which doubled as a design centre. Tiny fabric and wallpaper shops of all the famous brands lined the hall. They looked too impersonally European to Stella, all tassels and mock-Gobelin tapestry, like the suppliers for the lobbies of grand hotels.

Bob's office was reassuringly like Bob: flashy in a rather passé, eighties way. Every inch of wall space was covered with accolades to his various clients. Stella wondered what he did with the gaps on his wall when someone left him for another agent.

'Stella, how unexpected! How delightful!' Bob was halfway through reading a review in last night's *Evening Standard* which roundly criticised one of his clients, and was delighted to have someone who would appreciate quite how ignorant, philistine and *young* this idiot of a boy reviewer was. 'Always the same, bloody reviewers! Another kid trying to make his name slagging of a play the audience dared to enjoy!'

This was one of Bob's familiar themes. Stella didn't have to actually say anything; just having her there would be enough for Bob.

'Have you heard any more about the casting for *Dark Night*?' she finally interrupted.

'Opening here in October with Roxanne Wood as Millie. I don't suppose you'd change your mind and consider playing the mother? That's the part with the real meat on it. No, of course you wouldn't. Pretend I didn't say that.'

'I'll pretend you didn't say that,' Stella said glacially.

'Incidentally, this business about your son. It's the most extraordinary story. And he's such a looker. I don't suppose he can act? Think, you could do Gertrude and Hamlet . . .'

'I don't *do* mothers, remember, and as far as I know Joseph's never even been in a Nativity play.'

A stab of pain crackled through Stella. She really didn't know whether Joseph had played his namesake or third sheep to the left, or had felt left out at not being chosen at all. She didn't know if he'd liked climbing trees, or watching television, or what he liked in his sandwiches. She hadn't been party to any of his small griefs or triumphs. She knew none of the family labels and myths that were just as important to a person as their genetic imprint. Joe's whole childhood was a blank page to her. Only this dull, ordinary Pat, the woman Stella had given him to, could write the captions on the photo album of Joe's life and Stella, who ought to be grateful, found herself beginning to resent her for it.

'I wasn't thinking of a play necessarily,' Bob interrupted. 'But we really ought to stage a photo shoot. I'd bet you a hundred quid that boy's as photogenic as you are. It could give you a whole new lease of life. Look at Jerry Hall and her daughter Elizabeth. I can just see you both on the cover of *Vanity Fair*. It's exactly what you need, Stella darling.'

Stella stiffened her sinuous back, each of whose vertebrae had been kissed to such erotic effect, on and off camera, by her leading man in *Dead Men Can't Cry*. 'I don't give a toss about photo opportunities.'

'Stella, Stella . . .'

Stella ignored him.

Bob sighed. He hated to see a fabulous chance like this go to waste. Especially when Stella needed it so much. 'I think it's time you and I had a little talk. You know that film *Rock On*, about the ageing rock band, the one where you fancied playing the girl-friend? I didn't tell you what the shit of a young director actually said, did I? He said he'd always loved you since he was a teenager, but these days the lines round your mouth are too deep for the camera.'

'Has he seen the lines round Patti Boyd's mouth? Or Marianne Faithfull's?' snapped Stella. 'They're called Life.'

'That's not the point. She's still supposed to be fuckable.'

This time he had Stella's attention. 'And I'm not?'

Bob wished he hadn't been quite so brutal. 'You didn't get the part,' he pointed out.

'And they gave it to a sodding terrible actress ten years younger than me instead, you mean.'

Bob shrugged. 'It's becoming a bit of a pattern, Stella. There isn't one generation of actresses younger than you now; there are two. I'm sorry, love, but it's true. Maybe we should try Europe. The

British like their actresses to be dames or sluts. They don't have time for grown-up women here.'

'Are you trying to tell me I'm too old to be a slut?'

'You're the sexiest woman in the world, but Aphrodite herself had to put her clothes on at forty-five.'

'Tell me, Robert dear, where is all this leading, apart from Aphrodite putting her knickers back on?'

'Back to you, darling. Don't look a gift son in the mouth. We're talking centre spreads here. Don't let someone else break the story, because break it they will. It's too good to miss. Spill the beans yourself. I'll even fix it all up for you.'

'Bob,' Stella stood up, blazing with anger, 'you are a complete shit.'

'Of course I am,' replied Bob affectionately. 'That's why I'm such a good agent. Think about it.' He swiftly changed the subject. 'By the way, you are going to the Britannia fundraiser next week, aren't you?'

'I must be,' Stella said, and swept out. She didn't add that she'd asked Joseph to come with her. After all, he hadn't accepted yet and maybe it was better she kept him away from the seductive wiles of Bob Kramer.

Five minutes later she was walking out of the lift when a motor-cycle messenger, who couldn't believe his luck in bumping into Stella Milton on a dull Thursday afternoon, asked her for her auto-graph. 'Sign my helmet, Stella, will you? I've still got that poster . . .'

'. . . of me in my leathers. Here you go.' She signed her name with a flourish, half wishing she could make a bonfire out of those posters, half pleased that not everyone felt like that ignorant boy director who couldn't see beyond the lines at the sides of her mouth to the erotic woman within.

Do yourself a favour, Stella, she had to remind herself sharply, as she sashayed away, the rider's eyes still caressing her bottom, and stop believing your own bullshit.

From his window Bob watched the scene with wry amusement. Stella was right: she wasn't quite over the hill yet.

*

'Hello, Molly dear.' Molly was surprised to get a phone call from Pat during the week. Pat didn't ring up for cheery chats. Molly picked up the tone of anxiety in her voice and panicked. Had she somehow found out about Stella before they could tell her properly?'

'Everything all right?' Molly shifted Eddie on to her hip.

'As a matter of fact, Andrew's not well. He's come down with a chesty cough. Even given up his beloved garden and taken to his bed.'

'It must be serious then.' Andrew was the hardiest of men. Molly had never so much as heard him complain, even the time he had a minor stroke.

'I've finally persuaded him to call the doctor.'

'Can we do anything? I mean, Joe's at work, but Eddie and I could come and help. Pick up a prescription for you. Try and cheer Andrew up.'

'Thank you for offering, dear, but he just wants to sleep it off. I was really just ringing to tell you not to come this weekend. Andrew would prefer to take it easy and we wouldn't like Eddie exposed to a germ, bless him.'

Damn! That meant they wouldn't get the chance to break their news in person.

Molly felt an almost overwhelming urge to tell her there and then, but had to stifle it. It wasn't up to her, and anyway, Pat would only see it as an added sin and lay it squarely at Molly's door, and Joe would kill her. They'd just have to wait.

She'd hardly put the phone down when it rang again. 'Hello, Molly, this is Stella Milton. I wondered if Joe had mentioned the fundraising event I asked him to next week?'

Molly wished she were a dragon who could breathe fire down the phone. Stella hadn't even deigned to introduce herself properly, just assumed Molly would jump at her command. She wasn't bothering to ask if Molly would like to come to this stupid event full of arty-farty actors; in fact, she'd still shown no sign of wanting to meet Molly or Eddie at all. Presumably it was less ageing to have a handsome son on your arm than the handsome son's wife and especially the handsome son's baby.

'Cow!' Molly said to the receiver once she'd put it down. 'I wish I'd never found you. I wish Sister Mary had been a proper nun who didn't go round divulging details she ought not to. I wish Sister Bernadette who cleans floors on her hands and knees had been on duty. She would never have mentioned any Amandas.'

'What's the matter?' asked Joe when he got home, sensing that something was wrong. Though it would have taken someone deaf, dumb and blind *not* to notice Molly was on the warpath.

'This fundraising event Stella asked you to.'

'The one you said I oughtn't to go to in case I got spotted?'

'Yes. Well, I'd like to come too.'

Joe looked surprised. 'I'm really pleased she's invited you.'

Molly decided not to mention that Stella hadn't invited her. She didn't care if Stella wanted her there or not. It was a fundraiser. Her money was as good as the next person's. Or at least it would be if she had any. Besides, Stella couldn't just keep whisking Joe off to glam events and leaving Molly and Eddie behind like Cinderella all the time. 'You and I come as part of the package, don't we, Eds?' She tickled his tummy with her bare foot.

'Gah!' agreed the baby, and delivered a large fart as confirmation.

The tiny bar of the Britannia Theatre was so packed that actually crossing the few square feet to the bar seemed a physical impossibility. It looked more like the Tokyo subway on a bad day than sophisticated pre-theatre entertainment, and about as much fun.

Joe finally spotted Stella in the far corner and pushed Molly towards her. Stella had performed the major miracle of commandeering one of the few tables in the place. She was wearing a simple black linen dress which might actually have been described as understated if it hadn't boasted a slashed neckline so low you wondered whether her twin peaks had the remotest chance of staying hidden. Just in case any onlookers might have missed the scenery, a jewelled cross on a long black ribbon thump-thump-thumped between her breasts whenever she moved. Molly decided not to look in case she got hypnotized.

'Stella,' Joe murmured, not quite knowing where to put his gaze, 'I don't think you've ever met Molly.'

Molly felt Stella's eyes fasten on her with all the concentration of a jungle animal. Thank God she'd dressed carefully. How extraordinary, Molly thought, for all her fame and glamour, she sees me as competition. And a tiny part of Molly was glad. She had youth on her side after all, though that was hardly a match for Stella's sensuality.

'How lovely to meet you, Stella.'

'And you, too, sweetie,' Stella's lips swept up in a small, deliberate smile which didn't fool Molly for a moment. 'Now come and sit down.' She moved round about six millimetres so that Molly appeared to be squeezing an enormous bottom into the tiny space Stella had cleared next to her.

'So, Molly, what do you get up to all day while Joe's at work? Lots of lovely lunches?'

Molly bristled. You could certainly tell Stella had never looked after Joe herself. 'I lie around eating Turkish delight, drinking passion fruit juice and reading erotic novels,' she replied with a deadly smile.

Stella laughed nervously. 'But I thought you looked after the . . .'

'I think she's joking,' Joe pointed out.

Stella poured them each a glass of wine, piqued that Molly didn't seem as overawed as she ought to be. 'I ordered a bottle. This place before curtain up's worse than the Somme. You'd have no chance of fighting your way to the bar. Do you want to know who people are?' She pointed out various producers, directors, actors and actresses, set designers and other luminaries of the acting world. One of them, a man, turned abruptly, almost pouring his drink down Joe's neck.

'Sorry!' he apologised. 'Nearly baptised you with my beer there.'

Joe studied him in puzzlement. 'Haven't we met somewhere?'

146

The man grinned. 'I don't think so. You know my face but not my name. It happens to actors all the time. Don't worry about it.'

Joe took a sip of his wine. 'I know your name too. You came in and bought the new handbook on how to service your Saab, said you couldn't wait for it to be in the shops.'

The man looked at him with new eyes. 'You're absolutely bloody right. What a good memory.' He looked from Joe to Stella. 'And who are you?'

'No one you know, Neville,' Stella replied, obviously keen to change the subject from Joe's humble job. 'I didn't know you were a do-it-yourself buff.'

'I've got to do something with all the bloody time I spend waiting for parts in this ludicrous so-called profession of ours.'

'You can come and do my servicing any time you like,' Stella offered to raucous laughter.

'No, really,' Neville went on, staring at Joe, fascinated, 'who are you? You look so familiar.'

This time Joe winked at Molly. 'I'm the son Stella put in a basket of reeds on the river when he was a baby. A childless débutante found me and brought me up as an Honourable.'

Neville cracked with laughter and said, 'You're having me on!'

'Yes, Neville, you're absolutely right.' Stella glanced at Joe reprovingly. 'He's having you on.'

'Room for a little one?' interrupted a familiar voice. To Stella's annoyance, Bob Kramer squeezed into the spare chair at their table. Joe was amazed that someone of Bob's bulk could ever have got through the crowd.

'It's an old technique I learned from my boss. You put your hand on someone's arse and they either smile or hit you. In this gathering they usually smile.'

'Why don't you go and order another bottle, Bob?' Stella gestured towards the bar, knowing it would take him half an hour to get there and back. She didn't want him luring Joe into the limelight.

'I already rang ahead and ordered one bottle for now and another for the interval.' He reached behind him to a shelf where a row of drinks had been laid out with names written on cards in front of them. 'That was quite a bluff you carried off,' he said quietly to Joe. 'Did you ever act at school?'

Joe shrugged. 'The usual stuff. Actually I often ended up being the girl.' He simpered, and when he spoke again his voice had taken on a wily feminine tone. '"I left no ring with her: What means this lady?"'

'Oh my God.' Stella covered her ears. 'Not another bloody Viola. I've got to sit through forty of them tomorrow at the Southern's auditions. Why does every girl who wants to be an actress choose *Twelfth Night*?'

'I bet they're not a patch on mine,' Joe threw in. 'My Viola got a standing ovation. So did my Juliet.'

'It must be the eyelashes,' suggested Bob.

'Forget the eyelashes,' corrected Stella. 'It's in the genes.' She caught herself before Neville could ask her what she meant. 'He may have had acting in his family somewhere.'

'Good try, Stella,' whispered Bob as they got up and joined the throng pushing its way towards the theatre.

'I know what you're up to, and you can just stop now.'

'I don't know what you're talking about,' Bob said innocently.

'Oh yes you do. You're planning something. I know how your mind works, you reptile. You're trying to reel him in.'

'Sssh and enjoy the play now.'

Since school Joe hadn't really been that interested in plays, but this felt different. Sitting here amongst actors, glancing out along the rows at the famous faces, he felt a surge of excitement. He'd hardly been to the theatre in his adult life, it was far too expensive. Tonight he saw how well the actors worked together, the perfection of their timing, the way they said things not just through words but by using their bodies. The performance had real pathos and passion and it thrilled him. When the first act drew to a close, Joe was conscious only of disappointment.

When he looked round, he found Stella watching him, a small smile of satisfaction on her face. 'You were up there with them, weren't you?' she asked in a low voice soft with the pleasure of seeing him so bewitched.

Joe laughed, embarrassed at being caught out. 'You know what you said about acting being genetic, do you think it really is?'

'There are plenty of acting dynasties, aren't there? The Woods . . .' she tried to banish the thought of her rival Roxanne Wood, 'the Redgraves, and plenty of others – you could paper the walls with acting families.'

'Isn't that just environment, though?' Molly chipped in. 'Being imbued with acting from the cradle, getting *Macbeth* instead of bedtime stories?'

'Ssssh . . . don't say that here,' Stella corrected, turning round three times in the narrow confines of their seats. 'Bad luck. Call it the Scottish Play. Everyone does.'

'OK.' Joe watched, amused. 'So maybe it's contacts as well as imbibing an atmosphere.'

'I'm sure all those help,' Stella grabbed his arm, glowing with pride at his sudden interest in her world, 'but I'm a firm believer in genes. Genes account for most things in life, whether we like it or not.'

Although she didn't say it, Stella saw genes as her ally. They were, after all, what connected her so powerfully to Joseph, despite the years that had come between them.

After the play they went on to a restaurant in Camden Passage. Joe was amazed to find that their party had swelled to a dozen, including Bob Kramer and a couple of well-known actors. He was equally amazed that the restaurant, at first doubtful at the idea of producing a table out of the blue for twelve people, capitulated miraculously when they saw who the guests were.

'So what do you think of Stella?' Bob asked Molly, noticing that the seat next to her was empty and, in a rare moment of kindness, filling it.

'She reminds me of a praying mantis,' Molly said, in a low voice, smiling to mute her words, 'just as well Joe's her son not her lover.'

Bob laughed so that everyone looked at them. Stella had better not underestimate the little wife. She would, of course, because Stella always underestimated women.

After that, most of the chat was industry gossip: who was up, who down, who had got what part, usually grossly unfairly according to the assembled group. They talked of everyone on first-name terms, which Stella translated for Joe in a whisper. Some names he recognized, like Peter Hall or David Hare or Kenneth Branagh. Most he didn't.

It wasn't that different, he told himself between the goat's cheese blinis and the seared tuna with herb polenta, from any bunch of people talking shop. Even his own colleagues wouldn't sound so different gossiping about the awarding of a contract to some fly-by-night car dealer, or the shock waves when one car manufacturer took over another. This just seemed more glamorous and interesting. But then that might be because it *was* more glamorous and interesting.

Joe looked up from his polenta to see the man opposite considering him and Stella with unusual thoughtfulness. It was Tom Wall, the wildly popular actor who played a screen detective. 'You know,' Tom commented drily, 'now that I'm sitting opposite you, you two do look astonishingly alike. Are you sure you're not related in some way?'

'Weren't you there in the bar earlier?' Stella purred, her voice dancing with wicked humour, avoiding Bob Kramer's eye. 'He's my long-lost son. I put him in a basket in the river.'

Joe felt his stomach somersault wildly, but the assembled group all cracked with laughter.

Except Tom Wall, who simply smiled gently. 'I could almost believe you.' He reached a hand across and touched Joe's cheek. 'Look, he's still wet.'

Stella knocked his hand away with a shade too much force. Tom Wall, well known as a roaring queen, simply smiled in a catlike way. 'Tell me, Joe Meredith, what do you do for a living?'

For the first time in his life, Joe hesitated before answering.

The party broke up half an hour later. Somebody's agent picked up the bill. Stella explained that it was because the agent was trying to woo Tom Wall into leaving his long-standing representative and joining him instead.

'He won't, of course,' Bob Kramer pointed out acidly as they walked out of the restaurant. 'Actors only change agents when they're on the skids and they need someone to blame.'

Outside, Bob offered Stella a lift home, and she accepted.

'Goodbye, Molly.' She had to lean up to kiss her tall daughter-in-law. 'Goodbye, Joseph. Thanks so much for coming.' There was a tone of humility and gratitude in her voice that Bob had never heard before from Stella. She reached up and kissed Joe, bathing him in a look of longing and love so intense that it startled Bob.

At that moment a camera flashed from the alley opposite.

Stella turned and stared like a rabbit trapped in the headlights. 'Who the hell was that?'

'An admirer, maybe, someone who recognised you from the restaurant?' suggested Bob smoothly.

'I bloody well hope so.'

But Bob knew it wasn't. His tip-off to the *Daily Post* had been worth it. Stella would see that. If she wouldn't co-operate in reviving her own career, he'd have to do it for her.

'So what did you think of Stella?' Joe asked Molly as they walked to the tube station.

Diplomatically, Molly decided to hide her real feelings. Chopping your mother-in-law into tiny pieces and flinging them to the crocodiles might be seen as a slight over-reaction. 'A bit over the top, perhaps?'

Joe grinned. 'She is, isn't she? I think that may have been for your benefit. She wasn't like that the other day.'

Molly didn't add her other observation, which was that Stella was clearly totally, utterly, wildly besotted with Joe.

'More to the point, what did you think of the play? Wasn't it absolutely fantastic?'

Life at the *Daily Post* was always at its most frenetic before the first editorial conference of the day. Every department scrabbled round for today's breaking stories, follow-up features or ways of putting the *Post*'s particular spin on anything they could lay their hands on. It was at this time that competition between the different parts of the paper was at its most intense.

'You'd better come to conference today,' Tony barked bad-temperedly at Claire, one eye on the clock. 'Dorothy's off with flu.'

Dorothy, the deputy features editor, was an old stalwart who'd come to them when the Scottish paper she'd worked on had been taken over by their group. Tony had kept her on because most of the time she was calm as a whale basking in sunny shallows, but when the occasion called for it, she could instantly turn into Moby Dick.

In Claire's view she even looked like the great white whale.

Claire quickly marshalled her ideas for today's feature pages into sales-speak. You only got thirty seconds to pitch an idea to the editor, and even if he liked it he threw out impossible questions just to test you. On the other hand, if he noticed you and liked your ideas, it was wildly exhilarating.

Unfortunately today there was a crisis in the news section because an important story had just broken. The editor galloped through the conference in just over half an hour, too concerned to bother much with feature ideas. The various section editors were all about to rush off and assign writers when their gossip columnist arrived, exploding himself dramatically into their midst.

Rory Hawthorne was the highest-paid tattle merchant on any newspaper, and certainly the only journalist who'd become almost as famous as the people he wrote about.

'Hang on, everyone. My sources tell me that Stella Milton's been hanging round with a boy half her age, and last night we got a tip-off that they were in some restaurant in Islington. Before you all get back to your small earthquakes in Brazil, I need you to help me out.'

Claire bit her lip, hoping against hope that he wasn't about to say what she suspected he was about to say.

'There's just one catch.' He held up a black-and-white photo-graph of Stella, looking stunning, staring passionately up into the eyes of a strikingly good-looking dark-haired young man. 'Great shot, isn't it? The trouble is, no one in our department knows who he is. He's not an actor, or not one anyone's heard of. Is he a footballer or some new pop star we haven't caught up with?'

The sports editor shook his head. 'Never seen him before.'

The pop music editor grimaced. 'Sorry. No idea.'

The showbiz editor shrugged. 'Nice-looking boy. No one I know, though.'

'What about you, Eric?'

'No idea,' said the news editor.

'Surely someone in London must know who the fuck this boy is.'

Claire's heart wasn't just doing somersaults, it was positively trampolining. Her mouth was dry and her palms wet. If she didn't say anything, Rory Hawthorne would make it his concern to find out. It wouldn't be that difficult. If she admitted she knew him and was allowed to write the story herself, she could at least do it sympathetically.

'Yes,' she said quietly, hoping Molly would understand, 'I do.'

'Who is he then?'

Everyone in the room, Tony foremost among them, turned and stared.

'His name's Joseph Meredith. And he's not her toyboy, he's her son. She gave him away to be adopted and he's just managed to track her down.'

Chapter 15

'Bloody hell,' said the sports editor.

'Bloody hell,' said the showbiz editor.

'Bloody hell!' said the news editor.

'Are you sure?' said Rory Hawthorne.

'Yes.' Claire wished she could enjoy the moment of glory she'd fantasized about for so long. 'His wife Molly is my best friend. She was the one who traced his natural mother. Obviously she had no idea it was going to be Stella Milton.'

'That's some story,' said the editor. 'Rory,' he turned to the gossip columnist, 'you'd better get on to it before anyone else does.'

'Actually,' Claire interrupted, still feeling as if she were in the middle of some ghastly dream, 'I think you'd better let me follow it up.'

God alone knew what Rory would do with the story. A poisonous scorpion had more generosity of spirit than he had.

'Why the hell didn't you tell *me* about this?' Tony hissed angrily as they were coming out of the meeting. 'You know your job's been on the line. This is dynamite. And I looked a bloody fool for not knowing about it.'

'Loyalty,' Claire replied. 'Not a word in your vocabulary, I grant you.' Tony had the grace to look sheepish. 'Joe and Molly didn't want it to come out till they were ready.'

Claire was careful not to give too much away. The existence of Pat, the adoptive mother who probably felt hurt and aggrieved, hadn't occurred to anyone on the paper yet. It wouldn't take long before they saw how useful she'd be.

'You'd better get straight on it, then.' Tony tried ineffectually to take command.

'Yes.' Claire masked her reluctance with a brisk efficiency. 'I'll just drop round and see them now.'

She had no idea whether Molly was in or not, but she didn't want to start explaining things in the open-plan gossip-machine of the office. In the taxi driving across London, she felt physically sick. She'd done this out of loyalty, but would Molly see it that way?

When Claire arrived, Molly was packing up Eddie's baby bag to take him off for a jaunt.

'Claire! How lovely! We're just off to the park. Why don't you come with us? We'll pick up some sandwiches on the way.'

Claire hadn't even taken in what a spectacular day it was. Her world was hermetically sealed from considerations like weather and real life. Such a dull domestic project as a picnic would normally appeal to her as much as a session with the dentist's drill, but today it sounded wonderful. Partly because she knew she was about to shatter Molly's cosy world.

'I can't, Moll. Look, I'm afraid this is serious. Someone tipped off the paper that they'd get a cracking story on Stella last night. The paper sent a photographer and they've just worked out who it is in the photo with her.'

'Oh, God. I knew this would happen. Who on earth can have tipped them off?'

'Look, Moll, it was bound to come out soon. Stella's been flaunting him all over the place. Rory Hawthorne says they were spotted at the Ritz. She was apparently hanging on to his arm as if they were . . .' Claire broke off.

'As if they were what, Claire? What exactly are you implying?'

'I'm not implying anything. I know Joe, remember. It's Stella that's the problem. Someone ought to tell her this script should be *Listen with Mother*, not *9½ Weeks*.'

'So what exactly is your role in all this?'

'Now that it's all out, I've offered to write the story. At least you can trust me. I'll put the best possible slant on it. If we don't get it, another paper will. There was a tip-off, for God's sake. Someone wants to place this story. If I don't do it, Rory Hawthorne, our gossip columnist, will, and if Rory gets it, you'll all know about it. I'll try and sell it to the editor as a triumph-over-tragedy, that way the coverage won't be too bad. The only alternative is the full front-page film-star-abandoned-baby-for-career story.'

Molly briefly bathed in the fantasy of seeing Stella finally pay, then pulled herself together. That kind of publicity would hurt everyone.

'The thing is, they'll only let me do it on one condition.'

'Which is?' Claire could hear the suspicion in Molly's voice.

'That Stella and Joe tell their story exclusively to the *Post*.'

'I'll call Joe now. He'll have to get hold of Stella. One thing. Who could have tipped them off?'

'You'd be surprised. It could be anyone, even Stella herself. I wouldn't put it past her.'

'Oh come on! Stella's the villain of the piece, the actress who gave up her son. She's not that naive. This could be incredibly damaging to her.'

'She may think she's smart enough to manipulate the press.'

It just didn't ring true to Molly. Stella hated journalists, Joe said. A sudden thought occurred to her. But surely Claire wouldn't do that?

'You think it was me, don't you?' Claire read her thoughts.

Molly ignobly gave in to her anger and frustration that a lot of this was really her own fault. She was the one who had let Stella out of the bottle, and she'd compounded that by letting Claire, a journalist, in on the secret.

'And of course, my job has been on the line, hasn't it?' Claire went on. 'That would give me a reason to betray my oldest friend, wouldn't it?'

'Well . . .' Molly was beginning to see that perhaps she was being more than a little unfair.

'Fine. If that's your estimation of me, good. The trouble with you, Molly, is that you don't think, you just bloody well bulldoze! You're an emotional demolition service. They could have used you at Dresden and saved a few bombs.' Claire grabbed her bag and stood up. 'For the record, I could have told the paper any time, but I didn't, because, despite the fact that it was the scoop of a lifetime, I happened to feel an entirely misplaced loyalty to you. Not any more. I'm handing this over to Rory Hawthorne, and good luck to you all. Just don't expect him to tread gently on your dreams. And by the way, I'd watch out for Stella if I were you. From what I can see, she's getting an unhealthy obsession with Joe, and believe me, Stella Milton doesn't do anything by halves.'

She slammed out, leaving Molly shredded and furious. How dare Claire call her a bulldozer! She sat down, holding Eddie in a tight embrace, breathing deeply, trying to draw calmness from the scent of his baby skin.

As she hunted for a piece of kitchen roll to dry her face, the phone rang. She reached over for it, then stopped herself. Instead the machine picked it up and took a message. The call was from Rory Hawthorne of the *Daily Post*, asking her to ring him back urgently.

Molly closed her eyes. She'd read some of this man's stuff. Riveting, if it wasn't about you. He liked nothing better than to pull the Persian rug out from under the feet of the famous. She might resent Stella, but she didn't want to see her publicly humiliated and all their lives put under the spotlight. She'd have to find Joe and warn him.

But Joe was nowhere to be found. A highly irritated Graham came on the line to tell her that he had been summoned suddenly to London about an hour ago, and that she could remind him he had a job to go to, but not for much longer if this was how he repaid Graham's faith in him.

And then she remembered Pat. How long before this horrible man got on to her? What a story that would make: 'I Scrimped and Saved but He Dropped Me for Starry Stella'.

She'd have to warn Pat somehow, even if it meant breaking the news about Stella's identity herself.

Molly scooped up Eddie and hunted for her car keys. At this time of day the traffic was lighter than usual and the journey to Essex took her less than an hour. Buoyed by the desire to get there before Rory Hawthorne, the miles flashed by.

Joe should be doing this, not running to Stella as soon as she lifted her red-taloned little finger. It was possible, Molly had the honesty to admit, that Stella had been contacted by the dreaded Rory too and summoned Joe to talk about what they should do.

Pat was in the garden hanging out washing when she arrived.

'Nice to see you, dear.' For once Pat sounded as though she meant it. 'Beautiful drying wind.' She looked upwards at the neat portion of bright blue above her small semi. 'I'm not surprised you had to get out of London.' She chucked Eddie under his chin. 'You should be on a rug with your nappy off, young man.'

'He won't stay put. He's got crawling fever. Just as well Andrew's dahlias aren't out yet. How is he, by the way?'

'Much better. In fact, gone to the bowling club.'

Molly wasn't sure whether she felt relief or not that she'd have Pat to herself.

'I'll get us a nice cup of tea.' They both went indoors.

While Pat was away, Molly sneaked a look round the room. Everywhere were reminders of Joe: the hospital card, shaped like a blue teddy, with his birth weight on; his Percy Penguin certificates for swimming a width; landmarks of his achievements in the Cubs; prizes in a letter-writing contest to the local paper; every school report. She'd never noticed before quite what a shrine to Joe their otherwise rather anonymous sitting room was.

Pat brought the tea on a tray with a white embroidered tray

cloth. Molly had only ever seen real linen embroidered tray cloths like Pat's in antique shops, but Pat actually used hers. If Molly had owned them they would be covered in tea stains, but Pat had the knack of pouring tea without spilling any.

'Nicely mashed now, or meshed, as they say up north.' She stirred the tea in the pot. 'My American visitor from the Church Group said "steeped". Isn't that funny?'

Molly watched as Pat babbled on innocently. What had she made of having an adopted son like Joe? She must have seen that he stood out like a pearl in a pea pod. In looks and temperament, Joe was like a visitor from another planet. Surely, Molly convinced herself, Pat must have wondered where Joe came from and what his parentage was; why he had his extraordinary looks, his intro-spection, his taste for reading instead of rugby.

She couldn't put the purpose of her visit off any longer. 'Actually, Pat, there was a reason I came today. I wanted Joe to come too but I couldn't get hold of him.'

'Why was that, dear?'

'You know I was helping him look for his birth mother?'

Pat fidgeted with the tray cloth. 'You were the one who was doing all the looking, as far as I could see,' she corrected, as tart as the lemon curd biscuits on the plate in front of them. 'I thought you'd given up on all that.'

'No,' Molly went on as gently as she could, 'I didn't give up. I went on looking. The thing is, Pat . . .' She trailed off, her confidence deserting her, wishing she could run back to London.

'The thing is what?' There was a note of irritation in Pat's voice.

'We found her.'

'I see.' It was as if Pat had closed the shutters in some deep part of herself, in case a hurricane of emotion erupted that might make her spill her tea on the tray cloth. 'Has she agreed to meet him?'

For a moment Molly almost poured out the whole story: how Stella had not only agreed to meet Joe but was utterly thrilled and enchanted by him and had started showing him off to half of London.

'It's all been a bit dramatic,' she said quietly. 'You see, Joe's mother turned out to be someone rather famous.'

'So,' Pat's shoulder stiffened as if she were expecting a blow, 'who is she then?'

Molly took her courage in both hands.

'She's Stella Milton.'

Pat looked as if she'd been struck by lightning. 'Not *the* Stella Milton? The actress? But he used to have a poster of her in his room.'

'So did a lot of other people. It seems amazing, but it's definitely her.'

'Stella Milton,' repeated Pat softly. And then a line of bitterness, deep as a ditch, imprinted itself on her forehead. 'To think of all we gave up, all that scrimping and saving, not having a holiday for years, buying everything second-hand to send him to grammar school, and all the time his mother was Stella Milton.' She paused, suddenly fixing Molly with her gaze and asking the question that Molly had tried to answer herself: 'But why would someone like Stella Milton have to give away her baby?'

'I think she must have been very young; it must have been before she was famous. Maybe her parents wouldn't back her up and she had no money.'

A niggling doubt sowed itself in Molly's mind even as she said it. Would Bea really have thrown her only daughter out and told her never to darken her door again, like some Victorian matriarch? Molly thought of the kind, likeable, eccentrically extravagant Beatrice Manners and it somehow didn't add up. 'To tell you the truth, Pat, I don't really know.

'Look, I'm so sorry about all this. The thing is, there's a reporter called Rory Hawthorne from the *Daily Post* who's chasing up the story and he may try and get hold of you. It might be better if you didn't talk to him.'

'Better for who? What if I want to talk to him? Tell him what it was like to be making all those sacrifices while Joe's "real" mother was sipping champagne. It wouldn't look very good for her, would it?'

Molly listened, startled. A small smile of satisfaction lit up Pat's face. She was enjoying her moment of power.

'So have you been whisked off for a life of five-star luxury, courtesy of your new mother-in-law?'

'She's not really interested in Eddie and me,' Molly admitted. 'Only Joe. I think she's discovered the joys of having a handsome young son to fill up her life.'

'Poor Molly.' There was a note of triumph in Pat's voice as she said it. 'You sound as if she's stolen him away. This hasn't worked out quite the way you expected, has it?'

'I think we'd better go.' Molly gathered up Eddie's things and began to dress him ready for the journey home.

Eddie, who had been enjoying his nappy-free kick, was protesting at the sudden return to the prison of Pampers. Trying to quieten him down, Molly strapped him into his baby seat and cursed that, in her rush to get there, she'd left the car in the full sun. The burning metal of the seat catch touched Eddie's tender skin and he yowled in agony.

Molly, on the verge of tears herself, jumped in after him and roared off.

In the cool of the sitting room, Pat watched them go. If she were honest, she had always known Joe was different from her and Andrew: restless, sensitive, subtly resisting the suburban structures of family life she'd tried to impose on him. Her heartbreak at not having her own child had been so acute that she'd told herself he would be just like her own son, but he never had been, not really. And now maybe he wouldn't be their son at all.

She picked up the large photo of his college graduation from the mantelpiece where it had pride of place. Tears pricked at the back of her eyes and she felt a lump filling her throat until she could hardly breathe. She put the photograph back in its place, but she wasn't really watching what she was doing and it fell, its glass smashing into pieces on the tiled fireplace.

Usually the most houseproud of women, Pat ignored the mess and went into the kitchen. On the counter was a packet of rusks and a small carton of juice she'd got out for Eddie to have on the way home.

A thought suddenly winded her, painful as heartburn. What if she lost not only her son, but her grandson to Stella?

Her hurt, needing a target, settled comfortably on Molly. It was all her fault. Without her help Joe would never have carried this through.

By the time Molly got back to the flat there were three messages waiting for her: one from Joe, and two more from Rory Hawthorne, in which the man's tone veered from polite solicitude to clear irritation.

Suddenly the enormity of it all, the fact that their private concerns would become public, that the rifts she had been responsible for opening would deepen and perhaps engulf them all, seemed too much for Molly. She lay down on the bright red rug she'd chosen with such love and care, and wept into its woolly softness.

But Molly Meredith wasn't the type to collapse for long. Looking on the bright side was her religion. If God had sent her a plague of locusts, Molly would have decided they were good for greenfly.

So she pulled herself together and decided the only solution was damage limitation. Claire's mobile number turned out to be in her diary, and she wasted no time in calling it.

'Claire, I can't tell you how sorry I am. I must have been mad to suspect you. It's because all this mess is my fault.'

Claire listened, her feet in their ridiculously uncomfortable high heels perched on her desk. 'Exactly how many calls from Rory Hawthorne did it take to make you change your mind?'

'OK, OK,' Molly conceded, wiping away the last of her self-pitying tears. 'Three, as a matter of fact, not to mention the one my mother-in-law will be getting in Essex, and God knows how many Stella's had. Is there any way you can stop him?'

'As I said, only if you all offer me an exclusive interview. Then I can try and throw the velociraptor some fresh meat. That man doesn't give up easily once he's smelled blood. And for some reason he's got it in for Stella. Maybe she wouldn't autograph his willy when he was a callow youth.'

The truth was, Claire wasn't even sure she wanted to do the interview; she knew full well the whole thing might backfire and everyone would blame her. But if Rory wrote it, they'd all find themselves turning slowly on a spit with an apple up their bums.

'Thanks, Claire. Don't worry, I'll talk Joe into it.' Molly wished she was as confident as she sounded.

'Bye then. Call me as soon as it's sorted.'

Claire picked up her notebook and headed for Tony's office. Somehow she had to persuade him that they should follow the most sympathetic angle and not go for Stella's jugular. It wouldn't be easy, but her friendship with Molly depended on it.

She sat down opposite Tony, pretending to be supremely confident, and spoke fast and convincingly. 'Right then. There are two roads we could go down with the Stella Milton story. Stella as the heartless bitch who abandoned her baby, obviously. But I think we've got a better angle: Stella and her long-lost son in tearful happy reunion as told exclusively to the *Daily Post*, with pictures.

'The way I see it,' she bulldozed on before he could object, 'is that it's a story of our time. Shows how attitudes have shifted even from the seventies. Then it would still have been a disgrace. Now it's a happy ending.'

'And your preference for this angle has got absolutely nothing to do with your lifelong friendship with the leading protagonists in this story?' Tony asked suspiciously.

'Absolutely nothing,' brazened Claire. 'There's only one condition they've asked for: that you take Rory Hawthorne off the scent.'

'I can't do that. Only the editor can do that.'

'Then you'd better persuade him.'

She just hoped to God Molly could deliver what she'd promised.

'Remember, Claire,' Tony added as she was half out of the room.

'This is the big one. Probably the biggest you'll get in your whole career. And it's your lifebelt. Without it you go down. Don't screw up.'

'Thank you, Tony,' Claire said to herself under her breath. 'I certainly needed to be reminded of that.'

Molly finally tracked Joe down at Stella's flat. Stella answered the phone sounding remarkably sunny and unperturbed, before handing over to Joe.

'Molly, thank God.' Joe's voice was all tender concern. 'I've been trying to reach you. You may get a call from a journalist.'

'I know. Rory Hawthorne. I already have. Three times. But I haven't talked to him, I've just left the machine on. Joey, I was so nervous he'd get to Pat, and I couldn't find you. I hope I did the right thing. I went to Essex and told her what's happened.'

'Oh, Jesus, poor Mum. How did she take it?'

'She was shocked, as you can imagine, and pretty angry, as I suppose a lot of other people will be, at why someone like Stella needed to give their baby away.'

'I'm really sorry you had to tell her. I should have done it myself. I'll try and talk to her now. Thanks, Moll. Look, this must be hard for you too. I'm sure the bastards'll lose interest soon.'

'Claire rang as well. She says the only way to get this Rory taken off is if you and Stella agree to an interview with her. He's a complete shit, apparently, and only interested in demolition jobs. At least with Claire you'd know you can trust her.'

'And of course it'd be quite good news for her.'

'OK, Joe, go ahead with Rory Hawthorne. Just hope he doesn't get hold of Pat. The sob story she's just told me about how much they scrimped and saved to give you a good start while Stella was sipping champagne and taking her clothes off will make terrific reading.'

She slammed the phone down, the irony lost on her that she'd suspected Claire's motives too.

*

'I think you should go ahead and do the interview,' Bob Kramer advised Stella. When she couldn't make up her mind Stella always turned to Bob. 'It's not such a disaster. In fact, it's an opportunity.'

'You'd think a Third World War would be an opportunity,' Stella pointed out crisply, crossing her legs in that way Bob found so unsettling. God alone knew what she'd do to him if she found it had been him who'd tipped off the photographer.

'It's always better to be the one taking the initiative. You sound less defensive then, you can put your slant on the story. Once all the papers have got it you'll lose that. You'll be at *their* mercy. Look, you have a choice,' he went on silkily. 'Go with Hawthorne and you'll get amazing publicity but it's true he's not the kind of man who helps old ladies across roads. Maybe this girl would be a better option if she's a friend of theirs. She can mix altruism and self-interest, always a winning combination. Plus,' he eyed Stella cannily, knowing her pride in her new-found son was her Achilles' heel, 'this isn't just an opportunity for you. Joseph's a fabulous-looking boy, and he has real presence. Maybe he'll get some offers and you can make amends for all those years you dumped him in Boredom-by-Sea.'

Stella considered this. Bob had a point. 'All right. We'll do it.' She looked at him beadily. 'Did you really mean that? About Joseph?'

'Absolutely. Do you want me to deal with the paper?'

Stella wavered. 'This isn't about money, Bob. I don't want to be paid. I just want to tell my story, what a miracle it was for Joseph to walk back into my life and how I want to make amends to him if I can.'

'Very right and proper. It's always better if you can say no money changed hands. People who sell their divorce dramas and tales of children's wasting diseases always sound like shits.' In Bob's view this didn't, however, rule out a commission fee for himself, though he didn't think he would mention that to Stella.

'I'll set it all up then. It ought to be as soon as possible.'

'Fine.'

'Stella . . .' Bob hesitated slightly, unsure of whether Stella was capable of the complete truth. She had spent so many years pretending to be other people and creating her own version of reality that he wasn't sure she could still recognize it. 'There aren't any more skeletons in your cupboard, are there? Because you know, darling, I really hate surprises, and besides, the press might find them just when it's really embarrassing for you.'

'None,' insisted Stella, looking away so that he couldn't see her eyes. 'Isn't a totally gorgeous long-lost son enough for you?'

It was still only early afternoon when Stella left Bob's office. She thought about her promise to help out at the auditions at her old drama school. As a process it was both fascinating and excruciatingly boring, yet absolutely essential for the future of the profession. It would also be useful since she would be locked away where no journalists could find her.

One of the drama teachers, Suzanna Morgan, had been Stella's own teacher. Suzanna was one of those unpredictable, irascible, warm, loving types who considered drama to be several times more important than religion and an awful lot better for the soul.

Bob's words that this was an opportunity for Joseph as much as for her came back to Stella. He couldn't possibly be happy working on that dull car thing. A sudden idea occurred to her which seemed so right she had to act on it this minute. She hailed a taxi and asked to be taken to the Southern School of Speech and Drama, some of which was in Brixton..

Her old friend Suzanna was halfway through that day's batch of auditions when Stella slipped in at the back of the rehearsal room.

Suzanna hugged her most celebrated protégée. 'You're not due till the day after tomorrow.'

'I know. There was something I wanted to ask you. You've started auditioning, I see.'

'Yup,' Suzanna replied a shade wearily. 'Another thirty to see today. Still, it has to be done.'

'Come on then.' Stella took off her jacket. Once she'd put away her Ray-Bans and got out her new reading glasses, she looked like one of the other teachers.

She caught Suzanna's glance and offered a *moue* of dislike at her new bifocals.

'If it's any consolation,' confided one of the other staff, 'Tina Turner forgot hers at the Grammy's and someone had to read the result out for her.'

Stella laughed, a rich, likeable, unpretentious laugh. 'That makes me feel a lot better.' Any resentment at her sudden arrival dissipated like the sun lighting up a wet Wednesday in Wigan.

For the next three hours Stella sat through twenty auditions. The boys all chose 'Road' by Jim Cartwright, a vignette about life in a town in the north of England. Northern accents dipped dangerously at times.

Each time a new hopeful came on, Stella found herself asking one question. Did Joseph have more charisma and presence than they did?

At the end of the auditions, which yielded only a handful with enough spark and determination to stick to a profession more than ninety per cent of which was permanently unemployed, Stella captured Suzanna.

'I'm not one to ask favours,' Stella began.

'Don't, then,' responded the older woman, at her most Suzanna-ish. 'Save yourself the disappointment of a refusal.'

'How do you know it isn't going to be you who misses out? I wondered if you'd see someone for me. Not a real audition, just a chat, listen to them read something perhaps. And give me your assessment.'

'Someone who'd want to come to the school?'

'Possibly, although he's older than your usual students.' Stella tried not to think of the implications of what she was starting off. 'But for now just to see what he's like.'

'He? Stella, this isn't some young lover of yours you're bribing to keep him in your bed?'

Stella laughed uproariously. 'I sincerely hope not.'

'Then of course I'll see him, but it had better be soon. We have to make up our minds about places in the next few weeks.'

'Thank you, Suze. You're a friend.'

'Or a complete idiot. I can't help feeling you're up to something, Stella.'

'Me?' Stella smiled her cat-who'd-got-the-caviare smile. 'Surely not, Suzanna.'

Chapter 16

The interview with Joe and Stella was set up for the next day.
'Why don't you come too?' Joe asked Molly. 'I'd love your moral support. You can jump up and down and draw your breath in sharply if I'm about to say something particularly stupid.'

Molly had to admit she was consumed by curiosity about what Stella would say, and there was no point sitting at home feeling excluded. There was also the enticing thought that Stella would probably prefer her not to be there. She was damned if she was going to let Stella push her to the edges of Joe's life. From now on she would demand to stay with him, centre stage. Besides, this was one story she dearly wanted to hear. 'I'd love to.'

Stella, with her habitual distrust of the press, had insisted the interview took place in the anonymity of a hotel. She had surprised them all by opting for neither the opulence of the Ritz nor the exoticism of somewhere like Blake's, the usual backdrops for showbiz revelation. Instead she'd selected the minimalist and halogen-bright décor of Smith's Hotel.

Claire was suitably impressed. It seemed a no-hiding-place kind of venue and she hoped this boded well for the honesty of the interview. Maybe Stella really had decided to bare a little piece of her gilded soul, after all.

When Claire arrived she found Molly in the bar, sipping a mineral water. 'Where is everyone? Not backing out already, I hope?'

'Upstairs. Stella's agent arrived with some clothes for Joe to wear.'

'Oh my God,' Claire sighed. 'This isn't supposed to be a fashion shoot. It's a searing enquiry after the truth.'

'Pardon me.' Molly couldn't help laughing. 'I thought it was a newspaper interview.'

'Let's get up there,' Claire dragged her out of her chair, 'before Stella's agent smartens up the story as well as Joe.'

Molly knocked on the door of the suite. Bob Kramer answered. He stood back, grinning odiously. 'They won't be a moment. I had something sent over from Paul Smith for Joe. We want him to look his best, don't we?'

Stella emerged at that moment from one of the two bedrooms. She had dressed for the role of reunited mother in a modest but beautifully tailored black Jasper Conran trouser suit.

But, being Stella, the modesty was somewhat undercut by the absence of anything underneath it.

Then the bathroom door opened and Joe appeared, looking dazzlingly handsome in a narrow, taupe-coloured suit in some slubby fabric that made you want to stroke it. And something immediately struck Molly. She was expecting the slight embarrassment he usually showed when the attention was on him or his looks. Instead he actually seemed to be enjoying himself.

'Right,' Claire commanded briskly, 'let's get on, shall we, or our rival papers will get there before we do and all this will be a complete waste of time.'

Stella arranged herself with a little pout of rebellion at one end of an asymmetrical white *chaise-longue*.

'Where do you want me?' Joe asked.

'Next to Stella, please.'

Joe sat down with a trace of his old awkwardness, which cheered Molly no end. She couldn't bear it if he turned into a male model before her very eyes.

Sitting next to each other, the likeness was staggering.

'So,' Claire wasted no time, 'no one minds this little thing, do they?' She clicked on a tiny tape recorder, about the size of a matchbox, and placed it on the table between Joe and Stella.

'It must have been something of a surprise, Stella Milton, to suddenly find a grown-up son contacting you out of the blue. A son you hadn't seen for, what was it, twenty-five years?'

Stella laughed a rich, fruity, it's-my-birthday kind of laugh, a laugh, Claire noticed, tinged with warm possessiveness.

'It was absolutely amazing!' she agreed. 'Utterly extraordinary. I went home on some very ordinary weekday evening feeling that the world was a bit grey, and clicked on my answering machine. And there was this voice.' She looked at Joe and smiled, as if no one but them were in the room. 'It was Joseph, like that, out of the blue, saying he thought we might be related and telling me his date of birth. It was like having a grenade thrown into my life.'

'That's an interesting image. You make it almost sound threatening rather than joyous.'

'Yes,' flashed Stella, 'it was threatening. I don't know whether Joe realized that. I'd worked hard to get where I was. I wasn't sure I wanted this disturbance. To be reminded of what had happened all those years ago.'

'Were you angry with him for daring to contact you? To intrude on your privacy?'

Molly glanced from Stella to Joe, who was listening to every word as if he might learn the truth from them. Claire was an amazingly effective interviewer.

'Yes. But only until I met him. How could anyone be angry with Joseph? As soon as I saw him, I realized it was he who should be angry with me.'

Molly's eyes flicked to Joe but Claire's were still steadily fixed on Stella. 'Doesn't it make you regret the waste?' Claire asked. 'The years you could have had with him, as your own son?'

Molly held her breath. She could see from Stella's face that this thought had never occurred to her, and that it was, at this very

171

moment, lodging itself in her consciousness. 'Yes.' Stella turned the word around and examined it from all sides. 'I suppose it was a terrible waste.'

'Did you ever worry,' Claire pushed gently, 'over the years, what it might do to him, to be given away by his real mother? I mean, you weren't some penniless teenager, you *chose* to give him up.'

Stella's reaction was a sob. It hung in the air, as out of place in these smart surroundings as a stain on a wedding dress. 'Yes,' she whispered finally, 'of course I did.'

'That's why she wrote me the letters,' Joe broke in, his voice full of tender protectiveness.

'What letters were those?' Claire probed gently.

Joe answered before Stella got the chance. 'Every year she wrote me a letter on my birthday. She kept them all for me in case I ever turned up, to show me that she'd never forgotten me.'

Joe didn't notice Stella turn uncomfortably in her seat. But Molly did.

Stella bit her lip, overwhelmed by the love she could hear in Joe's voice, knowing she didn't deserve it. She'd written those letters out of the best of intentions, certainly, but would Joe understand if he ever discovered that they were loving deceptions?

'Perhaps this is the right time for the really tough question, Stella. You're obviously thrilled that Joe's come back into your life, anyone can see that.' The look that passed between mother and son would have convinced the most hard-bitten cynic of this. 'So why did you give Joe away?'

Stella fell silent, wrestling with some inner demon. Her lovely eyes darted round like a trapped bird banging on the bars of its cage. 'It was so different then . . . you just can't imagine.'

'Even in the seventies?'

'Even in the seventies. The sexual liberation thing was all a lie to most people. We were all so innocent. I wasn't ready to be a mother. I was still a child mentally. Even my parents wouldn't stand by me. Besides, I wanted so desperately to act.' She turned to

172

Joe as if he were the only person in the room. 'You must under-stand, Joseph, I just couldn't keep you, it wasn't an option, but it didn't mean I didn't love you.'

Molly felt a tear prick the corner of her eye and brushed it away. The genuine pain Stella still felt transformed her words from a cliché into a reality that dripped with suffering. If she had done something selfish twenty-five years ago, she had certainly paid the price.

Molly had been so angry with Stella on Joe's behalf, had blamed her for all Joe's problems, but she'd never thought about how it must have been for Stella herself, how frightening, how isolating. One careless act, and your life changed forever. Nothing like today, where single mothers and one-parent families were a fact of life.

Claire moved on. 'So, is this a story with a happy ending?'

'Absolutely,' purred Stella. 'Before there was just me. Now I have a great big handsome son.' She smiled at Joe like a python con-templating dinner. 'A great big handsome son who's about to be seen by the Southern School of Speech and Drama,' she added.

Joe's face lit up. 'You mean they've agreed to audition me?'

Molly felt as if she'd been slapped. Joe hadn't even told her he had the faintest interest in acting, let alone that there was an audi-tion for a drama school in the offing, yet it was clearly something he and Stella had discussed between themselves.

Claire had just asked her last question when the photographer turned up. He was about a year older than Joe, Norwegian, and though, according to Bob Kramer, he was flavour of the month, sought after by all the hot newspapers and magazines, the young man had gone into a panic when he'd heard who he was photo-graphing. 'She was the idol of my boyhood,' he kept repeating to anyone who'd listen, 'my icon.'

Stella was lapping it up.

While he was snapping away, Claire and Molly retreated to the other end of the suite. 'So what did you think of sainted Stella's sob story?' Claire asked in a low voice.

'I believed her,' Molly admitted. 'I've never liked her much, but it really made me think about how awful it must have been then. We have it easy now. How about you?'

'She's a selfish cow,' Claire announced in a low voice, 'with about as much concern for others as a drunk driver on a boozy Saturday night. And she hasn't even noticed you or Eddie exist.'

Molly felt as if Claire had removed a very heavy weight from her chest and she could suddenly breathe again. 'Do you know what,' she poured herself and Claire a glass each of the miniature bottle of white wine from the mini-bar, 'you're absolutely bloody well right. I've got to get him away from her.'

'Yep.' Claire clinked glasses. 'But she's got her claws in pretty deep. He's given her a whole new lease of life. Just when her flagging career could do with it. I don't think she gives a stuff about you.' She gathered up her notebook and tape recorder and turned back to Stella and Joe. 'Thank you, folks,' she announced with a professional smile. 'That was wonderful. I'll leave you now to go and write it. Can I give anyone a lift?'

'I rather fancy lunch,' Bob Kramer announced. 'What about you, Stella?'

'Lovely. As long as Joe's coming.'

'Sorry,' Joe apologized, taking Molly's hand as they all walked out of the hotel lobby, 'but I've got to go and see Pat and explain what's happening.' He looked at Molly. 'Want to come?'

Molly could have kissed him, especially when she saw the look on Stella's face.

'I'm sorry about that stuff about the drama school. I should have discussed it with you. I didn't know it was really happening. I thought it was just a wild idea of Stella's.'

Outside the tube station they passed a flower seller. 'Look, sweet peas. Pat's favourite flowers.' He chose a bunch in pale pinks, blues and lilac.

'Joseph Meredith,' Molly grabbed him, dizzy with relief that he hadn't forgotten his real obligations, 'have I told you lately that I love you?' She pulled him towards her in full view of the giggling pedestrians outside Tottenham Court Road station and kissed him on the lips.

When they arrived in Mere, the house was strangely peaceful. Normally Pat would be beavering away with some arduous task like washing blankets by hand or spring-cleaning the skirting boards with a toothbrush. Instead she was on the settee watching daytime television. Somehow in someone as energetic as Pat this was as shocking as if she'd been dancing nude in the driveway.

Pat's face was a picture when she saw both Joe and the flowers.

'Hello, Pat,' Molly said tentatively, remembering their last meeting.

Her mother-in-law nodded to her. Perhaps this was progress.

Joe handed her the flowers and she pretended to bustle about looking for a vase.

'I'll get one,' offered Molly.

Joe pulled Pat gently back on to the sofa. 'I just wanted to tell you that this has all been so weird and extraordinary, but I didn't want you to feel I'd forgotten you, or ever would. You were the ones who brought me up and gave me love and security, and I'll never forget it.'

Pat's downwards-sloping mouth curved in a brief smile. Poor Pat, thought Molly as she came back into the room with the flowers, she expected life to let her down and it always lived up to her expectations. She suddenly reminded Molly of a well-ordered budgie, the kind who kept a very clean cage, suddenly finding itself invaded by a glorious bird of paradise, in the form of Stella, who didn't respect any of those values of cleanliness and orderliness, but got all the attention anyway.

'I wanted to warn you that I've done an interview with Stella and it'll be in the *Daily Post* tomorrow,' Joe went on.

Shock registered on Pat's face, then unwilling fascination. 'So, what was her story? What guff did she give you about why she had you adopted?'

'That she gave me away because she couldn't face a life alone with a small baby and no support, just as she was starting out on her career as an actress.'

'Couldn't her parents have helped her out?' Pat interrupted acidly. 'Plenty of parents did; they might not have been keen at first but they usually came round in the end. That is,' she gave Joe a long look, 'if the baby's mother was really determined to keep it.'

'Well, her parents didn't,' Joe insisted defensively. 'She'd have been on her own and she couldn't face it.'

Molly fiddled with the flowers. She was on Pat's side with this one. She just couldn't see Bea in the role of unfeeling parent that Stella had cast her in.

Joe was still talking. 'I just wanted to say, Mum,' he emphasized the word carefully, but Pat turned her head away as if she were being stung, 'that I'll never be able to thank you enough for loving me so much, and that I'm sorry all this has happened.'

Joe jumped up and hugged Pat fiercely before she had time to protest about him mussing up her hair or that he might knock something over. 'And I do hope I haven't said anything in this interview that's going to hurt you.'

'I'm pretty strong really,' Pat asserted, dignified suddenly despite her flowery pinny. 'And, after all, I'm the lucky one. Her loss was my gain. I had you all those years, remember.'

Molly felt tears blurring her eyes at Pat's quiet stoicism.

When they got home, Eddie, who was being looked after by their downstairs neighbour, crowed with delight at seeing them.

'He such a love,' cooed Mrs Salaman, her English still reminiscent of Istanbul. 'You leave him with me any time. I have a granddaughter same age. Maybe they get married.'

'I'll start saving for the wedding,' laughed Molly.

It was a relief to be back in their ordinary little flat, just the three of them, with no mother-in-laws, adopted or otherwise, or interfering journalists. Molly went round opening all the windows, which seemed to have the effect of letting in waves of hot air instead of the breeze she was hoping for. The heat was so intense her shirt was sticking uncomfortably to her neck and she started to take it off.

'Here, let me help.' Joe stood behind her, pulling her body

against his. He undid the buttons slowly, kissing her neck as he did so until she felt her breath speeding up. She closed her eyes, forgetting all about everything, even Eddie. Each nipple felt like a sparkler, fizzing with delicious desire.

'Hang on a minute.' Her eyes snapped open in alarm. 'Where's Eddie got to?'

Joe turned her round slowly. She could feel his trousers bulging like a tent pole. 'Look. Sparked out on the sofa. I think he's overdosed on *Teletubbies* and Mrs Salaman's rum baba.'

'You don't really think she gave him rum baba?'

'I certainly hope so.' This time Joe picked her up bodily. 'All the more time for us.'

Molly woke early the next morning, before the others, as she usually did, and stretched deliciously. Every bit of her glowed and zinged. She didn't even want to wake Joe; just have five minutes to herself to rerun the erotic video of last night in her head. Joe had abandoned all the usual tried-and-true routines for something altogether more ambitious. If he went on like this she'd have to take up yoga. He'd certainly made her lotus blossom last night.

She sat up suddenly. Today was the day the interview was supposed to appear in the paper. Molly slipped out of bed and into her favourite dungarees, trainers and baggy sweatshirt. Her hair, untied from its usual fastening and tangling right down her back in a red cloud, reminded her of how Joe had buried his face in it last night, then arranged it carefully so that her breasts peeped through, like Lady Godiva's.

Enough! Molly found her purse and padded out. The newsagent on the corner had branched out optimistically into a small French bread stand which offered croissants, baguettes and pain au chocolat. These were wildly expensive, resembled the texture of leather and were made with processed flour despite their claim to be 'Fresh from France'. But still. Today was the day to throw normality to the winds and Molly bought a greedy bagful. She could always economize on lunch.

177

She then picked up two copies of the *Post* and scuttled back to the flat, holding her breath.

Joe was still asleep, so she laid their small kitchen table, made real coffee and put the croissants in the oven to warm. She even pinched a sunflower from the rather hideous dried-flower arrangement Pat had made them last year at her evening class, and put it in the middle of the table.

She could hear Joe stirring. His face appeared round the door, sleepy and smiling. 'Is that the smell of croissants I detect? Have I died and gone to heaven?'

'No croissants in heaven. Only spiritual pleasures.'

'Maybe I'd better go on living then. It's not my birthday?'

'That was last night. Don't you really know what day it is?' As a matter of fact she rather liked him for forgetting. At least he wasn't falling over himself with vanity. She pointed to the papers.

'Oh God.' He winced. 'Have you checked yet?'

'Thought I'd leave it to you.'

Gingerly, as if it might give him an electric shock, Joe picked up the paper and leafed through.

'It's not there,' he said, looking deeply relieved. 'Maybe a better story came up.'

Molly knew from Claire that newspapers had agendas of their own which sometimes meant stories didn't appear when they were supposed to, but she was surprised nevertheless. She began turning the pages of the other copy. It was bang in the middle of the paper, the centre spread; so huge that it was, curiously, easier to flick over.

She turned it round so that it faced Joe. 'Not there, eh? Then what's this? "Back Together . . . Sexy Stella and Her Long-Lost Son . . . Seductive film actress Stella Milton told of how, twenty-five years ago, when she was broke, desperate and only twenty, she gave away her baby son . . . 'There hasn't been a day when I haven't thought of him,' said Stella, forty-four. 'And now he's back I keep thinking my heart will burst with happiness.'"'

Joe stared at the words as if he'd never heard them before. His eyes sparkled shining and wet like dewy spider's webs caught in sunshine. 'All those years I thought my real mother didn't give a stuff about me, Moll, and she was thinking about me every single day. You don't know what it means to me. It's like being given another chance. I know I've been moody sometimes – you were right about all that even though I couldn't admit it. I was so bloody scared of being abandoned again. But it's all right, Molly, it's going to be all right. And it's all thanks to you for helping me find her. I love you so much.'

He went over to Eddie's cot and knelt next to the sleeping baby.

Molly half ran to join them and put her arms round the two people she loved most in the world, as if protecting them in some magic circle.

For this moment everything seemed to be perfect, just as she'd always dreamed it would be. And in that instant of perfection, Molly had no idea that before long it would be she who would hold the key to destroying it all.

Chapter 17

Once a month Anthony Lewis got up while it was still dark to go to the Peacehaven Antiques Fair. Not one of life's early risers, he found it harder and harder to pull himself out of bed, pile blankets into his van to protect any furniture he might buy, and set out for Peacehaven as the first sun dipped over the cliffs of the coast road.

The antiques market was held on a tract of former pasture several miles inland and attracted dealers from all over Europe. The really serious buyers arrived under cover of darkness and bought from the backs of vans, lit only by torches, giving the proceedings an illicit air, the natural legacy of the smugglers who were once rife along these coasts, stowing their contraband in caves and occasionally chucking some long-dead citizen out of his grave to replace his corpse with brandy.

After an hour hunting among the lorries, and one great find which ensured that coming here today had already been worthwhile, Anthony decided to shake off the fuzziness of a night in the Sun in Splendour with a black coffee. Next to him on the still dewy counter of the refreshment van someone had left a newspaper, which was sitting damply like a grey whale on a white plastic sea. Anthony was about to put it out of its misery when he noticed half of Stella's face. The other half had been acting as a plate for a bacon sandwich and was smeared out of recognition.

He unfolded the page. The story he revealed was so unexpected he choked, spitting a mouthful of coffee over the paper.

This time she'd gone too far.

He wiped off the coffee stains as best he could and studied Stella's beautiful face. The photograph was a good one, not some cheap Page Three snapper's vulgar attempt. Stella looked out coolly, her dark hair framing her face, her hand entwined through the arm of the young man next to her, the son she had given away for adoption. The resemblance was uncanny. And yet they didn't look like mother and son, more like some Greek brother and sister from ancient myth who had fallen in love only to discover, too late, the tragic fact that they were related.

Anthony Lewis started to laugh. Nothing Stella did was ever ordinary, not even finding her son.

'What a touching tale, Stella,' he said out loud, 'a real fairy story.'

He patted the damp newspaper with a piece of kitchen towel and tucked it into his pocket. Then he half ran, with long, lolloping steps, his black leather coat flapping, towards his van, a wolfish smile lighting up his usually lugubrious features.

'Hey, Ant,' called a voice from one of the lorries in the enclosure. 'Anthony! Come back!' The dealer turned to his next-door neighbour. 'He just bought a tallboy from me, five hundred quid's worth, and now he's buggering off without even taking it.'

Beatrice Manners was not a fan of the *Daily Post*. She had been a lifelong *Telegraph* reader and saw little reason to change her mind at her stage of life. It was all part of her morning ritual. Once she'd had her cup of tea and fetched her milk from the farm, she made herself breakfast of granary toast and heather honey which she consumed with a strong black coffee either in the sun room at the back of the house or in the garden under one of the apple trees, depending on the weather. By the summer months the apples were too much the target of fat, buzzy wasps, drunk and belligerent on apple juice, who considered the trees their property rather than hers, so she stuck to the shade of the horse-chestnut.

Now, as September beckoned, Bea was making the most of her outdoor breakfast. She would keep it up well into October. It might be high summer, but the end of August always seemed to her a gloomy time. It felt to Bea as if the knell of the season's departure was already being tolled. The best of the flowers were over, the grass dried out. She had already begun to look forward to crisper, clearer weather.

She had just finished her second round of toast and had folded her *Telegraph* neatly into manageable sections when she was roused by a greeting from someone leaning on the flint-and-wattle wall.

'Good morning, Bea.' To Bea's displeasure, it was Anthony Lewis. 'Lovely morning for reading the paper in the garden. I thought you might enjoy a change from your usual.'

He flourished a copy of the *Daily Post* in her direction.

'Never touch the rag,' Bea commented loftily, not stirring from her seat.

Anthony grinned. 'You might enjoy it today. Fascinating story about Stella. A work of true artistry. Stella's wasted on the stage. She should have taken up writing fiction instead. Such a vivid imagination. So brilliantly moving.'

Bea rose and sailed across the garden in her most *grande dame* manner. She'd never liked Anthony much and he'd always been most dangerous when he had this devilish air. But she'd never seen him look quite so full of himself before. He was behaving as if he'd just found a Van Gogh in his garage.

'I'm really not interested, thank you,' she said firmly, and headed back for the safety of her seat.

Infuriatingly he placed the newspaper on her garden wall. 'Have a read, Bea. I'm sure you enjoy good fiction as much as I do.'

He turned abruptly away, leaving Bea with the dilemma of whether to ignore the paper or get up to fetch it.

The temptation was too much for her, though she waited till he was out of sight so at least he didn't have the satisfaction of seeing her succumb.

She walked slowly back to her seat, feeling suddenly old, as if life had offered one too many battles. The paper was full of lurid accounts of philandering schoolmasters, giant marrows that looked as if they ought to be banned under the Obscene Publications Act, and payola politicians. When she came to the photograph of Joe and Stella she closed her eyes. Of course she had known this would happen, ever since Molly had turned up at her house all those months ago.

She read the interview twice.

When she'd finished she laid the paper down on the table. 'What utter cobblers!' she confided loudly to the drunken wasps in the apple tree. 'Has my daughter gone stark staring mad?'

They buzzed in agreement.

Bea got up and went inside to look up her train timetable. It was time she took a stand. Unless, of course, it was already too late.

In Mere-on-Sea Pat gazed at the newspaper photograph of Joe and Stella staring into each other's eyes. Andrew had been out to buy three copies.

'What's everyone going to think?' she demanded, an excruciating pain making it hard to even speak. Joe and Stella were so dazzlingly alike when you saw them next to each other that it was agonizing.

You did everything you could to love and care for a child, she told herself bitterly, even pretended to yourself that it was yours, and then Nature came and slapped you in the face with the proof that it wasn't.

She was going to lose him. What chance did she have against the glamour and sophistication of Stella Milton?

Pat, who was generally more prone to grumbling and resentment, felt the pure appeal of white-hot hatred. What right did this woman, this selfish, shallow woman, have to appear in her life and steal Joe away?

183

Andrew reached out and took her hand. 'You mean more to him than she does. You were there with the Elastoplast when he banged his knee, not her.'

Pat turned her face to the wall. 'He's going to need more than Elastoplast to hold himself together now.'

Andrew sighed. 'It's Molly I feel sorry for. It must be tough to find you've suddenly got a rival like her for your husband's affections.'

For the first time Pat looked more cheerful. 'Yes, but Molly's only got herself to blame, hasn't she? That girl should learn not to interfere in other people's lives.'

'She did it for the best. Molly isn't the type to sit back and watch the people she loves suffer,' Andrew pointed out, admitting to himself that it was why he liked his daughter-in-law so much.

'Then she shouldn't complain if she gets bitten,' retorted Pat.

Very softly, Pat began humming. Stella might be rich and successful, but right was on Pat's side. And she might just decide to prove it.

'My God, have you seen this?' Joe's workmates were all gathered round the paper in stunned amazement.

Graham, Joe's boss, didn't know whether to be angry or impressed at this new revelation about the exciting lineage of his star employee and – though he perhaps hadn't made this as clear as he ought to Joe – heir apparent.

'Tell you what, I wouldn't mind having her as *my* mother,' offered Brian, the technical manager, then paused, realizing it wasn't his *mother* he'd like to have her for.

'It must be a bit weird, don't you think? I mean, mothers aren't supposed to be shaggable.'

'Well, mine certainly isn't.'

'Do you think he'll stay on after this?'

'Of course he'll stay on,' Graham replied testily. 'He's still got a living to earn. She's not a millionairess.'

'She must be pretty well off, though.'

'That doesn't necessarily mean she's going to start supporting Joe and his family. It'll probably just mean his Christmas presents get better. Where is the lad anyway?'

Joe appeared at that very moment, ducking his head slightly as if to avoid a blow when he saw them all gathered round the paper.

'Bloody hell, Joe!' they chorused. 'You're a dark horse. What's she like?'

'She's a very nice lady.' Joe's tone implied that that was the end of the story. 'Now, who's got the artwork for the new Vieira Coupé?'

Joe's colleagues looked as if they'd been deprived of a very juicy bone, but they knew Joe better than to try and get more out of him now. They'd just have to wait till later for some tit-bits.

Meanwhile Graham stomped off, half impressed, half annoyed, to phone his wife. It wasn't often he knew something before she did.

A delicious thought occurred to him which he decided to keep entirely to himself for the moment. Maybe now they had the connection through Joe, Stella would agree to pose for the front of their Peugeot handbook.

Bob Kramer cracked his knuckles in glee at the coverage. The *Post* was low-rent, of course, but the story would still be all round every other paper in seconds. The photograph was fantastic too. For once they hadn't used a talentless undo-your-top-button-for-me-darling merchant but someone with real style. It had the quality of a glossy magazine. Stella looked wonderful, but it was Joe who was the revelation. There was something dark and full of repressed passion about him that came right off the page and grabbed you.

Bob was usually a lifelong exponent of the let-them-come-to-you philosophy, but now and then he liked to help things along. Today he sent out a runner to buy an armload of papers and dispatched them off to various useful people. The last, almost as an afterthought, was the producer of *Dark Night and Desire*, the play Stella wanted so much to act in.

*

185

Perhaps the last person to see the article was Stella herself. She liked to join the world gently and late. If she wasn't actually working she began each day about ten thirty making herself a glass of hot water with lemon in it, or sometimes, if she needed a lift, ginseng. She would take it back to bed where she would then fling open the windows of her bedroom and listen to the world below.

Stella could judge the time of day just by the sounds that rose up to her from the Covent Garden street below. Her favourite time was the rush hour, when she could hear everyone scuttling in to work, pausing only to get their skinny lattes at Pret à Manger, or the cigarettes they would have to stand outside their offices to consume. Then, a little later, taxi doors banging as the bosses arrived. Like Eustacia Vye, Thomas Hardy's heroine in *The Return of the Native*, Stella preferred weekdays to weekends, when she could better savour the leisure most people weren't lucky enough to enjoy.

Today she would be doing the auditions, but not until this afternoon. It was late morning, almost lunchtime in fact, when she heard a taxi draw up outside her own building, and a loud, bossy, entirely English voice rise up through the ether. 'Thank you, young man,' it said, 'for going to the trouble of opening the door.'

The biting sarcasm in the tone painted the picture below for her vividly. Her mother was arriving and the driver had failed to bestir himself.

Stella dressed quickly, not wanting Bea to find her *en deshabille* at ten to one, or she would be given the usual lecture about people in dressing gowns after ten looking like tarts. Since most of the parts Stella played *were* tarts, albeit tarts of sophistication and class, this seemed a particularly pointless criticism, but even at her age Stella cared more about her mother's opinion than she cared to let on, so she threw on her clothes in record time. Her dresser would be proud of the fact that in under a minute, the celebrated Stella Milton could put on her own clothes, brush her hair and even add a pout of damson lip gloss before her mother had time to barge in firing criticisms from both barrels.

Seizing the initiative, Stella conceived the brilliant idea of opening the front door before Bea had time to ring the bell.

'Hello, Ma.' She did a passable performance of being thrilled to
see her mother. 'What a lovely surprise.'

'Lovely surprise, my arse,' replied Bea rudely. 'What the bloody
hell do you think you're doing, Stella? Have you gone completely
off your head?'

Stella ushered her swiftly inside, grateful she didn't have any
neighbours to eavesdrop.

'Cup of tea?'

'I didn't come for a cup of tea. You know perfectly well why I'm
here.'

'Don't be so dramatic, Ma. This isn't the stage of the Chowringee
Empire.'

Bea swept her lilac pashmina round her, the one she'd actually
bought in Pakistan forty years ago, not during the current wave of
pashmina passion sweeping London's trendies, forcing them to
cough up the kind of money that would have fed a Pakistani family
for months.

'Stella, this is serious.' She took out a copy of that day's *Post*.
'What on earth were you thinking of?'

'Don't make so much fuss, Ma. I had to get the press off my back
so I gave one little interview.'

'It's not the quantity that matters,' Bea flashed. 'It's what you
said. It was pure fantasy.'

'It was for his sake. He was unhappy. Since finding me he says
his life makes sense for the first time. Look at him, he's gorgeous;
he never fitted in to the family that adopted him. I'm sure they're
nice enough people, but Joseph is exceptional.'

Stella could see that her mother still wasn't convinced. 'Look,
Ma, I did it because it was what he needed. He'd never recovered
from feeling rejected, and that was my fault. Can you imagine what
it was like to finally see that?' Stella's voice curdled with sudden
pain. 'To look at this glorious young man and see that he was dam-
aged, and all because he hadn't felt loved by his real mother,

because she'd given him away like a bundle of old rags. I had to show him it wasn't like that!'

'Wasn't it, Stella?' Bea asked quietly.

'No, it wasn't! I suffered too. Maybe now it seems as if I made a mistake, but it didn't seem like it then.'

'And what about these letters you wrote him?'

Stella flinched so slightly that most people wouldn't have noticed. But Bea did. 'You made them up, didn't you! You didn't sit down and write to him every year. You forgot all about him.'

Stella looked as if she'd been struck. 'All right. But they're not fakes. They're what I feel, what I would have written. I just didn't write them when he thought I did.'

Bea closed her eyes, feeling like a worn old tyre which has been on the road way beyond its natural life. 'Stella, what have you done?' She opened her arms and Stella folded herself into them.

'I just wanted to make it right for him, Ma. I couldn't bear seeing all the pain I'd caused.'

Bea patted her as she'd done when Stella was a small child. 'Surely it would be better just to say you're sorry and admit you were in the wrong than construct new lies?'

Finally, after all these years, her daughter was finding out not only that she could love someone more than herself, but that love was inextricably tied up with suffering. She wondered how to break the worst news of all to Stella.

'Darling, I know you want to help Joseph, but I don't think this is the way. Creating more lies can't be the answer. I think you ought to go away for a little while. That way things might quieten down.'

'But I don't want to go away! I've only just found him.'

'Then you must stop trailing him around like a mascot. He has a life and a family. Imagine how Molly must feel.'

'Don't be so ludicrous, Ma. I haven't taken him away from anyone.'

'You don't realize your own power. You're rich and glamorous. Molly and Joe live in a little flat. They have an ordinary life. He does an ordinary job.'

'I'm lonely, Ma,' Stella blurted. 'It's been so wonderful finding him.'

'What about Richard? That man loves you, God alone knows why. Get yourself a proper relationship and stop being the third person in Molly and Joe's.' Bea knew it was brutal, but it had to be said. 'Just remember, if Joe's hurt twice he'll *never* forgive you.'

Stella could hear a shiver of fear crumbling the edges of her mother's voice and it terrified the life out of her. Bea had always been so strong. 'What is it, Ma?'

'I don't read papers like the *Daily Post*. Anthony brought it for me. He said he thought I might be interested.'

Stella's shoulders slumped, and the sinews of her neck stood out sharply, making her look suddenly middle-aged and not at all sexy. 'All right. I'll try and back off.'

Bea hugged her again. 'My poor Stella. I'm sure that's for the best. And now I must get back to my dahlias. I hate London these days.'

After her mother had gone, Stella sat down on her balcony, feeling sick and shaky. Anthony wasn't as harmless as he seemed. He could do her a lot of harm if he chose to. Now that she'd found Joseph, she couldn't bear to lose him again. And that was exactly what she'd do if he were to find out the truth.

To her relief, today was the day of the auditions she'd promised to help out with at the Southern. That would mean an entire afternoon in a darkened theatre away from prying eyes.

She thought about Joe all the way in the taxi. Her mother was right. From now on she should stay out of his life.

Her old friend Suzanna leaped on her as soon as she arrived. 'You're a deep one, aren't you?' she teased. 'This young man you wanted me to see – Joseph Meredith, didn't you say his name was? Funny you didn't mention that he happens to be your son.' She brandished a tattered copy of the *Post*. 'My God, Stella, he's certainly a looker. If he can even act his way out of a paper bag then I'll see what I can do.'

Stella bit her lip. She had a feeling this was just the sort of thing Bea would disapprove of. Thinking she could play the fairy godmother and rescue him from his ordinary life. 'Well, as a matter of fact, Suze, I was going to ring you. I think Joseph may have cooled on the acting front and decided to stick to something where he might actually earn a living.'

'Really?' Suzanna couldn't remember when she'd last felt so disappointed. 'But you said he was so eager?'

'Yes. Well, I think reality's stretched out its freezing fingers and he's remembered he's a family man with a mortgage.'

'How bloody depressing.'

'Not for his family. Thank you for agreeing to meet him for me. I know how busy you are.'

Suzanna knew Stella well enough to leave the matter there for now. She smiled sweetly and they both settled down to watch two dozen more hopefuls auditioning for the precious few places at the school. But later that day, when Stella had gone, she flipped open her mobile phone and fished in her bag for her copious, tattered address book.

She found Bob Kramer's number and dialled it. 'Bob, Suzanna from the Southern. Look, can you enlighten me? Stella was incredibly keen for me to meet this young man who turns out to be her son. Now she's suddenly changed her mind. But after seeing him in the paper, I think he's certainly got something. I'd really like to talk to him, but she's put a lid on the whole thing.'

'Don't mind Stella,' Bob said with more than a touch of irritation. 'She's just being mother hen-ish. She'll come round. She'd better. I've had three casting directors on the phone, as well as the creative honcho at the ad agency which does her Peugeot ad. He's come up with a follow-up campaign to use her and Joseph together. Stella doesn't see it yet, but Joseph could turn out to be the best thing that's happened to her career in years.'

'Maybe she's frightened of feeling she's using him?'

'Stella frightened of using someone? It'd be the first time.'

'Maybe it's mother love. It can hit you like a force-ten tornado. Believe me, I know. I've got three kids. I recognize the symptoms.'

Bob thought about this extraordinary possibility. He had always respected Stella's talent, but even her best friends wouldn't have described her as maternal. This would be a new and frankly astonishing side to her.

On the other hand, surely it was also an opportunity? It couldn't be beyond his capabilities to show Stella that this was a life changing opportunity for Joe too and it would be unfair to stand in his way. Bob had no children, and no intention of ever having any, but it was his view that any mother, especially a newly discovered one who had a lot to make up for, ought to be encouraging the talents and interests of her offspring, not sabotaging them before they had a chance to take off.

It took Bob only fifteen minutes to jump in a cab and get to Stella's flat. He even ran up the stairs instead of waiting for the lift.

He was somewhat shocked by Stella's appearance when she answered the door. She looked as if she'd been crying. She kept her sunglasses on and kept flicking her dark hair across her face as if she didn't want anyone to know who she was.

'I suppose you've come to tell me to stop making a fool of myself just like my mother keeps telling me. It's all right. I'm getting the message. I should leave Joseph to get on with his life and concentrate on getting on with my own.'

'Well, actually, darling, I don't think that at all. My phone's been positively jangling with opportunities for both of you. The ad agency for Peugeot want to talk to you about doing a commercial together, the producers of *Dark Night and Desire* want a meet because, guess what, Roxanne Wood's pregnant . . .' He smiled, waiting for her enraptured response, not even noticing that it wasn't forthcoming before he built up to the climax of his exciting revelations.

'And, wait for it, this bit's even more amazing. The director of the Millennium Film Festival called this morning. They want to honour you with a special award and have you say a few words at the Big Opening. You're hotter than you've ever been, Stella darling!'

It all seemed to Stella like an empty victory. She ought to be thrilled but instead her mother's warning reverberated in her head that she must stay out of Joe's life or disaster would enfold them all.

Oh Christ, what the hell was she going to do now?

Bob hadn't been Stella's agent for eighteen years for nothing. He understood her moods even before she did.

'Look, Stella love, Joseph's a grown man, not the little baby you gave away. Surely it's up to him to decide on all this for himself?'

Stella's shoulders slumped. She knew all too well what would happen if Joe were consulted. When fame, or even the slenderest chance of it, came and tapped you on the shoulder, nobody ever told it to go away and wait till they were ready. Joseph would be no exception.

Joe had long ago departed for work and Eddie was crawling around nappy-free when the doorbell rang and Claire's voice sailed up through the intercom.

'Just popped in on my way to work to make sure you were both still speaking to me.'

By the time Claire arrived, out of breath, at their door, Molly was clearing the debris away from their celebratory breakfast.

Claire picked up an uneaten croissant.

'Here, let me make you some coffee,' offered Molly. 'And how come Peckham's on your way to work when you live the other side of London?'

'OK, I admit it. I was feeling nervous that you'd hate the interview. You both mean a lot to me.'

Molly felt overcome with guilt that she'd ever suspected Claire of tipping off that photographer. 'To tell you the truth, Joe lapped it up. He's gone off in glory to be ribbed by his workmates.' Molly suddenly hugged her friend, bubbling over with relief that everything seemed to be working out so well. 'It's like a miracle. He just seems so much more at home in his skin now that he knows Stella loved him and that she didn't just chuck him away and forget about him. The funny thing is, he isn't even angry with her. I'm sure I would have been, but not Joe. He's got this kind of touching gratitude.'

Claire let out a sigh that sounded like a fast puncture. 'I hope she deserves it. There's something about Stella's story that I didn't quite buy. Maybe she's just too much of an actress for you to ever believe she's genuine even when she is.'

Molly, who'd been conscious of the same feeling, changed the subject abruptly. She didn't want Claire pursuing the matter, however close their friendship.

'Anyway,' Claire sounded relieved, 'I'd better go and join the world of the working. I'm so glad you and Joe are still talking to me.' She paused, not wanting to put a pin in Molly's happiness. 'A word of warning. I hate to be a party pooper, but if Stella *is* hiding something, some other hack is bound to find it. I doubt if our rivals at the *Press* will want to settle for a happy ending, especially if it's the *Post*'s happy ending. It may be open season on Stella from now on.'

As if to endorse Claire's words, the phone rang almost the moment she had left.

'Hello,' said a voice Molly didn't recognize. 'I'm a reporter on the *Daily Press*. Could I speak with Joseph Meredith, please?'

Molly slammed down the phone, finding that she was shaking, her glorious happiness evaporating, leaving her with an ominous sense that she'd known all along it couldn't last.

Somehow there was only one person in all this she could really trust, one person who wouldn't lie to her and who was wise enough to help them all through the emotional quicksands that were opening up around them.

With her usual swiftness of purpose, Molly gathered up Eddie, pausing only to grab a nappy and sunhat, and dashed down the stairs with the baby under one arm and his buggy under the other. She didn't bother to check up on the trains to Cliffdean. They were so frequent she wouldn't have to wait long. Eddie, as ever, was enchanted by railway stations and viewed the whole venture as a grand day out.

In less than two hours Molly was on the small rural bus that weaved in and out of the valleys to Lower Ditchwell. Eddie oohed and aahed with delight as if Postman Pat's van might at any

193

moment come cresting over the hill in the opposite direction to complete his happiness.

Molly strapped him in his buggy to walk the last few yards, grateful she would soon be in the shady garden of Bea's cottage. She rang the doorbell three times but there was no answer. Eventually she walked right round the house, but everything was shuttered and locked. The one person who could tell her if Stella was telling the whole truth wasn't here.

'She's gone to London,' said someone from a few yards behind her, someone who was leaning casually on the flint wall. It was Anthony Lewis, the antique dealer. Molly got the impression he'd been there a few minutes watching her. 'I saw her going off in a taxi.' The man's skull-like face was fixed into a grin designed, Molly suspected, to be deliberately disconcerting. He looked like a life-long bit player who has suddenly seen his opportunity to be a star.

'I don't suppose,' Molly asked reluctantly, 'you know via the village bush telegraph when she's coming back?'

He shook his head, still smiling. His lank hair swung as he did so. 'No idea, I'm afraid. Is it anything I could help you with?'

Molly almost cringed in instinctive revulsion. 'No thanks. I'll call her when I get home.' She turned Eddie's buggy sharply and almost raced back to the bus stop.

'What a lovely little boy,' Anthony Lewis commented. 'The bus won't be back for half an hour. It goes right up to the head of the valley. Are you sure you don't want to come into the shop and wait where it's cooler?'

Molly shook her head.

'I see you found Stella.' His grin had broadened still further. 'How did she take it when you produced her long-lost son?'

Molly couldn't bear his goading tone. It implied that everyone's motives were somehow suspect. 'Actually, she was overjoyed. She'd never stopped thinking about him. In fact, she missed him so much she wrote him a letter every single year on his birthday.'

'Did she indeed? Every single year? Now that's what I call heart-warming.'

When she looked out of the bus window twenty minutes later, Anthony Lewis had disappeared, but just meeting him had soured her trip. He dripped a kind of contagious bitterness that made her want to have nothing to do with him.

When she got back to Peckham, hot and tired and disappointed, there were two more messages on their machine. Molly flopped down on the sofa. She played them both back with a sense of misgiving she wasn't entirely proud of. One was from Bob Kramer, Stella's agent, asking Joe to call back as soon as possible to discuss some very exciting opportunities that had come up. The other was from someone called Suzanna Morgan from the Southern School of Speech and Drama asking Joe to call her. Bloody Stella! This had her fingerprints all over it. This acting idea was entirely hers. Joe would never be able to resist any of this.

Molly made herself a cup of tea and examined her conscience. It wouldn't be that surprising if Joe was getting fed up with his job, or at least found it secure but limiting. OK, he might not have discovered this sudden interest in drama had Stella not burst so dramatically into their lives, but some kind of change would probably have come along. And although Molly loved looking after Eddie, she'd enjoyed the freedom when Mrs Salaman had taken him. Would it be so terrible if Joe had a crack at acting? Couldn't she find some childcare – Mrs Salaman herself, since she seemed to adore Eddie – and get a part-time job?

She remembered with distaste how the wife of one of Joe's colleagues kept ringing Graham and asking how her husband was getting on at work. They'd all despised her for it and felt sorry for him that he was taken for such a meal ticket. But wasn't Molly becoming the same sort of person? A wife who simply saw her husband as someone who paid the bills? She had always loathed people like that.

In fact, had Molly known, she would have been astonished to find that Stella was also having doubts about encouraging Joe to act.

Stella's first instinct on meeting Joe and finding he was so hand-some, and so wasted working in some motoring backwater and living in a shoddy flat, had indeed been to rescue him. But Bea's visit had made her think. Had acting really made her so happy? Here she was in her mid-forties, terrified of losing her beauty on the one hand, or becoming a ludicrous face-lifted parody of herself on the other; and having a half-hearted relationship with Richard, probably only because he adored her and he was all that came between her and an empty life. She had even given up her child for acting.

She had been motivated by passion, by determination and by a capacity to put steel-mesh barriers between herself and certain uncomfortable truths. Joe wasn't like that at all. He was an emotional, sometimes thin-skinned young man who had a job and a family. Perhaps all those things, though quiet and unglamorous, were actually worth rather more than five minutes of fame.

Stella had therefore resolved to try and dissuade him from being too dazzled by all this sudden interest. She had also come to another, far more painful resolution. She should start to drift firmly into the background of his life. Before that, though, what she wanted, more than anything else in life, was for him to be at her side for the Millennium Awards, when the whole profession would reassure her that her life had some meaning despite her stupid mistakes.

In fact neither Stella nor Molly had to discourage Joe from becoming a media star because Joe had no inclination to be one.

'You can't say no to the cover of *Tatler*,' pleaded Bob Kramer, feeling slightly faint.

'Can't I?' asked Joe, smiling infuriatingly. 'But you never asked me if I wanted to be a male model.'

There was only one offer he showed any enthusiasm for. The following Tuesday, instead of dressing in his usual work clothes, Joe put on black jeans and a T-shirt.

'What are you doing?' Molly asked, intrigued. 'A spot of cat-burgling, or auditioning for "All because the lady loves Milk Tray"?'

Joe looked embarrassed. 'Actually you're pretty warm. I'm going to talk to Suzanna Morgan at the Southern Drama School. She's an old friend of Stella's.'

Too late he realized this was about the worst thing he could have said. Molly's face closed over like a shutter slamming out the sunlight.

'Come on, Moll. It's a fantastic opportunity. These ad people keep telling me I've got "presence", whatever that is. I used to love acting at school. I've got to have a shot at it.'

'Is that what Stella says?'

'I'm not sure she even knows.'

'Oh, Joe, for heaven's sake. Don't be so naive. Stella's obviously set this up. Drama schools don't just summon in writers of car manuals every day of the week and audition them. This woman probably owed Stella a favour.'

'You could be a bit happier for me,' Joe said. 'Anyway, don't worry. It'll probably come to nothing.'

'Are you really bored at work?'

'It's hardly Nobel prize-winning stuff, is it, telling people how to service their own Mondeos?'

He kissed the top of Eddie's dark head. 'You'll wish me luck, won't you, squire?'

Molly watched him go in dismay. This wasn't how she'd wanted things, Joe already feeling he'd compromised with life at the age of twenty-five. How had everything got so bloody complicated?

Joe had absolutely no idea what an audition should be like. His only ideas came from films like *A Chorus Line* or *Fame*. He was supposed to read something, he knew. Would they give him something or should he bring his own? He hadn't done enough acting at school to have a repertoire and he was screwed if he was going in for any of that Once-more-unto-the-breach stuff.

In the end he'd decided to go for poetry. At least he was familiar with that.

The Southern School of Speech and Drama was based in Brixton, next to the Ritzy Cinema. Suzanna Morgan herself came to fetch him from the porter's office and took him up to a small room. It was nothing like he'd imagined, no stage, no row of critical observers, just her. She was a surprise too, after Stella's chic flamboyance. She could have been a civil servant. She seemed surprised that he'd turned up. 'I'm sorry. I'm a bit confused. I understood from Stella that you'd changed your mind about wanting to act.'

Joe seemed so thrown she had to come to his rescue. 'Never mind. Have you brought something to read?'

'I didn't want to do Shakespeare,' Joe explained. 'I thought I'd have a crack at Marvell.'

'"To His Coy Mistress"?'

Joe felt a small thud of disappointment. From her tone he'd obviously picked a cliché. Without any conscious thought, the words of another of his favourites, John Donne's 'To His Mistress Going to Bed', a poem which was far more deeply explicit and erotic than Marvell's, came into his mind and he started to recite it.

'Come, Madam, come, all rest my powers defy,' he began, startling Suzanna with his sudden tone of sexual command. 'Until I labour, I in labour lie . . . Licence my roving hands, and let them go, Before, behind, between, above below . . . O my America! my new-found-land, My kingdom, safeliest when with one man mann'd . . .'

Suzanna, who had thought herself ready for anything, who had seen and heard almost everything, from the sentimental to the shocking, found herself taken by surprise, rather like the object of the poem she was listening to, by the powerfully seductive charm Joseph Meredith brought to the words.

The shy young man of a few minutes ago had metamorphosed into a forceful and tempting lover. The words sounded every bit as impossible to resist in this small, hot room as they must have done when they were first written.

'That wasn't "To His Coy Mistress",' she rebuked, shaken by his sexual commando tactics.

Joe grinned. 'I know, but I could see you're not much of a Marvell fan so I tried you with something a bit earthier.'

'Yes, well. So you can do the obvious stuff. See how you get on with some David Mamet.'

Suzanna listened with mounting excitement, telling herself she shouldn't jump to conclusions. All right, he was good. He seemed at first sight to possess subtlety and range, and, most important of all, the power to move his listeners. Added to his easy charm and astonishing looks it was quite a package. But she had to be hard-headed. Reading a bit of poetry hardly constituted an audition to one of the toughest acting schools in the country. He would have to come back and be seen by her colleagues doing a more conventional piece.

All the same, over the years Suzanna had seen more than five thousand hopefuls and her instincts were finely honed. Joe definitely had something. Maybe Stella was right. Acting was in the DNA after all.

'Right. Thanks. Joe, I thought your performance was terrific, but would you be prepared to come back and read again for myself and a few other people?'

'To be frank, I'd be prepared to do more or less anything you asked,' Joe confessed engagingly.

Suzanna laughed at the hackneyed casting-couch implication that could be read into his words.

To her absolute amazement, the six foot two of nigh-perfect manhood in front of her actually reddened in embarrassment as he followed her thoughts. 'I hope you didn't think I meant . . .'

'No, Joe,' she reassured him, 'I didn't think you meant that.' Actually, reflected Suzanna for about the first time she could ever remember, it was rather a pity he hadn't. 'Shall we say next Monday at two p.m.?'

Joe knew he should say no, that Mondays were the worst possible day at work and two p.m. one of the busiest times on that day. Perhaps it was an act of rebellion, a semi-deliberate spanner in the works of normality, that made him agree and decide to sort it out with Graham later.

It was only after Joe had gone that Suzanna remembered his family situation. Stella said he was married with a baby. Pity, it was much easier if students were single. It was one thing putting a passion for acting above anything else, but it could be damn tough if you had a family.

Back in her office she couldn't wait to call Stella, even though she might not be pleased.

'Stella, love, I just had to ring. I know you wanted to put me off but I've just seen your Joseph and he was brilliant. He didn't read a proper scene or anything, just some poetry, and I need a second opinion, but I think he's extraordinary. I've asked him to come in again on Monday. What's all this about him not wanting to act? He seemed pretty keen to me.'

Stella almost banged the phone down. How dare Suze see Joe after she'd asked her not to? But it was clearly too late now and she couldn't help being intrigued. 'OK. I'll come clean,' Stella admitted. 'I was the one who changed their mind. I've been interfering too much in his life. He has a wife and baby and a steady job. Maybe he should try and hang onto them.'

'Come on Stella, you don't really mean that. If he's got the acting bug it would probably have come out anyway. What if he's destined to be a talent of our times?'

'With a broken marriage and a child he never sees?'

'Oh Stella, this isn't like you! You've got to think about passion and intensity, not mortgages!'

'I don't suppose there's any chance you're wrong about him?'

'After five thousand applicants?'

Stella sighed. She could foresee trouble ahead.

On the day of Joe's second audition, Molly gave herself a lecture about being unwifely. He'd been so excited she had to face reality. If Joe got a place and desperately wanted to go to drama school, they'd have to try and find a way. All right, she'd wanted to look after Eddie herself but maybe she'd have to compromise. If she got a part-time job, even if Joe was at drama school, they could probably share looking after him. After all, actors were often around in the day, she'd seen one or two she recognized in the park with their kids. She glanced longingly over at Eddie, who was just learning to sit propped up on a pile of cushions. She really didn't want to trust him to the care of a childminder, but maybe between her and Joe, if he got in, they could work something out. After all, who said life was perfect?

Being Molly, she felt a million times better. Bitterness and introspection just weren't part of her make-up. She swooped down to pick up Eddie, feeling like an old radio with a new battery. As she lifted him, his head knocked against her breasts, making her gasp out loud in pain. It wasn't even time for her period. Unconsciously she slipped a hand down to feel them.

It couldn't be, God, let it not be, not . . . But some primitive instinct told her that it was precisely that. Breast-feeding gave you some protection against pregnancy, but lately he'd almost weaned himself.

In the post-baby stage of broken nights, sex hadn't been much on the agenda, with one or two notable exceptions. She'd been meaning to have a coil fitted, but you had to go to the doctor at the right time of the month and she'd simply forgotten.

How they'd all laughed in the maternity ward when the family planning nurse had appeared to talk about contraception to new mothers still woozy from giving birth. They'd all been in stitches, literally and metaphorically, at the very idea. None of them ever intended having sex again. If only they'd stuck to it.

She felt a cold film of sweat on her brow and her breath speeded up. If she was right and she had fallen pregnant again, Joe might see this as a deliberate trap to stop him following his dreams.

Chapter 18

For once Molly's famous resourcefulness was bugger all help. No matter how much she tried to be positive, the situation was dire.

Feeling beyond hopeless, Molly retreated to bed with a hot-water bottle and a packet of chocolate Hobnobs while Eddie gurgled on the floor and tried to eat his Duplo.

Joe came back early that evening. One look at his face told her the outcome. 'I got it,' he shouted picking Eddie up and swinging him round. 'They can offer me a place from October. Oh, Moll, I know it'll be tough but I'm sure I can freelance for Graham. Homeworking's all the thing these days. We'll be all right. I'll work like ten men.'

October! That was so soon he wouldn't even have the chance of a payoff. Graham would feel left in the lurch by someone he'd trusted. 'As a matter of fact, Graham sounded pretty pissed off when he rang earlier.'

'Oh, he'll come round. I'll persuade him it's in his interest, don't you worry.'

Joe's enthusiasm was so infectious and he looked so handsome all lit up with excitement that Molly couldn't bear to tell him her suspicions. How could she have been so careless and dimwitted?

He sat down on the edge of the bed. 'It's so incredible, Molly. I'd always done a few parts at school but I didn't know I had any real talent. These people at the drama school, they really believe in me!' He took in Molly's lack of enthusiasm. 'Do you really mind? I couldn't have gone on working for Graham for ever, you know.'

'It's just that it's all so sudden.'

Guilt made Joe defensive, and just as Molly started to tell herself she had to be more sympathetic, he blew the whole thing. 'We never really discussed it, whether we'd have children straight away. It just kind of happened.'

'Eddie just kind of happened, you mean.'

'Yes, but because you wanted to look after him you assumed I'd start on the gold watch route, but I'm not really a gold watch kind of person, am I?'

Joe finally noticed the Hobnobs and hottie and the fact that his energetic wife was actually in bed. 'Are you feeling ill? Can I get you anything? Look, I know money will be tight if I do it, but I could get an evening job too. We'll get by.'

Molly's heart dank like a stone. If he did that they'd never see him. If this offer had been next year or even in six months' time they'd have had time to save at least. Their attitude to money had always been, as Joe put it, 'To our income and beyond!' Their bank manager hadn't always seen the funny side.

She sat up, about to ask him whether there was any possibility of the drama school holding his place for a year while they got sorted out, but the phone rang and interrupted her. It was Stella asking Joe if he would accompany her to the Millennium Awards.

Suddenly it was all too much for Molly. She always seemed to be the one who was accommodating everyone else, trying to make their dreams come true, but what about her own dreams? All her feelings of being excluded and upstaged by Stella boiled over in her. She was sure Stella was behind this scheme of Joe's to throw up his job and be an actor, yet she hadn't offered any solid help, like some grandparents did. She hadn't even asked to meet her grandson and hold him. Molly came to the shocking realization that she hated Stella and wished she'd never found her.

'Yes,' she screamed when Joe came off the phone, so out of character that Joe stared, 'why don't you accompany your darling mother to the Millennium Awards? In fact, why don't you bloody well move in with her? That's what she'd really like, isn't it, her darling son back where he would have been if she hadn't made the small error of giving him away twenty-five years ago. Your new life as an actor would be far more fun without the baggage of a wife and baby. After all, you've got a big future, you don't want to be saddled with boring old responsibilities, do you?'

She picked up her hot-water bottle and flung it at him as hard as she could. Her aim had always been good and it caught him on the left temple.

'Oh yes,' he lashed back, eyes blazing, 'and I've got plenty of those, haven't I?' He thumped into Eddie's room where they kept their clothes, since there was no room for a double bed *and* a chest of drawers in their room, and tossed clothes into a sports bag. 'Fine. I'll take up your offer. At least she doesn't live in bloody Peckham!'

Molly heard the door bang shut and sobbed noisily. She hadn't even dared tell him about the newest and most unexpected of his responsibilities. Maybe she was just imagining it after all? But even as she tried to reassure herself with that thought, she felt the tenderness in her breasts that was all too recognizable.

Stella stood in front of her favourite mirror in the harsh light of her bathroom. She'd replaced the old-fashioned dressing-room-style bulbs with halogen, which seemed to illuminate every wrinkle as if it were the Grand Canyon. She was entirely naked and was holding a very convincing blonde wig which had arrived, in a beautiful hat box, together with a highly scented single rose and a copy of the script of *Dark Night and Desire*. The play's producers had invited her to meet them in three days' time.

Stella was, in many ways, her own harshest critic. She knew without Bob having to tell her that the film parts had started drying up. The theatre, at least for the moment, was kinder. She had, she reckoned, a few more years as a siren on stage.

Still standing in front of the mirror, she pinned her dark hair up as she had seen the make-up artists do, pulled a rubber cap tight over her hair to flatten it and carefully pulled on the wig. The effect was extraordinary. She felt like a different person. Luscious, amoral and sexually voracious. When she read the first line of the script, her voice had subtly altered into a caressing yet dangerous Tennessee Williams twang. Even if she thought it herself, she looked pretty damn good. And anyway, this wasn't a part, like her first Juliet all those years ago, where she had to walk across the stage totally naked. She simply had to let her clothes slip a little, and no one – certainly not any actresses ten years younger than she was, like Roxanne Wood – let their clothes slip better than she did.

She smiled gleefully at the thought of Roxanne Wood's pregnancy and how annoyed the younger actress must have been at its timing. And then another, more unwelcome thought sneaked into her mind. Who was the real winner: Stella who got the part or Roxanne who got the baby?

Stella was pondering on this when her entryphone buzzed. It was probably a minicab that had come to the wrong place.

'Hello, is that Stella? It's Joseph here.' Joe's voice threw her entirely. 'I wondered if I could come up?'

'Yes, of course. I'll press the button.'

Feeling totally ludicrous, she dashed to her bathroom and grabbed the silk shirt and trousers she'd had on before. She was still barefoot but had done up the final button when the lift doors opened.

Joe smiled shyly as he walked the few feet between the lift and her flat.

'You look amazing.' The wonder in his voice touched her so deeply she could hardly bear it. 'The blonde hair changes your eyes somehow.'

She still had the wig on. 'Oh, this stupid thing!' Before she could think about it she'd pulled it off and stood there with all her hair pinned to her head under a rubber cap. No one had ever seen her looking so ugly, except her dresser. 'God, now I'm like something out of *Alien*. The things we do for Art.'

She was feeling strangely nervous and gabbled on. 'I've got to read for a play. In a blonde wig. My agent says I shouldn't read, I'm too grand apparently, but I don't give a damn about things like that if I want a part.'

She eyed his sports bag in alarm. Perhaps he was passing through on his way to the gym. 'I'm sorry to barge in,' he apologized with a smile so disarming it would have melted the heart of even a traffic warden. 'Molly and I have just had the most God-awful fight.'

'I see.'

He followed her inside and put his bag discreetly by the door.

'Would you like a glass of wine?'

'I'd prefer a beer if you have one.'

'I'll have a look. My friend Richard has one occasionally.' She opened the fridge to reveal its magnificent emptiness. Two bottles of white wine, one of champagne and a small pack of feta cheese.

'Don't you even have any milk?'

'Only wine, I'm afraid.' She followed his astonished gaze. 'I eat out a lot and I take my coffee black.'

They sat down on opposite sofas and Joe reflected how different their lives were, his so domestic and trammelled, hers so entirely self-absorbed and full of choices.

'The thing is, I've been offered a place at the Southern and Molly thinks it's all your fault.'

Damn. Suzanna had obviously not paid a blind bit of attention to Stella's plea.

Stella felt a pang of guilt. Her mother would agree with Molly.

'It's pointless Molly blaming you,' Joe went on. 'I was getting bored out of my mind with what I was doing.'

'Did Molly know that?'

Joe looked guilty. 'We don't talk about work much.'

'Maybe she feels you've sprung this on her without any warning.'

'I suppose so,' conceded Joe. 'But Molly never used to be like that. She used to believe in passion and spontaneity.'

'Then you had a baby.'

'Surely you can have a little of both.'

'Don't ask me, Joseph. I chose freedom, remember. But I'm not sure I can recommend it.'

'I thought you at least would understand. So do you think I should pass up the offer?'

Here it was, that awful question.

'I think you should involve Molly in your decision. She'll feel differently about it then. Maybe there's a way round it. She sees acting as my thing and she doesn't like me much. I can't blame her.'

'The thing is . . .' Stella could see how difficult Joe found it to ask her a favour, and the knowledge cut into her. She was his mother. He should be able to ask her for anything. 'I wondered if I could doss down here for a day or two.'

Stella struggled with a flurry of contradictory emotions, a suspicion that it might not be fair to Molly, apprehension at her mother's reaction, uncertainty about giving up her cherished privacy. But there was one emotion which overwhelmed all the others. It was like a powerful and irresistible tidal wave: the desire to have Joe to herself and to look after him for the first time in both their lives.

'All right.' She struggled against a crazy sense of excitement at the prospect of having him there. 'But just while you and Molly try and work things out.'

'Thank you, Stella. It means a lot to me.'

'The only condition is that you have to ring Molly now and tell her where you are.'

Stella considered trying to explain to Molly that Joe coming here was for the good of their marriage, but she wasn't sure Molly would begin to understand. To Molly it would look like a betrayal. But that was something Stella was just going to have to live with.

When Claire happened to call it was like a miracle from heaven. Molly hadn't even been able to drag herself out of bed, stunned by the fact that she'd sent Joe off to Stella when what she really wanted to do was keep him away from her.

'What's happened?' Claire demanded as soon as Molly opened the door, her tear-stained face all puffy and red with crying.

'It's Joe.'

'Of course it's Joe,' Claire tried to joke. 'When is it not Joe? It's the same with all my girlfriends. Whenever you find them in pieces all over the floor, *cherchez l'homme*. What's he done this time?'

'He's left and gone to stay with Stella.'

'What happened?' Claire folded Molly into a tight embrace, patting her friend's wild red hair.

'He's had an offer from drama school and he wants to throw up his job. It's all Stella's doing, she always thought his job with Graham was far too lowly. Then she rang up to ask him to take her to some fancy awards ceremony and I lost my rag. I hated her so much. All she wants is to take him round and show him off and she doesn't give a stuff about us, and Joe's going along with it. So I told him to just go and move in with her and be done with it!'

Claire led Molly back to the bedroom. 'Look, let's have a glass of wine. Pain always seems more bearable with a Chardonnay in your hand.' She foraged in the small but pretty kitchen for a couple of glasses.

She took them back and sat down on the edge of Molly's bed. It was amazing to think that both Joe and Molly slept in this tiny bed. It was now covered with all the paraphernalia of misery: wet tissues, chocolate biscuits and a cordless telephone.

'He accused me of interfering. He said I'd been the one who really wanted to find Stella.'

'Interfering? Not you, Molly, surely?'

Molly's face crumpled.

'Sorry.' Claire reached out and took her hand. 'I shouldn't have said that. Me and my big mouth.'

'Even *you* think I'm an interfering busybody.'

'No, I don't. Honestly. You're a doer, that's all. Most people sit about complaining and never really want things to change. Or they haven't got the energy or the courage to make them change. You're not like that. It's why you're so lovable, Moll.'

'Joe doesn't think so. Maybe he didn't really want things to change either. Maybe I just thought he did.'

'Joe's a bit of a dreamer; that's probably why he fell for you, so you would *do* things for him. He knew what you were like.'

'And what did I *do*? I got pregnant.' She didn't even dare mention that she'd done it again.

'Yes, but that's being Molly again. You wanted a baby, so you had one. Look at me and most of the women I know. I'm stuck with a hopeless married man and most of my friends are married to their jobs and neurotic as hell. You were the one who went out and got what you wanted. You're the real mover and shaker. And Eddie's wonderful.'

'Oh, Claire,' suddenly Molly didn't feel like the strong one who did things any more, 'I thought finding Stella would be the answer to everything.'

'Nothing's ever the answer to everything. Besides, finding Stella's been fantastic for Joe. Any fool can see that. He's obviously been hurting for years, and you've made that right for him. He knows she loved him after all. That shone through that interview, it's why it was so touching. You've given him the greatest gift anyone could. Without you he'd still be going round with a great gaping hole inside. You're wonderful, Molly.'

'And now he's gone to her. I said he'd have a much better time without the baggage of a wife and baby and he took me at my word.'

'Don't worry. Stella will be a complete pain in the arse to live with. She's never put herself out for anyone; she probably doesn't even know how. She's had some poor boyfriend she can't commit to hovering in the background. It's admiration Stella thrives on, not real love. He'll soon find that out. She certainly won't be spoiling him with home cooking and doing his washing like most mums. I doubt Stella knows what a mixed load is.'

'There are other ways of spoiling him.'

'Corruption by fancy lifestyle, you mean?'

'Stella's world is full of first nights and famous people. I can't compete with that. Joe wants to jack in his job in October and go to drama school. In October! And we haven't got a bean in the bank. It's all Stella's doing. She got him the audition at the Southern. This has got her fingerprints all over it. She always hated his job. She's making him into someone suitable to be Stella Milton's son.'

'Do you really want to know what I think?' Claire knew she was taking her life in her hands here. Friends didn't always want to know harsh truths. 'I think you're going to have to let him go for a while, in order to get him back. What about this drama school idea? It'll be tough, I know, but Joe does have something special about him. She was right about that. He was never really cut out to be a motoring hack.'

Claire's words bit into Molly, but she knew the pain came from facing something she already knew. Had her own desire for a home and security made her not want to see the truth? That Joe was never really happy in what he was doing, and that it was nothing to do with finding Stella?

'I mean, he must be good,' Claire went on. 'The Southern is a tough number. They wouldn't actually offer a *place* just because of Stella. They've got too much at stake. Has it ever struck you that Joe might be really talented?'

Molly was shocked to find that she hadn't really considered that. 'I suppose I saw acting as being Stella's thing, and Joe wanting to do it simply as choosing her over me.'

'Maybe he might want to act *and* have you. I can see it'll be hard, though. You depend on his income, don't you? And you always wanted to be with Eddie. Perhaps he could wait till Eddie's a bit older.'

'Except for one thing.' Molly suddenly slumped down against the pillows. 'I'm pretty sure I'm pregnant again, and Joe doesn't even know.'

'Ah.' Claire let out a deep breath of frustrated solidarity. Even she hadn't got a solution to this one. 'You poor thing, you really are up shit creek, aren't you?'

Chapter 19

Claire was right. Joe did find staying with Stella unsettling. He lay in Stella's luxurious spare bedroom, between crisp cotton sheets, not sleeping and half listening out for Eddie. He missed them both. But he knew this rift was a deep one. Secretly he hoped Molly would ring, yet he knew she would probably be too proud to do so. He was an adult now and he couldn't expect either Molly or Stella to make decisions for him.

This was down to him.

Stella's life was wildly different from theirs. He hadn't imagined himself as particularly domesticated, but he could at least make an omelette. But Stella didn't even have eggs. She never had milk or bread either. Joe hadn't imagined a world where you ate every meal out, even breakfast. But Stella claimed she never ate breakfast anyway.

He discovered a Tesco Metro a few hundred yards away, whose existence Stella was totally unaware of and from which he bought a few basics.

'Aren't you amazing?' Stella marvelled, her voice brimming over with admiration and wonder, as if he'd just discovered the source of the Nile rather than a late-night supermarket.

'Don't you ever eat at home?' he asked, moving the feta cheese and champagne to accommodate milk, butter and cheese.

'Not if I can help it. I'm either dieting, in which case I don't eat anything, or I eat out.'

Joe opened a packet of Clusters and looked for a cereal bowl.

'I don't have any,' Stella pointed out gaily. 'Use a cup.'

She stole a mouthful. 'These are delicious.'

Joe wandered round with his cup of breakfast, studying Stella's expensively minimalist sitting room. She had fewer knick-knacks than anyone he'd ever come across. Molly was the opposite. She collected mementoes everywhere she went, from days out on Southend Pier to beer mats from pubs they'd drunk in as students. She'd once confessed she'd kept the condom wrapper from the first time they'd made love.

At the back of one of Stella's beautifully crafted built-in book-shelves, he noticed the tiny sock that had once been his. Stella had tucked it into a small glass frame. The image of Eddie's fuzzy dark head flashed into his mind, and now, looking at that small sock, he yearned to hold his little son.

He turned sharply to Stella, a blinding question suddenly occur-ring to him. 'You've never said much about my father. It's as if he didn't exist.'

Stella, startled, dropped a glass of the orange juice Joe had just bought down her white silk dressing gown. She looked away, avoiding his eyes. She ought to tell him now, but she couldn't bear how much he would hate her, that she might lose him just when she was getting to know and love him. When she had a horrible decision to make, Stella had always been a coward who took the line of least resistance. She did the same thing now.

'He hardly did exist.' Her voice was so soft he could barely hear it. 'It was just a brief thing. I was so young and inexperienced I didn't realize what was happening until it was too late.'

'Did he know?' Joe had forgotten he was still holding the frame with the tiny sock in it. 'About me, I mean?'

Stella's voice seemed to fade even further, as if someone had turned down the volume. 'I didn't tell him. I felt it was my decision.' Her eyes fastened on to Joe's. 'I'm so sorry. He wouldn't have been much of a father.'

'Just like me.'

The pain in his voice cut into Stella like the blade of a sharpened knife. This was her fault. The sense of loss and failure and devastation in Joseph's tone. She had taken the decision, expecting not to feel the guilt. It had seemed so simple all those years ago. Motherhood just wasn't for her. All that leaking and oozing and exhaustion.

In the end the decision to give him up had been relatively straightforward. Of course, it had hurt at the beginning, but over the years there had been only the occasional manageable twinge. Nothing that could have prepared her for this.

It was only on meeting Joseph, and loving Joseph, that the tide turned and drowned her. Now she could see for the first time the enormity of what she'd done.

The realization that before Joseph she had never loved anyone, not even her own mother, hit her like a terrifying blaze of lightning. Love hurt, she saw, and there was no getting away from it. She wanted to turn to Joseph and hold him so that nothing could ever hurt him again.

A sudden sense of nausea flooded through her. There was something he didn't know that could hurt him very much indeed, and she hoped to God he would never find it out.

'What would you like to do today?' she asked, swiftly manoeuvring the conversation away from the terrifying rapids. 'Or do you have to go to work on Saturdays?'

'No. Only in a crisis.'

'Then let's have lunch together. Then we can go and get you something to wear for the awards tomorrow. Unless, that is, you slipped a dinner jacket into your sports bag.'

'I don't have a dinner jacket kind of life.'

The statement, obviously true, made him think of Molly and the life he did have. Suddenly he missed her optimism and her capacity to make so much out of so little. By now she would be awake and would have taken Eddie into bed with her.

Without saying anything to Stella, he picked up the phone extension and dialled their number. He was startled to find that the machine was on. His disappointment at hearing his own voice instead of Molly's was devastating. He couldn't bring himself to leave a message, but hoped, ludicrously, that Molly might dial 1471 and know it was him. Perhaps even call him back.

But Molly was either out or too pissed off with him, and no call came.

'Right,' Stella said brightly. 'Ready to go?' She tried to contain the fizzling sense of ludicrous excitement she felt at actually going out, alone, with her son and having him all to herself.

Ignoring the lift, they skipped down the stairs and out into the Piazza. It was mid-morning and the place was already packed with shoppers and tourists, browsing the market stalls for silly gifts to take home, clothes-buying in Hobbs, or filling up brown paper bags of wonderful exploding bath salts from Blush.

They ate croissants from a stall, and Stella took him to the lower level to show him the wonderful shop full of mechanical toys. A gaggle of small boys had their noses pressed up against the window, reminding her painfully of what Joe would have been like at a similar age.

Then they set off across the Piazza, arm in arm. Stella had never felt happier in her life.

As they sauntered, Joe realized with a shock that he'd never actually walked down the street with Stella before. It was a strange experience. Everyone noticed her. Some people recognized her openly; others glanced slyly sideways or nudged their friends.

Stella stared directly ahead.

'The trick is never to catch anyone's eyes,' she whispered. 'That way you can pretend it's not happening.'

'Do you ever get used to it?' Joe asked, appalled.

She laughed one of her sexier laughs. 'Actually, I rather like it.

Isn't that a terrible confession?' And as she said it, Stella realized it was the sad truth.

Lunch was enormous fun. Stella laughed and drank and half flirted sometimes with Joe and sometimes with the waiters, who were about his age. At first he'd found it disconcerting – she was his mother, after all – until he understood that flirting was simply Stella's normal means of communication. It was, he saw, another of her distancing devices. She didn't like engaging with serious things. Maybe she saved that for her work.

It was almost four when they finally left the restaurant.

'Right,' Stella insisted, taking his arm, 'where shall we start? If you don't have a DJ I'd love to buy you one.'

'I'd rather hire one. My life isn't exactly littered with black tie occasions.'

'Only if you'll let me buy you something else.'

It was a curious sensation, going shopping with Stella. Pat had always sent him off to Burton's with Andrew and a detailed description of what they had to buy. Molly bought him loud but funny ties to brighten up his taste for black, but otherwise he rarely thought about his appearance.

The dress hire shop was in Exeter Street, its window decorated with a James Bond-style arrangement featuring a dummy in a white tuxedo plus a touching attempt at Ursula Andress with a knife in her bikini. The mannequin was so ancient she even managed to make Ursula Andress seem young.

'No,' Stella shook her head, 'white tuxedos are too tacky. How about a kilt?'

Joe fell about laughing. 'I'm about as Scottish as roast beef and Yorkshire pudding! Absolutely no way.'

'It'll just have to be a boring old dinner jacket then. Come on.'

The sales assistant took one look at Joe and beamed. Rarely did he get a customer worthy of his loving attention to detail and creative flair. Today it looked as if his luck had changed.

'He thinks his ship has come in,' whispered Stella. 'Most of his customers are probably flabby old gentlemen.'

Much to the salesman's disappointment, Joe turned down all suggestions of a tartan silk ensemble, a Mr Darcy-style ruffled shirt and a satin waistcoat, and opted for a simple black DJ, white shirt and blue bow-tie. 'Hang on a minute, sir,' implored the salesman. 'Just one little touch.' He reappeared with an indigo silk cummerbund. 'Just the shade of sir's eyes,' he breathed. 'If you don't mind me saying so.'

'I do mind you saying so.' Joe looked as if he might expire with embarrassment.

'But I don't,' cooed Stella. She stood at his side, her eyes fixed on his in the mirror. She caught sight of herself next to him, and the likeness between them hit her like a brick in the windpipe.

It should have been pure pleasure: a mother and son, as similar as if they had been turned from the same mould. Instead it was agonizing. For twenty-five years she could have enjoyed seeing him grow, been there when he cut his knee. For all that time, when Joe was becoming himself, she could have been part of his emotional landscape, knowing him better than any other human being could. But she had thrown all that away, like some savage discarding a precious stone, without appreciating its value. If only she could have rolled back the years, it would have been worth it at any price. Now, twenty-five years later, it seemed the most tragic loss she could conceive of.

To hide her agony she pretended to study a glass cabinet displaying cuff links. One pair, representing the two Greek masks of tragedy and comedy, caught her eye. They somehow symbolized her own inner turmoil. She asked the salesman to get them out.

'Here,' she said to Joe, 'just what you need for tomorrow.' She pushed back his sleeve to find the buttonhole of his hired white shirt. As she did so, she exposed a small blemish on the inside of his left wrist, the slight darkening of the skin she hadn't seen for twenty-five years.

Stella thought she might quite literally die. The pain that pulsed through her stopped her from breathing or speaking. She was transported back to that moment when she had first been handed her baby. She had taken him unwillingly, not wanting to bond, and then, almost against her will, she had opened his shawl and seen his dark perfection, the black peak of hair, the cloudy navy eyes, the long eyelashes and that tiny mark on his inner wrist.

And another, even more painful barb twisted into the opened wound of her loss. Why had he really left Molly and come to stay with her? Had her selfishness made him into someone who found loving difficult, just as she did?

She would make it up to him. She would love him so much that the damage she'd done all those years ago would have to heal under the sheer power of her devotion. But in some hidden, honest part of herself, buried away under the layers of self-deception, she knew that life wasn't as easy as that.

She made herself do up the cuff links and pull his sleeve down to blot out that little blemish.

'Great. Thank you.' Joe kissed her on the cheek, unaware of the deep river of her pain. 'Thank you, Stella. They're fantastic.'

Stella noticed, with a sudden shock, that he always called her Stella, never Mum or Mother.

Outside in the street, Joe turned to her. 'You're not to argue, but I want to get you something too. Why don't I see you back at the flat in about an hour?'

Stella wandered through the Piazza, smiling like an idiot. She even stopped and watched the line of robot imitators, five or six of them, all painted different colours from chalk white to bronze and silver. What a way to make a living! Standing stock still for hours on end, with only the tiniest, barely imperceptible jerky movements to show that they were alive, in exchange for a meagre pittance and the dubious glow of feeling that they were entertainers. And this was the road she'd selfishly encouraged Joe down.

In one of the back streets she came across an Italian deli she'd never seen before, perhaps because of her habit of never buying food and travelling everywhere in taxi. The thought struck her

217

that she and Joe could stay in tonight and that she could actually cook for him. Stella's concept of cooking, it had to be admitted, consisted of buying every salami in the place, a sliver of eight different cheeses, four kinds of olives, sundried tomatoes and ciabatta.

'Now,' she announced, eyes glowing like a priest's in an off-licence, 'how about the main course?'

'We've got some nice fresh pasta,' offered the young man behind the counter, salivating at the thought of who he was serving and what a tale it would make later. 'How many is it for?'

'Just two.'

'We've also got a nice putanesca sauce, home-made,' he suggested. 'You know putanesca means . . .' He stopped and reddened, realizing what he'd got himself into.

'Prostitute,' supplied Stella. 'My usual role.' This wasn't quite true, but it was the public perception of her. 'I'll have a tub of that and two portions of the tiramisu, please.'

Stella took her two bulging bags and headed through the throngs of tourists, out-of-towners on their way to shows, and schoolgirls giggling outside Accessorize in the Piazza. The thought that she had someone to go home to, to cook for, maybe even to iron shirts for, filled her with delicious excitement.

At home she had a mantelshelf full of invitations, most from people or organisations she didn't really know, but who wanted the cachet of Stella Milton coming to their party. It was bliss that she could ignore them all and spend the evening with Joe.

He wasn't back when she got home, so she had the chance to unpack her booty and keep it as a surprise. She could hardly believe how much fun it was to put on a pinny and prepare a meal for someone else.

She was halfway through laying out the olives, salami and cheese on a platter, whistling to herself at the same time, when she stopped short. The tune that had come into her mind was 'Molly Malone'. The pleasure drained out of her like a spilt wineglass. Joe oughtn't to be here. She was being selfish, not genuinely loving. Even after all this time, she was taking not giving.

The phone rang, jangling through her consciousness like the wail of a siren. For a moment it seemed so loud it paralysed her.

It was her mother.

'Stella, what on earth are you doing?' Bea's tones accused her across the miles as clearly as if she were standing two inches away. 'Molly's just told me that she and Joe have quarrelled and he's staying with you. That's quite wrong. A mother should never get between husband and wife. I know it's been wonderful finding Joseph, but you've got to send him home.'

Stella, who had been within a gnat's breath of deciding this for herself, felt instantly mutinous. Why did her mother think she had the right to tell her what to do, or that Stella was incapable of coming to a moral decision on her own?

'I'm taking him to the Millennium Awards tomorrow. It's my big night and I want him to share it. At the moment I'm not prepared to think beyond that.'

'I wish you'd reconsider. Stella, darling, you're far too glamorous, you don't know the impact you can have. You're turning that boy's head. Molly tells me he's got a bee in his bonnet about acting now, and it's all to do with you.'

'It's more than a bee in his bonnet. And actually I tried to discourage him, but Suzanna Morgan says he's got real talent. Maybe I'm doing him a favour.'

'And maybe you're not. Ninety-five per cent of actors are unemployed, as you well know, and the successful ones turn into sociopaths like you and me who travel the world or give our children away. Of course Molly's worried about him wanting to act. Acting's a disease. I'm very glad I'm over it.'

'Balls.' Stella wasn't taking this lying down. 'If the National Theatre offered you a nice little cameo you'd jump at it. In fact, if the Bexhill Pavilion offered you Widow Twankee you'd jump at it.'

'That isn't the point, Stella. The point is that you're coming between Joe and Molly.'

'But it's so wonderful having him here.'

'You should have thought of that before you gave him away,'

Bea pointed out brutally. 'You must make him go back to Molly. Molly gives him the steadiness you didn't. She's a resourceful young woman and she loves him.'

'I don't know whether I can.'

'Stella, darling, if there's one thing I've learned, it's that loving someone means doing the best thing for that person, no matter how it hurts.'

'Come on, Ma,' Stella replied waspishly, 'stop sounding like a greetings card.'

The conversation was cut short by the arrival of Joe holding a big gift-wrapped parcel. 'Ma, I've got to go,' Stella whispered, 'Joseph's back. I'll think about what you said, I promise.'

In Lower Ditchwell, Bea sat in her chair under the apple tree and thought hard. Stella had never sounded so happy. It seemed as if she'd finally discovered that loving someone else made you happier than loving yourself. What a catastrophe that it happened to be twenty-five years too late.

Bea thought about the two women in Joe's life: his mother and his wife. How unfair for Molly to find herself eased out of her own life by Stella's seductiveness. What was worse, Bea decided gloomily, was that she suspected Stella rather enjoyed the fact that she outshone Molly so effectively. Yet the reality was that Stella's glamour was a cloak for her inadequacies. Molly, who didn't bother to make the most of her own appearance, was actually a stronger person underneath. Somehow Bea had to find a way of opening Joseph's eyes to what he already had.

Molly was beautiful too; it was just that she chose to downplay it. Perhaps she should stop hiding her attractions under all those tomboy layers and give Stella a run for her money. It was time Joe noticed that it wasn't Stella who held all the cards.

As she sat in her shady garden, where she'd chosen to retreat and tend flowers instead of actors' egos, an idea came to Bea which made her laugh out loud.

She might be a sad old bat buried in deepest Sussex, but she still had her contacts, and not all of them were dead. Yet.

Bea fetched her ancient address book. By fair means – or possibly foul – she was going to have a table at the Millennium Awards to share the honour about to be bestowed on her daughter – and to make sure that Molly got the chance to remind Joe that she was a stunning young woman as well as his wife.

But first she had to find something for Molly to wear, something so stunning and yet so subtle it would put Stella in the shade, which, if she knew Stella, would take some doing.

On the spur of the moment she called Stella back.

'Stella, darling, I know it's your big night tomorrow and I wanted to mark it with a corsage for you. What are you going to be wearing? I assume you've already decided.' Since clothes were Stella's passion, it was a fair assumption that she had spent weeks coming to this decision.

Stella found the sudden change of tone from stern to saccharine deeply suspicious. Her mother was behaving very strangely indeed. 'My red satin,' Stella said guardedly.

'The backless, sideless one held together with the odd bit of chain? Or the backless, sideless one with the halter neck?' Bea enquired, trying not to sound gleeful. It didn't really matter which; both were wonderfully tasteless. It was strange how Stella could have an unerring knack for daywear, and yet give her a smart occasion and the whore won over the madonna every time.

'The halter neck.'

'Would you like an orchid? Or a white camellia like Greta Garbo?'

'Ma, I don't want to be rude, but corsages went out with the Coronation. People only wear them to weddings in Sidcup.'

'Ah. Would you prefer a bunch of flowers for your flat instead?'

'That would be lovely.' Stella decided she ought not to be so ungracious. 'Thank you, Ma, it's a really nice thought.'

Bea felt the tiniest flash of guilt. Still, she reminded herself, Stella was behaving with complete insensitivity and it had to be stopped.

For the next hour Bea rang dozens of people, calling in favours, reminding important figures in the industry that their fathers or mothers had been her bosom buddy (even if she'd actually hated them). Eventually, she'd achieved what she wanted.

All she had to do now was talk Molly into it.

As it happened, Molly had been through the whole emotional range that day, from fury to despair. She had even considered lobbing a brick through Stella's window, except that Stella's windows were so high it would probably have fallen back to earth and hit Molly instead. She'd been rescued from the more extreme of her fantasies by the arrival of Claire with a bottle of wine and a box of feminist fortune cookies, every one guaranteed a put-down.

When the doorbell rang, hope surged in Molly that it might be Joe, bashful and contrite, with a bunch of flowers and his sports bag.

The last person on earth she was expecting was Stella's mother, wearing what appeared to be fancy dress, plus a floppy straw hat, clutching a plastic suit carrier and smiling beatifically.

'Hello, Molly dear. I know you're not expecting me. A bit of a surprise. Can I come in?'

'Of course.' Molly stood back, Eddie on her hip. 'This is my friend Claire, the one who did the interview with Joe and Stella in the paper.'

'Nice to meet you.'

There was something extraordinarily cheering about Bea's arrival. In spite of her eccentric appearance, Beatrice Manners exuded no-nonsense confidence. Somehow when Bea was on the scene you felt, as in one of those comforting Agatha Christies with Miss Marple, that things were going to take a turn for the better.

'How are you holding up in this horrid mess, darling? I'm so glad your friend's here.' The genuine sympathy in Bea's voice was Molly's undoing. Tears flooded down her face, blurring her mascara and making her hiccup with misery.

'We were just considering chucking a brick through Stella's window, as a matter of fact.'

Bea held out her arms and Molly buried herself in the older woman's bony embrace.

'I've got a better idea,' Bea announced. 'My daughter is behaving disgracefully and I can't apologize for her enough. But it's time we *did* something. All this silliness has gone on too long.' She took off her coat and led the two of them to the sofa. 'What a lovely room. You have fabulous taste, my dear.' She dropped her voice. 'Much better than Stella's. Now look, Molly, it's time you and I started fighting back. In Stella's defence, I think she's genuinely found she loves Joseph, but being Stella, she thinks he's come gift-wrapped just for her. She's simply forgotten your existence. And I think the way we should remind her, pathetic though it may be, is by you proving you're not someone who can just be pushed aside when it suits her.'

'Right on,' endorsed Claire, raising her arm in a mock Che Guevara salute.

'You mean I can throw the brick after all?' asked Molly, brightening.

'I totally sympathize, but as a matter of fact I've got a subtler scheme. And more deadly.' She opened the suit carrier and removed two dresses. One of them was pale cream silk which fell in soft, shimmering folds. 'This one's for me. It's Givenchy. An original. I know that because I had it made in 1935. It cost three thousand pounds even then, but given the number of times I've worn it, it's probably better value than something from Miss Selfridge.'

She shook out a second dress. This one was black and slender, a beaded column dress with a single shoulder strap. 'It doesn't look much on the hanger, but believe me, when it's got a body inside, it's a wow. Especially with your body. I was always too flat in the chest department and had to wear falsies. Here, try it on.'

Bea took Eddie from Molly's arms and put him down on the floor. Then she handed him the wooden cane with an ivory fox's-head

223

handle that she'd brought with her. 'That should keep him quiet, for a minute or two anyway. Now, slip it on, Molly, while the going's good.'

Shyly at first – after all, she hardly knew Bea – Molly removed her Caterpillar boots, her dungarees and lastly her plain white T-shirt. She stood, blushing slightly, in her bra and pants.

'When you've toured in all the countries I have, with a quick change for every act and God-awful facilities, you get to see more bosoms than the editor of *Playboy*.' She winked outrageously. 'And not just bosoms, either. You soon get to know who's a natural blonde, I can tell you. I'm afraid a bra's out of the question with this frock.'

Molly removed her bra as ordered and wiggled into the dress. It slipped up easily as far as her hips, then stuck. 'Oh God, I've put on so much weight since Eddie, I'm like a bloody hippopotamus trying to get into a size eight tutu!'

Bea looked momentarily defeated, then, brightening, she delved into the lining of the dress and removed two safety pins. 'I remember now. I was in India and I'd had a touch of Delhi belly. It was falling off me.'

Without the pins the dress slipped over Molly's hips as if it had been made for her. Bea zipped it up and stood back to give her opinion.

'My God. On me, people just looked at the dress. On you, it's the body they'll notice. You are a very lovely girl, you know. At least you will be when we've done this.' She pulled off the double scrunchie Molly always used to keep her luxuriant hair under control and it billowed in red waves round Molly's lightly freckled shoulders.

'My God, Mol,' marvelled Claire, stunned, 'you're Rita Hayworth to the life!'

Molly peeped at herself in the mirror and almost gasped. She looked as she'd never looked in her whole life before. The slinky one-shouldered dress both clung to and somehow supported her newly voluptuous breasts without the need for a bra, and her loosened hair lent her an air of luxurious sexual promise. She looked like one of those Burne-Jones models who enslaved nineteenth-century painters with their erotic wiles, and made them abandon their respectable wives and families for a life of dangerous passion.

'I know you modern girls probably think this is all a bit ante-diluvian, but it's time you used a bit of that sex appeal of yours to remind him that Stella doesn't have a franchise on it.'

'I never see myself as having sex appeal,' laughed Molly, as fascinated by her new appearance as Bea was. 'I'm Managing Molly who'll sort it all out.'

'And look where that got you,' teased Bea. 'Time for a new image, definitely. How about Man-Eating Molly, or maybe in this case Mother-in-Law-Eating Molly.'

'It's weird, though, isn't it?' Molly frowned. 'I mean, it's almost as if I were competing for him sexually.'

'That's the only way Stella knows how to respond. The sad thing for Stella is that I suspect she *has* no genuinely sexual feelings. In Stella's case, what you see is what you *don't* get.'

Bea lifted Eddie up and faced him towards his mother. 'What do you think of Mum's new look? Good enough to eat, eh?'

At which point Eddie stretched his chubby hands towards Molly's boobs.

'Sorry,' laughed Bea gaily. 'I could have put that better, couldn't I? By the way, do you think I could stay here tonight? It seems a frightful performance to have to go back and forth to Sussex.'

'Beatrice,' Molly acknowledged, meaning every word, 'it would be a pleasure.'

And it was. The wine was finished so Bea and Claire tripped down to the corner shop and managed to extract two halfway decent bottles from Mr Sawalha which no one suspected he stocked.

'They were round the back,' Claire explained. 'I think he was quite attached to them, but when Bea regaled him with her success in *Salad Days* at the Rangoon Palace, he refused to sell us any of the stuff on the shelves and insisted we take these. I think they're really rather good.'

Molly raided the fridge and impressed herself by knocking up a pasta sauce using a pound of tomatoes and the last of the droopy basil leaves from the plant on her windowsill. It reminded her of that poem by Keats she'd always loved: 'Isabella, or the Pot of Basil'. Poor Isabella's lover Lorenzo had been killed by her jealous brothers and she cut off his head and planted it in a pot of basil. Maybe Molly should do the same with Stella's. This gruesome but pleasurable thought sustained her as she chopped onions – and for once didn't cry – throwing in some coriander for good measure.

'I hope you like pasta,' Molly called gaily, coming back into the sitting room to join them.

'My dear, when you've travelled like me you can eat anything. Curries in India, dim sum in China, noodles in Singapore, dried fish in Thailand, sheep's eyes in Afghanistan. I've been to more out-posts of the Empire than Dr Livingstone.'

'You must have had a fascinating life,' said Claire.

'Yes. But it wasn't what I wanted really. I would rather George had been able to get a job here, but his range wasn't wide. When the musical comedies had had their day, so had George. So travel-ling abroad was our only way of keeping working. I thought I was doing my best, but it wasn't good for Stella. She was a lonely child, and now she's a lonely adult, despite all the fans.' She raised her glass. 'Not like you and me. We're blessed with energy and drive. If we feel lonely we do something.'

'Pity the thing we do isn't always very sensible,' sighed Molly. 'Like finding long-lost mothers.'

Bea took her hand. 'Perhaps something would have happened anyway. Joseph has to work out what it is he wants from life.' She winked outrageously. 'We've just got to make sure we nudge him in the right direction. And if anyone can, you can. I think Joseph is a very lucky young man.'

Molly raised her own glass, feeling wildly cheered. 'Well, it's about bloody time he saw it.'

Bea smiled delightedly. Her granddaughter-in-law was finally beginning to sound like she'd get somewhere. 'We'll drink to that, won't we, Claire? In fact,' she smiled the smile she'd kept for adversities from Shanghai to Newfoundland, 'I think Mr Sawalha would approve of us opening the second bottle.'

The next day Mrs Salaman, Molly's downstairs neighbour, was only too thrilled to look after Eddie, and Molly found herself in the unusual yet rather delightful situation of dressing up like a starlet on the cover of *Hello!* magazine at 2.30 in the afternoon.

'Are you sure we aren't going to look absolutely ridiculous?' she asked Bea anxiously.

'You wait,' promised Bea.

'You're going to knock 'em dead.' Claire hugged her. 'I only wish I were there to see it.'

'I'll take pictures,' promised Bea.

Going to the Millennium Awards that afternoon was one of the strangest yet most exciting experiences Molly had ever had. They arrived in a taxi at the back of the Grosvenor House Hotel in swish Park Lane to find a long line of limos disgorging their starry occupants in front of a sea of photographers all jostling each other to get the best pictures.

Molly put one foot tentatively out of the taxi and found herself faced with a long red carpet that stretched for what seemed like miles to the entrance of the hotel. On one side was a huge bank of photographers about two hundred strong. On the other was a line of TV cameras and their just-out-of-kindergarten-looking presenters. Molly suddenly knew how Moses must have felt when God cleared a path through the Red Sea. Except that Molly had to fight the temptation to get straight back in the taxi and stay in Egypt.

'Smile!' hissed Bea, more experienced at the demands of celebrity, taking her firmly by the arm.

The cameras flashed even though, as far as Molly knew, they had absolutely no idea who she was.

'Could we have some of the young lady on her own?' demanded a young snapper in the front row.

Bea retreated, smiling delightedly. 'Come on, Molly, remember why you're here. Pose as if your life depended on it!'

Suddenly the whole thing seemed incredibly funny to Molly: the ludicrousness of fame and the need these men – for they were all men – had for fresh meat, not really caring who she was. She began to pose as if she really were a starlet eager to make it into the gossip columns.

'Great!' congratulated one of them. 'Shoulders back! Toss your hair a little, let's see you shake that glorious hair!'

Molly obliged.

'Who did you say you were?' asked one of them when they'd stopped snapping.

Before Molly had the chance to admit the truth, Bea had a brain-wave. 'She's Stella Milton's daughter-in-law. The wife of her long-lost son. You probably read about it in the papers.'

At the sudden hint of a story, and hence saleability, they started snapping again furiously.

At that moment, the stretchiest of stretch limos arrived and the photographers swivelled their lenses to capture what looked like the catch of the night. In a blaze of flashes, Stella herself stepped smiling from the car.

Red satin wasn't the best colour for mid-afternoon, especially teamed with sunglasses. Stella had clearly had a recent hairdo and her hair, usually a soft dark brown, had taken on a hard blue tone. In the blinding afternoon sun, there was more than a suggestion of Morticia Addams.

'Stella! Stella!' shrieked the photographers. 'This way!'

With exaggerated calm, every languid movement designed to convey that it was she who was in charge, Stella turned first one side of her face, then the other, towards the cameras.

'A couple with your son, Stella!'

Stella's smile of absolute possession, as she entwined her arms around Joe, made Molly, as yet still unnoticed by her mother-in-law, want to hit her.

'And how about,' one of the more enterprising photographers quested, turning back towards Molly and Bea, 'a quick snap with your lovely daughter-in-law?'

In that glorious, crazy instant Molly knew there had to be a God after all. She would treasure the expression on Stella's face for the rest of her life. It was a heady cocktail of stunned amazement and frozen horror, with just a spritz of jealousy.

'Molly!' Joe exclaimed, stunned. 'What on earth are you doing here? And where on earth did you get that amazing dress?'

'We hired it,' insisted Bea firmly before Molly could reveal it was one of Bea's old costumes.

'But why are you here?'

Molly's confidence was growing by the second. 'To see you, of course, and to watch my mother-in-law get her award.'

'As a matter of fact,' Bea announced grandly, 'we were invited by Sir Ronald Wood.'

Stella gaped. Sir Ronald Wood was the grand old man of British theatre, father of the recently pregnant Roxanne, whom Stella hoped to replace in *Dark Night and Desire*. 'But you don't even know him.'

More famous faces were arriving behind them and they had to break up the traffic jam they were creating on the red carpet. 'Yes I do.' Bea smiled infuriatingly. 'In fact we were quite close at one time.' She didn't add that she had begged, cajoled and finally given a hefty donation to the Theatrical Benevolent Society to get her hands on two places at Sir Ronald's table, and that the two people who had been ceremoniously dropped would probably never speak to her again. 'See you at the party afterwards. You know, Stella,' she added, 'red doesn't really suit you. It makes you look like a tart on a sofa.'

'And you're as sour as an old yogurt!' snapped Stella. 'You should look in the mirror yourself, you old bat.'

Bea and Molly swept into the ballroom, helping themselves to a glass of champagne as they went in. Molly tried not to gawp as famous face after famous face swanned by, quite often stopping to say hello to Bea as they passed.

'I must do this more often,' Bea commented wryly, 'while I'm still alive to enjoy it.'

Across the other side of the room, Stella looked livid and Joe sheepish. To Bea's delight he kept glancing over at Molly, as if he were desperate to talk to her but didn't know what to say.

When Bea was halfway through yet another conversation with a long-lost friend, Molly went across to him.

'I'm sorry about all this. It was Bea's idea.'

'You looked as if you were enjoying yourself.'

'I was. I mean, this isn't my world, but it's fun to watch.'

'You're looking incredible.'

'Thank you. All part of Bea's plan to annoy Stella and show you both I'm not just a mousy little housewife you can walk all over.'

Joe looked serious. 'I don't think anyone who knows you would mistake you for a mousy housewife, least of all me.' Molly found herself smiling. And then he went and spoiled it. 'A heat-seeking missile, perhaps . . .'

Molly was suddenly white-hot with fury. Joe didn't seem to have learned much in their days apart. 'Oh, just get lost, why don't you? At least I *do* something about life. You tell me you've been unhappy working for Graham, but it took me finding Stella for you to notice. I was the mover in our relationship because you just swim with the tide. Even this audition for drama school was because Stella organized it for you. You've walked out on me and Eddie, apparently, although even that isn't clear, and gone straight to Mum to be idolized. At least my motives were reasonable. It strikes me yours are just selfish.'

The dress helped. So did the hair. They gave Molly the courage to turn dramatically on her heel and leave him to it.

'Well done,' congratulated Bea when Molly flopped down next to her at their table. 'That told him.'

Molly glanced back at Joe to find him standing alone, as uncomfortable as she was. She was tempted to get up and run to him, grab his hand and make for the exit. But she'd been the decision-maker too often. This time it was his turn. He had to make it clear that it was she and Eddie he wanted.

Joe looked as if the same thought might be going through his mind and Molly's spirits rose like the fizz in her glass of champagne, but just as he took a step towards them, the Master of Ceremonies announced that the Millennium Awards were about to take place.

Stella had always felt there were far too many award ceremonies, with too much back-patting and showing-off, but tonight, with so many familiar faces here and Joe at her side, she wouldn't have minded it going on forever. Even her irritation at her mother's outrageous behaviour in getting herself invited and then holding court like an ageing courtesan on one of the most influential tables in the room didn't matter.

Famous faces were buzzing like sycophantic flies round the Wood coterie, and shots of their star-studded table would be caught by the TV cameras all evening. Well, they were all in for a surprise that would knock the smug smiles off their faces.

Stella had to admit that Molly did look quite attractive. She glanced at her own reflection in the mirrored column behind her.

Damn Bea, she was right as usual: red was too obvious a colour to be wearing. At an occasion like this she should be acting like the respected wife, not the slutty mistress.

Tomorrow, her choice of outfit would be torn apart in the newspapers and on daytime television. When poor Sarah Killen, another vampish actress of Stella's vintage, had worn a stunning minidress, which admittedly hadn't left much to the imagination, the newspapers had run double-page spreads asking readers whether she was too old to get away with it.

Feeling more sensitive than she wanted to admit, Stella helped herself to a glass of wine and leaned towards Joe. 'Not long now.'

In fact, the string of awards took up well over an hour. And then, at last, her moment had come. She heard the MC start to announce the award: 'And finally, to mark the Millennium and to celebrate Britain as a vital part of Europe, the industry would like to congratulate one of its most alluring – and enduring – exports . . .'

'He's making me sound like corned beef,' hissed Stella, causing Joe to start giggling.

'. . . star of stage and film, our very own – Stella Milton!'

Stella rose graciously to her feet, ignoring the fact that only several cobwebby straps, already straining on their moorings, were keeping up her dress, and walked up to the platform.

'Before we give you the award, Stella, we'd like to show a few brief extracts of the films that have made you famous,' the MC grinned in a misguided attempt to be saucy, ' and occasionally infamous!'

Stella tried not to look as the clips appeared. She knew exactly which they would be: *Family Ties*, *The French Mistress* and of course *Deceptive Bends*. There they were again, the boobs that launched a million poster sales, encased in skin-tight leather.

'That film was shot,' the MC continued gallantly, 'impossible though it is to believe, nearly twenty years ago. And now I'd like to present you, Stella, with the Millennium Award for enhancing our industry with your presence, your glamour and your talent. Thank you, Stella Milton!'

After the applause had died down, Stella smiled. 'I thought I was going to get my gold watch for distinguished long service tonight. I'm not *that* old, you know.' She turned directly to the camera. 'Sorry, chaps, I'm about to throw out your running orders because, contrary to habit, I'm going to make a speech.'

The TV cameramen looked at each nervously. It was a live performance, timed to the last second. This was going to be hairy.

Stella ignored them. 'I'm thrilled to get this award because I've been incredibly lucky in my career. To have a career as successful as mine you have to make sacrifices, but there was one sacrifice I made that didn't just involve me. When I was just starting out as a young actress, I found myself pregnant, and I gave away my baby son.' People at the furthest tables who had still been chatting fell instantly silent. 'I could say it was for my art or for the needs of creativity, but actually I did it because I was selfish. I was luckier than I deserve. My son found me and I've been given a second chance.'

Stella's voice cracked with emotion and she clutched the podium for support. 'So tonight I'd like to apologize to my son from the bottom of my heart and to ask him to come up here so that I can dedicate this award to him: Joseph Meredith, the son I didn't deserve to be reunited with.'

Joe found every pair of eyes in the vast room trained on him, and the world froze for a moment as he realized he had no choice but to go on stage. He stumbled towards the dais, followed by a cameraman recording his every move, as, all over the room, people began to clap. By the time he reached the stage the applause was thunderous.

Stella, waiting by the podium, turned him round for everyone to see. 'My lovely son, Joseph Meredith. Joe, can you ever forgive me?'

Even the producer of the live OB, whose timings had been blasted to smithereens by Stella's outburst, watched mesmerized. 'She certainly has a sense of theatre, I'll say that for her.'

All over the vast and glittering room, guests jumped to their feet, cheering now.

Despite her anger with Stella and her frustration with Joe, Molly was washed along with all the others on the tidal wave of emotion. It was as if the thousands in the room and the millions watching at home were all included in this mother-and-child reunion, and had some personal investment in it.

Only one guest sat steadfastly in her chair, unnoticed in the emotional intensity that hung in the air.

'Oh God, Stella,' Bea murmured under her breath, wiping away tears not of emotion but of apprehension, 'you bloody silly girl. Why do you always have to go and push your luck?'

Chapter 20

From all over the vast room, dozens of guests, many of them as well known as she was, swarmed to Stella's table and hugged, kissed or congratulated her.

Joe found himself embraced by complete strangers with tears in their eyes, who behaved towards him like long-lost relatives themselves.

Bob Kramer was one of the first to rush up. 'Brilliant, Stella, brilliant. Even the director of *Dark Night* had a tear in his eye, and he's so excited about seeing you. Congratulations!'

In the midst of the excitement Molly noticed how white Bea was looking, how fail and suddenly old. With her daunting will power drained out of her, she looked almost breakable.

'Come on, Beatrice,' Molly said gently. 'I think we should be moving. Will you come back with me and stay at the flat?'

'I'd prefer to go home, thank you, dear. There's a train at eleven and a taxi will meet me. I wish Stella had told me she was going to do that.'

'Was it such a mistake? Why?'

But Bea would say no more.

'At least let me take you to Victoria,' Molly insisted. She looked round to find Joe, but he was in the middle of a group of fawning celebrities. Molly saw that at least he had the grace to look over-whelmed, and not entirely happy.

'Stella has trumped us, my dear.' Bea glanced over at the group. 'But in a way she may live to regret.'

'How dare she!' Pat switched off the TV furiously to blot out the image of Stella and Joe hugging each other. The thought that it was being relayed to millions of people, including everyone she knew, made Pat crease up with pain and humiliation. 'She gave him away! She threw him out because he got in the way of her career! It's not fair, it just isn't bloody well fair!'

The anguish in his wife's voice tore at Andrew's gentle heart. Had he been wrong to help Molly find Joe's mother? But then, how could any of them have known it would turn out like this? 'He needed to find her, love. Molly was right about that. Joe's never been really happy despite all the love you gave him. There's always been part of him that has held back. Maybe having his importance recognised so publicly like this will really help him.'

'He doesn't need help; he's fine. You're beginning to sound like Molly. You always did think the sun shone out of her backside.'

Andrew tried to put his arms around her. His wife's body shook under her shapeless dress. She'd put on weight lately and lost inter-est in clothes. 'Look, Pat love, I know it's hard, but you've never given Molly any credit for loving Joe as much as you do. That's why I helped her. She wanted Joe to feel accepted by his real mother.'

'Well, he's certainly been accepted now, so she should be bloody well thrilled, shouldn't she?' Pat's voice sounded like a razor rip-ping through precious fabric. She tried to suppress an anguished, hiccuping sob. 'Oh, Andrew, she can offer him so much. She just swans into his life and everything's suddenly fine, and all those years – all the endless nappies and the sitting up with him when he was ill, and the economizing – none of it counts now. He's proba-bly forgotten about us already.'

'Not Joe. He's a good lad. He'll come round. He loves you too, Pat.'

'Does he? Ashamed of me, more like. Stella Milton probably lives in a palace. Look at us, Andrew, in this shabby little bungalow. We haven't bought anything new in thirty years.'

'Then maybe we should start.' Andrew hid his hurt that his wife thought so little of the life they'd built together. But then he'd always been happier with his lot than Pat. She seemed to have a restless yearning for some unnamed rainbow. Andrew couldn't help wondering if it was something to do with childlessness, and he felt sadness pinch at his heart that he'd never been able to give her a baby of her own.

'Think how Molly must feel,' he said.

Pat's expression closed over. Her face, once pretty, looked pinched and unpleasant. 'Molly's only got what she asked for.'

'Pat, love,' Andrew felt a small clutch of despair that things were turning out so differently from the way he'd hoped, 'try and be a bit more understanding. Molly loves Joe every bit as much as you do.'

'Does she? Then she's got a funny way of showing it,' Pat plumped up the cushions on their brown tapestry sofa, as she'd done every night for thirty years. 'You know, I've never liked this sofa.'

It was on Andrew's lips to say 'Buy a new one then, love.' But it wasn't the sofa that was wrong with Pat's life, Andrew saw sadly; it was something deeper, something that a new three-piece suite couldn't cure.

There was a big crowd that night in the Sun in Splendour in Lower Ditchwell, which meant ten rather than three people. Early Sunday evenings were not the pub's finest hour. Even though the front door stood invitingly open, people preferred to make the most of the late summer evenings outdoors rather than spend them in the ancient pub with its smoke-blackened beams and uneven rough-tiled floor. It came into its own in late autumn and winter when the pungent tang of woodsmoke and the lure of hot toddies brought in the crowds as if to some pagan ceremony.

'Here, Ant,' remarked the morose landlord to one of his few

faithful regulars, 'isn't that the old bat who lives on the corner? That actress lady?' He indicated a camera shot featuring Bea in all her finery at the awards ceremony.

'So it is,' endorsed Anthony Lewis, moving himself into a better position to see the television. 'And that young girl with the baby. Another lot of bloody poncey awards. They'll give each other a statuette for Best Fart in a Motion Picture next. My God, look at them. Our culture's finest, God help us all. What's it for this time? Albanian Aid? Sell the dog and have a refugee instead?'

'Something called the Millennium Awards. Look, there's that sex bomb Stella Whatsername.'

'Milton,' supplied Anthony, sitting up and watching, all traces of his cynical lethargy evaporating.

'It says here she's getting an award for being our sexiest export.'

'Pity they didn't export her altogether.' Anthony watched Stella climb the dais to get her award and silently toasted her with his glass of whisky. She was wearing some indecent red dress. Stella loved playing up the scarlet woman to the point of parody, yet she managed to stay just inside the borderline. Damn her, she was as alluring as ever, though Anthony had long ago realized that invitation wasn't for him, or anyone else. It was a general, not a personal invitation, and as such entirely hollow. He doubted whether Stella had invited any man she'd ever met into what passed as her heart.

He watched as she received her award then beckoned to a young man seated at one of the tables.

Anthony wobbled on his bar stool and almost knocked over his drink. The likeness in the flesh rather than a flat newspaper photograph was staggering. The same nearly black hair, the indigo eyes fringed with long, dark eyelashes, the same knack of somehow looking you straight in the eye. And yet Anthony sensed an uncertainty in Joseph that Stella had never been troubled by. For all his arresting looks, the young man seemed faintly ill at ease in his own skin. As well he might, given the circumstances of his birth.

An unexpected anger buried deep under Anthony's layers of

237

self-loathing and protective cynicism scorched suddenly through him and he swept his glass off the bar.

'Bloody hell, Ant,' the landlord squawked, 'watch what you're doing with that glass.'

'Bloody hell, Ant,' echoed the mynah bird. 'Bloody hell!'

'You're lucky I didn't throw it at the sodding television.' Anthony climbed off his stool. 'Sorry about the mess,' he said, making no attempt to pick it up. He couldn't look at the screen. The sight of Stella and Joe locked in an embrace was too much to take. 'I'll see you.' He lumbered off out of the bar, his long black leather coat swishing, reminding the landlord of an injured crow.

'I wonder what's eating our Ant,' murmured the landlord to the empty bar. 'Seems to have a thing about Stella Milton. I hope he's not one of them stalkers. He's weird enough sometimes.'

'Weird enough,' repeated the mynah wisely, nodding its black head as if it knew exactly what the link was between the scene on the television and Lower Ditchwell's unreliable antiques dealer.

When he got back to the shop Anthony rang the number Molly had left with him when all this was starting. Her answering machine clicked on and he almost replaced the receiver. Of course she wasn't in. The awards were live.

'Hello,' he said reluctantly, 'this is Anthony from Ditchwell.' He realized he sounded like a bloody phone-in guest and pulled himself together. 'I'd like to speak to Joseph Meredith on a matter of urgency. Tonight if possible. It doesn't matter how late.'

For the rest of the evening he paced around his small beamed sitting room as if it were a prison cell. He wished he could hate Stella, as he'd tried to do many times before, but the truth was that even after all this time she was still part of him, like a virus, drumming through his blood, to the deepest place in his heart.

It was almost midnight before Molly carried Eddie up from Mrs Salaman's flat. Her kind neighbour had said he was welcome to stay the night, but Molly needed his small warm body for comfort. He was the only thing that kept her sane just at the moment.

Absent-mindedly she pushed the button on their ancient answering machine to playback. Eddie must have been fiddling around with the volume and Anthony Lewis's voice suddenly filled the room like the Wizard of Oz's.

Eddie, frightened, gave a whimper and Molly had to calm him. What on earth did the man want? He said to call no matter how late. Molly glanced at her watch: 11.45. Did he really mean as late as that? She suspected Anthony Lewis of being a night owl. With his long, thin body and lanky hair, he reminded her of a vampire played by Alice Cooper.

She was too tired to think about it, so she dialled his number.

He answered almost at once.

'Hello, Mr Lewis. You left a message for us. I'm afraid Joe's not here. He's staying with Stella for a few days.' She hoped her voice didn't betray her anger and frustration with both of them.

'Gone home to Mum, has he? I'd like to be a fly on the wall there.'

'So would I,' confessed Molly before she'd had time to think better of it.

'You've been a bit sidelined by stunning Stella, haven't you? She does that to everyone. But I'm here to give you the chance to upstage her for once. Can you meet me in Cliffdean tomorrow?'

'Why on earth in Cliffdean?'

'Neutral territory.'

Molly's curiosity got the better of her. 'All right.'

'One o'clock. In front of the pier. I'll buy you lunch.'

Of course it was the one day that Mrs Salaman couldn't have Eddie. He'd just have to come with her. He'd love the pier anyway.

Much to her surprise, Molly slept soundly and didn't wake till after nine. There was plenty of time to get Eddie up, give him breakfast, pack up his nappy bag with juice, a bottle and baby food and head off for Victoria. Although the holiday season was well past, the station still had a festive feel to it, with lots of young people dressed in ludicrous red, white and blue pinnies, berets

239

and strings of onions, looking faintly embarrassed as they gave away free bits of croissant. Eddie was thrilled.

Molly had to admit, she loved Cliffdean. You would have to be a strange person not to, in her view. Some people called it London-by-the-Sea, partly because, unlike the average seaside town, it was chic and sophisticated. But it was far more than that. It was a real place. Smart in some ways, seedy in others. A seaside town with style. It had somehow survived the influx of homeless and jobless who hung about in other coastal towns. Or if it had its fair share, it absorbed them with better grace, partly because Cliffdean, like California, was full of people who had migrated there looking for something special, a way of life that was neither urban nor provincial. Cliffdean was simply Cliffdean.

She was surprised to find him already waiting for her by the pier entrance; she'd had him down for someone who would probably be late. There was, Molly thought, an air of suppressed excitement about him which was distinctly unnerving.

'Shall we go on the pier?' he offered.

Molly, still unsure of why he'd got in touch, nodded.

The wind was cold and refreshing and Eddie leaned out of his buggy looking at the sea through the cracks in the pier. Those cracks had terrified Molly when she was a child; she'd been sure she would fall through them and drown. At the age of twelve she'd made herself stare down them and willed herself to be brave, a quality she suspected she might be needing again soon.

'You're wondering why I asked you here.'

'Just a bit.'

'You saw the affecting scene at the awards ceremony last night?'

'I was there.'

'Of course you were. And were you moved to tears like the rest of the nation?'

'I was, actually, even though I could happily strangle the pair of them. I suppose it made me realize how it must have been for Stella, only twenty, on her own, just starting out as an actress, finding herself pregnant with no one to help her.'

Anthony Lewis laughed. It was a curious, rasping sound which set off a fit of coughing. He dealt with it by lighting a cigarette. 'Except,' he drew the smoke in deeply and held it, 'that Stella wasn't single and starving with no one to support her, touching though that picture might be.'

'What do you mean? What exactly are you implying?'

'I mean,' Anthony stopped and leaned against the railings at the side of the pier, 'that Stella was married to me.'

Molly felt as if she'd been kicked in the pit of her stomach. '*Married*?' For a moment she thought she'd have to lean over the railings and be physically sick. 'Stella gave Joe away when she was *married*?'

Molly couldn't conceive, couldn't begin to imagine, how anyone could give away their baby under such circumstances. It would be like her giving Eddie away because she and Joe were in difficulties.

'But what happened?'

'I worked in the theatre then, not very successfully, it has to be said, but we weren't starving. The truth was, Stella never wanted children. She'd had a bout of anorexia and she thought she was infertile. When she found she was pregnant she was horrified.'

'But surely you had to give your consent to the adoption?'

For the first time Anthony lost his cocky combativeness. 'I thought it was the only way to save our marriage. I knew Stella wouldn't make a mother. She didn't even like children. She was focused absolutely on her career. If you put your hand to Stella's ambition, it would burn you. I know. I found out the hard way.' The bitterness in Anthony's tone seeped out into the air between them. Could he be making this up? 'She'd have had an abortion if she could have but she found out she was pregnant too late. Her periods were always up the creek so she didn't miss them. It just never occurred to her she could get pregnant. The truth is, Stella never considered keeping Joe for a moment; she couldn't get shot of him fast enough.'

Molly leaned forward, holding on to the railings to steady herself. If Joe found out any of this it would destroy him. He'd finally constructed an image of himself as a baby who had been loved, whom Stella had only given away because she couldn't cope.

'But how could Stella lie like that? She must realize it could all come out.'

'She probably believes it herself. Stella's a fantasist. That's why she's such a good actress. She actually persuades herself she's the person she's playing – nun, whore, Juliet, it doesn't matter. She probably convinced herself it actually happened that way. If it weren't for the small inconvenience of me.'

Molly dipped down and put her arms round her baby son in a gesture half of protection, half need. Stella had actually given away her own baby when she was married to its father. The truth hit her with blinding force. The man standing next to her was Joe's father!

He bobbed down next to her, reading her thoughts, and took Eddie's small hand in his. 'I don't suppose I'm an ideal grandad.'

His expression was inexpressibly sad, and for the first time, Molly wondered what all this must have been like for him. Stella, with her ambition and her fantasies, had a lot to answer for. 'You still love her, don't you? After all she's done.'

Anthony Lewis climbed brusquely to his feet.

'Just like you love Joseph. Poor us. Right, I'm off. Nice to meet you again. I knew all this would come out from the first time you walked into my shop. You weren't the kind to give up. You're a very determined girl.' To her amazement he grinned at her wolfishly. 'Not unlike Stella. I think what you should do next is take Stella on face-to-face. She never did like confrontation. Manipulation is Stella's forte.'

Molly watched him leave, her stomach churning, then slumped down next to Eddie's buggy and buried her face in her hands. It was true that none of this would have come about if it hadn't been for her. Joe would have given up; she'd been the one who'd pushed on in her insensitive belief that she knew best.

The realization hit her, like another twist of the knife, that now that she knew the truth about Stella, she had to decide what to do about it. If she told Joe it would shatter all his illusions and might bring him back to her, but equally it could destroy him in the process.

For once in her life all her usual certainty lay in pieces around her. 'Oh, Christ,' she muttered into her damp red hair, billowing wildly around her, 'what the hell am I going to do now?'

Next to her a small hand clutched a lock of her hair and pulled it gently. She looked up into Eddie's concerned little face, with its long, long eyelashes, a tiny replica of his absent father. She thought of the baby inside her and its uncertain future. Joe had grown up without the love of his real parents, she was damned if the same thing was going to happen to Eddie or to the baby she was carrying.

Chapter 21

Cliffdean station was crowded, but Molly was so preoccupied by Anthony's suggestion that she confront Stella, she didn't even notice.

Without consciously coming to a decision, she found herself standing at the ticket office and asking for a ticket to Ovington, from there she'd get the bus to Ditchwell. Bea would know. Bea would listen and advise her. The one person in this God-awful mess she could actually rely on was Bea.

Beatrice Manners had her own sense of foreboding about the situation and had dealt with it in her time-honoured manner, by gardening. Hollyhocks did not have divorces, abortions or affairs. Delphiniums cast their seeds to the wind and that was that. An enviable state indeed. In fact, the self-propagating flower, which didn't even need a male of its own species, seemed to her the highest pinnacle of God's planning. Pity he'd screwed up when he got to humans.

The sudden sight of Molly, red hair flowing wildly, pushing her great-grandson in his buggy briefly cheered Bea, until she saw the look on Molly's face. She reminded Bea of a crushed pre-Raphaelite angel.

'What's happened, Molly darling? Come and sit down.' Bea

indicated the rustic wooden bench under the chestnut tree. Its leaves were already falling. She knew how it felt.

'There was a message waiting when I got home after the awards.'

'From Anthony Lewis?'

'How did you know?'

Bea took off her gardening gloves and sat down on the bench beside her. 'I thought that performance the other night might be a sob story too far for Anthony. Anthony's not a horrible man, but he's a bitter one. I knew he would feel Stella was airbrushing him out of her past and that he might finally rebel. God knows why Stella couldn't see that for herself.'

'It's true, then? They were married?'

'Yes. He had a lot of promise then, but no application. Anthony isn't a sticker. Except perhaps in terms of Stella.'

'What do you think I should do?'

'I think you should tell Stella you know and that you will tell Joseph unless she does first. It's bound to come out some time, with all these journalist types digging around, and it would be better coming from Stella. As long as she finally tells him the truth. Would you like me to keep Eddie for you while you go? In fact, why don't you both stay here for a day or two? You could catch the train and be with her in an hour or two.'

It was beginning to get cold, and Molly's celebrated energy felt as if it was seeping out from some invisible crack in her being. She didn't know if she had enough fire in her for a scene with Stella. At least the thought of having Bea to come home to made her braver.

'Off you go then.' Bea pushed her gently.

'What if she's not in?'

'She is. She was on the phone a second ago. I'll tell her you're coming.'

'I'm not sure I should leave Eddie.'

Bea picked Eddie up in a glow of great-grandmotherly adoration. He beamed back. There was no excuse not to go.

The next hour passed in a cloud of anxiety for Molly. How could she get through to Stella? Under the veneer of sensuality, Stella was pure steel.

At Victoria she spent a pound on going to the de luxe lavatories and smartening herself up. She felt as if she were dressing for the guillotine.

'Oh, for God's sake,' she told her reflection sternly, making the shopper next to her jump guiltily, 'she's not the monster out of *Alien*. She's only your mother-in-law.'

'Actually,' the shopper confided, '*my* mother-in-law is the monster out of *Alien*. You show her!'

'I will,' promised Molly.

Stella, warned by Bea of Molly's impending visit, had also dressed for the part, or rather under-dressed for it, which had even more impact. There was no sign of her trademark slinky black, no glaring red lips, no high heels. Stella – deliberately, Molly was sure – had chosen a pared-down look: white sweat pants and a hooded white top, with bare feet and not a shred of make-up. She looked like someone about to check into a very expensive clinic.

'Would you like some herbal tea? My mother said you wanted to talk to me, so here I am.'

Molly looked around for some sign of Joe's presence, even for Joe himself. But there was none.

She decided to waste no time. 'When I got back from the awards there was a message for Joe, and he wasn't there so I returned the call.'

'Efficient as ever.'

Molly's chin shot up. She was damned if she was going to let Stella patronize her. 'It was from Anthony Lewis.' She paused pointedly. 'Your husband.'

'Ex-husband,' Stella corrected calmly. 'And what ridiculous stories has Anthony been spinning to you?'

Stella's tenuous grip on reality was too much for Molly. 'Don't you ever face the truth about yourself, Stella?' she blazed. 'You were *married* when you had Joe. Married people don't go giving their babies away. I can't conceive of giving a baby away in those circumstances. You weren't single or starving and unable to cope. You could have had Bea's support, or Anthony's. You just didn't want a child, so you handed Joe over without a second thought. It doesn't quite fit with what you've been telling the *Daily Post* and your adoring millions on TV, does it? Not to mention Joe himself. What is he going to feel when he finds out? You're a cow, Stella. Although that's giving cows a bad name. At least they don't give their calves up willingly.'

Stella listened, her sense of indignation mounting. What did Molly, with her unshakeable certainties and her blundering attempts at righting the world's wrongs, know about choices like Stella's? The only choice Molly had ever had to make was what colour to wallpaper her poky little flat.

'You dislike me so much that you swallowed every word Anthony said,' Stella flashed back. 'Didn't you? You can't wait to brand me as a heartless bitch. Anthony wasn't exactly queuing up to be a father either, you know. He can't stand children. And for your information, my supportive mother was in Jakarta doing *Private Lives*. It's all so easy for you, isn't it? Little Miss Molly with your overflowing boobs and your limited horizons. Earth mother and home-maker. You never wanted more than that, did you? You snared Joe at twenty-four and set him on the road to being a nice steady husband with attitudes as dull and narrow as your own.'

Molly flinched at the cruelty in Stella's accusations. Was this what Joe had told her? And if he'd felt like that about her first pregnancy, what the hell would he make of another?

'And let's face it, Molly, how did you take it when Joseph decided he didn't want to be your meal ticket any more and wanted to try acting instead? That upset your housey-housey fantasies, didn't it? You couldn't deal with the fact he might want more out of life than security. And for your information, it actually wasn't that easy even for a heartless bitch like me to give away my baby. I cried myself to sleep missing Joseph, but I was an actress and my marriage was crumbling and I couldn't have got where I wanted with a child to look after.' She swept the searchlight of her bright blue eyes round on to Molly. 'You don't understand it, do you? You can't see that a career can matter as much as nappies and playgroup. You've never felt the excitement of being brilliant at what you do, of being praised, fêted, of feeling no one could do it like you do. Especially when you're too young to know that feeling won't always last.' Her voice quivered like a finely pitched violin at the memory of how heady it had all been when she'd started out. 'Of course I regretted it later, when I saw that acting was only part of life and I didn't have anything else in mine. But it was too late then.' She looked Molly squarely in the eye. 'Until you gave me a second chance. Can you imagine what it was like to have him walk back into my life and not hate me? It was miraculous! A dream come true.'

The white-hot purity of Stella's selfishness was too much for Molly to take. 'You're amazing, you know that, Stella? Even after all that's happened, you're only thinking of yourself. *Your* sacrifices, *your* ambitions. What about Joe? I tried to find you because I thought it would help Joe, who, thanks to you, has never felt he fitted in, who's so frightened of rejection that he hasn't been able to really love anyone – maybe not even me or his own son! Don't you see, Stella, he's repeating what you did to him!'

'You want me to send him home, don't you?' Stella turned away, and Molly was staggered to see that her cheeks were wet with tears. 'You don't know what it's been like in the last few days. Just to have him here, to be able to look after him, to know when I go to sleep he'll be here in the morning. It's been the best time of my whole life.'

'But you've taken him from us, Stella.' Molly's voice was no longer angry now. Just tired. And scared. 'We love him too.'

'And you want me to give him back.' It was a statement, heavy and flat and anguished.

'You'll have to tell him the truth about Anthony, you know,' Molly said gently. 'Because he's going to find out sooner or later.'

'From you?' Stella reminded Molly of the goddess in *She*, turning into an old woman before her eyes.

'Not necessarily. But it's bound to come out.'

'I love him more than anything else in the world,' Stella said quietly. 'I couldn't bear it if he turned against me now.'

For once Molly's confidence wavered. Every instinct she had was for openness, for facing up to truths, for never keeping secrets. But where had it got her? 'Then you'll have to decide what the right thing is to do. To be perfectly honest, I'm not sure any more. I've screwed things up pretty badly myself. Maybe I'm not the one to hand out advice. I just know I love him and I miss him so much.' She turned away, close to tears; she was damned if she was going to break down in front of Stella.

Stella stared at her. 'You seem very quiet. What's happened to Molly the missile?'

'Perhaps she scored an own goal in ever trying to find you.'

'Perhaps she did.'

'And now she's scored another. I'm pregnant again and I haven't even told Joe yet.'

'What a surprise for him. Just like last time.' Stella's voice held the slightest sneer of superiority, as though accidental pregnancy were something that had never happened to her.

Molly was within a millimetre of hitting her. 'So what's your advice then, Stella? Have an abortion, or wait till it's born and conveniently give it away like you did? What's your considered view on this one?'

Molly didn't wait for an answer. She'd been mad to think she could ever appeal to Stella's better instincts.

Chapter 22

Claire finished printing out her ideas and read them through. Since the interview with Joe and Stella had appeared, her position on the paper seemed more secure. Tony had stopped dropping heavy-handed hints about her being top of the redundancy list, and occasionally, like today, she'd even been asked to sit in again for the deputy features editor, who was off sick. A big privilege, and Claire knew it. She was beginning to feel almost relaxed. Which was of course a very unwise thing to do.

The editorial conference was always fast, sweaty and stressful, and today it seemed even more so than usual. It was held in a meeting room next to the editor's office, and the atmosphere was usually thick with aggression, competition and paranoia. Even though the room was large, it was hard to fit all those egos in any enclosed space.

Today everything went through straightforwardly, without any section trying too hard to rubbish the others' ideas. All the same, Claire was rattled by Rory Hawthorne's smug attitude. He sat silently through the conference, smiling, and it wasn't until they were all about to leave that he finally deigned to speak.

Claire was instantly alerted to trouble. Rory's face, normally just smarmy, had taken on a whole new slick of self-satisfaction.

'Just one more little thing,' he announced, waving his mystery titbit in front of all their noses. 'I think you might be interested in some information that's just come in.'

They all sat down again.

'That story you wrote about Stella Milton and her long-lost son, Claire dear, the story you were allowed to write instead of me because of your intimate connections with the protagonists . . .'

Claire sat up as if someone had just stuck a pin in her bum. The man's voice was thick with insinuation.

'Yes?' the editor answered for her, toying with his felt-tip, something he only did when he was particularly interested but was damned if he was going to show it. 'Claire did a good interview. Brought a tear to the eye. The interest from the rest of the media's been massive.'

'Pity it left out one very salient fact.'

'And what was that?'

'That Stella Milton didn't give away her baby when she was starving and single, as she told Claire so movingly. She gave him away when she was married and perfectly comfortably off.'

Married? Claire's heart thudded so hard she could hardly think.

'She simply thought a child would stand in the way of her career,' Rory went on smugly.

'How the hell do you know?' Claire demanded.

'Because her ex-husband's just been on the phone offering us the story.'

The editor turned to Claire. 'Well, what do you make of that?'

Claire had a horrible feeling it was true. There had been something about Stella's revelations that had never quite fitted. This was obviously it. 'Pure crap.' She forced her tone to sound combative. 'How do you know this man's not some creep with a grudge against Stella?'

'Because he also says he's happy to produce the evidence.'

Claire felt like crumpling up. Poor Joe, this would devastate him. But she certainly wasn't going to let Rory know her suspicions. 'I still don't think we should run it. If this man was married

251

to Stella, his consent would have been necessary to have Joe adopted. Why would he have given it?'

But hideous Rory Hawthorne was still looking superior. 'Because he says he thought it was the only way he could hold on to Stella.'

'He wasn't much of a father then, was he?' Claire scrabbled around for ways of discrediting the story.

'We're not discussing the man's paternal attributes,' the editor cut in testily. 'We're discussing whether what he claims is accurate.'

Claire went on the offensive. After all, her good journalistic name was at stake too.

'I think you need more sources to back him up. Stella will sue if we get this wrong.'

The editor eyed Claire beadily, making a rapid assessment of her motives. 'All right. Rory, you'd better check out this man's story. What about Stella's mother, that old actress biddy? And the adoptive parents, they may know something.'

'I'll do them,' Claire offered. She knew from what Molly had said that Pat might blab, especially in the skilful hands of Rory Hawthorne.

'No thanks, Claire,' the editor said quietly. 'You stick to the story you're working on.'

That was when Claire knew she was in trouble. She couldn't wait to get out of the room to warn Molly. She had to do it via her mobile from the ladies' loo. 'Moll, it's Claire!'

Molly stopped skipping through the Situations Vacant column. 'What's the matter? Why do you sound as if you're in the middle of a swimming bath?'

'Don't worry about that. Moll, this is serious. They're on to Stella. She's got a husband, the stupid cow. She was actually *married* when she gave Joe away. And she lied about it. The husband's trying to sell his story to the paper. This is turning nasty, Molly. They'll really go for her now. The full Heartless Bitch number. Rory Hawthorne's already on his way to Essex to find Andrew and Pat.'

For a moment Molly allowed herself the luxury of imagining

Stella's career in ruins, her true nature revealed, loathed and reviled by everyone; but almost instantly the effect this would have on Joe brought her back to reality. 'Shit. Pat's already got it in for Stella. She'd probably love to co-operate. I think I'd better get up there too – pretty damn quick.'

'I'll take you,' Claire offered. 'Rory's good but I might be able to deflect him.'

'Thanks, Claire. You're a real friend.' A thought occurred to her. 'By the way, aren't you sticking your neck out here?'

'Don't ask. I'm beginning to wonder if I'm cut out for journalism. I seem to have some normal human instincts like affection and respect. Hopeless. See you in half an hour. I'll come in a cab and we can take it up to Essex.' Since this might be her last assignment, she might as well go in style.

While she was waiting for Claire to arrive, Molly left two warning messages on Stella's machine. One for Stella, and the other for Joe in the hope that he'd somehow get it.

'I just hope Rory hasn't got there first,' Claire prayed as they crawled through the lunchtime traffic of east London. 'He's a fast worker. That man could worm his way on to Scrooge's Christmas list.'

The first thing they saw outside Andrew and Pat's modest bungalow was Rory Hawthorne's Alfa Romeo Spyder.

'Shit!' said Claire. 'Shit. Shit. Shit.'

Andrew opened the door, looking concerned and unhappy.

'Don't say anything to him,' insisted Claire, shoving her way into the sitting room where Pat had already loaded a trolley with coffee and fancy biscuits on white paper doilies. Rory Hawthorne sat next to her with an encouraging expression.

'Molly! What are you doing here?' Pat almost dropped her cup in surprise. 'I wasn't expecting you. This is Mr Worthington. He's an old school friend of Joseph's.'

'Is he, my arse?' demanded Claire. 'And what school was that exactly, Mr Worthington?'

Rory's eyes narrowed. 'I take it you're abandoning your career as

253

from now?' he asked nastily. 'Because you certainly won't have one after this.'

'Mr Worthington is really a reporter on the *Daily Post*, Pat,' Molly explained. 'His name's Rory Hawthorne and he's doing an exposé on Stella Milton.'

Rory Hawthorne was a clever journalist, and he took in two things: the adoptive mother didn't like Molly; and, even better, she loathed Stella. All might not yet be lost.

'We have just discovered,' he added smoothly, 'that Stella Milton was actually married when she gave her son up for adoption, and we feel that puts her touching story of not being able to cope as a single mother rather into question.'

'That's wicked!' Pat was genuinely appalled.

'Apparently she thought he'd get in the way of her career. We – that is, the paper – wondered if you would like the chance to put your side of the story. I mean, it must have been tough for you, bringing up her son with not much money, and there she was, getting rich and famous. And now she's being photographed everywhere with him; in fact, I understand he's actually living with her at the moment rather than with his family. When was the last time he got in touch with you, as a matter of interest?'

Pat stood up and walked over to the window, weighing up the man's proposition. This was it, her chance to say how *she* had felt when glamorous, self-absorbed Stella waltzed into her life and stole Joe's affections.

But Rory, unable to stand the tension, miscalculated.

'Of course,' he added, as if it were the most natural thing in the world, 'we wouldn't expect you to give up your time for nothing. Perhaps two thousand pounds might be adequate?'

Molly closed her eyes. She could hardly blame Pat if she wanted to get her own back on Stella. She and Andrew *had* struggled and gone without things, and made sacrifices to give Joe the best they could, and it must have been terrible to have Stella swan into her life and steal him.

She of all people knew how that felt.

Pat turned back from her contemplation of the garden. Her faded face looked years younger and her back somehow straighter. Pat the whinger seemed to have disappeared altogether.

She's going to do it, thought Molly.

'As a matter of fact, Mr Hawthorne,' Pat answered with more spirit than Molly had ever seen her show, 'I heard from my son Joseph three days ago. And no thank you, I wouldn't like to tell my story, even for ten thousand pounds. I can just imagine what you'd do with it. I've never liked the *Daily Post*. Tittle-tattle and innuendo. Always printing things while it's pretending to condemn them. Andrew and I may be unimportant people but we have our standards. We'll sort this out in our own way, thank you very much.'

She held out his coat to him.

Rory Hawthorne looked at Claire as if she were something unpleasant on the sole of his shoe. 'You'll be hearing about this.'

'Yes,' Claire agreed pleasantly, 'I expect I will.'

'Well done, love,' Andrew congratulated his wife as soon as Rory had left. 'You really told him.'

'I did, didn't I?' grinned Pat. 'But don't think Stella's getting off scot free. It's time I told that woman a few home truths of my own. Could you run me to the station? I'm going to London and I'm not coming back till I've seen her.'

'No need for a train,' Claire offered, grinning. 'I've got a taxi outside. We'll take you.'

Pat nodded. She suddenly reminded Molly of Queen Victoria in her later years: small, faded, plump, but with extraordinary inner strength of purpose. 'I've just got a few things I need to take with me.'

The journey to London was silent and tense. No one felt like asking what Pat would do if Stella were out or refused to see her.

It didn't take long to reach the hinterland of superstores and DIY warehouses that marked the beginning of the city. Almost an hour later they were in Covent Garden.

'Shall we come up with you?' asked Molly when they reached Stella's block in the Old Flower Market.

'No thanks. This is something I'd rather do alone.'

Pat pressed the buzzer on Stella's intercom. There was no reply. She waited ten seconds and tried again. Stella must have gone out. Pat felt all her nerve begin to ebb away like a departing tide. Who did she think she was, a nobody from Mere-on-Sea, taking on Stella the Sex Goddess?

'Yes?' a voice finally replied. 'What is it? Could you please stop pressing my bell?'

Pat wasn't even aware she'd been leaning on the buzzer all this time.

'It's Mrs Patricia Meredith.' Pat wished she hadn't used the Mrs. It made her sound as if she had to rely on it for some pathetic attempt at status.

'Sorry? Who?'

She'd been going to add 'Joseph Meredith's mother', but now chose her words carefully. 'Joseph Meredith's adoptive mother.'

'I see,' said the distant voice. 'I suppose you'd better come up.'

As she climbed the steps, Pat wished she had changed into something smarter, but what was the point? She would never be anything other than a provincial nobody to someone like Stella Milton. All the same, it might have given her more courage for the battle ahead.

Stella Milton, in the flesh, was a disappointment. She wasn't dressed as an upmarket tart, or a sex-addicted schoolmistress, or a leather-clad biker. In fact she wore, rather disconcertingly, a white towelling dressing gown. In her bare feet she was hardly taller than Pat. Pat felt obscurely cheated, yet cheered. She'd come across more glamour on the Women's Institute outing to *Evita*.

'I apologize for not hearing you. I was in the shower. I'm going out in an hour.'

Pat breathed in. An hour would be plenty. Maybe Stella would just have to cut short her beauty routine for once.

'May I sit down?'

'Of course.'

Pat sat down cautiously, aware of feeling as out of place in these ultra-sophisticated surroundings as a nodding dog in a Mercedes. 'A reporter just came round to my house researching the story of how you gave Joe away when you were married.'

To Pat's satisfaction Stella's attempt at superiority collapsed in a heap. She looked as if she'd been kicked. 'Your husband's sold his story to the *Daily Post* and they were just checking the facts. They also asked me how I felt about bringing up your child while you were making yourself rich and famous.'

Pat was enjoying her moment of theatricality as much as Stella had ever enjoyed her own stage triumphs.

'And what did you say?'

'As a matter of fact,' Pat said quietly, 'I told him to get lost.'

Stella bit her lip, feeling suddenly humble at the sight of this dowdy woman's dignity. 'Should I thank you?'

'I'm not sure you'll want to. You see, I wouldn't tell the man from that paper, but I'm going to tell you instead, because this is private, between you and me. You disrupted Joe's life once by giving him away – that's forgivable, because you were young and we all make mistakes, even if you were married. But now you're doing it again. And this time there's no excuse. Have you ever thought, really thought, of the damage you're doing just so that you get the pleasure of having a grown-up son?'

Stella sat opposite Pat, mesmerized, as if she could never move again.

'You gave Joe away. No one pressured you. You weren't like some poor girls I knew, whose families blackmailed them, told them they couldn't come home with a baby. Those girls didn't know where to turn because they were seventeen, with no money, so they gave up their babies and it broke their hearts. You weren't like that. You were twenty-four and you were married. You gave Joe away because it suited you. Just like it suited you to take him back.'

'What else could I have done? I didn't just take him back,' Stella said quietly. 'I would never have gone looking for him. I didn't feel I had the right. He was the one who looked for me, remember. Or rather Molly did.'

Pat waited till she'd finished speaking. 'I can see what a good story it was for the press, Joe finding his mother and her turning out to be someone beautiful and famous like you. A real fairy tale with a happy ending. Except that it wasn't for me. To me it felt like he was rejecting everything I'd given him. You don't know what it feels like to bring up a child, do you, Stella? It means giving things up and going without so that they can have a new school uniform; it means not having holidays so they can get a decent education; it means staying up at their bedside when they're ill even if you're so dog-tired yourself you could sleep standing up. You don't even know Joe had meningitis, do you? I stayed in hospital with him, camped out for two weeks, hardly eating or sleeping because I thought he was going to die, and then he came through, and do you know what the first thing he said was, the very first thing?'

A harsh hiccuping sound of pain burst out of Pat. 'He opened his eyes and said, "Hello, Mum." But I'm not his mum, am I? Not any more. You've taken that away from me and I hate you for it. And all he is to you is a handsome face to take to a première. It flatters your ego. You don't love him,' Pat almost spat, 'you don't know the meaning of the word love.'

Stella said nothing. With her back as stiff as a board, she walked across to the bookshelf and took out the tiny sock. 'What do you know about me? For months after I gave him up I used to sleep with this. I would put it right up to my face. For months I could smell his smell, clean and milky and a little antiseptic.' She held the delicate sock up to her nostrils and breathed in deeply, as if it might still hold the same sad aroma twenty-five years on. 'I could only sleep if I had it with me. I've never washed it. Not once in twenty-five years.'

Pat listened, disbelieving. 'But if you felt like that about Joe, why did you give him away?'

'Because it was only after he'd gone that I felt it.'

'But you had three months to change your mind. I remember every minute. They were the worst three months of my life. Each time there was a knock on the door I thought you'd had second thoughts and come to take him away from me.'

'It wasn't so terrible at first. I threw myself into acting. I'd just had this incredible offer to be Juliet. The first nude Juliet.' She smiled in bitter irony at the memory. 'Very Stella Milton. That was my first real chance. When it ended I realized what I'd done but it was too late. You had Joseph. And my marriage to Anthony was disintegrating before my eyes. So I just got on with life. There was plenty of work. I never had any gaps. I just filled the hole Joe had left with acting.'

'I brought you something.' Pat delved into her large bag and pulled out a photo album. 'I meant to use it to rub in all the things you missed. His first steps. Every birthday. Learning to swim. His school plays. He was a lovely boy, my pride and joy.'

'And I've taken him away from you.'

Pat looked Stella steadily in the eye. She had acquired a dignity that Stella almost envied, like a medieval saint who knows right is on their side. 'Then maybe you'd better give him back. Not to me, to Molly and to Eddie. They're his future. You and I, we're just the past. They're his real chance of happiness. Molly knew finding Joe's mother was a risk, that I'd hate her for it, and she was right, I did. But she loved him enough to take that risk. Now it's our turn. Here', she handed the album to Stella, 'this is for you to keep.'

Stella was startled. 'But you can't give me that. It's Joe's whole childhood.'

'I had the reality, remember. You deserve the photos at least. Time I went.'

Stella turned her face to the wall. The pain was too great to speak, even to say goodbye. Pat gathered up her things. 'I'll see myself out.'

When Pat had gone, Stella began slowly to turn the pages of the childhood she'd missed. When she'd finished she got up, feeling like an old woman, and opened the door to her spare room.

Joe's things were everywhere. She found his sports bag and began to pack it. Socks, underwear, jeans, lastly a pile of polo shirts. She picked up an indigo one, the deepest blue of the ocean, the colour of Joe's eyes. In an echo of her earlier gesture with the baby sock, she held it to her face. It puzzled her that the fabric was damp, until she saw that it was her own tears that were wetting it.

As she buried her face in it one last time, she heard Joe's key turn in the door.

It felt like a death sentence.

Chapter 23

Joe stood in the doorway of Stella's flat, an eyebrow raised in teasing question. 'Looking for my dirty washing? I don't quite see you as the Persil mum.'

'As a matter of fact,' Stella returned his smile even though inside she felt like dying, 'I was just packing up your stuff. Time you went home, darling. It's been great fun playing mother and son, but I expect you've guessed by now, I'm not really the maternal type.'

The look of hurt in his eyes sliced into her, but she turned away and went on putting things in his bag. 'Besides, Bob rang. I've been offered a tour.' She scrabbled around for something that would sound convincing. '*The Importance of Being Earnest*. Edinburgh, Scarborough, Bristol and Guildford. Amazing money. Too good to refuse.'

If Joe had never tracked her down, it struck Stella agonizingly, she would never have known what she'd been missing.

She could have gone on with her well-run, well-heeled life full of civilized pleasures and safe, empty adulation. She wouldn't have had to feel all this pain, the everyday longing to be part of Joe's life, to wash his clothes and shop for the things he liked to eat, to simply have his ready smile greet her instead of coming home to a beautiful yet empty flat.

But her own act of selfishness all those years ago had cost her these ordinary pleasures, the easy rhythm of intimacy between mother and son. She had no one else to blame.

The worst thing of all was knowing that Joe had come to trust her and perhaps even forgive her. Now she was going to have to risk all that again.

'When are you leaving?' Joe asked.

'Tonight. It's all a bit sudden. The leading actress has got mumps, poor thing, most unglamorous, and I'm replacing her. Richard's coming back to flat-sit.' She added this part in case Joseph asked if he could stay on here.

'That's that, then, is it?' The bitterness in his tone burned into her like acid.

'Just for the moment. Joseph, before you go, I need to talk to you.'

'How ominous does that sound?'

Together they sat on the roof terrace. The jasmine had finished and there was a sad tang of autumn in the air. Stella closed her eyes, savouring their last moments of happiness together.

'So,' Joe prompted, his tone brusque and wounded, 'what was it you wanted to talk about?'

'There's still something I haven't told you.'

'Not more deep dark secrets?' he asked warily.

'Just the one. I had hoped not to have to admit it, selfishly, but a journalist is digging about.' She took his hand and pressed it between hers until it almost hurt. 'I love you, Joe, and I want you to always hold on to that fact.'

'So what is this journalist going to reveal?'

'That I wasn't twenty and single when I had you adopted.' She braced herself almost as if she expected a blow. 'I was twenty-four and married.'

'You were married! To my father?'

'Yes. Though I knew the marriage was over by the time I found myself pregnant. The whole thing had been a disastrous mistake.'

'And I was an even more disastrous mistake,' Joe threw in bitterly. 'The baby that would keep you stuck in the marriage.'

Stella nodded grimly.

'So you gave me away? What did he say, my father? Didn't he try and stop you? Surely he could have stopped you?'

'He wanted to save the marriage. He would have done anything I asked.'

'Including giving your baby away.'

'Even that. I was the villain, not him. I was so young and unhappy. I just wanted to get out. Out of Ditchwell. Away from Anthony. All I wanted to do was act. I would give anything to take back those years, to have brought you up myself and given you the love you deserved.'

She wanted to look deep into those dark blue eyes, so like her own, and into his soul, hoping for forgiveness, but Joe had turned his face deliberately away. Suddenly it seemed vital that he listened to what she had to say, not for her sake, but for his future happiness. 'Joe, listen to me. I've watched you with Molly. I see how you can't quite trust her love, how you have to push her to crazy limits to prove it, and I know it's all my fault. I rejected you and now you don't trust anyone, even Molly. But think about this. Think what a risk she took in finding me. And she did it for you. Molly loves you, Joe, and you've got to go back to her. For both our sakes, don't make the mistakes I have and lead an empty, lonely life.'

'You have Richard.'

'Whom I never commit to.'

'Molly hasn't made much attempt to get me back.'

'Because it's you who should be trying to get *her* back. For God's sake admit it. You're in the wrong. Go back and ask her to forgive you. Before it's too late. I love you, Joseph, and I hate to admit this, but no one could love you more than Molly.'

Joe finally faced her and she saw that his eyes sparkled with unshed tears. 'I love her too, but I'm so bloody scared she'll abandon me that I had to abandon her first.'

'If there's one thing in this life that's certain,' Stella said, realizing it was the truth, 'it's that Molly won't abandon you.' She touched his cheek, wondering if Molly would kill her for her next words. 'Especially now she's going to have another baby.'

Stella wasn't sure he'd even heard. He gave no sign, but grabbed his bag and headed for the door. It was as though, having made the decision, he couldn't wait another second. She had to catch hold of him while she still had the nerve. 'One last confession. Those letters I gave you. I didn't write them when you were growing up. I wrote them all the night before I met you. The timing might have been fake, but every word I said in them was genuine.'

To her utter amazement, Joe cracked with laughter, his eyes like the sea after a sudden storm has lifted. 'You know what you remind me of? One of those Russian dolls. You think you've got to the truth, the essential Stella, but there's always one more. Why did you pretend you'd done one every year?'

'Because I had to somehow prove I hadn't forgotten you and that you were loved and valued.'

He held her eyes for a moment, as if imprinting them in his mind. 'It's all right. I do feel loved and valued. Now.'

Stella beamed with joy and relief. 'And let me categorically insist, you *have* got to the smallest Russian doll.'

'Thank God for that. Goodbye, Stella . . .'

He thundered down the stairs, too excited to even wait for the lift.

Stella went slowly back into her flat, to find the telephone ringing, as if from another world. 'Yes,' she asked distantly, feeling like an old tyre with the air let out.

'Stella!' Bob Kramer's voice exploded. 'What the fuck are you playing at? You're supposed to be at the St Anne's rehearsal rooms meeting the producers of *Dark Night and Desire*. They've been sitting on their expensive arses for the last half-hour waiting for you.'

Shit, shit, shit, Stella repeated to herself. For months she'd been longing to get this role, polishing up her Southern accent and trying to pin down the precise shade of neurotic neediness the part demanded.

She'd even meant to prepare herself for this last hurdle with a chemical peel or some lip injections a friend of hers had had in Paris. Well, she'd just have to convince them by the sheer strength of her acting talent.

She spent a final ten minutes fixing the blonde wig in place and touching up her make-up. Even if she said it herself, she didn't look too bad. Not thirty, but nothing like her real age. What should she wear? She found a transparent white blouse with a frill down the front, which had seen better days, but then so had the character in *Dark Night*.

At least her luck was in on the taxi front. She spotted one almost outside her flat and jumped into the back.

St Anne's Place was only five minutes away, in Soho, tucked round the back of St Anne's Church. Stella used the final moments to read through the script.

Bob, looking like an agitated budgie, was hopping up and down with impatience. 'You only just caught them.'

'Right,' Stella announced, feeling the power flood through her. This was going to be good; she could sense it.

She read the first scene, where her character taunted her inadequate husband by outlining her sexual fantasies, and then another where she virtually seduced her brother-in-law on stage. She could see the casting director and the producer watching her, enthralled. She had them in the palm of her hand.

And then, from nowhere, came the distracting thought of Joe, how he must be home by now, perhaps even holding his baby, the baby she had not yet held in her own arms yet.

Stella stopped mid-flow. 'One question.' She fixed the producer with a kestrel-like stare. 'How old is my character, do you think?'

'Thirty-one, thirty-two,' he replied, 'but along with the promiscuity, there's flashes of innocence. At times she can seem like a young girl.'

'Gentlemen,' Stella pulled off the wig, then the rubber cap that held her hair in place, and tugged at the hairgrips, 'I'm sorry. I can't go on. You see, the thing is . . . I'm a bloody grandmother!'

And while the three onlookers stared at her, appalled, Stella burst out laughing. In that mad moment she realized she'd never felt freer in her life. No more obsession with dieting and wrinkles and continually assessing how she looked in other people's eyes. From now on she'd eat what the hell she wanted and dress in anything she felt like.

As she walked fast out of the rehearsal rooms and into her new life, she heard her agent speaking for everyone. 'God protect me,' he shouted after her departing back, 'from fucking crazy actresses.'

Molly trudged exhausted up the final steps to the flat. She just wanted to lie down on the scarlet sofa and put her head under a cushion. If she'd known this was how everything would turn out she would never have dreamed of starting it.

Just inside the door there was a note from Mrs Salaman telling her that she'd taken Eddie downstairs with her.

Molly didn't even know if she had the energy to go and get him. The flat felt cold and she tried to cheer it and herself up by putting on the glowing red lamps either side of the sofa, and lighting the gas-effect fire. But even though the flat brightened up, Molly's spirits didn't. Half an hour later she was still sitting there when there was a knock on the door.

It was Mrs Salaman with a bathed and beaming baby in her arms. 'He hear you come back. He wants his mummy.'

Molly took Eddie from her neighbour and held him tight. At least *he* always had the power to cheer her up. The world could never be entirely dismal with a blue-eyed, beaming bundle like Eddie in it.

'Also,' Mrs Salaman had a smile wider than if she'd won the lottery, 'I've got surprise for you. Always I tell my son about your house, how it look like a beautiful harem, like in Istanbul. And now my son, he's doing up his restaurant, and he hate designers, he says they all poofs, so I bring him here today and he went crazy.

Said it was perfect. Exactly right for his restaurant. He's waiting downstairs to talk to you now.'

Molly was touched to the core. She knew Mrs Salaman's son had a restaurant in the high street, but she'd no idea business was booming enough to do it up.

'It seat one hundred fifty people,' Mrs Salaman announced proudly. 'And soon he open another. He wants to spend five thousand pound.' She winked. 'Up to you how you spend. My son not good with receipts.'

Molly gulped, her mind already tenting the restaurant's roof with yards and yards of exotic – yet cheap – fabric from the market. She'd done it here; why not on a larger scale in a restaurant? Even though she had little experience Molly knew this was something she could do.

'Thank you, Mrs Salaman. If your son's serious, I'd love to!' She kissed the old lady, who blushed pinkly. 'Would you mind keeping Eddie for half an hour more while I go and talk to him?'

For the first time in ages, Molly felt cheerful and purposeful. Perhaps one of the reasons she'd been so obsessed with finding Stella had been because she herself needed a challenge. It might have been safer for everyone if that challenge had been doing up The Dervish restaurant instead of tracking down Stella Milton.

Joe was almost out of breath by the time he bounded up the last steps to his own front door. He had run all the way from the tube station, and in a final burst of anticipation, took the stone steps three by three.

He decided not to ring the bell but use his key to get in.

In his mind's eye he'd been expecting to hear music, maybe U2, Molly's favourite, and see Eddie kicking on his sheepskin.

The silence and desolation of the flat felt like a sharp kick to the stomach. And then, irrationally, cold fear flooded through him. Maybe Molly really had had enough. She could have gone away, he had no idea where to, taking Eddie with her.

In that moment of panic he saw that life without Molly would be colourless and empty. She was the rock from which he dared to swim into dangerous waters, and without her he would feel like a drowning man.

Then he noticed the remains of a fire in the grate, and a huge wave of gratitude broke over him. She was simply out. Next to the fire, under the light of one of the red lamps, he saw the local paper open on the jobs page. She'd ringed a number of part-time options.

Joe sat down and closed his eyes. Perhaps he'd been behaving more like Stella than he'd guessed. Stella only seemed to think of herself, and he had too. He had never really considered what Molly wanted from life, that she had longed to look after Eddie herself, see his every tiny but momentous change, to hand on her own distinctive values to their child. How could he have thought of throwing up his job and going to drama school without so much as consulting her? He had shouted that his life was full of responsibilities as if they were a burden, but actually he liked them. Molly and Eddie were part of him.

His spirits soared when the doorbell rang, and he sprinted to open it. Mrs Salaman stood there holding out Eddie. 'Oh,' she apologized, while still managing to give him a beady look of female suspicion, 'I thought you was Molly.'

'I'm waiting for her,' he explained sheepishly, taking his son into his arms. Then he added, on the spur of the moment, 'Mrs Salaman, I'm really sorry for all the trouble I've caused. Thank you for helping Molly out.'

'Hhhmmph!' replied their neighbour, with all the withering sarcasm she could muster for the male gender. 'Don't tell *me*. You better tell Molly.'

'Where *is* Molly?'

'She out with my son deciding how to do up his restaurant. I hear you come in and think it was her.'

When the door had closed behind her, Joseph carried the baby into the sitting room and lay down on the sofa, holding his small son tight against the beat of his own heart. 'I'm sorry, little man, but

I promise from now on everything's going to change around here. I love you both so much.'

A quiet click of the front door told him Molly was back. She stood looking down at them, holding a big coffee table book, her expression serious.

He reached out an arm, still holding the baby tight, and folded them both against his chest. 'Can you ever forgive me for being such a selfish prat?'

Molly paused for a fraction of a second, then made up her mind.

'Depends if you're going to stop being one.'

'I'm sorry. The drama school idea was mad. I'll call Graham in a moment. I must have been crazy to think I could drop everything like that. It was just a silly fantasy.'

'I certainly hope it wasn't, since I've just done a five-grand deal to do up a restaurant, and maybe even another if this one works. I'll have to start feeling guilty unless it's for a good cause.'

Joe laughed, stroking her wild red hair. 'Molly, you're amazing.'

'Too bloody right,' she seconded. 'Pity it's taken you all this time to see it. How has Stella the Siren taken your sudden return to hearth and home?'

'She's going on tour.' He paused, a question occurring to him about this mother's motivation. 'At least she *said* she was going on tour. She also said that although she loved me, no one could love me as much as you do, and that you and Eddie needed me.' He paused, his eyes flitting downwards. 'As well as the new baby.'

Molly's hand stole down to her belly, but her face was radiant. 'Well, good for Stella! Who would have thought she had such a grasp of life back on earth?'

'I love you, Moll. Thank you for being the brave one.'

'Or the stupid one. Are you sure about this baby? I mean, you didn't really choose it.'

Molly thought her heart might explode with relief and delight when she saw the look in his eyes. 'Then I'm choosing it now. Come here and I'll prove it to you.'

It was just as well that Eddie had finally fallen asleep and could be placed gently on his sheepskin rug and so missed the scarlet sofa being used for purposes definitely not intended by its designer.

Beatrice Manners, standing at her kitchen window watching two redwings and a fieldfare squabble over the windfalls from her Bramley apple tree, was stunned to see a London taxi slowing down outside her door and Stella emerge with two huge suitcases.

'I sent Joseph home to Molly,' Stella announced blithely. 'And I thought you and I might take a well-earned break. A long cruise in the Med, perhaps? Up the Nile and down again? Something fairly time-consuming which would require our absence while they patch things up.'

'How long did you have in mind?'

'About three months should do it.'

'Who's paying?' asked Bea suspiciously.

'I am, you old skinflint.'

'I thought you hated cruises,' smiled Bea, 'full of old people.'

'You could teach me bridge.'

'Stella,' Bea couldn't keep a smile from her face, 'I don't think I can stand this new role. You're the most glamorous woman of your generation, not some OAP saving on the gas bill.'

'Where then?'

'As a matter of fact, I've always rather fancied Las Vegas.'

'Las Vegas it is then. I'll get on to my travel agent to fix it up.'

They stowed Stella's suitcases in the conservatory while she made the call.

'Stella?' Bea watched her daughter with quiet satisfaction.

'Yes?'

'This is good of you.'

'Don't mention it. I needed a holiday.'

'I don't mean that.'

'I know what you mean. Now come on, get packed before I change my mind. And while you're looking for your passport, I might hop down and pay Anthony a visit.'

'Well, that should certainly give him a surprise.'

'A long-overdue one. I haven't been kind to Anthony.'

From her upstairs bedroom, Bea watched Stella walk down the village street under the darkening sky.

It was the end of October already. Bea loved the winter here: the pheasants wandering into her garden from the bare fields to forage for food in the early morning mist; listening to the Canada geese honking overhead at dusk; the ritual of removing her summer bedding plants to the greenhouse to wait under glass till spring. This year she would miss all that, but she couldn't think of a better cause.

Halfway through packing, she made a brief telephone call, then finished off her suitcases humming to herself and thinking of the warm Nevada winter. She might even get a purple tint to match all the other old ladies.

Stella looked at the sign on the front of Anthony's shop that said 'Back in Five Minutes' and ignored it. He was probably just trying to discourage customers.

The door opened easily enough, but the interior of the shop was cold and gloomy, reminding Stella faintly of an undertaker's.

'Hello?' she shouted, peering into the dimly lit passage that led to his workshop. There was furniture piled everywhere: chests of drawers, lacquered cabinets with mirrors that were losing their silvering, a vast French armoire made of wood and ornately decorated with bamboo.

Anthony Lewis emerged holding a sanding machine in one hand. He'd had a haircut. The short crop was a vast improvement on the lank, shoulder-length arrangement he'd had before.

'Hello, Anthony.'

'My God,' Anthony stuttered, almost dropping the heavy sander. 'Stella.'

She looked absurdly like she'd always done. Gilded and glamorous and ever so slightly superior. As out of place in these surroundings as a silver fox coat in an Oxfam shop. 'I suppose you've come to try and stop me talking to the papers,' he concluded.

'I'm sure your analysis of my character is probably better than anyone's – and so it ought to be – but no. Sell your story with my blessing. You might as well get some reward for the appalling way I've behaved. Actually, I came to apologize. I've been in a kind of trance ever since Joseph appeared in my life, terrified of him finding out the truth. That's why I said all those crazy things. It must have hurt you, being cut out of the story like that.'

'I sometimes hate you, Stella.'

'I can understand that. I'm not always my favourite person myself.'

'Still successful?' he asked, despite himself.

'Fading fast. But not bothered. It seems like progress.'

'You're still very beautiful.'

'Thank you, Anthony. But not on screen, unfortunately. My beauty is best seen from the back stalls, and then through opera glasses.'

Anthony smiled. 'You never used to have a sense of humour.'

She picked up the remaining shepherdess from the pair of figurines he'd smashed. 'That's pretty.'

'There used to be two. Now there's only one.'

'Like life.' She leaned forward to examine the delicate china.

'You've got a grey hair.' He sounded stunned.

'I've got a whole posse of them. I am forty-five, after all.' She caught his eye and laughed. 'OK, I mean forty-seven.'

'What's he like? Our son?'

'He's wonderful. But troubled. I think perhaps things will be better now. At least he's got a wife who loves him more than anything on earth.'

'Lucky Joseph.'

'Yes. Lucky Joseph. Goodbye, Anthony, I'm sorry I wasn't a better wife.'

'You were a fucking awful wife, as it happens. But memorable.'

'Maybe that should be my epitaph.'

'Why?' he asked. 'You're not thinking of dying, are you?'

'No. Only going to Las Vegas.'

Anthony watched her leave, wishing he really did hate her. His revenge had been so close, but typical of Stella, she'd just robbed him of it. And he didn't even mind.

After she'd gone, he picked up the shepherdess she'd just been holding. For a moment he held it over the concrete floor. It would be symbolic to lose both. No more Stella in his life. Instead he put it on a high shelf, where it sat illuminated in a shaft of evening sunlight.

Then he rang the *Daily Post*.

Claire was packing all her possessions from her desk into a plastic container. The *Daily Post* kept a stack of these brightly coloured boxes, known by the journalists as heave-hos because you were given one when you'd just been fired.

To be honest, Claire didn't really mind. She'd had enough of Tony and his lack of imagination, in bed and out of it, and the whole of the Stella story had made her see journalism differently. It wasn't often you were involved in both sides of a story and could appreciate that the facts were more complicated than newspaper reporting ever allowed.

Admittedly, the business with Rory Hawthorne meant that she'd been fired rather than given any redundancy money, but a funny thing had happened to Claire. She felt the urge to go back to her hometown. Her dad's values seemed suddenly more alluring than superficial London ones. It probably wouldn't last, but at least she could get her washing done before she changed her mind.

Rory Hawthorne was watching her with satisfaction. 'Hurry up, Claire dear. Security will be up any minute. I'd suggest a farewell drink but I don't think you'll have time.'

For a tempting second Claire considered tipping the contents of her box over his head. Instead she handed him the Venus fly-trap plant that had stood on her desk. 'Have this, Rory. It likes eating things alive. Just like you.'

She was cut short by the phone on her desk ringing. She hoped it wasn't Tony calling to offer his apologies, the rat.

'Hello. I want Rory Hawthorne on the line, please. Now.' The voice on the line was unfamiliar, and at first Claire didn't pay much notice to it but the next words grabbed her fullest attention. 'Tell him it's Anthony Lewis and I want to retract my story. Tell him I made the whole damn thing up.'

Claire grinned, savouring the moment. 'Call for you, Rory,' she shouted gleefully, and picked up her box. It seemed lighter now. If she grabbed a cab she'd be able to drop in at Molly's on the way home. 'I think it may be important.'

When Stella got back to the cottage Bea was packed and ready to leave. She was sitting at her fruitwood bureau writing a list for her cleaner of everything that needed to be done in the house and garden during her absence. She looked up at her daughter's return. 'The travel agent rang back. The flight's tomorrow morning. How was Anthony?'

'Looking a lot better than usual. He's had a haircut at last, and got rid of that frightful leather coat.'

'Perhaps he's decided it's finally time to move on.'

They finished up the contents of the fridge for their supper, and Bea fussed about how her cleaning lady would ever manage the pot plants.

By ten o'clock they were ready for bed. 'You go up,' Stella suggested. 'I'll make us some cocoa.'

'Stella Milton in bed with cocoa at ten o'clock?' asked her mother, scandalized. 'Are you sure you wouldn't like a bed jacket and some Horlicks?'

Stella waited until Bea was safely upstairs before making one last brief phone call.

Pat was halfway through laying the breakfast table for tomorrow morning. After that she would plump up the cushions on the settee – small, comforting rituals to make her feel secure and in control. She could never sleep unless everything was tidy and ready for tomorrow.

'Hello, Pat. It's Stella here. I just thought you'd like to know

that Joe's gone home. My mother and I have been called unavoid-
ably away. On a trip to America. We may be some time.'

'I hope you enjoy the trip.'

'It's largely thanks to you. Your generosity with the album
embarrassed me into it. Though actually, self-sacrifice has its unexpected pleasures. I feel like Bogey in *Casablanca*.'

Pat laughed and said goodbye.

She didn't think she'd bother with the rest of the tidying-up.
Tomorrow would arrive whether the cushions were plumped up or
not. In fact, she might just go out and buy a whole new three-piece
suite instead.

Next morning Stella said goodbye to Lower Ditchwell just as the
pale pink glow of the sunrise was beginning to light up its ancient
mellow walls. The taxi driver grumbled at the amount of luggage
and said he would have brought a minibus if he'd known they
were emigrating. It felt to Stella like the end of an era. It struck her
that Lower Ditchwell looked too pretty to be real.

Real places, just like real people, always had a few imperfections.
It had taken her a long time to see that.

Gatwick Airport was crowded with travellers, who stopped in their
tracks at the sight of Stella Milton arm in arm with an older woman
wearing jodhpurs and a frilly shirt. They were even more surprised
that Stella had declined the discreet hospitality of the executive
lounge and was mingling with *hoi polloi* in the main terminal.

Once they'd actually got to the airport, a sudden feeling of let-
down and disappointment had crept in to Stella's world. She hadn't
said goodbye to Richard; Joseph had gone back to Molly. Bob Kramer
would probably never speak to her again. Stella suddenly had a
clearer sense of what she was giving up than what she was gaining.

Bea looked at her. 'Feeling regret? A good deed never goes
unpunished, as Oscar Wilde said.'

An incomprehensible squawk came out over the loudspeaker
and Stella strained to listen. 'Come on, Ma, I think that's our flight
they're calling. Two old bats hit Vegas. We're all we've got now.'

But Bea was looking around restlessly. 'You usually like to be one of the last,' she reminded Stella. 'By the way, did you ring Richard?'

'I'll call him when I get there.'

'No you won't. You'll call him now. There's a phone over on that pillar.'

Bea began assembling her numerous make-up cases, flight bags, and packets of boiled sweets, plus her enormous floppy hat, taking an infuriatingly long time to do it all.

Stella rejoined her a few minutes later, smiling to herself. 'He said yes,' she confided.

'What to? The great honour of watering your plants? That man's too good for you.'

'To moving in with me when we get back.'

'Stella, darling.' Bea's face split into a huge grin. 'That's a wonderful idea!'

'I know. Pity it took me quite so long to come up with it.'

By now they were the last in the line. Reluctantly Bea picked up her vanity case, big enough and ancient enough to have been aboard the *Titanic*, and they walked slowly towards passport control.

Seconds later there was a commotion the other side of the departure lounge. Joe and Molly, with Eddie in his buggy waving a streamer, ran across the emptying hall, followed by Pat and Andrew and the girl who'd interviewed Stella for the *Daily Post*.

'Really!' Stella looked at Claire in distaste. 'You people have no respect for privacy, do you?'

'None at all,' agreed Claire gaily. 'That's why I'm giving up newspapers and going home.'

'She got fired, actually,' Joe explained, 'for stopping Rory Hawthorne exposing you.'

'My God, I'm sorry. I do seem to have caused havoc for everyone.'

'I wouldn't have missed it for the world,' said Claire.

'Thank God we caught you,' said Joe breathlessly. 'Molly would have killed me if we'd been too late!'

Neither Bea nor Stella needed further explanation that Molly and Joe had buried their differences. The way they smiled at each other with a secret, slightly self-conscious relief was testament to that.

'Joe's starting at the Southern next week,' Molly announced proudly. 'His boss has been brilliant. He's agreed to give Joe enough freelance work to keep us solvent. There's only one condition,' she added, laughing. 'We have to call the baby Graham!'

'But as Molly's convinced it's going to be a girl anyway, we're not too worried. We'd much rather it was a Stella, wouldn't we, Moll?'

'Far too actressy,' Stella insisted. 'I'd stick to something nice and down-to-earth like Jane, or Mary. Or even better,' she turned towards Pat, 'I've always thought Patricia's a very nice name.' They exchanged a secret smile.

While Joe relieved Beatrice of her vanity case and they all started to walk towards the departure gate, Molly took Stella's arm and held her back for a moment. 'I wanted to thank you for sending Joe home to us.'

Stella shrugged. 'He would have gone anyway. I just hurried him up. Thank you for letting me borrow him. They were the best moments of my life. Not that I deserved them.'

Passport control loomed ahead and Bea shouted to Stella to hurry up or they'd miss the plane.

On the spur of the moment, Molly undid the straps of Eddie's buggy and placed the baby firmly in Stella's arms.

The intellectual sexpot of the British stage held him as if she weren't sure what to do with him. Then she laid his cheek against her own and looked deep into his blue eyes. 'Hello, little Eddie,' she said. 'I'm your grandma.'

Behind her sunglasses, Molly saw Stella blinking something from her eye.

'I must go.' She handed the baby carefully back. 'That's our last call now. The other passengers will assassinate us. By the way, Joseph, did I tell you? I've got a wonderful new part.'

'In that play you were after?'

277

'No, I turned that down. Bob was livid. In real life. I've decided to act my age.'

'Well, I certainly haven't,' tutted Bea. 'Now come on or we won't get there while we're still alive.'

'Just one more thing,' Stella shouted. 'My flat will be empty for three months if you want to live in it and rent yours out. A small contribution to your living costs.'

'I thought Richard was moving in?' Joe said, confused.

Stella winked. 'He is. But only when I get back. We've decided to give living together a try. I must have got used to having a man around the place. Till then the flat is yours.'

They all waved as Stella and Bea finally headed through passport control to catch their plane.

'You know,' Molly confessed, holding Eddie, 'I think I might be able to get on with Stella after all.'

'Especially if she's three thousand miles away,' pointed out Joe.

Molly laughed. Joe was hers again thanks to Stella, and there was a carefree lightness about him she'd never seen before. 'And who knows? Maybe even when she's living just around the corner.'